Sharon Kendrick once won a national writing competition by describing her ideal date: being flown to an exotic island by a gorgeous and powerful man. Little did she realise that she'd just wandered into her dream job! T̶ ̶ ̶ ̶ ̶ ̶ ̶tes for Mills & B̶ ̶ ̶ ̶ ̶ ̶ ̶ ̶ubborn but always̶ ̶ ̶ ̶ ̶ ̶ ̶who bring them ̶ ̶ ̶ ̶ ̶e best books̶ ̶ ̶ ̶ ̶st like life…

**Jackie Ash̶ ̶ ̶ ̶ ̶ ̶tes dark, emotional stories with alpha heroes who've just got the world to their liking, only to have it blown apart by their kick-ass heroines. She lives in Auckland, New Zealand, with her husband, the inimitable Dr Jax, two kids and two rats. When she's not torturing alpha males and their gutsy heroines she can be found drinking chocolate martinis, reading anything she can lay her hands on, wasting time on social media or being forced to go mountain biking with her husband. To keep up to date with Jackie's new releases and other news sign up to her newsletter at jackieashenden.com.

DEMAND FOR 'I DO'

SHARON KENDRICK

JACKIE ASHENDEN

MILLS & BOON

First published in Great Britain 2025
by Mills & Boon, an imprint of HarperCollins*Publishers* Ltd,
1 London Bridge Street, London, SE1 9GF

www.harpercollins.co.uk

HarperCollins*Publishers*, Macken House, 39/40 Mayor Street Upper,
Dublin 1, D01 C9W8, Ireland

Demand for 'I Do' © 2025 Harlequin Enterprises ULC

Greek's Bartered Bride © 2025 Sharon Kendrick

King, Enemy, Husband © 2025 Jackie Ashenden

ISBN: 978-0-263-34466-0

06/25

GREEK'S BARTERED BRIDE

SHARON KENDRICK

MILLS & BOON

For Eileen and George Riddiford, for all their help
whilst researching the magical city of Venice.

And also to Guy Black, for introducing me
to the marvellous Riddiford family!

CHAPTER ONE

THE COLD BLAST of emotion to his heart was unprecedented and extremely unwelcome.

Oblivious to the chill of the February day, or the spray of the speedboat as it powered towards the shore, Odysseus narrowed his eyes to stare at the instantly recognisable skyline.

La Serenissima, they called her. Venice. He had seen pictures of the place. The dark, silent waters. The intricate buildings which edged the canals. The spellbinding light, even in winter. At times he had even dreamt about it. But this was his first visit. His mouth flattened into a grim line. Surprising, really, given his ancestry.

With the faint mist of rain clinging to his face, he tensed as the boat approached the Academia Bridge and once again found himself asking the question which had been plaguing him for weeks.

Why the hell had he come here?

To free himself from the ghosts which had haunted him for as long as he could remember?

Or was it something more primitive? Something bone-deep and atavistic for the Greeks had a very satisfying word. A word he could almost taste on his lips—bitter and sweet.

Ekdikisi.
Revenge?
No.

His lips curved into a smile which people always observed never really reached his eyes. Revenge implied victimhood and Odysseus had never considered himself a victim, despite the savage circumstances which had forged him and spat him out. This trip to his mother's homeland was motivated by curiosity, or perhaps that was too mild a description for something which felt like the drawing of a final line. A desire to meet with his only living relative before the old man died.

'*Siamo qui, signor,*' announced the driver as he anchored the bobbing boat and turned to his passenger, his gaze watchful.

What did the boat keeper see? Odysseus wondered, pressing a wad of notes into the man's palm before leaping from the boat with an athlete's natural grace. A powerfully built man with an unruly mane of dark hair who would have looked equally at home on a ramshackle old fishing boat? Or did he simply register the expensive clothes—the sophisticated exterior which marked him out as one of the richest men in his native Greece and beyond? The costly coverings which hid the true nature of the man within. A man who women complained had a heart of ice. A man his rivals described as unknowable. The lone wolf, they called him in the handful of the countries in which he operated, but he could live with that. In fact, he rather approved of the soubriquet, even though it wasn't intended to be flattering. His mouth hardened. But other people's approval had never been high on his wish-list.

The ancient edifice of his hotel was only a few steps away from the mooring and the doorman sprang to attention as Odysseus walked up to the main desk. One of the female receptionists automatically pulled her shoulders back to draw attention to her breasts, but he failed to react as he signed his name. Registering her disappointment, he gave the ghost of a smile as she handed his passport back and he headed for the elevator.

Within minutes he was established in a suitably lavish suite overlooking the Grand Canal, which his assistant had booked, along with the requisite costume for tonight's ball, which was hanging in the wardrobe, awaiting his arrival. He cast a curious gaze over it, for it was essentially a fancy dress costume. But he had wanted a condensed Venetian experience, and this was all part of it. Satin breeches. A voluminous cloak. Buckled shoes and a tricorn hat. And the mask of course. An elaborate covering of the eyes, which should guarantee him a certain anonymity.

Not that anyone knew him here.

Not even his grandfather. At least, not yet.

He turned away from the wardrobe to study the milky waters of the lagoon.

Tomorrow he had an appointment to meet with Vincenzo Contarini though he hadn't yet worked out what he intended to say. A pulse began to beat at his temple as he thought about all the things he *could* say. About how much blame and bitterness he could apportion towards the old man. But that was not his style. He didn't do emotion. He had learnt to temper his reaction to things beyond his control because in every aspect of life there was immense power and advantage to be gained from not reacting.

But he wasn't going to think about that. Not tonight. Tonight he would watch the Venetians at play—for his assistant, Andreas, had procured him a ticket to the city's most exclusive ball.

'Only one ticket, Kyrios Diamides?' Andreas had enquired curiously.

'Neh,' Odysseus had growled. 'Only one.' For although a hundred women would have dropped everything to be seen on his arm, he did not need the distraction of a partner. He was here as an observer, nothing else. To confront the past, after so many years of ignoring it. Would it achieve some kind of closure? His mouth hardened. Who knew? Maybe it would be better to leave the wound open and untreated. To remind himself of how toxic families could be and thus reinforce his determination never to have one of his own.

But for tonight, at least, he would participate in something he'd never done before and the novel was always a tantalising prospect. So many of life's big prizes had come glittering his way at a prodigiously young age. Money and women had been there for the taking and Odysseus was aware that lately his attitude had grown jaded—a crazy situation for a man barely thirty-four years old and at his sexual peak. Didn't Andreas and even his personal pilot sometimes drop large hints that all work and no play posed their own danger?

Perhaps once he had attended to this assignation and returned from Venice, he would address the recent absence of sexual intimacy in his life, which certainly wasn't due to a lack of opportunity.

Yes, recreation would definitely go to the top of his to-do list.

But not right now.

For now there was work. There was always work. His refuge and salvation. Opening up his computer, Odysseus sat down at the antique desk, the beauty of the Grand Canal forgotten as he stared intently at the screen.

'Oh, Grace. You look *gorgeous*! Like something out of a film!'

But Grace barely registered her friend's excitement, or the lavish compliment, even though she wasn't usually known for her looks or her dress sense. She stared in the mirror of the staff restroom, at the very summit of the fifteenth-century Venetian palace which Kirsty had smuggled her into earlier. A whole hour ago actually, but it had taken that long to shoehorn her into this elaborate costume.

She knew the whole point of a masked ball was to disguise the way you looked, but even so. Who could have thought she could ever look like...

This?

The flowing scarlet silk dress was cinched in so tightly around the waist that she could barely breathe. It was doing things to her body she hadn't thought possible. The boned bodice clung to her ribs, pushing her modest breasts upwards and close together, resulting in the rather startling effect of making her look incredibly busty, so that she was practically spilling over the embroidered edge of her bodice. An elaborate hat covered most of her chestnut-brown hair with a cascade of scarlet feathers, and the gleaming golden mask left only a pair heavily kohled eyes and vermillion lips on show. What on earth had happened to Grace Foster, the colourless mouse who always faded into the background with her nondescript clothes and ordinary features?

That woman was nowhere to be seen. Tonight, she looked like an exotic bird. In other words, nothing like her at all. The bland functionary was nowhere to be seen—her usual uniform a distant memory. She'd never done anything remotely like this. Never even imagined she could. Yet here she was...

'I don't know if I can go through with it, Kirsty,' she gulped.

'Are you kidding?' Her friend's voice was disapproving as she indicated her own black waitressing dress with a disparaging wave of her hand. 'If you really think I've gone to all the trouble of sneaking you in and risking my job, only for you to have cold feet at the last minute—you're wrong! I've worked out exactly how to get you in there without having to go through the official entrance bit.'

'But what if I can't carry it off?' Grace swallowed. 'With no ticket?'

'Of course you can carry it off!' retorted Kirsty. 'Nobody's going to bother asking for your ticket. Anyway, the others are in there and they'll be looking out for you.'

This much was true. Grace made another unnecessary adjustment to her hired dress. Over the years she'd built up a small network of friends and Cara and Sophia were both here...somewhere...with legitimate tickets they'd saved up for, unlike her. But they didn't have her responsibilities, she reasoned. And although she happily sent most of her wages to pay for her grandmother's care in England, it did mean she missed out on a lot of the stuff which other women her age were doing. She didn't spend much on clothes. She didn't go out much. Which was why she occasionally found herself wishing that life could be a bit more...well, exciting.

But wasn't that the whole point of tonight?

Wasn't this a chance to enjoy one of the more sensational aspects of her adopted home city, rather than contending with the downside of the busy Venetian Carnival? Like having to fight her way through marauding hordes of tourists every time she went to buy a loaf from that little shop near the corner of Campo San Barnaba. Or being half startled to death every time a cloaked figure emerged from the shadows, wearing one of those white, unmoving masks which she still found scary, even after all these years.

'Does your boss know you're here?' asked Kirsty.

'Are you kidding?' answered Grace. 'He'd have an absolute fit.' Vincenzo Contarini was a self-confessed snob, who believed that everyone had their station in life and, as his general dogsbody, Grace was very definitely near the bottom of the heap. But he paid well and provided free board and lodgings in a city which was eye-wateringly expensive. She could never have afforded to live here otherwise. And if sometimes it felt a bit like living in a gilded cage, she always tried to push that particular thought away, because those kinds of thoughts got you nowhere.

Kirsty gave her a little shove. 'Now, grab your bag and let's go. The ball awaits you, Cinderella. And don't forget...' She paused dramatically, but her words were tinged with seriousness. 'Tonight you can be anyone you want to be.'

Rather nervously, Grace nodded and followed Kirsty

from the cloakroom, through a confusing number of back stairs, until they found their way to a discreet door which was obviously a staff entrance. She could hear chatter and music and laughter in the distance. In her narrow and delicately buckled shoes, her footsteps faltered and if Kirsty hadn't given her another gentle push, she might have fled.

Inside, it was as spectacular as everyone had said it would be. The sparkle and gleam of lavish costumes. The rising chatter of voices and cliquey little groups. Beneath chandeliers which cascaded from the high ceilings like diamond waterfalls, people were dancing, the women wearing jewels which glittered like flashing lights. In a distant alcove of the giant space, a string quartet was playing, and in another stood a trio of young men, juggling with gleaming golden balls.

But everyone else was mingling at the far end of the ballroom and Grace felt stupidly self-conscious and alone as she stood there, her fingers gripping her sequined bag.

Her main objective had been getting into the venue— she hadn't thought much beyond that and she couldn't see her friends anywhere. Hurriedly, she moved forward, aware that her palms were damp with nerves but not daring to wipe them on the hired dress. Terrified that people were looking at her and recognising her for the usurper she was, she felt achingly self-conscious, her progress slow, and as she paused deferentially to let an older woman pass, her gaze drifted upwards to the balustrade which overlooked the ballroom.

And that was when she saw him. Standing on a balcony directly above her. Grace's footsteps came to a halt as their eyes met and, beneath her tight bodice, her heart began to pound.

If only she had wings and could fly!

Because there, silhouetted against a tall window, stood a man who made every other man in the room shrink into nothingness. Why? Was it because he was so much taller than all the others? His shoulders much broader? His legs indecently long? Or because he exuded an aura of experience and danger which was almost tangible? Which should have made her want to run a mile in the opposite direction, but instead she found herself rooted to the spot.

He was dressed entirely in black. A tricorn hat sat rakishly on his slightly too long ebony hair, making him resemble a figure who'd stepped out of a fairy tale. Or a dream. He stood alone and watchful, as if daring anyone to come close. As if personal space was something he guarded jealously. Was that why people were circling him so warily, the men appearing to acknowledge an unassailable rival while the women slowed their speed whenever they passed, though he seemed oblivious to their lash-batting attention?

She wondered if their gazes really *had* connected, or whether that was wishful thinking on her part, because why would he have noticed someone like her—small and insignificant and out of place in this grand setting? But he was definitely looking at her now. Behind his mask, she couldn't see his facial expression—obviously—but there was something subtly challenging about his stance. Something which was calling out to her and bringing her senses to life. How mad was that? Blood flooded to her cheeks as Grace found herself remembering Kirsty's parting words.

'Tonight you can be anyone you want to be.'

Could she? She swallowed. Because right now the person she most wanted to be was the kind of woman who would stride up to the powerfully built man who was standing on the balcony and boldly ask him to dance. And he would say yes. Of course he would. He might even give a delighted laugh as he pulled her into his arms. Beneath the tight bodice her nipples grew hard as she imagined herself melting into that impressively honed body and...

'Signora?'

An unfamiliar voice breaking into her wayward fantasies, Grace turned to see a man, his name badge marking him out as an official rather than a guest, his face sour and slightly malicious. Her breath froze. Had she been rumbled? Had slipping in through the staff entrance made it obvious she didn't have a ticket?

'Yes?' she answered, in English rather than her more usual Venetian dialect, hoping the man might treat her more deferentially if he thought she was a wealthy tourist.

But annoyingly, he immediately switched to the same language. 'Your ticket, please, *signora*?'

Grace swallowed. It was her worst nightmare come true. She pictured herself being publicly ejected and word getting back to her boss. Wouldn't he accuse her of bringing his aristocratic name into disrepute and wouldn't those be grounds enough for him to sack her? Her contract wasn't formal—in fact, she didn't even *have* a contract.

Desperately, she considered her options. She could turn tail and flee, or she could try to brazen it out. But how? She glanced up to see the man in black, who hadn't moved. He was still there. And unbelievably, he was still watching her, a small curve playing around his sensual lips as he studied the reaction between her and the official. Was it her imagination, or had he just imperiously bowed his head in her direction—as if he were granting her permission to approach?

'*Signora?*' repeated the official. 'Your ticket, please.'

And suddenly she knew exactly what she was going to do. For one night only she was going to forget about being careful Grace Foster. Timid Grace Foster who never put a foot wrong, who always bowed to authority and rules. Tonight was supposed to be about doing what *she* wanted, although she wasn't exactly sure what that might be. The only thing she did know was that the brooding figure in black looked commanding and indomitable. A safe haven, she thought with sudden certainty—which was surprising, given the undeniable edge of danger he exuded. Could he rescue her from this annoying little man?

Sucking in a deep breath, she began to hurry towards him.

CHAPTER TWO

FROM HIS VANTAGE point on the balustrade, Odysseus had watched the woman in red stumbling into the ballroom, looking almost as if somebody had pushed her and, unexpectedly, he had been deliciously and unusually fascinated. By her tiny waist and diminutive frame, yes, both emphasised by the rich hue of the scarlet gown she wore. But by something else, too. Her movements were jerky, as if she were a puppet whose strings were being pulled. As he had watched her startled gaze roaming around the groups of exotically clad guests before coming to rest on him, it had crossed his mind that she was behaving like an outsider.

And that struck a chord within him. Because wasn't that *him*?

Always.

Even now.

Despite the billions he had accumulated in his bank accounts, despite the generous contributions he made to his charities, and the party invitations which flooded into his life like a river—deep down wasn't he the same person he'd always been? The outcast boy who had never fitted in, who had become a man with those same square-peg qualities.

But he didn't care how he appeared to others. He was never diffident, nor apologetic. Not like the woman in red, who had almost jumped out of her skin when one of the staff stopped to say something to her. His eyes narrowed as he observed the awkward interchange between them and as she glanced up in his direction again, he sensed the appeal emanating from her petite frame.

Almost imperceptibly, he inclined his head and she began to move towards him, jerkily negotiating her way through the crowds. In a swirl of scarlet silk, she made her way up the stairs leading to the balustrade, the official following closely behind. Odysseus watched as she approached and said, 'I'm sorry,' as she brushed past a woman nearby. But something made him smile as she reached him, for she was even smaller than he'd thought.

'Hi!' she exclaimed, her voice bright and slightly brittle, before she added in an undertone, 'Can you act like you know me? Please?'

His interest very definitely alerted now, he curved his lips into a smile. 'Of course,' he murmured softly.

The official stepped forward. 'Do you know this woman, *signor*?'

The man's tone of entitlement and judgement set Odysseus's nerves jangling, for he was sensitive to both. 'Do I know her? I most certainly do. I've been standing here waiting for her for the best part of an hour, but you know what women are like,' he drawled.

She raised herself up on tiptoe and touched her lips to his jaw in a butterfly brush of temptation. 'Sorry I kept you,' she said.

'I'll forgive you this time, *darling*,' he said, looping his arm around her tiny waist and drawing her into the contours of his body. Her sigh of relief was audible and he found himself wanting to echo it, because she fitted so deliciously against him, as if she had been designed for no other purpose than that. Something visceral made him splay his fingers around her waist, which had the effect of making her nestle even closer, giving him the opportunity to breathe in her perfumed warmth. And he took it. Briefly indulging his senses with her subtle scent before turning to speak to the man in a whisper which every person who had ever crossed him would have recognised, and feared. 'Is there something wrong?' he demanded silkily.

'Er...no.' The man's Adam's apple began to work convulsively. 'No. Nothing is wrong. My mistake, *signor. Scusi.*'

Waylaying the official with a peremptory elevation of his free hand, Odysseus glanced down at the woman by his side. 'Has he been bothering you, *darling*?'

She shook her head. 'I... No.'

'Sure?'

A grateful smile curved her scarlet lips. 'Honestly, it's okay.'

'Well, in that case—' Odysseus slanted the man a look of dismissal '—I was just about to ask the lady to dance. So if you wouldn't mind...?'

'*Sì, sì, signor. Mi dispiace!*' The hapless man backed away before scuttling off and being swallowed up by the crowd.

'Mission accomplished,' murmured Odysseus, a quiet sense of satisfaction washing over him as, reluctantly, he removed his hand from her waist. 'I don't think he'll bother you again.'

'Thank you. That was very…kind of you,' she said, in that soft English voice, but he could sense her hesitation. As if she didn't want to go. Which happened to coincide with his own sentiments exactly.

Do you think we should make some moves just for the hell of it, in case he's watching?' he suggested silkily. 'Or would you prefer me to deliver you safely somewhere else? There might be a man waiting for you. Your date, perhaps?'

She shook her head so that the elaborate concoction of feathers fluttered in a blur of scarlet and gold. 'There's no man. I'm here on my own, though my friends are here… somewhere,' she added vaguely.

'So, nothing to stop you from dancing with me.' A slow smile curved his lips. 'If you want to?'

Grace swallowed. If she wanted to! But daydreaming about marching up to the masked man to demand he whirl her around the floor was one thing—actually going through with it was quite another. Because up close, he was even more arresting. The firm jut of his jaw was dark, the curve of his lips shockingly sensual. And his eyes were incredible. The most unusual shade of piercing blue—brilliant and burning, like the flames of that old-fashioned gas fire in England which her nana used to have. And he was still waiting for an answer. Better she indicated her hopeless lack of ability, rather than making a fool of herself in front of so many people. 'I'm not very good at dancing,' she admitted.

'In that case, I will teach you.' Behind his mask, his blue eyes gleamed. 'I'm a very good teacher.'

His soft boast was underpinned with sensual promise and her body was reacting to his words in the most disturbing way. Beneath the boned bodice of her dress, her breasts were tightening, the nipples puckering into exquisite little nubs. Was it normal to respond to someone in this way, when you barely knew them? Was she risking making a complete fool of herself? Maybe it was that which made her hesitate to leave the fairy tale intact in case she ruined it…

'I might step on your toes?'

'I won't let you.'

She stared up into his masked face, so mesmerised by the curve of his lips that she completely forgot her self-consciousness. 'How will you stop me?'

'I will lift you up before your tiny foot makes contact with mine.'

'How do you know my foot is tiny?'

'Because the rest of you is. Small and perfectly formed.'

Stupidly, she blushed. 'Actually, I'm heavier than I look.'

'Ah. Shall we test it out?'

'Go on, then,' she agreed recklessly.

He gave a soft laugh before placing his hands on her hips and lifting her up into the air, before putting her down again, seemingly oblivious to the wild tremble of excitement which rippled over her skin. 'You were saying?'

Grace's heart was racing so fast she could barely get the words out. 'I can't believe you just did that!'

'You liked it,' he observed softly.

'Yes,' she whispered. 'I did.'

The air between them was thrumming with a sense of expectation so potent that Grace forgot to be shy, or nervous. Because this was flirting, she realised. Real, grown-up flirting. She'd witnessed it all her life because the Italians had managed to turn it into an art form, but had never properly engaged in it herself. She was always too self-conscious—too aware of her shortcomings and responsibilities—not to mention the fact that she'd never met anyone she'd particularly wanted to flirt with. Her job meant that she led a monastic sort of life, which made her fade into the background in so many ways. But now? Now she was having X-rated thoughts about a man in breeches, which she couldn't help noticing were lying so tautly and provocatively across his powerful thighs.

'Shouldn't we… I don't know…introduce ourselves? I'm Grace,' she added, resisting the desire to hold her hand out to be shaken.

'Odysseus,' he replied silkily.

She nodded. Of course. She'd been trying to work out the origin of that delicious accent, which sounded like a mixture of gravel and honey. 'That's Greek.'

'So it is.' Suddenly his gaze was hard and piercing. 'And?'

What were the rules of flirting? she wondered, with a novice's desperation. Wasn't she supposed to dazzle him with her humour and wit? 'Isn't there something about having to beware of Greeks?'

'Only if they're bearing gifts, which I'm not, and if you're angling for one, let me warn you that it's way too soon for that, *darling*. So stop blushing,' he instructed softly. 'And come and dance with me.'

Grace was acutely aware of eyes watching them as he led her downstairs to the dance floor. Or rather, they were watching *him*—every eye drawn to his tall and powerful frame. This section of the ballroom was still relatively quiet and the string quartet was playing an Italian melody she knew very well, but it sounded as if she were hearing it for the first time.

She moved into his arms and the sensation was distracting. No. It was more than that. It was *electrifying*. This time, the touch of his hands on her waist felt shockingly intimate—and annoyingly frustrating—as if his fingers were burning through the delicate fabric of her dress and branding her with his touch. Beneath the heavy swathes of silk-satin, she could feel her skin growing hot as she moved in time to the music. How could she have worried about something as unimportant as taking the right steps when dancing with him felt so easy?

She looked up to find his blue eyes studying her with amusement. 'So what was all the fuss about?'

It took a moment for her to realise what he was talking about. 'I was asked for my ticket.'

'Which you haven't got?'

'Which I haven't got,' she agreed. 'I'm afraid I'm a gatecrasher.'

'Just not a very good one,' he mused.

'You aren't shocked?'

He gave an odd kind of laugh. 'Why would I be? Most of us have had to blag our way into something or other at some point in our lives.'

'What, even you?'

'*Neh*, even me,' he agreed, his voice edged with a sudden trace of bitterness. 'So let me give you a tip for next time, *poulaki mou*. You might as well have held up a placard outing yourself as a trespasser when you arrived. You looked so damned guilty.'

'I was trying to be confident,' she confessed. 'But it's a pretty intimidating place to walk into and I was... I was as nervous as hell.'

'But you're not nervous now?'

'Funnily enough, no. I'm...enjoying myself.'

'So am I.' Odysseus pulled her closer, his heart beating very hard beneath his ridiculously frilly concoction of a shirt. Her shy candour was as enchanting as her neat little body, though his usual preference was for tall and rangy. She intrigued him, because these days he met only supremely successful women, who would rather have died than admit they couldn't afford a ticket.

His throat grew dry. Her body was pressed so close to his. He could feel the narrow curve of her hips beneath the span of her tiny waist and a surge of lust flooded his body. When was the last time he had danced with a woman? He couldn't remember. And never like this. Was it the fact that they were wearing so many clothes which added to the intensity of the moment—the constricting layers of satin and lace only adding to his growing frustration?

He wanted to pull the feathered hat from her head.

To rip that scarlet dress from her body and feast his eyes on the soft skin beneath.

The dance had finished but neither of them moved. He didn't know how long they stood there but as her body melted against his, Odysseus knew if they stayed like that much longer, he might be issued with a public indecency order. So finish it, he told himself sternly. She's a distraction you don't need, especially tonight. Send her away and go back to your room to prepare for tomorrow's grim appointment.

'Won't your friends wonder where you are?' he said.

She pulled away, mortified embarrassment burning her cheeks. 'Yes, I expect they will. I should probably go and find them. I'm so sorry. You've been really kind. I didn't mean to keep you.'

He wondered what had made her so suddenly servile. 'You aren't *keeping* me from anything,' he told her impatiently. 'I'm just giving you an excuse to get away, that's all.'

Grace blinked up at him in bewilderment—not sure of what to do next. He might just be saying that to be polite, of course, but he didn't strike her as a people-pleasing kind of man. Should she play safe and hurry away into the night and forget the way he was making her feel? She pushed the thought away. 'And what if I don't want an excuse to get away?' she questioned.

There was a pause before he tilted her chin with the warm cradle of his palm, so that her eyes were locked in a collision course with his. 'Are you always so totally without guile, Grace?' he questioned softly.

'I'm not sure I know what that means.'

To her disappointment, he let his hand fall. 'It means that you need to be clear about what will happen if you stay with me, because I don't want there to be any misunderstanding. We can go through the motions of grabbing ourselves a glass of prosecco, or finding something to eat, or we could dance some more—all of which are undeniably enjoyable pursuits. But ultimately...' He appeared to choose his words carefully. 'Ultimately, I want something else.'

'Go on,' she encouraged uncertainly.

'I want to take you back to my room, which is not so

very far from here, and then to remove that exquisite but very constricting costume. And then I want to make love to you. All night long.' His voice dipped with unholy humour. '*Neh*. You look shocked, Grace, and perhaps you should be. Perhaps I am a little too honest for your particular tastes. So why not use this opportunity to make your escape, *poulaki mou*? Find yourself someone more suitable. A nice, safe man who will take you on three chaste dates before politely asking permission to hold your hand. But I suggest you go now, in case I'm tempted to try to change your mind by breaking the rule of a lifetime and kissing you in public.'

Grace's lips fell open because in truth she *was* shocked—but less by the things he'd just said than the fact that someone like *her* was capable of making a man like him come out with such a passionate declaration. She almost asked whether he was sure he wasn't mixing her up with someone else, until she remembered Kirsty's words.

'And what if I don't want to go?' she said slowly.

'Ah. Then that puts an entirely different slant on the situation.' The hardening of his lips might or might not have been a smile but when he spoke again, his voice was very definitely edged with a note of warning. 'But you need to understand that I'm flying out of here tomorrow—alone—and I don't intend ever coming back.'

'But everyone comes back to Venice,' she protested.

'Not me,' he contradicted softly. 'The choice is yours, Grace. I've told you what you can expect and it's the only offer on the table. Take it or leave it.'

It was the most unromantic statement imaginable but at least nobody could accuse him of falsely raising her hopes. Grace sucked in an unsteady breath, unable to ignore the insistent pulse beating low in her belly, knowing she would never forgive herself if she let this opportunity slip away.

'I'll take it,' she said boldly.

CHAPTER THREE

HIS HAND WAS rucking up the voluminous folds of her ball gown and Grace gasped as his fingers whispered over her knee.

'Oh, please,' she moaned helplessly, feeling the rough rasp of his jaw against her neck. 'Odysseus. Please.'

'With pleasure, *poulaki mou.*' Taunting provocation coating every syllable, he pushed her up against the wall. 'All you have to do is ask.'

At least the hard surface provided some sort of anchorage and Grace held her breath as his hand reached her thigh at last, his fingers impatiently pushing aside the satin and lace until they alighted on the tender skin. 'Oh!' she gasped, then gasped again as he located the damp panel of her knickers to brush a teasing finger over the swollen mound before making a fractional retreat. 'Oh, please don't stop.'

'God, you're responsive,' he observed with unsteady admiration as he pushed the fabric aside and continued to stroke her.

Sweet waves of sensation tantalised and frustrated her so that even if she'd been able to think of a suitable reply, she wouldn't have been able to choke the words out. Instinctively, she parted her thighs and he gave a low growl of approval and once again she pleaded for release—jumbled half-sentences of words she scarcely recognised because she had never thought she would ever *beg* a man for anything. His hard kiss silenced her but his hand continued to work its magic, until suddenly she was spasming violently against his fingers, hearing his soft laugh as she slumped back against the wall, and if his other hand hadn't been wrapped tightly around her waist she might have slid to the floor.

Her eyes fluttered open at last to find his hot blue gaze raking over her and Grace realised how bizarre this scene would appear to an observer because neither of them had even removed their masks.

There hadn't been time.

He had led her quickly through the crowded ballroom, past the gimlet eyes of that same official who had stared at her resentfully, along with several women who clearly thought they should have been in her place. She thought she'd seen Sophia moving towards them but something about Odysseus's body language must have warned her off, because her friend had quickly taken a step back. And within several breathless minutes they had arrived in his suite, a few floors up from where the ball was still taking place. A vast, high-ceilinged series of rooms, lit only by the gleam of the canal and the moonlight out-side, which picked out an abundance of gilded fittings and a huge, canopied bed.

But they hadn't made it as far as the bed.

As he'd pulled her roughly into his arms his tricorn hat had fallen off, and his laugh had been unsteady as he'd started to kiss her. And Grace had kissed him back with a hunger which seemed to take him by surprise—

as if she'd given him the green light to be as rough as he wanted. And rough seemed to be what she wanted, too. Suddenly his hands had been all over her, peeling back the layers of slithery fabric until he'd found what he was looking for, locating the sweet, wet spot where she was most vulnerable. With a carnal growl of satisfaction, he had thrummed his thumb against the swollen nub, and the resulting orgasm had been so incredible that Grace wondered if she would ever feel normal again.

Her heart was slowing down as he reached above her to turn the light on, but Grace shook her head.

'No, don't,' she whispered. 'It's more…'

'More what?'

She very nearly said romantic until a small voice of reason warned her against it. Because his words had made it clear this liaison was to be the very antithesis of romance. And wouldn't extra lighting run the risk of illuminating her hopeless inexperience? 'Atmospheric,' she amended quickly.

'I think what will make it more atmospheric is if we remove these damned clothes as quickly as possible,' he said unevenly. 'And I also think it's about time we got rid of these, don't you?' He tugged off his mask and threw it aside and Grace's breath caught at the back of her throat as she drank in the sight of his naked face.

Had she thought he looked gorgeous before? Well, that was nothing to seeing him properly for the first time. He was like some sort of god, she thought dreamily—and far too beautiful to be human. High, sculpted cheekbones contrasted with the lush sensuality of his full lips and a mane of magnificent hair which gleamed like polished jet. But it was his eyes which were the most arresting feature of all. No longer framed by the elaborate mask, they were thick-lashed and bright with desire and even in the moonlight you could see how blue they were.

'Now you,' he instructed throatily.

A little unsteadily, Grace pulled off first the feathered hat and then the scarlet and golden mask, carefully placing both on a nearby bureau because she had to return them to the hire company tomorrow in pristine condition and she certainly couldn't afford to pay for replacements. She wondered if Odysseus would be disappointed with her rather ordinary face but he wasn't actually looking at her face. His attention was elsewhere and there was nothing but hungry preoccupation tightening his features as he reached out and began to undo her tightly boned bodice. There were so many hooks that it seemed to take for ever, and she held her breath as the tension mounted, her frustration growing as his fingertips brushed against her heated flesh and then brushed away again. Closing her eyes, she squirmed her hips in silent entreaty.

'You want me to hurry?' he asked, his voice amused.

'Well, yes.' She swallowed, hostage to this incredible desire which was pulsing through her body and obliterating every other thought and feeling other than need. A need so strong that she couldn't help but voice it. 'If you could.'

'You're very greedy, aren't you, Grace?' he questioned, with a touch of amusement. 'I should make you wait. For, ultimately, that will only increase the pleasure.'

She opened her mouth to tell him that if the pleasure increased any more than this, then her heart might actually stop beating. 'I'm rather hoping you won't,' she told him honestly, her eyelashes fluttering open.

Her thready statement seemed to impact on the rigid self-control he must have been exercising, because now she could sense his own impatience as he finished unbuttoning the heavy dress.

'Imagine having to do this every time you wanted sex,' he commented wryly. 'Those sixteenth-century aristocrats must have had gold medals in patience.' And then he raised his eyebrows. 'Although perhaps you're used to this kind of undressing?'

'You mean…' she sucked in a breath as his fingers sizzled over her skin '…do I regularly wear scarlet ball gowns?'

'Well, presumably not when you're out shopping,' he murmured and then his fingers stilled in their unbuttoning, and a sudden steely note entered his voice. 'I was just wondering if this was an annual event for you.'

Did he mean the ball? Or was he intimating that she hooked up with a new man every year and did…this? She opened her mouth to protest that she was not that kind of woman but by then he was lifting her out of the heap of rich fabric and there were far more immediate concerns on Grace's mind than protesting her innocence. Any minute now and he would see her completely naked. He would realise that her curvy body had been nothing but a mirage—or rather, a miracle of corsetry. Would he be disappointed with the real her and feel she had given him a false impression?

Trying to distract herself from these spirals of negative thinking, she began to tug at his costume, shrugging off the heavy cloak and scrabbling at the fine lace shirt until she had bared his torso. Her sigh of appreciation was instinctive as she smoothed her palms over the oiled silk, wondering if she dared touch the daunting hardness which was straining so flagrantly against his satin breeches.

Did he sense her sudden shyness? Was that why he put his lips close to her ear?

'I'm all done with waiting,' he growled. 'I'm all yours, *poulaki mou*. Do what you want with me.'

His steely interrogation seemingly forgotten, Grace shivered with anticipation as he pulled off the last of their clothes. She was naked now but there was no place for insecurity—not when she could see his face growing taut with lust as he tumbled them down onto the canopied bed.

Liquid fire flooded through her as he wrapped himself around her, her softness contrasting with his hard muscle. His mouth was on her breast, his teeth teasing at a nipple, a powerful thigh pushing in between hers. Lost in a haze of heat, she flickered her hand towards his groin, not in the least bit shy now, which was curious. She'd never touched a man intimately before but instinct told her to be gentle and that instinct was proved right, because he groaned helplessly as she feathered her fingertips over his straining hardness.

He allowed her nothing but a few frustrating seconds of exploring his rocky length when, with a sudden rush of air, he moved away and got up off the bed. Hungrily, her eyes followed him as he walked over to the desk, his powerful frame bathed in silver. She saw him bend and remove something from an overnight bag and suddenly understood its significance as moonlight flashed upon the metallic paper. For one appalled second, she stilled as she realised she'd been so caught up with what was happening that she hadn't given contraception a second thought.

Because it was something she'd never had to consider before.

In breathless silence she watched him return to the bed and he flicked her a rueful glance as he rolled the protection over his thick shaft.

'I'm finding it difficult to concentrate when you're looking at me like that,' he admitted huskily.

'Do you…want me to look away?'

'No,' he husked fervently. 'Most definitely not.'

Which was confusing. But there was no time to think about that either, because now he was moving on top of her and Grace was eagerly opening her mouth to him. Her legs, too. She was so pent up with desire for him that she didn't have time to grow nervous, even when she felt his blunt tip brushing against the wetness of her quivering flesh. Maybe that was what made the pain much less than she'd expected. There was just one moment of exquisite tension before he thrust deeper inside her, filling her completely and making her cry out.

'Odysseus,' she choked, the single word filled with disbelief and wonder that something could feel so *incredible*.

His own muttered response was incomprehensible. Momentarily, he grew still, before driving his lips down on hers again and kissing them so thoroughly that she felt as if she were being consumed by him. By his mouth and his body. By the stroke of his fingers and that sweet, rhythmic thrust which seemed almost to reach her heart. Did she say something? Was that why he briefly halted his movement?

'Is that good?' he demanded shakily.

'God, yes,' she choked back. 'You…you wouldn't believe how good.'

'Oh, I think I would.'

She tried to savour every second. To enjoy it for what it was. She was blown away by his obvious skill, but this was interspersed with an unexpected tenderness which took her by surprise. He was being very *careful* with her, she realised. As if she was delicate and precious. And that was her undoing. That was what made her tumble over the edge, just like last time.

Only this was nothing like last time.

This time he was inside her. With her. Part of her. The dreamy fairy tale complete. Powerful spasms tore her apart, lifting her up before tumbling her down in dreamy slow motion, to a place where everything was golden and pulsing. Reality shifted in and out of focus as he increased his speed and, as his body tensed, Grace risked glancing up at his face. Was she hoping for some kind of connection—a moment of silent communication which would acknowledge this incredible intimacy between them? But his eyes were closed, his features shuttered, as if he were deliberately blocking her out. He ground out something in Greek, and then began to pulse inside her.

She stroked the damp tendrils of his hair until his big body stopped shuddering, but she didn't say anything, even then. She didn't want to break the spell and risk shattering this fragile perfection. And anyway, what was a woman supposed to say in a situation like this? That it had been the best thing which had ever happened to her? Wasn't that the kind of statement they warned you never to say to a man after the first time?

But in the end, it seemed she didn't have to say anything because he got up from the bed without a word and disappeared into the bathroom and when he returned, there was no sign of the condom, just the faint smell of soap. And if Grace hadn't been lying in bed feeling so ravished and replete—she might almost have thought she'd imagined the whole thing. Because, despite the fact he was naked as he walked over to a tray of bottles, Odysseus seemed utterly composed.

No.

Not composed.

Remote.

Grace sat up a bit and stared at his expressionless features.

'Drink?' he suggested coolly, snapping on a light so that the room was instantly bathed in a soft, apricot glow.

'Yes, please.'

Feeling exposed in the lamplight, she escaped to the bathroom herself while he was busy with glasses, pleased to wash and refresh herself and repair her appearance, though slightly shocked by the image reflected back at her in the mirror. With her flushed face, bright eyes and smudged lipstick, she thought how different she looked.

Because she *was* different. She was no longer naïve Grace Foster who'd never been to bed with a man. She'd just had unbelievable sex in a luxury hotel room with a complete stranger and the weird thing was that she didn't feel in the least bit guilty about it.

Combing her fingers through her hair, she returned to the bedroom to find Odysseus lying amid the rumpled sheets, having placed two glasses of water on either side of the bed. So, no celebratory champagne, then, she thought, with a slight beat of disappointment. But he patted the empty half of the bed beside him and she headed towards it, trying not to be self-conscious about her nakedness. His eyes were watchful as she climbed in beside him and she had to resist the temptation to cover herself up with the duvet, or at least conceal the nipples which were hardening beneath his narrowed gaze. Because it was a little late in the day for modesty, wasn't it?

'You enjoyed that,' he observed.

'I...' Sinking back against the pillows, Grace turned towards him, feeling his hard thigh brushing warmly against hers. 'Well, yes, I did. Very much.'

His smile was easy but there was the glint of something cold in the depths of his eyes. 'It isn't always like that for women the first time.'

She shrugged, a little self-consciously. 'You could... tell?'

'Yes, I could tell.' There was a pause and she wondered if she was imagining the tinge of ice in his voice. 'Which makes my question of earlier redundant. This obviously isn't an annual event.'

'Obviously,' Grace responded as lightly as she could, even though she found his reaction more than a little... disheartening. Had she been hoping he would be secretly flattered that she'd given him her virginity, or maybe furious she hadn't given him a heads-up beforehand? Or at least that it would have produced *some* kind of emotion, rather than those clipped and cool observations he'd just made. As if he didn't care, one way or another.

Until she forced herself to remember the things he'd told her. That he was flying out of here tomorrow. Alone. He hadn't spun her any lies, or led her on with false promises. He'd been pragmatic from the outset and she had been the same. She'd helped undress him and urged him to touch her with throaty entreaties which had seemed to come from somewhere deep inside her and hadn't he seemed to *like* that? So what was the point of stoking up indignation and ruining the memory of what had just happened by behaving as if he'd done something wrong? Shouldn't she be just as matter-of-fact as him?

'How about you?' she questioned. 'Do you do this kind of thing often?'

'Having sex with masked strangers, you mean?'

She blushed. 'That's one way of describing it, I suppose.'

Odysseus brushed a strand of hair away from her flushed face. Would she be shocked to discover he hadn't had sex with a woman in over a year? Probably. The trouble was that might make her triumphant and start reading too much into it. And it wasn't fair to encourage make-believe, especially given how innocent she was. 'The answer to your question is no, but I'm still leaving the city tomorrow afternoon.' He reached out, his thumb tilting her chin upwards, searching her face with his eyes. 'Unless you thought that what just happened might change my mind?'

'That's a very arrogant supposition,' she said quietly.

'Maybe. But I happen to be a very arrogant man, *agape mou*,' he announced unapologetically before his voice dipped. 'Who wants very much to kiss you again.'

Some of the tension left her body, to be replaced with a different kind of tension, and he could see her amber eyes growing smoky.

'I'm not stopping you,' she whispered.

'No.' He tiptoed his fingers over her belly and the sheets rustled as she opened her thighs for him, his throat thickening as he encountered her honeyed heat. 'You're not, are you?'

This time he did make her wait. Kissing her from her eyelids to her thighs, he trailed his lips slowly over every inch of shivering flesh until she was begging for release. But he didn't heed her breathless pleas, telling himself that delayed gratification would only intensify her pleasure, knowing all the while that this was solely for his own benefit. He was testing his own resolve and denying the urgent hunger in his blood, as if determined to demonstrate to them both the icy control for which he was renowned.

Yet by the time he reached for another condom, his hands were trembling so much that he could barely get the damned thing on. And by the time he had slipped in-side her again—rock-hard amid all that honey and silk—he had to fight the urge to come. She felt like no other woman had ever felt, though he'd never slept with a vir-gin before. Was it all that taut newness as she took him into her body which was making him feel so powerful and so primitive? Or was it her naïve enthusiasm? The way she was sucking eagerly at his nipples—which im-mediately made him think about where else he would like her to suck him. Next time, he promised himself dazedly as she began to orgasm again and, with a helpless moan, he followed her over the edge. Definitely next time.

He hadn't planned to sleep. He had intended to make the most of the few remaining hours by exploring every inch of her body and satiating his lust for her until he had eradicated it completely. But a strange contentment was whispering over his skin and there didn't seem to be a thing he could do to stop it. Irresistibly, he found himself being dragged into a deep sleep, and it wasn't until he felt a movement beside him that he forced his eyes open and saw that Grace was no longer in bed, but in the process of picking up her discarded lingerie. Strange, came his first inconsequential thought once he'd managed to drag his gaze away from the silky globes of her bare bottom. He hadn't noticed that her knickers were so plain when he'd been in the process of removing them.

'What's going on?' he murmured, rolling onto his back and feeling the instant stir of an erection.

The sensible navy fabric of her panties hugging her hips, she glanced up at him, startled. 'I didn't mean to wake you.'

'Well, you have.' Pillowing his head on crossed arms, he yawned, watching as she walked over to where the rest of her discarded clothes lay in a billowing heap of scarlet silk, right next to his tricorn hat. 'Where are you going?'

'Isn't it obvious?' Ignoring the voluminous petticoats, she was shrugging on the red dress, fumbling to do up the hooks he had so painstakingly freed. 'Home.'

'Why?' He slanted her a speculative look and patted the vacant space beside him again. 'At least stay until morning.'

Grace hesitated under the influence of that sexy smile, torn between doing what she knew was sensible and what she really *wanted* to do, which was to climb straight back into bed with him. But she carried on doing up the fiddly red dress, because she had no alternative, not really. What could she tell him? That she'd glanced at her watch and been horrified to see it was four a.m. and she needed to get back before she was discovered?

That if she waited until morning, the hotel would be buzzing with life as people made their way towards one of the dining rooms for their breakfast. That right now the place was quiet and shrouded in welcoming darkness and nobody would be around to notice her drifting down the shadowed stairways in her bright silk gown. That her everyday clothes were in the staff cloakroom and she needed to get changed before first light and then to slip quietly over the dusky bridges, through the narrow Venetian streets she knew so well, until she arrived at the place which was officially her home but didn't really feel like home. That if she left it much longer she wouldn't be on hand to serve Signor Contarini his morning coffee and there would be all hell to pay. Why ruin the gloriousness of what had happened with the dull reality of the everyday, especially as it was only ever intended to be one night?

'I can't,' she said bluntly.

He looked surprised. No doubt he was. She couldn't imagine many women choosing to leave in similar circumstances, not when he was lying there looking so delectable with invitation oozing from every pore of his spectacular body. He obviously hadn't had enough sex, but the weirdest thing was that neither had she. How was that even possible? How had she gone from novice to addict in a few short hours? He had awoken a powerful physical hunger inside her and satisfied it beautifully on three occasions, but she was left wanting more. Grace would have given almost anything to have gone back over to curl her hand possessively over the hardening ridge she could see outlined beneath the bedding, and then to position herself so that he could push inside her again.

Almost anything.

But not her whole existence. She couldn't risk her job and her reputation and her very livelihood. Not on something he'd told her at the outset wasn't going to last.

'I don't know why you're choosing to leave at this time of night,' he said impatiently. 'But if you won't change your mind, at least give me five minutes to throw on some clothes and I'll put you in a water taxi and see you home.'

'No!' The word came out more sharply than she had intended but the idea of him escorting her to the front door was making her feel almost dizzy with fear. 'Thanks, but no, thanks. I can see myself home.'

Beneath that blazing blue scrutiny she did the rest of the buttons up and bent to put on her buckled shoes, glad to hide the flush of emotion from her hot cheeks. She needed to compartmentalise this, she told herself fiercely, because that was one of her skills. Putting things in their rightful place. Accepting situations for what they were and not what she'd like them to be. So that by the time she straightened up to face his rumpled beauty, she had composed herself enough to present him with a smile she hoped held just the right amount of appreciation which was appropriate in the circumstances.

'Anyway. Gotta go,' she said lightly. 'Great night.'

'Come over here and kiss me goodbye.'

Grace was sorely tempted by his soft command. Especially when he moved one hard thigh beneath the thin sheet. She cleared her throat. 'Better not.'

'Why not?' His voice was mocking. 'Scared I might persuade you to stay longer?'

'In a word…yes.' As she grabbed her little sequined bag, she flashed him a rueful smile. It was fairly obvious that within a few seconds of being kissed she would be flat on her back again and there simply wasn't enough time if she wanted to get back before the Contarini household woke up.

But it was more than that. She was scared of the way he could make her feel. Scared of the mass of contradicting emotions he had stirred up inside her, like a hornet's nest. In his arms, she had discovered a side of herself she hadn't known existed. Like one of those hard-boiled sweets which were meltingly soft on the inside when you sucked them for long enough. She'd felt like a woman instead of a dogsbody. A real person and not just an invisible functionary. And she couldn't allow herself the luxury of feeling that way because there was no future in it. The sooner she got back to her humdrum existence, the better.

'Thanks for the memory!' Picking up her feathered hat and jewelled mask, she blew him a kiss, wondering if it was admiration or irritation which flashed so briefly in his narrowed eyes.

This is all for the best, she told herself fiercely.

But her heart was pounding with regret as she turned away and headed for the door.

CHAPTER FOUR

SILHOUETTED AGAINST THE WINDOWS, staring out at the sun-splashed water of the canal, the old man must have heard the heavy door open, but he didn't bother turning around as Odysseus was shown into the formal salon.

'Signor Diamides,' announced the startled-looking maid who had greeted Odysseus on his arrival, then kept him waiting in a gloomy anteroom which had made him think of some medieval torture chamber. He suspected it had been a poor attempt to intimidate him, but naturally it had failed—because nothing and nobody ever intimidated *him*. His mouth twisted as he studied the old man standing at the far end of the salon, surrounded by coloured glass ornaments which glowed emerald, ruby and golden in the sunlight.

'Leave us!' barked Vincenzo Contarini but still he didn't turn round, not even when the maid shut the door behind her.

This was a classic demonstration of power-play, thought Odysseus, his irritation at the *obviousness* of the old man's delaying tactics giving way to a slow beat of anger as he wondered what he was hoping to gain from this meeting.

A grovelling apology?

Regret on the aging tyrant's part?

Because if that was the case, he suspected he would go away empty-handed. And besides…even if the old man broke down—even if he got down on his knees and begged his forgiveness for what he had done—would that really make any difference? It wouldn't bring her back, would it? It wouldn't change anything. The loss, or the bitterness, or the guilt.

Refusing to stoop to his grandfather's level of game-playing, Odysseus stood in silence, letting his gaze flicker around the prestigious salon. Despite the world-famous glass artefacts which had been produced by the Contarini family for centuries and the priceless antiques which stuffed the room, it was a curiously sterile room. There were no photographs. Nothing in any way personal. More like a museum than a home, he thought disparagingly.

But who cared how the old man lived? He was here to ask questions, nothing more. And if he wasn't firing on all cylinders this morning, then didn't he have only himself to blame? Odysseus felt his pulse quicken as his mind took him back to the memories he'd been failing so spectacularly to suppress. He had woken up alone this morning, his body pulsing with frustration as he recalled his liaison with the woman in red.

He remembered her exquisite tightness. The way she had wrapped her soft legs around his back and made those helpless little cries as he had driven into her. He didn't know a damned thing about her apart from her name, though she might have lied about that. She had certainly been a mass of contradictions—her foxy exterior disguising a remarkable innocence and he couldn't deny that it had blown his mind when he'd discovered she was a virgin. If he'd known, would he still have bedded her?

Probably.

He had been accused of many things in his life but never self-delusion. And he had found her so utterly irresistible… He remembered lying amid the rumpled sheets, hard and aching as he'd watched her go. His inability to get her to stay was a first, which had only added fuel to his desire. Over breakfast he had wondered how difficult it would be to trace a masked woman who had gatecrashed a party of over two hundred guests. But surely, the whole point was that he didn't *want* to trace her. The memory was perfect because he knew he would never see her again. He would never have the chance to grow bored or impatient with her, or wonder how best to end it without breaking her innocent little heart.

'So. My unexpected guest.'

A rasping voice shattered his thoughts as the old man turned round at last, his handmade suit hanging loose on his shrunken frame, and Odysseus was unprepared for the jolt of shock which rocked through him. Despite having planned this trip since his father's death, the impact of seeing his grandfather in the flesh took him by surprise. This was a man he'd only heard about and read about and he hadn't expected to feel anything other than contempt. But suddenly it was way more complicated than that. He acknowledged something close to recognition as their gazes clashed. Was it because the eyes set in those wizened features were an extraordinary shade of blue? Blue like my eyes, Odysseus thought, with a bitter sense of recognition. Blue like my mother's eyes.

An unfamiliar sorrow welled up inside him, but he kept his expression impassive, as he had taught himself to do since he had first become aware of the notion of self-will.

'Surely you must have expected a visit from your only grandson at some point?' Odysseus enquired, his tone deliberately measured.

'I had no such expectations,' negated the old man.

'That is…surprising.'

'Why should it be? I have nothing to prove.' Vincenzo stuck out his jaw. 'Not to you. Not to anyone.'

'Is that so?' Odysseus asked the question with soft deliberation, but suddenly he could see the other man grow tense.

'Just tell me what it is you want!' The old man glared, his Adam's apple working furiously above the too-loose collar of his shirt. 'Is it my money you're after?'

Behind his implacable expression, Odysseus felt the warm flicker of rage. 'I have money of my own.'

'Yes, so I believe. You've made quite a name for yourself, I understand. The billionaire fixer, they call you.'

They called him many things, thought Odysseus sardonically, but he said nothing, just continued to study the old man objectively, finding solace in the power of silence, as always.

'So why are you here?' The old man's voice quavered. 'And why now?'

'I want to ask you a few questions.' Odysseus raised his eyebrows. 'Let's start with the main one, shall we?'

'Go on, then,' goaded Vincenzo, the light of challenge entering his faded blue eyes. 'Ask away.'

'Why did you kick my mother out onto the street?'

'Because she brought the family name into disrepute!

Getting herself pregnant by some *wastrel*!' The old man spat the words out. 'She had everything. Everything! The best education in the world. A generous allowance. A trust fund. And there were men, too. Wealthy men, waiting in the wings until the time was right, eager to make her their wife. Her golden future was right there—at her fingertips—until she had her head turned by a...nobody!'

'And that was her choice,' Odysseus said flatly. 'But even if you despised my father and everything he stood for, she was still your daughter. Your only child. Yet you didn't even come to her funeral.' There was a pause and, unexpectedly, it took a moment before he could bring himself to speak. 'You didn't even come to pay your last respects.'

'Why would I? She threw her life away and I wanted nothing to do with the man who was responsible! She made her bed, so I let her lie in it!' The old man was clutching at his throat, as if he couldn't get enough air, and suddenly he reached towards a brass bell, ringing it surprisingly loudly with gnarled and trembling fingers. 'Grace!' he rasped. 'What the hell is she doing this morning? Grace! *Venite! Venite!*'

For one extraordinary moment, Odysseus felt as if the old man had trespassed into his thoughts, because hadn't that been the name which had been paramount in his mind all morning? He shook his head. He must be going mad. Or was he? Because 'grace' was also a type of prayer, wasn't it? Was it possible the old man was asking forgiveness for what he had done to his only child? And if a form of contrition was expressed then surely he could go away with some sense of closure. Wasn't that all he had ever really wanted?

The door opened and a woman dressed entirely in grey stepped inside, her eyes downcast and her red-brown hair pulled back into a tight bun.

'Yes, Signor Contarini?' she said quietly.

And then Odysseus really did think he was going mad because her soft voice sounded like…

Sounded like…

He shook his head, his gaze raking over her slender form as if seeking reassurance. He must be mistaken. Last night's Grace had been passionate and bright. This morning's Grace was drab and lacklustre.

And yet…

Wasn't there something about the set of her shoulders and the way her heart-shaped face seemed balanced on a neck which looked like a delicate stem, which reminded him all too vividly of the tiny temptress who had so eagerly given him her innocence?

Look at me, he willed silently.

Look at me.

As if obeying his voiceless command, she raised her head and for once Odysseus's ability to remain neutral deserted him. His whole body stiffened, his hands clenching into tight fists by the shafts of his thighs as his heart began to pound like a piston. It could not be her and yet it *was* her.

No mask today. No scarlet lips, nor clinging crimson gown. Just a pale face without a scrap of make-up and a dowdy dress which did her no favours. And eyes which darted to him in silent appeal.

Odysseus met her frantic stare. What did she think he was about to do—inform his hated grandfather how they'd spent the night together? A pulse began to beat at his temple. Who *was* she?

'Where have you been?' demanded Vincenzo Contarini. 'Why didn't you answer the door earlier?'

'I'm sorry...' she stumbled. 'I'm afraid I didn't hear the bell and I—'

'The shutters! The shutters!' interrupted the old man impatiently, waving his hand towards one of the vast windows.

But Odysseus noticed a certain watchfulness creep over Vincenzo's demeanour, his faded eyes suddenly studying the woman in grey intently, his curiosity clearly aroused. The wily old fox had missed nothing, he realised.

'Yes, of course,' answered Grace quickly.

Odysseus watched as she moved across the room and began to fiddle around with the shutters until an obelisk-shaped shadow fell over her petite body, making her outfit look even greyer than before. He gave a faint shake of his head, still trying to get his head around her dramatic change of appearance—a bright bird of paradise transformed into a dull sparrow.

'Is that sufficient, Signor Contarini?' she questioned quietly.

'Yes! Fill up my water glass and then leave us,' he demanded querulously. 'And then wait outside the door until I summon you.'

'Yes, *signor.*'

Praying she wouldn't slop water and the all-important squeeze of lime all over the priceless desk, Grace managed to accomplish the simple task without mishap and handed the drink to her employer, wondering if he had noticed the slight trembling of her hand. And then she made her way back across the room, trying not to hurry, terrified she would stumble and draw attention to herself. Painfully aware of two sets of eyes watching her self-conscious progress, the short journey seemed to take for ever. Her breath was coming in shallow bursts as she closed the heavy door behind her and she had to fight very hard to resist the urge to sink onto one of the spindly antique chairs which adorned the reception hall—because imagine if they came out and found her, sitting there as if she had a right to. From inside the room she could hear the muffled sound of voices, her thoughts splintering into bewildered fragments as she wondered what the two men were saying.

This was like her worst nightmare. Actually, it was worse than that—because at least you could wake up from a nightmare. But didn't it go some way towards explaining why her boss had been even crankier than usual these past few weeks? There had been whispers from other staff members about the identity of the mystery guest who had been due to arrive this morning, but nobody had a clue who he was. Excitements were rare in the Contarini household and in an effort to distract herself from the distracting memory of losing her virginity last night, Grace had been peeping from an upstairs window when she'd heard the doorbell ring. Her heart had frozen in her chest as she'd seen the man standing on the doorstep, before her mind had gone into a complete flap of denial.

It couldn't be.

It couldn't.

But it was. Even if she hadn't known him quite so

intimately, there was no mistaking that powerful physique, or the blue-black gleam of his hair. Who else was built like that, with shoulders broad enough to carry the weight of the world? Last night he had looked swashbuckling and sexy, but he didn't need the tricorn hat or close-fitting breeches to achieve the same effect in the cold light of day. Even the immaculately cut designer suit couldn't disguise the honed muscle of his hard body, or detract from those incredibly long legs.

Rooted to the spot, she felt her mind begin to race. What on earth was her Greek lover doing here? Surely it couldn't be to do with *her*? And yet, why else would he be here? Signor Contarini never received visitors—he had become an increasingly difficult recluse. She'd become so twitchy when she'd seen him that she had let the maid answer the door even though, strictly speaking, that was her job—and there would probably be hell to pay later. But she couldn't run away now. Odysseus had seen her. That icy blue gaze had registered her presence with impassive scrutiny. And she dared not risk angering Vincenzo further by beating a retreat to some quiet corner of the palazzo.

Her heart started hammering as she heard the loud summons of the bell and, pinning a wobbly smile to her lips, Grace returned to the reception room, trying to look anywhere but at Odysseus. But ignoring him took a monumental amount of willpower and not just because of the powerful magnetism he exuded, or the fact that the last time she'd seen him he had been stark naked in bed, his groin growing hard beneath the bedsheet.

The problem was more to do with her and her reaction. Beneath her grey uniform, her breasts felt like twice their normal size and that now familiar ache was beginning to melt, low in her belly. And there didn't seem to be a thing she could do about it. It was as if her body was determined to taunt her with memories of how sweet her induction to sex had been, leaving her feeling dizzy and breathless in the wake of the powerful storm he had invoked. Sucking in a huge breath, she extended her smile.

Just a few more minutes and he'll be out of here, and everything can go back to normal.

But wasn't it funny how you could try to convince yourself of something you knew just wasn't true?

'Show Diamides out, will you, Grace?' barked Vincenzo.

'Yes, *signor*,' she answered quietly, acutely conscious of her boss's probing stare.

As she walked beside the powerful Greek towards the grand entrance hall, Grace thought how much taller he seemed than yesterday—but that was because he was. In her carnival shoes she'd been a far more respectable height, but today, in her working flats, she felt positively diminutive in comparison.

She pulled open the front door and then she *had* to look at him because it would have been impossible not to. Or maybe it was just temptation winning out as she succumbed to the desire to feast her eyes on his beautiful features at last. As she lifted her gaze, Grace met an unknown expression glittering from his sapphire eyes and tried to communicate with one of her own. Please don't say anything, she prayed silently. Don't accuse me, or question me, or mention what happened last night, not now—not with Vincenzo now standing just a few steps away, watching us like a hawk.

'Thank you,' he said formally, holding out his hand to her and, although it was highly inappropriate for a visitor to shake the hand of a humble housekeeper, surely it would have been the height of rudeness not to take it.

But Grace couldn't prevent the shiver which rippled over her skin as their flesh made contact, her instinctive response belying the apparent innocence of the gesture. She was just about to snatch her hand away when she felt a small rectangle of cardboard being nudged into her palm. She closed her clammy fingers around it, grateful for the fact that he had turned away to speak to Vincenzo, the brief distraction allowing her to conceal the business card in the roomy pocket of her grey dress.

'It was an *interesting* meeting, Signor Contarini,' Odysseus bit out coldly. 'But we will never see each other again.'

'And a good job!' snapped the old man.

But Odysseus simply inclined his head with imperious dignity and Grace wondered who he was, that he could get off with speaking like that to one of the most powerful men in the city. He stepped outside and she watched him heading off towards the Academia Bridge, with the pale sunlight gilding his blue-black hair. A couple of young women stopped in their tracks to stare at him, though he didn't pay them the slightest attention. And her heart twisted with pain at the thought that she would never see him again.

But as she shut the door she remembered the business card he'd handed her and surreptitiously patted her pocket.

'Grace?'

Composing her face, she turned round to face her

boss, her heart plummeting when she saw Vincenzo's expression. It was a wily look she recognised and she needed to be on her guard because she knew how ruthless he could be. He might pay generously but he was a privileged tyrant and not for the first time she thought what a poisoned chalice this job could be. 'Yes, Signor Contarini?'

'So what was all that about?' he questioned slyly.

She played the innocent, self-protection prompting her to field his veiled question. Because what else could she do? She couldn't afford to lose this job. Not now. Not after everything she'd been through. Unflinching beneath his accusing stare, she fixed him with a look of mild bemusement. 'I'm not sure I understand.'

'Don't take me for a fool, Grace!' he spat out. 'You know him!'

And in a way Grace was grateful that the old man's accusation was so specific because it meant she could answer it with a certain amount of truth, though her voice wasn't quite steady as she shook her head. 'No, *signor*. I don't.'

Because she didn't know him. Apart from his name and the fact that he had taken her to heaven and back, she didn't have a clue who Odysseus Diamides was, or where he'd come from, or why he was meeting with her employer.

But one thing was for sure.

She needed to find out.

CHAPTER FIVE

ODYSSEUS SIPPED HIS coffee and waited, keeping his gaze trained on the street leading to the little backwater café where Grace had suggested they meet. It was an out-of-the-way spot largely unfrequented by tourists and as he watched the locals coming and going, he was reminded that this wasn't just a holiday destination of breathtaking beauty but a place where people lived normal lives. Two businessmen drinking wine together beneath a shady canopy. A working boat unloading crates to the back entrance of a small restaurant, to the sounds of whistling from within. A young child, walking with his mother, school finished for the day, smiling contentment on the little boy's face.

And he wondered what it must be like to grow up like that...

By rights he should be high above the Adriatic on his private jet right now, thinking about the meeting which had just taken place between him and the grandfather he had been schooled to despise. His father had always been vitriolic about the old man, blaming him for his wife's untimely death and reinforcing that terrible loss whenever he got the opportunity. Odysseus felt his jaw clench, remembering that the finger of culpability had sometimes pointed in other directions, too...

Yet, unexpectedly, his shock sighting of Grace working as some kind of maid in his grandfather's house had temporarily driven the torturous past from his mind. Or maybe it was simply the realisation that Vincenzo Contarini was never going to express any remorse for what he had done—so why bother kicking against a locked door?

It had been easier to focus on Grace and the reaction which had flooded through him when she'd walked into the room with her hair scraped back, her slim body swamped by that ugly grey uniform. His disbelief at her dowdy appearance had warred with a vivid and visceral flashback of easing himself into her slick tightness and hearing her gasps of pleasure. Unusually compromised yet strangely turned on by the unspoken but apparent need for secrecy, he had pressed his business card into her hand, feeling the unmistakable shiver which had rippled over her damp palm as their eyes had met. Was that the moment when he'd realised how much he still wanted her?

But wasn't the truth that he hadn't stopped wanting her since she'd walked out of his hotel suite that morning, leaving him high and dry and aching?

His erotic recall cleared as he saw her making her way towards him, over a narrow bridge which crossed the canal. Small. Unremarkable. Straight brown hair streaming over her shoulders, though the sunlight revealed the occasional warm highlight. The drab grey dress had given way to jeans and trainers and some sort of raincoat, which was knotted tightly around her waist. He'd half wondered if she would show, after that stilted conversation when she'd phoned him, speaking in a stage whisper as if afraid of being overheard. But then he'd reasoned that of course she would. She couldn't afford not to. Wouldn't she want to know why he was meeting with her boss, as much as he wanted to know why she was working there?

She came into the café, said something in Italian to the man behind the bar and slipped into the seat opposite him. Undoing her trench coat, she hung it on the back of the chair and he could see the stiff set of her shoulders as she turned her face to his. Beneath the subdued artificial lighting of the café, her bare lips looked as though they were trying not to tremble and her hands were clasped together in her lap.

He narrowed his eyes, still trying to work it out, his usual cynicism banished by the intriguing riddle in front of him. Not one woman but three, he mused.

A virgin temptress.

A downtrodden servant.

But now…

Odysseus ran his thumb along the rough edge of his jaw. Now she was simply an ordinary, fresh-faced young woman who was radiating good health and vigour. Her eyes were shining and her lips were bare. Her eyebrows were thick and dark and her hair was spilling over her shoulders in a cascade of natural colour. Not his usual type at all. And then his attention was caught by a fragment of scarlet nail varnish, clinging to the edge of one fingernail, when all the rest were unpainted. She must have missed it in her hurry to erase evidence of last night's ball, he thought, assailed by the provocative memory of those red talons stroking over the taut flesh of his straining erection. And, surprise, surprise, he thought wryly. It was happening all over again. Uncomfortably, he shifted his weight in an attempt to divert his attention from his hardening groin.

'So.' Swallowing against the sudden dryness in his throat, he leaned back against the wooden chair. 'That was some entrance you made.'

Her amber eyes were bright and very direct and only the faint shadows beneath hinted at the fact that she'd had very little sleep last night.

'Are we talking about last night, or this morning?' she enquired.

'We both know what I'm talking about, Grace,' he snapped. 'And it isn't your skill in managing to close a pair of shutters under the obviously suspicious gaze of your employer.'

She pursed her lips together. 'Thank you for not saying anything.'

'What was I going to say? That I was pleased you'd found your way home safely at that time in the morning, or that I was sorry I'd made you miss out on so much sleep? I found your obvious need for secrecy…intriguing. And curiously tantalising.' There was a pause. 'Do you realise, I don't even know your surname?'

'Foster,' she supplied unwillingly.

'So, Grace Foster.' He flicked his gaze over her bloodless cheeks. 'Why did you look so scared when you saw me?'

'Why do you think?' she demanded heatedly. 'I work in an old-fashioned environment and my boss is really particular about status.' She picked at the single red fingernail before continuing. 'Believe me, it would have gone down like a lead balloon if he knew that I'd spent the night with a…friend of his.'

'He's no friend of mine,' he said, his voice harsh.

'No. I thought not.' Her amber eyes were huge in her face. 'So…who exactly *are* you?'

There was a pause as the waiter deposited a glass in front of her and began to pour water and seemingly inexorable seconds ticked by before the bottle was emptied. But Odysseus was grateful for the brief hiatus before the man walked away, because it gave him time to work out how to answer the inevitable question. He had told nobody about his meeting with Contarini—not even his assistant—because there was nobody in his life close enough for him to ever make such a disclosure. He guarded his personal space obsessively. He didn't want people getting to *know* him and bought silence whenever he could. And though he could do nothing about the inevitable conjecture which came with the territory of being a billionaire—he never confirmed or denied rumour.

Whenever anyone tried to get him to open up—as they invariably did—he blocked their interest with a smooth expertise which was second nature to him. His upbringing might have been lacking in many of the things other children took for granted, but it had helped him develop a stony carapace which protected him from the chaos of feelings. He prided himself on his emotional self-sufficiency and it should have been easy to bat away a question from a woman with whom he had shared nothing but a brief night of sex. To tell her it was none of her damned business.

Yet inexplicably, in this tiny café, in a glittering city which had fascinated him ever since he had found out about his mother's birthplace, Odysseus found himself wanting to do the opposite. Was it because she was someone who lived on the inside of a life which, by rights, should have been part of his? A life he had never known and never would. Today's terse meeting had confirmed what he had always suspected—that there was never going to be a fairy-tale ending with Vincenzo Contarini. The blood ties severed before he had been born weren't going to magically meld together. He wasn't going to find himself in the difficult position of having to 'forgive' the old man. And wasn't that a kind of liberation, of sorts?

'I am Vincenzo's Contarini's grandson,' he informed her.

She looked completely shocked. Her amber eyes had widened and she gripped the table as if for support. Was that surprise genuine? he wondered cynically.

'His *grandson*?'

'You didn't know?'

'No! He's never mentioned a grandson before.'

'Why would he?' he said, surprised by the sudden harshness which had entered his voice. 'We don't exactly have what you'd call a traditional relationship.'

'I'd kind of worked that out for myself. But even so.' She pressed her fingertips to her lips. 'I mean, I had no idea you even existed—'

'Are you sure?' He leaned forward. 'What about when you first met me?'

She blinked in confusion. 'You mean, at the ball?'

'As far as I am aware, that was our first encounter.'

The bewilderment on her face changed to a look of

comprehension. 'Are you suggesting I deliberately targeted you?'

'Well, you did,' he pointed out. 'There were a hundred men you could have chosen, yet you chose me.'

'*How* am I supposed to have targeted you when you were wearing a mask and a hat and I didn't even know you existed? I'm not that smart!'

'So why, then?' he persisted coolly. 'Why me?'

Still reeling from his bombshell disclosure, Grace hesitated, tempted to take him to task for his arrogant assumptions about women in general and her in particular, but something stopped her. Maybe it was that brief flicker of pain she'd seen in his eyes when he'd come out with the unbelievable fact that Vincenzo Contarini was his grandfather. Why had she never heard about him? Yet despite his cool countenance, it was obvious he was hurting—even if he was pretending not to—and the caring side of her nature felt a sudden rush of compassion. This wasn't about *her*, she reasoned, so why attempt to be coy, or repair what was left of her reputation? She'd gone to bed with him, hadn't she? She'd let him touch her intimately while he was still wearing his mask! There was absolutely no point in pretending she hadn't fancied him—especially as she was never going to see him again.

'If you want the truth, I chose you because you looked as if you wouldn't take any nonsense from anyone,' she said slowly.

Dark eyebrows raised, he studied her curiously. 'Explain.'

She shrugged. 'You seemed taller and stronger than

anyone else in the ballroom, and also, you were watching me.'

'A lot of people were watching you, Grace,' he said
softly. 'You were a very eye-catching proposition in that
red dress.'

'I didn't notice anyone else but you,' she admitted,
her cheeks growing warm at the compliment but when
she saw his eyes narrow, she wondered if she'd been a
bit *too* honest. 'I didn't want the shame of being thrown
out of the ballroom and people finding out I didn't have
a ticket,' she continued quickly. 'Venice is a small and
very gossipy city and it wouldn't have gone down very
well if it had got back to my boss that I'd been gatecrash-
ing. So I threw myself on your mercy.' She wriggled her
shoulders self-consciously. 'You were my knight in shining armour, if you like.'

But he didn't bother acknowledging her weak joke,
just continued to subject her to the iron-hard gleam of
his eyes, which cut through her like a blade. 'How old
are you?' he asked suddenly.

'Twenty-three.'

'Twenty-three,' he repeated slowly. 'Intelligent, attractive and articulate.'

'Why, thanks very much,' she answered flippantly.

'Yet you're working as a rich man's servant.'

'And your point is? You strike me as a pretty rich man
yourself, Odysseus.' Deliberately, she studied the lapel
of his handmade suit, her gaze drifting over the exquisite cream shirt and a tie of silk which matched his blue
eyes exactly. How dared he look down his privileged
nose and start *judging* her? 'Are you saying you don't
have servants?'

His voice was impatient. 'That's different.'

'How?' she argued. 'Don't I fit your perceived idea of what a servant should be? Wrong age, wrong marital status, wrong shape?'

'That's not what I said.'

'But it's what you meant, isn't it?' she demanded. 'And why wouldn't I do it when I happen to be very good at it? I really love this city, but I'm sure even you can appreciate how much it costs to live here. I could never afford the market rent but this way I get to live on the Grand Canal *and* I get paid well.' She knew she wasn't providing him with all the facts, but nobody said she had to. She wasn't going to see him again but she could certainly influence the way he remembered her. A virgin conquest was one thing, but she wasn't going to come over as some sort of hard-done-by *victim*. '*You* may live in a lofty ivory tower looking down on the world, Odysseus, but surely you can understand that not all of us do.'

A faint smile tugged at the edges of his lips.

'Are you suggesting I'm a snob, Grace?' he questioned softly.

She shrugged. 'I'll let you be the judge of that.'

Odysseus met the defiant challenge sparking from her eyes and wondered if she had any idea how much her outspokenness was turning him on, because his great wealth and his power often made women people-pleasers when they were in his presence. But that wasn't the only thing which was making his blood grow heated. Last night's attraction had been mutual—a flash of something extraordinary, sharpened by the fact that they had both been dressed as other people. A cocktail of anonymity and flirtation which had gone further than it should have done and had ended all too abruptly.

But today she wasn't coming onto him one bit and that in itself, was alluring. In fact, she seemed to have gone out of her way to dress in a manner which made her fade into the background and that also set her apart from just about every woman of his acquaintance. Her hair was windswept, her jeans and sweater unremarkable. So why this sudden longing to shove aside the scratched café table and pull her into his arms? Was it the memory of her sweet responsiveness which made him want to behave so uncharacteristically, or because a woman playing hard to get was outside his realm of experience?

He'd been targeted by the opposite sex for as long as he could remember. At fifteen he'd needed to get away from home and the predatory stepmother who had watched him like a dog on heat. He'd found himself a job on a yacht sailing around the Greek islands, and the daughter of the luxury vessel's owner had watched him with eyes which had been just as hungry. But she hadn't been married to his father, which meant he was able to consider having sex with the gym-honed heiress.

Yet Odysseus had resisted the pleas to visit her cabin in the dead of night, or to linger when she flaunted her topless body in front of him while her parents were ashore. If anything he had savoured testing his own resolve and witnessing her growing frustration at his resistance. He'd waited until the very last day of his employment, when his pay cheque had been safely in his hand, before taking her down to the beach, where he'd spent the whole night exploring her body beneath the stars.

She had whispered that he was her 'bit of rough' and

he had stored away that piece of information thoughtfully. She'd gasped into his ear that he was the best lover she'd ever had and he hadn't had the heart to tell her that he'd been a virgin. But even at the height of his first penetrative orgasm he had remained curiously detached, despite her demands afterwards to know how he *felt* about her. The words she had tried to corral him into uttering had remained unsaid and she had been unable to hide her disappointment.

That had been the beginning of his sexual journey and he had plotted his future course accordingly. Physical satisfaction coupled with an emotional distance were the only things he ever guaranteed and not once had he ever strayed from that path. He chose his lovers carefully. Wisely.

Until now.

'So Contarini doesn't know you're meeting me?' he questioned.

'Of course not!'

'Because you sense he wouldn't approve?'

'Something like that.'

He raised his eyebrows. 'His approval naturally being something you always seek?'

'He's my boss, Odysseus. He pays my wages. And since he'll be here long after you've flown off into the sunset—' she put her hands flat on the table, as if she was preparing to lever herself to her feet, and the rogue scarlet fingernail winked at him provocatively '—it would be pretty stupid to do something which annoyed him. Jobs like that don't exactly grow on trees.'

He saw a sudden rush of colour flood into her cheeks and she dropped her gaze to the table, as if she'd said too much, and for a moment Odysseus studied her bent head, his mind a mass of conflicting thoughts.

The best thing would be for him to say goodbye. To take a water taxi to the airport where his plane was waiting and lose himself in work and preparation for his upcoming trip to Tuloranka. But something was holding him back. He felt a rush of desire as potent as a raw slug of retsina and suddenly he gave in to it, let it wash right over him.

'Turn your hands over,' he instructed huskily. 'And look at me.'

Raising her puzzled gaze to his, she nonetheless did as he asked, exposing the palms which last night had pressed hard into his buttocks as she'd urged him even deeper. Was she remembering that, too? Was that why she suddenly bit her lip as a flush of colour spread over her cheeks? He began to trace a slow and deliberate circle over her skin and to anyone watching, it would have appeared to be the most innocent of touches. Yet to Odysseus it felt unbearably sensual. He heard her suck in a shuddered breath and then expel it—a sound of pure capitulation made all the sweeter by her obvious unworldliness. He could see the smoky dilation of her pupils as she fixed him with a bewildered amber gaze.

'Wh-what are you doing?' she whispered.

'I'm reminding you what happens when I touch you. It's pretty remarkable, isn't it?' He paused. 'Are you as turned on as I am right now, Grace?'

She didn't answer straight away. Her gaze flickered down to their hands before she lifted her eyes to his once more. 'You…you know I am,' she breathed shakily.

Yes, he knew, and for a moment Odysseus cursed the

fact that he'd already checked out of his hotel, while she was clearly in no position to take him home. But even if she had been, he was damned if he would ever set foot in his grandfather's house again. He studied her trembling lips and considered his options. Finding another room wouldn't be a problem for a man with his connections, despite the fact that it was a busy carnival week. But a snatched afternoon of sex wasn't what he wanted. After a whole year of self-imposed celibacy, she had awoken his sexual hunger in a way which felt new and raw and urgent. She had set his blood on fire.

He slid his thumb over her skittering pulse as he thought about his upcoming schedule. A trip to Tuloranka, to advise King Kaliman on how best to develop his country's highly prized lithium resources, thus increasing the national wealth by billions. A big job, yes. A very big job. But not without setbacks. Odysseus frowned. It was a country steeped in somewhat archaic tradition and, as a single man staying at the palace, celibacy would be a necessity, not a choice. So why not make the most of what was available on offer now? Surely he would be crazy not to capitalise on this incredible chemistry with the petite housekeeper who was staring at him with darkened eyes which mirrored his own frustrated thoughts exactly.

'When's your next free weekend?' he asked suddenly, pulling his hand away.

Grace blinked, wondering why he had stopped touching her and thinking it was probably a good thing because her swollen breasts felt as if they were about to burst right out of her bra. Her mouth was dust-dry, and she had to lick her lips before she could frame a coherent answer to his question. 'Not till the end of the month,' she croaked.

He shook his head. 'That won't work. Can't you bring it forward?'

'I can try,' she said doubtfully. 'Why?'

'I thought you might like a trip to Paris.'

'Paris?' She stared at him. 'Are you serious?'

'I'm not in the habit of saying things I don't mean,' he offered drily.

'Paris!' She sat up very straight, her heart beating fast. 'Oh, my God. I've always wanted to go there.'

'You've never been?' He frowned. 'You do have a passport?'

'Of course I have a passport, but…' She hesitated. 'Why do you want to take me to Paris?'

'Oh, come on, Grace.' His voice dipped. 'Surely you must have a few ideas?'

Refusing to take the erotic bait, she shrugged. 'Maybe you want to grill me about your grandfather.'

'I'm not interested in him.' There was a heartbeat of a pause. 'I'm interested in you.'

Grace's sense of disorientation increased because fairy-tale invitations to the most romantic city in the world didn't happen to someone like her. There must be a million other women he could have taken who would have been way more suitable. 'But you still haven't told me,' she persisted stubbornly. 'Why me?'

If she hadn't been so innocent then Odysseus would have dismissed her question as disingenuous. The kind of breathless words women uttered when they were seeking flattery. But she *had* been innocent. *His* innocent. And that was significant. The lust which had rocked his body when he had made love to her had been primitive. He'd never experienced anything like it before and he wanted to experience it again. 'I have never slept with a virgin before,' he admitted huskily.

A faint shadow crossed her face, as if his anatomical candour had disappointed her, but then she gathered herself together, as if determined to match his bluntness. 'And is it very...different?'

'*Neh*. Very different. It was...incredible.' He gave a short laugh. 'If you must know, I've been aching for you ever since I woke up this morning. I am aching for you right now. I wish we were alone so I could do something about it. I would like to reach my hand underneath the table and feel how wet you are. I would like to make you come again,' he continued, his voice dipping into a caress. 'Does that shock you?'

She looked down at the scarlet fingernail and then up into his face again, her colour still very high, but her amber eyes were bright and challenging. 'A bit,' she admitted.

He shrugged. 'I could dress up my desire for you with flowery language, but I don't want you to get the wrong idea. I am a straightforward man, Grace, and my needs are equally straightforward. I like sex and, judging by your response last night, you like it too.' There was a pause. 'But as a novice, you have much to learn.' His gaze raked over her flushed face. 'If you like, I can help with that.'

Her fingertips fluttered to her throat, as if attempting to conceal the rapidly beating pulse, and suddenly he wanted to flicker his tongue over the delicate skin.

'Is that a boast?' she husked.

'I have no need to boast.'

'You want to whisk me off to Paris and teach me everything you know about sex?'

'I think *everything* would be too big an ask. And certainly not achievable in a single weekend,' he murmured, with an unashamed hint of sensual mastery. 'But I can certainly get you started.'

'Why, that's…outrageous,' she breathed.

'Mmm. I agree. It is. But so what? What you did last night was pretty outrageous.' He picked up her palm again, enjoying her corresponding shiver as he curved his fingers over the bare flesh. 'You strike me as someone who is ripe for adventure. So why not just reach out and embrace another one, while you have the opportunity?'

CHAPTER SIX

AGAINST THE LAVISHLY appointed backdrop of the hotel suite, Grace found herself fixed in the sapphire spotlight of Odysseus's gaze.

'There's no need to look so frightened,' he said softly. 'I won't bite.'

'Oh!' From somewhere, Grace manufactured a wonky smile. 'That's disappointing.'

She could tell from the answering curve of his lips that her feeble attempt at flirting was exactly what he wanted and she was doing her level best to fulfil that particular criterion, which she'd managed with such aplomb in Venice. But back then she'd been on familiar territory. This time it wasn't easy to slot into her brand-new reality and she still couldn't quite believe she was here.

In Paris, with a billionaire lover she barely knew.

The getting here had been disorientating enough, even though she'd known the travel plans in advance and had nursed them to herself like a particularly delicious secret. But nothing could have prepared her for the journey. The private jet which had whisked her from Venice and the limousine waiting in Paris, with the driver carefully explaining that Kyrios Diamides was busy and would meet her at the hotel. Grace had smiled politely and pretended it didn't matter.

But it did.

She had *wanted* him to be there. She hadn't been anticipating him clutching a bunch of flowers, or standing there with a soppy smile of expectation on his face—she wasn't *that* naïve. She just didn't want to be left feeling like an inconsequential package which was being delivered to the powerful billionaire by his driver. Wasn't she important enough for him to juggle his schedule so he could meet her in person? Clearly not. She'd started wondering if she had been naïve in agreeing to his suggestion that she join him in Paris and during the drive through the early spring sunshine, her doubts had multiplied. By the time she had arrived at the swanky hotel, with its bright boxes of flowers adorning every wrought-iron balcony, she'd been sorely tempted to tap the driver on the shoulder and ask him to take her straight back to the airfield.

But to her surprise, Odysseus had been waiting to greet the car. He had even managed to dwarf the presence of the famous actor who was being ushered into a nearby blacked-out SUV. He had carried her small suitcase as if he were a valet—though she'd seen his faint look of surprise when he had observed its modest dimensions.

'This all you've got?' he verified.

'I hope it's enough.' She had been aware of the note of defensiveness in her voice. 'I'm only here for two and a half days, aren't I?'

But his question had been enough to stoke a growing sense of insecurity which was never far from the surface. In the elevator, she'd been stung into self-conscious

silence—mostly by a beautiful blonde who kept stealing hungry glances at the Greek billionaire. And now
Grace was standing alone with him in this lavish suite,
stricken by that same dumbness, scarcely able to believe
that someone like him had chosen someone like her.

Because…

She was acutely aware of how much she was punching above her weight. She'd looked him up online, deciding that forewarned was forearmed, although there
was regrettably little to get her teeth into. It seemed he
was a crazily successful fund manager, which apparently
meant investing money for rich people so they became
even richer. He had a reputation for tact and silence,
which was why he had landed so many high-profile cli-
ents. And although he had been photographed with lots
of beautiful women, he seemed resolutely single—the
latter fact giving rise to much conjecture. But that was all
it was—conjecture. Any interviews he'd given were fo-
cussed solely on his successful business empire—and information about his background was sketchy. He'd grown
up near the docks in Athens, but there was no mention
of his mother—or indeed of Vincenzo Contarini.

As she feasted her eyes on his magnificent physique
her sense of disbelief kept growing, because just how gorgeous did any man have a right to be? His eyes glittered
like sapphires against the burnished gold of his skin and
although he was wearing pared-down jeans and a silk
shirt, you could just *tell* how wealthy he was. He looked
vital, she thought, while she was feeling increasingly invisible—terrified of doing or saying the wrong thing.

His narrowed gaze lingered on her face assessingly.
'Good journey?' he enquired conventionally.

'Oh, you know,' she said. 'It was a bit weird getting used to being waited on hand and foot by all your various members of staff. And the plane was...well, it was much bigger than I was expecting and...'

He reached out his hand as her babbled words tailed off and for one breathless moment she prayed he was going to kiss her, but he simply pushed a heavy lock of hair away from her cheek.

'You look...tired,' he observed softly.

Was that a criticism? Grace touched her fingertips to the shadowed area beneath her eyes, which no amount of foundation had been able to erase. 'Yeah. I suppose I do.'

Blue eyes lasered into her. 'Any particular reason?'

Now was not the time to inform him that Vincenzo Contarini had been making her life a misery ever since she'd told him she was going away. Grace had been vague about the upcoming weekend, batting off her boss's barrage of suspicious questions with an air of assumed innocence she was terrified he would see through. She hated the idea of deceiving him, but what else could she do? He'd been in a foul mood ever since his estranged grandson's visit, finding fault in everything she did and even making her stay up past midnight to sew a mother-of-pearl button onto a shirt she was certain he would never wear. Imagine his reaction if she told him she was spending the next two days with Odysseus—a man he clearly loathed, though she still didn't understand why. Would he have tried to stop her?

Of course he would.

'Oh, just running around before my trip,' she admitted carefully. 'Making sure that everything gets done.'

'You don't get away much?'

Now was also not the time to tell him that her only trips abroad were long train journeys back to England, because that would involve telling him about Nana. And it would inevitably be a downer on what was supposed to be a romantic weekend if you started telling your lover about your beloved grandmother who had been suffering from dementia for the last two years. 'Not really,' she told him honestly.

'I think I'm going to run you a bath,' he said softly. 'Let you chill for a while.'

Grace stared at him, because although the thought of somebody doing something for *her* for a change was making her feel stupidly emotional, this wasn't what she had been expecting. He hadn't kissed her. Hadn't even touched her. Did that mean he'd gone off her? Keeping her expression bland, she nodded. 'That sounds great.'

'So why don't you go and unpack your clothes next door and come and find me when you're ready?'

'Sure,' she said. Glad to get away from that piercing gaze, she picked up her minuscule suitcase and went into the room he'd indicated, which was dominated by a huge four-poster bed. Removing her trainers and dropping her denim jacket onto a dusky pink sofa, she slid the remainder of her clothes onto the fancy padded velvet hangers and hung them in the wardrobe, aware that her fingers were trembling with nerves. She felt like an actor who had been parachuted into a play at the last minute without being given any lines or stage directions and she didn't have a clue what to do next. She wanted to behave like that woman she'd been on the night they'd met, or the woman who had let him turn her on in the café the next day. But she couldn't seem to access all that sassiness and brio, and Odysseus wasn't making it very easy for her.

She'd thought…

What?

That by now he would be pushing her down onto that vast bed and sliding his hand hungrily beneath her cotton dress? Yes. Of course she had. Because that was the fantasy. That was what had been preoccupying her thoughts since the travel details had pinged into her inbox and she'd stared at them in disbelief.

Shutting the wardrobe door and following the sound of running water, Grace entered the steamy bathroom, her senses instantly assailed by the heady scent of jasmine, but even more by the vision which greeted her. It was an incongruous sight—the Greek billionaire with his shirt sleeves rolled up, next to a tub filled high with bubbly water. He straightened up as she appeared and his image was reflected back from the many mirrored surfaces, as if taunting her with all those different angles of a powerful body which suddenly seemed so far away.

'Would you like me to bring you a glass of champagne?' He raised his eyebrows. 'Or perhaps you'd prefer to wait until afterwards?'

After what? Grace wondered with a touch of hysteria, but somehow she managed a smile. 'I've never drunk champagne in the bath before,' she informed him nervously.

'No, I don't suppose you have.' His eyes glinted with something she didn't recognise. 'In which case, I'd better go and pour you some, hadn't I?'

Turning away from her obvious embarrassment, Odysseus beat a hasty retreat, aware of the pulse hammering at his temple as he walked along the long corridor and into the grand salon. For long moments he stared down at the steady stream of traffic on the Avenue Montaigne before, eventually, he sighed, plucking a bottle of vintage champagne from the ice bucket and tearing off the foil with impatient fingers.

When would he learn that nothing ever turned out the way you expected? His body had been as tight as a coiled whip all morning—something he'd put down to the frustration he'd experienced since leaving Venice and breaking his self-imposed celibacy with a woman he couldn't seem to stop thinking about. A woman who was wrong for him on so many levels. How easy it was to be wise after the event, he thought acidly.

He had decided not to meet her at the airport for many reasons and not just because of ever-pressing work commitments. He'd been in such a state of heightened anticipation that he didn't trust himself not to start making out in the car and public lovemaking was something he never indulged in, no matter how powerful the provocation. Plus, he didn't want her thinking he was the kind of man who met women off flights like an ardent suitor, because he wasn't. Achingly aware of her relative innocence, he had decided it was important she understood his boundaries from the get-go, and he didn't want to mislead her.

He had paced around the hotel suite distractedly all morning, eagerly awaiting her appearance. Bearing in mind that he hadn't been able to keep his hands off her and she clearly felt the same, it should have been simple and straightforward. But then the limousine had arrived and all his plans of instant sex had been blown out of the water.

She'd been sitting upright in the back seat and he'd seen the look in her eyes as she'd peered out of the window. The anxiety and the trepidation—but, even more than that, the way she'd been chewing on her lip. She had looked unbearably vulnerable and something in his gut had clenched as she had stepped from the car, all bare legs and a light cotton dress. Her diminutive stature and wide eyes made her seem impossibly fragile and his once clear agenda of sexual tutelage now seemed burdened by a sudden and unwanted sense of responsibility. In that moment she had looked less like flesh and blood and more like some delicate piece of porcelain and he was terrified of touching her. Of breaking her. A cloud had passed over the day and somehow he couldn't seem to shift its shadow.

But then, hadn't everything taken on a more sombre hue since his return from Venice, when he'd walked away with the sickening discovery of how little his mother had meant to her own father? And hadn't that only reinforced his cynical conclusions on the toxic nature of families? Silently, he cursed his lack of judgement.

Why the hell had he brought innocent Grace Foster here when he should have been seeking solace with a woman who was more like him? Somebody without a heart, who knew the rules. Somebody who had nothing to do with a past he wanted to shut the door on for ever.

After pouring two flutes of champagne, he returned to the bathroom, lingering in the doorway as he took in the intimate scene in front of him. Up to her neck in foam, Grace was lying with her head resting against the back of the bath, her eyes closed and a damp strand of hair curling on her cheek. She looked soft. Relaxed. All blurred and hazy—like an out-of-focus photo. She might almost have been asleep. But she wasn't. She must have heard him because her wet lashes fluttered open and she smiled and Odysseus was unprepared for the sudden clench of his heart in response to that simple smile. She hauled herself up a little, the water slopping away from her, giving him a distracting glimpse of a pair of rosy nipples.

'You look more…relaxed,' he observed.

'Mmm. I feel it.' She gave a self-conscious little shrug. 'It's amazing what a little hot water can do.'

'Here,' he said, handing her the drink.

'Thanks.' She took a sip and blinked rapidly as the bubbles flew up her nose, before fixing him with an inquisitive look. 'Aren't you having any?'

'Not right now.' He put his glass down on the floor and studied the shiny expanse of her wet shoulders. 'I'm tempted to get in there and join you.'

There was a pause and her cheeks grew even more flushed. 'So…what's stopping you?' she questioned shyly.

'Logistics,' he husked and, taking the glass from her fingers to place it next to his own, he leaned forward to touch his lips to hers, unprepared for his reaction to that first kiss. Because didn't he find himself almost *resenting* the surge of surrender which flooded through him as she kissed him back, her wet hands cupping the sides of his face as if to anchor herself? Her tongue moved greedily inside his mouth as if she were as eager to reacquaint herself with him and he could taste the sharpness of the champagne and the sweetness of her lips.

With a hungry growl he slipped a hand beneath the frothy water and cupped her breast and the contrast between the warm globe of flesh and the silken caress of the water on his skin was delicious. She gasped as he flicked his thumb over one thrusting nipple and he couldn't resist exploring further, down over the flat belly before flickering his fingertips between the thighs which had so willingly parted for him.

'Yes,' she breathed hungrily, but as water began to slop over the side of the bath, he pulled away, his heart hammering hard against his ribcage.

'Not here,' he announced huskily, ignoring the disappointed pucker of her lips as he lifted her out of the water and wrapped her in a voluminous towel. He heard the ragged breath she sucked in as he became engrossed in the erotic task of drying her. He paid particular attention to her nipples and the honeyed slickness between her thighs before recognising, with a sudden urgency, that he needed to get her into bed before they both ended up on the unforgiving marble floor.

He carried her to the bedroom, lowering her onto the cover so that she looked tiny against the vast mattress, her nakedness framed by a backdrop of dusky pink satin. He began to undress and her eyes were huge as they followed each movement with fascination and he wondered if it was her innocent preoccupation which made his fingers uncharacteristically unsteady as he peeled off his shirt and reached for the button of his jeans.

'It is very distracting when you look at me like that,' he murmured.

'In a good way, or a bad way?' she questioned.

Could she really be that innocent? he wondered wryly. 'In a good way,' he conceded, rolling onto the bed beside her and pulling the tie from her hair, so that the damp chestnut-brown locks tumbled down in wild profusion. She gave a little yelp of what sounded like relief as her arms snaked sinuously around his neck to press herself close to him, and her enthusiasm drove away the last of his habitual cynicism. With a low growl of anticipation, Odysseus began to rediscover her petite body with the practised drift of his fingers. Her slim hips and tiny waist. The rocky nipples, which fitted so neatly into his waiting mouth. The soft curls and honeyed folds.

Unable to ignore her moans any longer, he groped for the condom he'd had the foresight to place beside the bed but sliding it over his aching hardness seemed to take for ever. And maybe it was the delayed gratification which was responsible for the incandescent burst of pleasure which arrowed through him as he thrust deep inside her. Because what else could it be?

It was over too quickly. He heard her gasp just before she started to spasm and then he was coming too, he just couldn't seem to stop himself. The words he choked out were incomprehensible as he spilled his seed inside her and afterwards, he felt... He stared at the ceiling with faint bemusement. He felt *different*. He turned his head to look at her. Her eyes were closed, a flushed satisfaction had made her cheeks grow pink and there was a small, secret smile curving her lips. For the first time in his life, Odysseus could feel the true and intimidating danger of a woman's power, and he didn't like it.

Who *was* she? he wondered bitterly.

'Better?' he questioned, his tone deliberately nonchalant.

'Mmm?' Unwillingly disturbed from a sensation of complete bliss, Grace opened her eyes and gave a lazy yawn as she met the sapphire glitter of his gaze. 'Better than what?'

'Than when you arrived. Despite sending me a text from Venice, telling me how excited you were about the trip, you looked as I imagine Marie Antoinette might have done on the morning of her execution,' he murmured. 'Which wasn't so very far from here.'

'Yes, I know. I read it in the travel guide on the way over. And I *was* very excited about coming on this trip,' she added truthfully. 'But the reality was a bit of a life shock. I've never travelled by private jet before, or been picked up by a chauffeur in a flashy car and then brought to an amazing suite in an equally amazing hotel. It all felt a bit overwhelming and... I don't know, almost...' she wriggled her shoulders '...cold-blooded.'

'But it doesn't now?'

'No,' she answered softly and all she wanted was for him to kiss her again.

But he didn't. It was disappointing. It was frustrating. Worse than that, it felt a bit *controlling*.

'So tell me, because I'm curious.' He turned onto his side so that his gaze was icing over her, cool and blue and forensic, and Grace found herself instinctively tensing as she waited for his next words.

'What the hell are you doing, working for a man like Vincenzo Contarini?'

CHAPTER SEVEN

Acknowledging the bitterness of Odysseus's words, Grace wondered if she should deflect them—perhaps by asking for another glass of champagne, or remarking on how pretty the view of the Parisian street outside was. The last thing she wanted was to discuss her often horrible boss—especially not with the man who was lying naked next to her. This weekend was supposed to be about fantasy and escape. She'd wanted to keep the difficult areas of her life on the back burner. To pretend they weren't happening so she could forget what she was going back to—a life of grim service. But Odysseus was studying her with such cold intensity— and surely it would be naïve to suppose that her boss's estranged grandson *wouldn't* want to quiz her, given the circumstances?

'Why do I work for Vincenzo?' Wriggling up the bed a little, she raked her fingers through her messy hair and wondered when it would be diplomatic to go in search of a hairbrush. 'Well, for a start, he pays well.'

'Of course he does,' he said softly. 'And money means everything, right?'

'It's all very well for you to be so dismissive when you're obviously loaded, but I happen to need the money,' she retorted, because suddenly she felt as if he was judging her.

'For what?' He glanced across the room to where she'd left her not-so-white trainers and the rather faded denim jacket she'd bought from a stall near the Rialto Bridge. 'Forgive my bluntness, but you obviously aren't feeding a fashion addiction.'

Grace didn't have the heart to be offended by his rather brutal assessment of her clothes because wasn't he only speaking the truth? She'd never been into fashion—never really had the opportunity. Because first she'd been a broke student and then a housekeeper. Sometimes she felt old before her time. She dressed simply and cheaply and always had an eye for a bargain, yet she made light of her thrift because she didn't want people feeling sorry for her. And though she wished she could tell Odysseus Diamides that none of this was his business, she could see from that intense expression in his blue eyes that he was determined to find out.

'If you must know, I'm paying for my grandmother's care,' she told him, mollified yet indignant when she saw the condemnation on his face replaced by a look of surprise. So he *had* been judging her!

'Tell me about her,' he said.

'Honestly.' She shook her head, a stupid lump rising in her throat. 'It's a long story and I'm not going to bore you with it.'

'Tell me,' he insisted softly.

Grace met his commanding stare, recognising that he had enough quiet authority about him to coax blood from a stone and something was tempting her to confide in him. She told herself he wouldn't understand about the hardships in her life—this man who owned an aero-plane, whose shoes probably cost more than she earned in a month. Yet some kernel of pride was making her want to justify her servile position in the house of a man with more enemies than friends—a man he clearly hated. Odysseus Diamides knew her body better than anyone, she realised suddenly—but he knew nothing about her as a person, and suddenly it became important that he did. She didn't just want to be some dim blur in his back catalogue of lovers. If ever he remembered her in the future, she wanted it to be as a real person.

'So my mum took me to Venice when I was seven, after my father died,' she began, meeting the question in his eyes. 'It was her dream city and she hated Devon, where I was born. But it's also one of the most expensive cities in the world and having a child hampered her opportunities, so she got a job working as housekeeper for Signor Contarini. It was only supposed to be temporary but it turned out to be permanent. You know how life just happens and you just chug along with it?' She shrugged. 'I think she thought she'd meet someone else and fall in love, but she never did.'

'So you grew up in Vincenzo's house?'

'Well. Sort of.' She took the opportunity to grab a silken throw from the bottom of the bed and slid it over her body, because her nakedness was only adding to her feeling of vulnerability. 'We had our own section of it, where the rest of the servants lived—so I never had much to do with him on a day-to-day basis. He didn't really like children, to be honest, so I kept out of his way as much as possible.'

'And did he…?' She could see a pulse flicker at his temple. 'Did he ever mention my mother?'

She saw the flash of something indefinable in the depths of his eyes and she wanted to tell him what she suspected he wanted to hear, but Grace knew she couldn't tell a lie just to make him feel better. Something told her he would see right through her efforts and then despise her for even attempting to try. 'Never, I'm afraid. Some of the older staff mentioned that he'd had a daughter but that was years before our time and...well, there was no evidence of any family. No photos, or anything like that.' She looked up into a face that might have been carved from granite and prayed she hadn't been too brutal. 'What...what happened to her?'

'That's irrelevant,' he said, in a cold voice which was unequivocal. 'We're supposed to be talking about you.'

She nodded. 'We used to visit my nana whenever we could and though she used to try and persuade us to move back to England, my mum never wanted to.'

'Did you?'

'Not really. Venice is an amazing city and it's all I really know. Devon had too many cows for my liking,' she joked, but didn't manage to raise a smile from those carved and implacable features. 'I went to school there like any normal child and then enrolled in the local university.'

Dark eyebrows swooped upwards. 'You have a degree?'

Grace didn't attempt to keep the exasperation from her voice. 'Why? Did you think I was only qualified to answer the door and pour glasses of water for irascible men?'

'I didn't say that.'

'You didn't have to. It's pretty obvious that's what you were thinking.'

'Is that so?' He stared at her mockingly. 'Do you have a particular talent for reading people's minds, Grace, or is that something which just happens with me? In which case, should I be worried?'

If he hadn't been so sarcastic, she might have explained that when you were a servant—or a servant's child—you got good at reading body language because you were supposed to anticipate other people's needs. But, unwilling to risk his derision, she stuck to the facts.

'I did a language degree and qualified as an interpreter,' she continued stiffly. 'I'd just been offered a job in Brussels when my mum…' And this was why she didn't talk about it. Because this was what happened. Every single time. That annoying lump in her throat, which was making it difficult to get her words out, had made its presence known and if she'd been telling anyone else, they might have gently suggested she halt her story. But not Odysseus. There was no gentleness in him, she realised, despite the fact that they'd just made love. That cold blue gaze was slicing through her like a blade and the angles of his face were hard and shadowed. She remembered her friends urging her to seek counselling when all this had happened, but so much had been going on that she never had done and, anyway—who would have paid?

'It was a freak accident,' she told him flatly. 'Contrary to popular belief, very few people drown in Venice but one night…' She swallowed. 'One night there was a terrible storm and Mum must have lost her footing on her way back from the market and…that was it. At first light the Polizia di Stato came to say they'd found a body in the canal. She…she wasn't even forty.'

Grace waited for him to come out with conventional expressions of regret but he didn't say anything and after a moment or two it occurred to her that he was a man who seemed very comfortable with silence. Was that a ploy he'd developed over the years, she wondered, which would make other people want to fill it? Because if that was the case, it was working.

'My grandmother was so shattered by news of her daughter's death that she had a stroke,' she said slowly. 'The doctors said that sometimes shock can do that to a person. At first, they said she should get better, only it was much worse than they thought and she didn't recover and needed to go into care, which is unbelievably expensive. She's got dementia now. And since I'm her only living relative and the only person who can help contribute, I...' She pressed her lips together, trying to sound brisk and matter-of-fact, because she had loved her nana so much. Still did. Even if she stared at her only grandchild with eyes which were blank and unrecognising whenever Grace paid her a visit. 'I took over my mother's job and that's what I've been doing ever since.'

'Wait a minute.' His eyes narrowed. 'Why did you take your mother's job? Why didn't you go off and use your degree and send money to your grandmother that way?'

It was at this moment that Grace lost patience, because what did a man like Odysseus Diamides know about how ordinary people dealt with all the horrible stuff which life threw at them? 'Why do you think? Because I was broke. I couldn't afford care fees *and* rent. And there was Mum's funeral to pay for, too. You wouldn't believe how expensive that is in Venice. But Signor Contarini stepped in. He offered to pay for everything if I just carried on from where Mum had left off and became his housekeeper. And we...we gave her a lovely send-off,' she said, trying to stop her voice from wobbling as she remembered the black gondola, decked with flowers and the cold tears which had streamed down her cheeks as she had watched its slow glide. 'Plus he gives me enough salary so that I can pay for Nana's care, though not a lot else. Hence my rather drab wardrobe choices.' She shrugged. 'It's what you call a win-win situation. And I'm indebted to him.'

Or trapped, Odysseus thought to himself. Stuck inside a gilded prison.

But Grace's explanation about her servile role had surprised him and, though it further fuelled his contempt for his grandfather, it had also stimulated his interest. Pluckiness and stoicism were strangely attractive qualities and it occurred to him that he had never come across a woman so willing to put someone else's needs ahead of their own.

'Come on. Isn't it your turn now?' she ventured, into the pause which had followed. 'Isn't it time I learnt something about you?'

'I guess so,' he answered, with practised skill. Bypassing the kind of intrusive detail he suspected she wanted, he chose instead to recount the rags-to-riches account of his time as a runner on the floor of the Athens stock exchange, to the announcement made just a decade later that he was the richest man in all Greece. It was a smooth and potted history he'd got down to a fine art, knowing when to skate over detail, when to elaborate and when to pause for laughs. It left people feeling they understood him. They never did, of course—that was just an illusion and one which he had carefully cultivated. 'Now my job takes me all over the world and I live on an island—alone—and very happily so.' He narrowed his eyes, deliberately keeping his tone dismissive. 'So. Does that tell you everything you want to know, Grace?'

She began to pluck at the silken throw, inadvertently drawing attention to the outline of her body beneath. 'Well…'

But he shifted the focus, deliberately peeling away the cover to reveal her breasts, allowing his thumb to trace a lazy circle over the peaking nipple. 'I think we've done enough talking,' he murmured. 'Isn't it about time I made you come again?'

'Oh, yes please,' she whispered, with shy eagerness.

Which he did. On every available surface. Odysseus had never wanted a woman so much as he wanted Grace. He was hard all the time, vacillating between intense pleasure and intense frustration. He couldn't seem to get enough of her and couldn't seem to work out why. Was it her innocent willingness to learn how to pleasure him which was making him feel as if he could explode with lust every time he looked at her, or the fact that he'd never met anyone quite like her? She was humble and polite. She thanked the staff and made a point of chatting to them in French. In between room-service meals and non-stop sex, he realised that in a little over twenty-four hours they hadn't even left the hotel and that he hadn't thought about work. Not once.

'Let's go for a walk,' he said suddenly.

From within the deep cushions of the extra-long sofa where he'd left her dozing, she blinked those extraordinarily long black eyelashes at him and, in the spring sunshine, the amber of her eyes resembled molten gold. 'A walk?' she echoed in surprise, and he felt an unexpected touch of guilt that his preoccupation up until now had been so relentlessly carnal.

'It's a beautiful day and Paris is a beautiful city, of which you have seen very little. The Tuileries Garden isn't far from here.' He raised his brows. 'Does that appeal?'

'Well, yes, it does. Very much,' she answered shyly and once again he felt an unexpected punch to his heart.

'I'll leave you to get ready while I catch up on some work next door.'

'But it's Saturday,' she objected.

'I am well aware of what day it is, Grace,' he said coolly as he reached for his jeans.

Grace watched him go, feeling like a fool. What was she *like*? Of course he knew what day of the week it was! He was probably using his work to emphasise the boundaries of their relationship, which he'd been reinforcing whenever he got the opportunity. And he wasn't exactly subtle about it. She knew what he was doing. Warning her off ever daring to dream of any kind of future between them. He liked living alone, as he'd told her on more than one occasion. He didn't like commitment. Definitely didn't want children of his own, although it seemed he had several adoring godchildren scattered all over the world.

After spritzing herself beneath the shower, she pulled on a dress and trainers and, at the last minute, crammed on the floppy hat with the polka-dot ribbon which Sophia had insisted she borrow. 'Because men love hats,' she had informed Grace knowingly. 'And they hide a multitude of sins.'

It seemed her more worldly friend had been correct because when Grace went to find Odysseus—tapping out something on his computer—he went very still when he saw her, his smoky blue gaze travelling all the way up from her feet, to linger on her head.

'Mmm. Nice…*hat*,' he murmured, his eyes glinting with provocation.

'I… Thank you.' Dreamily, she touched the brim, trying not to think about the sinful curve of his lips, or get too carried away by the careless compliment.

He flipped the lid of his computer shut and rose abruptly to his feet. 'Let's go.'

Outside, the warmth of the sun beating down on her only increased Grace's feeling of contentment as they began to walk towards the famous gardens and she drank in the landmarks she'd only ever seen in books or films. The glint of the River Seine. The Robocop structure of the Eiffel Tower. The Palais Royal and the Place Vendôme. And, of course, cars—living in Venice, she wasn't used to cars. They sat at a pavement café and drank Kir Royale and she watched elegant women passing by with their handbag-sized dogs.

By the time they reached the Tuileries, Grace was feeling totally relaxed—especially when Odysseus managed to commandeer a vacant bench. Was it something about his commanding presence which made a young couple spring to their feet, as if compelled to give the powerful billionaire the space he needed?

'You don't mind if I make a few calls?' he said, pulling out his phone.

'I don't suppose it would make any difference if I did?'

'Correct,' he affirmed.

Punching out a call, he began speaking in Greek and, with a jolt, Grace realised she hadn't looked at her own phone all day. She hadn't wanted to. It was as if the outside world no longer existed and this powerful man had become the centre of her universe. And surely that was dangerous.

Was it?

She stared at the way the sunlight sparkled on the water of the central fountain and wondered what advice her darling nana might give if she weren't lying in a coma. But deep down, she knew. She'd tell her that life was short and to get out there and enjoy herself, instead of spoiling it by worrying about the future. And that was what she intended to do. No more entertaining impossible dreams about a man who was totally out of her reach. She was just going to enjoy what they had now. She was here to learn about sex…so bring on the next lesson! A tiny white dog came yapping up to her and she giggled as she bent to ruffle its soft ears and it rose up on its back legs and performed a little dance.

'That's better,' purred Odysseus.

Retracting her fingers from the playful canine, Grace looked up, noticing Odysseus was turning off his phone before sliding it into the back pocket of his jeans, and she felt a blissful clench of anticipation as she met the gleam of his eyes. 'What is?'

There was a pause. 'I wonder if you have any idea of how beautiful you look when you smile.'

Don't react. Do *not* react. Remember what you've just been thinking. 'I'll bear that in mind,' she said lightly, holding onto her hat against a sudden gusty breeze, aware that Odysseus was studying her with a look she now recognised. A smoky longing. A burst of sensual flame, which flowed between them like lava. Desire in its purest form which made her go weak at the knees.

'I think we should go back to the hotel as soon as possible because I want you, Grace. Very badly,' he stated unevenly.

'I want you too,' she whispered.

'And later I'm going to take you somewhere very special for dinner.'

Grace was on such a high that she didn't even stress about what she was going to wear, especially as Odysseus took her straight to bed and ravished her so thoroughly that afterwards she was left feeling completely sated. They slept wrapped in each other's arms and it was only when she woke up amid the rumpled sheets that her doubts started to emerge.

'Is this restaurant you're taking me to very posh?'

'Reasonably. Why?'

'I'm wondering what to wear...*obviously*.' She threw him a reproving look. 'Especially after those snide comments you made about my fashion sense.'

'I take it all back. You look good in anything. Better still in nothing.' He trailed a slow finger over her hip. 'But there's a dress shop next door. We could easily go down and find something for you to wear.'

She couldn't deny being tempted by his careless suggestion and Grace supposed that purchasing a designer dress would be a drop in the ocean for someone like Odysseus. And there was no doubt that a sumptuous gown bought in this expensive part of the city would help her blend in and look the part. But she shook her head, because that was definitely a line and she didn't want to cross it. 'I'd rather not,' she said. 'I'll just tart up something I've brought with me and do my best not to let you down.'

She could tell he was surprised—perhaps even a touch irritated—by her refusal to accept his offer, but in the end she pronounced herself pleased with what she accomplished. Her simple black dress adorned with masses of silver chains which caught the light as she walked, she slid her feet into a pair of barely worn black heels which brought her almost up to his shoulders. She was just about to add to her supposed look of sophistication by piling up her hair, when he stopped her.

'No. Leave it down. I like it best like that,' he commanded huskily, and Grace felt a flutter of delight as he stroked his fingers through the newly washed strands.

His car sped them to a restaurant high on the sixth floor in the fifth arrondissement of the city, overlooking the glitter of the river and Notre-Dame Cathedral. It was, indeed, very grand, but the light touch of Odysseus's hand at her back filled Grace with a sense of self-belief and although everyone in the room was looking at him, he seemed only to have eyes for her. In the candlelight, they ate duck with polenta and drank rich, red wine and she found herself thinking that this was, without doubt, the best night of her life and she wanted to savour every second of it.

He didn't take her straight to bed when they arrived back at the hotel, just tugged off his tie and kissed her very thoroughly before disappearing into the bathroom, and that felt comfortable and intimate. It felt real. Hugging herself with anticipation about the night ahead, Grace suddenly heard a vibrating sound coming from the depths of her small rucksack and pulled out her phone, her heart sinking when she glanced at the screen.

Because, intoxicated by sex and enclosed within this bubble of rarefied luxury, it had been ridiculously easy to forget that she had another life. And the reminder of that life came crashing down like a rock when she saw that there were fourteen missed calls from Vincenzo.

Fourteen.

Why the hell had she put her phone on silent? was her first thought.

But her second thought was to wonder why she worked for such an unreasonable man.

Yet she knew the answer to that question. She did it because she had to. Sucking in a nervous breath, she was just about to ring him back when the screen started flashing and, barely registering the fact that Odysseus had returned and was standing in the doorway, she swiped the call to accept.

'Signor Contarini,' she trilled nervously. 'Is everything okay?'

CHAPTER EIGHT

IT WAS NOT in Odysseus's nature to accept the unacceptable, but he resisted demanding that Grace terminate the call to his grandfather, because this was really none of his business. She could, of course, talk to exactly whom she pleased—because she was a free agent, as was he. But despite all his best intentions, his indignation that she was being bothered on a well-earned break was dispelled by a growing fury as he listened to one half of the conversation.

It began with her apologising and some bone-deep instinct made him flinch as he observed the craven attitude which seemed to have diminished her.

'I know. I know,' she was saying. 'I'm really sorry. I should have told you I was leaving the country. Still, I'm glad that nothing's wrong and that Maria is looking after you okay.'

As she listened to the response she glanced up at him and her face flushed a deep red. 'No, I do realise that. But does it honestly matter who I'm with, Signor Contarini?'

A long tirade followed though Odysseus couldn't make any sense of it out, other than the rising volume of ire coming down the phone.

'But I'm not supposed to be back until tomorrow evening,' Grace croaked, and then listened. 'Well, yes, I suppose so. Of course I can come back earlier if—'

Unable to tolerate any more, Odysseus took the phone from her, shaking his head and holding his finger against his lips as he listened.

'Let me stop you right there,' he interrupted at last, when he could stand no more of the old man's tirade. 'You're talking to Odysseus now, do you understand? And I'm not having Grace upset or, indeed, my weekend ruined by your unreasonable demands.'

The old man's voice changed. He tried bullying, then bluster and Odysseus felt the bile rise up from his stomach as he heard the old man's increasingly desperate inducements. Suddenly, he cut the call, seeing Grace's amber eyes widen in horror.

'What have you done?' she breathed, trying to grab the phone back. 'What have you *done*? You can't just hang up on him like that! I'll have to leave. I'll have to go back! Give me the phone. Let me ring him.'

'No,' he negated, and then softened his voice because her genuine distress was making a slow rage begin to build inside him. 'You can ring him in a minute if that's what you still want, but first you must hear me out.' He walked over to the window, trying to compose himself, trying to gather his racing thoughts—rejecting the impossible and then embracing it, before turning round to stare at all her flushed and natural beauty. 'You can't work for him any more, Grace,' he stated flatly.

'Oh, can't I? *Can't* I?' Anger rose up inside her and for the first time in as long as she could remember, Grace started to lose her temper. 'You can't just barge into my life and ruin it like this!' she raged. 'This is nothing but posturing on your part, with a whacking great dollop of male ego thrown in! You're just making a stand against someone you don't like, but this is *my* livelihood. Vincenzo isn't going to win employer of the year any time soon, but that's just the way it is. Don't you understand? I've told you that I need the money for my nana and yet you...you...'

She began to blink back the helpless tears which had gathered at the backs of her eyes, furious with him, but furious with herself, too—for putting herself in this vulnerable situation. What had she been thinking? 'You've managed to single-handedly ensure that I probably won't have a job when I go back to Venice unless I do something about it pronto. So I'd better start packing and leave right now—or at least first thing in the morning. I need to try and repair the damage before it's too late.'

'Please don't.' The words were soft and so was the hand which he placed on her shoulder and Grace's attempt to shake it off was half-hearted because it felt so good there. As if she had been born to have him touch her like that. He had shrugged off his dark dinner suit and undone a couple of buttons of his snowy shirt—and he looked as hot as hell.

'Listen to me, Grace.'

'I don't want to listen.'

But he paid no attention to her stubborn response. 'Do you want to know what he said to me?' he demanded. 'He offered me money, and when I didn't bite he then offered me shares in the family business if I promised to leave you alone. Do you realise what that means? He was *bartering* you, Grace, and that is outrageous.'

'Yes, it's outrageous—but so what? Like I told you, I'm not in a position to object to his morals.'

'I know you're financially dependent on him because you have responsibilities,' he ground out impatiently. 'But there *are* alternatives.'

'Oh, really? Like *what*?' she demanded spikily. 'I don't actually *do* the lottery.'

There was a pause. 'There is a solution of breathtaking simplicity,' he said at last.

The amber gaze she fixed on him was filled with suspicion. 'I'm dying to hear what that could be.'

'Marry me.'

At first Grace thought she must have misheard him. And when she realised she hadn't, wasn't there a part of her which allowed herself to buy into the idea with an eagerness which should have acted as a warning? She stared at him—waiting for the unique behaviour which traditionally accompanied a proposal of marriage. Some previously unseen smile to transform his features perhaps, before murmured words of love, which he would sheepishly admit he'd never said to anyone else.

But naturally, none of that happened. She must have been temporarily deluded to even imagine they might. His face was as impassive as she'd ever seen it and his eyes were a cold and steely blue. 'Well, well, well,' she said, with soft sarcasm, because that seemed the only way of subduing the stupid hope which had briefly flared as she'd contemplated escaping the gilded prison of the Contarini house into this man's arms. 'This is all very unexpected. I must say, I had no idea of your true feelings for me, Odysseus.'

'I don't *have* any feelings for you, other than de-

'sire,' he responded softly, before quickly tempering his words—presumably when he saw the look of dismay she must have failed to hide. 'Well, I do. I like you—'

'You hardly know me,' she objected, wondering why his brutal words had hurt so much.

'I have good instincts around people.'

'That's hardly the basis for everlasting bliss, is it?'

'But I don't believe in everlasting bliss, Grace. And that isn't the type of marriage I'm talking about.' He paused, as if painstakingly selecting which words would cause the least offence. 'I'm proposing an expedient arrangement which could benefit both of us.'

In spite of everything, her interest was spiked and, even though she told herself she was simply gearing herself up to get knocked back again, Grace stared at him from between hooded eyes. 'Go on.'

'You know that job I was telling you about? The royal trip I have coming up?'

'I'm very pleased your career seems to be doing so well, Odysseus, but I don't see what that has to do with me.'

He gave a lazy smile, as if her feistiness was turning him on. 'I don't know how up to speed you are with Tuloranka, but the regime only changed a couple of years ago. King Kaliman is dragging the country into the twenty-first century, but much of its ethos remains entrenched in the past, and it's a struggle.'

'Thanks for the lesson in world affairs,' she offered drily. 'But what does this have to do with your bizarre proposal?'

There was a pause. 'Because while I am there, I must observe the country's draconian laws. As a guest of the

King and a single man, I will be unable to have sex outside marriage.' There was a pause and now his eyes glittered, like sunlight on a blue glacier. 'You are obviously inexperienced, Grace, but you must have noticed by now that I find you utterly irresistible. You are fire to my blood,' he concluded huskily.

As his words sank in, she stiffened. 'You mean it isn't like that for you with everyone?' she asked, genuinely taken aback.

'No. It isn't.' He nodded his dark head reflectively. 'Perhaps it the knowledge that I am the only man to have ever physically possessed you which is so endlessly provocative.'

'Odysseus!' she said, but the darkening of her eyes belied her shocked response.

He shrugged. 'I know it is an unfashionable and anachronistic point of view, but it's the way I feel.' There was a pause. 'Or perhaps my year-long celibacy is the real reason why I can't seem to keep my hands off you.'

Grace tried to remain calm, although her head was buzzing like a jarful of wasps. Why on earth had someone as sexy and as gorgeous as Odysseus Diamides been celibate for a whole year? 'But… I mean…why?' she questioned. 'What made you swear off women like that?'

'It wasn't a big deal,' he growled. 'And as a lesson in self-control it was exemplary.'

'But that wasn't the only reason?' she fished.

'Well, no,' he conceded. 'I happen to have a very low boredom threshold and the predictability of women had begun to irritate me. Particularly, their incessant demands for things I wasn't prepared to give.'

'Such as?'

'Well, *love*, mostly.'

'Because you don't believe in love?'

He shook his head. 'No. Most emphatically, I don't.'

She sucked in a deep breath, trying not to act as if she was hurt by that sardonic statement, because she had no right to be. 'So...you want to marry me because you're obsessed by my body and this way you can have sex in a strict country without offending anyone, have I got that right?'

'Pretty much, *neh*,' he purred. 'But perhaps it will have another benefit, and the marriage will put an end to the endless speculation about why I have never taken a bride. Every interview I've ever given always starts off with that same damned question and it drives me mad.' He tilted her chin with his finger and his deep voice grew smoky. 'So why not enjoy our remarkable chemistry until it burns itself out?'

'And is that...inevitable?' she questioned carefully. 'That it will burn itself out?'

'Always. Attraction is like oil. A finite source.' He shrugged again, as if the death of desire were of no consequence.

'So what's in it for me, Odysseus?' she asked, qualifying her question when she saw the outraged expression on his face. 'Oh, I get that most women would probably bite your hand off to be your wife, but you've hardly bombarded me with inducements, have you?'

'Then why don't I spell it out for you in more favourable terms?' he suggested softly. 'As my wife, you will receive an allowance that will more than cover the cost of your grandmother's care and, when we divorce, you will walk away with a generous settlement. Which means you don't have to go and work for someone like Contarini ever again.' A note of something implacable entered his voice. 'You can do whatever you want to do. Use your degree. Become a linguist. Travel the world. I'm setting you free, Grace.'

'But why?' she asked bluntly. 'Why would you do that?'

There was a pause, and as he shrugged he was the personification of cool, male arrogance. 'Because I can.'

Grace was breathing rapidly as he studied her expectantly because his suggestion was completely bonkers and yet... She swallowed. The thought of not having to worry about the ever-escalating cost of Nana's care was hugely tempting, but so too was the thought of living a normal life and doing normal things. Because lately the miserable nature of her job had become ever more apparent—like the slow drip of a tap which gradually became a big puddle—and for the first time ever, she allowed herself to consider an alternative. No more rising at the crack of dawn and going out in all weathers to procure the only cornetto in the city which her boss would contemplate eating for breakfast. No more cancelling stuff at the last minute because Vincenzo had some trifling complaint. No more sitting in that big, dark house most evenings while the clock ticked away the hours and her life.

But that life was the only one she had ever really known, locked into a situation which was highly unusual for a woman of her age. Restrictive, yes but undoubtedly safe—and sometimes the outside world seemed a little... *daunting*. Because Odysseus was only talking temporary. She wouldn't have him by her side for long. What if she took a leap and everything came crashing down around her ears? 'And if I said yes, what would happen?'

'You collect your things and fly to my island home in Greece. We'll get married there. Don't expect romance, because I am not a romantic man. No fuss. No frills.' His sapphire eyes glinted with mockery. 'So I hope you weren't holding out for a big dress on your wedding day.'

Ignoring his sarcasm, she bit her lip because she had far more immediate concerns on her mind. 'And what if Vincenzo tries to stop me?'

Suddenly all that mockery and humour was gone. '*Kalós theós epifónima*, Grace,' he bit out. 'He's your employer, not your damned jailer! But just to reassure you, I will ensure that a bodyguard will be at your side at all times.'

And then she asked him, because she *had* to ask him, 'Why…why do you hate him so much?'

The silence which followed seemed endless as he seemed to weigh up whether or not he could trust her. 'Because he rejected my mother,' he said at last, his words harsh and bitter. 'He kicked her out when she was pregnant and she…' He shook his head. 'The rest doesn't matter. That's all history. Vincenzo Contarini is history,' he ground out. 'And I forbid you to worry about him any more, do you understand?'

Forbid was a powerful word, but right then it was making Grace feel protected. As if he were warding off the unsavoury elements of her life and rescuing her from all the drudgery, and she was too caught up in the violent swirl of her emotions to recognise just how dangerous a concept this was.

And she wanted him, that was the thing. The single element which dominated everything else. She wanted him with a hunger she'd never experienced before. He had awoken her senses. Made her feel like a woman. Made her feel as if *this* was the person she was always meant to be. How could she contemplate going back to that miserable existence and saying goodbye to him, knowing that this unlikely relationship could never work as an affair?

But she could only say yes if she accepted his boundaries and, really, there was only one which mattered.

She mustn't ever fall in love with him.

No matter what the provocation, nor how great the sex.

'Okay, then,' she said carelessly, not wanting to scare him off by sounding *too* eager. 'I'll marry you.'

CHAPTER NINE

'Wow,' said Grace softly and then, because the word seemed hopelessly inadequate, she said it again. 'Just *wow.*'

'You like it?'

She could hear the note of pleasure in Odysseus's voice and who could blame him? Once again, she took in the panoramic view, shown at its breathtaking best from their viewpoint on the hilltop. The island of Kosmima was nothing short of paradise—no wonder the Greek billionaire had chosen to live there.

There were beaches of silvery sand, citrus trees heavy with bloom and the mingled scents of thyme and salt perfuming the warm air. Directly behind her stood Odysseus's home—a dazzling white villa set in flower-filled grounds and featuring a vast infinity swimming pool. Inside, his taste was for quiet opulence and superb art. The house was bright and spacious and couldn't have been more different from the dark and twisty house she'd grown up in, but Grace had loved it on sight. His offices were in a separate part of the sweeping grounds, though she couldn't help noticing that they hadn't been included in her tour of the property—as if he were erecting boundaries and keeping her out of his private space. She'd met his housekeeper, Evangelia, whose son, Marinos, was visiting from university in Thessaloniki, as well as Evangelia's cat, a black and white ball of fur which had hissed at Grace in a very unfriendly manner.

She had flown in from Venice earlier that day and, as they had circled the crescent-shaped island, the pilot had pointed out the solar panels and wind turbines which made Kosmima self-sufficient for energy. With its abundant olive-oil crop and a daily catch of fish which was apparently haggled over by pretty much every Michelin-starred restaurant in Europe, the tiny island was thriving.

'I love it,' she said honestly, meeting the question in Odysseus's sapphire eyes.

'So you won't object to getting married from here?'

'Is that a joke? How could anyone possibly have any objections about this place?'

'It is a little isolated for some tastes,' he observed.

'But not yours, obviously.'

'It's one of the main reasons I bought here.'

She raised her eyebrows. 'And the other reasons?'

'You mean, apart from its natural, unspoiled beauty and some of the best sailing in the world?' A slow smile curved his lips. 'Mostly, I like the fact that nobody comes to see me without my permission.'

'And what about leaving?' she said, her voice very deliberate. 'How does that work?'

'That can happen at any time of your choosing, Grace,' he answered softly. 'Or mine.'

A flicker of foreboding whispered over Grace's skin as she realised what he was saying. He was making it clear that he wouldn't really care when the time came for her to go. But she already *knew* that—all she needed to do was remember it. She was never intended to be here for the long haul. First there would be the wedding, followed by a brief honeymoon and after that they would be jetting off to Tuloranka.

As man and wife.

The firing of her pulse bore testimony to her state of excitement, which just kept growing, no matter how much she tried to contain it. But who could blame her? How could you possibly look at a man like Odysseus and do anything but desire him?

Did he know that?

Was he aware that, physically, she was completely in his thrall?

Forcing her gaze away from the distraction of his carved features, she stared down at the little cove, where the transparent water lapped so invitingly against the shore, thinking about the dizzy action of the last few days.

She'd said a tearful farewell to Kirsty and Sophia while being deliberately evasive about her rapid engagement, suspecting her protective friends might have attempted to talk her out of the marriage if they'd known the cold-blooded truth about the contractual arrangement. They would have flagged up the potential for getting hurt—a potential which hadn't escaped her. Until she thought about Nana and the financial security Odysseus was offering. She was doing this for her grandmother, she reminded herself fiercely, and nobody was going to talk her out of it.

Thankfully, the trip to the Contarini house had passed by without incident. The hulking presence of a Greek bodyguard had helped, though he'd been safely out of earshot when Grace had asked Maria to convey the message to Vincenzo that she would like to say goodbye. But the old man had refused to see her, and, though she'd told herself it was for the best, it didn't lessen her sadness that her time there should have ended on such a sour note.

And yet the sadness had been quickly replaced by a rush of gratitude and excitement as it began to sink in that she really *was* free.

'I have missed you,' said Odysseus suddenly and Grace turned round to see him watching her.

His unexpected words took her by surprise but, although it had only been a couple of days, she had missed him too. 'Have you?' she prompted, her throat thick with longing.

'*Neh.* I have ached for you, *poulaki mou.* These last two nights I have barely slept, thinking about your incredible body and how good it feels to be inside you,' he admitted huskily. 'And I want to take you to bed,' he concluded hungrily. 'As quickly as possible.'

She wanted him to illustrate the fervency of his words with some action on top of that windswept hill—surely the most stunning spot in the world for a passionate kiss—but all he did was lace her fingers with his and lead her back towards the villa, as if this were nothing but a continuation of her guided tour.

Doing her best to conceal her disappointment, Grace entered the air-conditioned cool of the house, angry with herself for feeling that way. Because only someone extremely stupid would wish he hadn't been quite so clinical about his physical needs.

Don't expect romance, she told herself, remembering his coldly emphatic words.

Yet when they reached the vast white bedroom, with its full-length terrace overlooking the dazzling blue sea, she wondered if she had been wrong in her assessment, because this didn't feel in the least bit clinical. His kiss was slow and searching, his removal of her sundress almost leisurely—so that by the time she was easing his jeans down over the daunting ridge of his erection, Grace was breathless with burning need. With the tentative whisper of her fingertips, she touched him intimately, and as she saw him grow harder before her eyes, she failed to hold back the instinctive note of wonder in her voice.

'How eager you are, *poulaki mou*,' he observed unsteadily.

Her question was uncertain. 'Do you like me being eager?'

'I like it very much,' he affirmed softly, the flicker of an arrogant smile playing at the edges of his lips. 'It means you are taking your tuition seriously.'

She wanted to tell him not to be so damned *patronising*, but she wasn't going to ruin the mood by being picky about a definition. And besides, he was scooping her up into his arms and carrying her across the bedroom, laying her down carefully on the bed, his fingers lightly stroking her naked flesh and his mouth trailing a teasing line of kisses from breast to belly, until she was wriggling with frustration.

'Don't be so impatient,' he chided softly.

'It's hard not to be,' she answered truthfully. You're so bloody gorgeous.'

'You are always...' above her puckering nipple, his finger momentarily stilled, but his deep voice was filled with something like amusement '…so totally without guile.'

Hadn't he said the very same thing in the ballroom in Venice? 'And is that a good thing, or a bad thing?' she ventured cautiously.

'You just must take care not to be vulnerable, Grace, that is all.'

A different note had entered his voice now. Hard and implacable, it was very definitely a warning, and she knew he was right. But could she honestly be any more vulnerable than she was at this moment? When she was lying there naked, just waiting for him to make love to her, her whole body quivering with expectation. He had placed each of his thighs against her hips, so that she was enclosed within those powerful legs, and she felt safe within their warm anchor. His body was taut with tension, his desire almost palpable. Yet still he didn't move and this momentary restraint seemed significant. Was he demonstrating his awesome powers of self-control? she wondered dazedly.

But suddenly a low groan of hunger erupted from his lips as he spread open her thighs and entered her and every thought was obliterated by the blissful sensation of having him inside her again. Grace clung to his shoulders as he made thrust after thrust, unprepared for the welling up of something nameless inside her as the excitement built to an incredible crescendo. And wasn't she grateful that her orgasm chose that moment to ambush her—swift and sharp and sweet? So that the choking cry she uttered sounded like sexual satisfaction, rather than the helpless words of emotion which were hovering dangerously on her lips.

He buried his face in her neck, his breathing warm and ragged, and she must have fallen asleep, because when she woke he was no longer beside her. He was standing at the window, naked, his back to her as he stared out at the blue sweep of the sea—like an emperor surveying his domain. Still revelling in the afterglow of sex, she allowed herself a few moments of silent contemplation just to drink in his beauty. The broad shoulders and muscle-rippled back. Those narrow hips and endlessly long legs.

'Hello,' she said sleepily.

In the split second which followed her murmured greeting, Odysseus took the time to compose himself, impatient with himself for allowing her to orchestrate this inexplicable change to his mood and trying to talk himself out of it. There wasn't anything *special* about her, he reasoned savagely. She didn't possess some other-worldly power which had made him feel as if she had touched his icy heart with the fiery heat of her passion.

It had been particularly good sex and that was all.

That was all.

He turned round. *Theo*, but she looked amazing, all the same. Flushed and rumpled and utterly ravished. He wanted to get straight back into bed with her, but something told him he needed to build up his resilience—and he wasn't thinking about the physical. 'I thought we could go down to the cove for a swim,' he said abruptly.

'A swim?'

'Why are you looking at me as if I've just suggested a walk in a snake pit?'

'Because I can't swim,' she stated baldly.

'What do you mean?'

'I may be a linguist but surely you don't need a translation for such a simple phrase?' A shadow of embarrassment had darkened her eyes. 'I know it's shameful to admit, in this day and age, but I can't. It was an extra-curricular activity at school in Venice and I was usually... Well, I had to help my mum, because it was a big house and there was a lot for her to clean on her own.'

Odysseus's jaw tightened as he thought of her as a schoolgirl, scrubbing floors for his hateful grandfather. 'I can teach you,' he said.

'First sex, now swimming—whatever next?' she said, with a stab at humour. 'But I don't have a costume with me.'

'I anticipated this,' he said. Walking over to a drawer, he produced a package, which he tossed onto the bed. 'Look on it as a wedding gift.'

He observed the tremble of her hand as she tore open the tissue paper and stared askance at a tiny pair of bikini briefs and an equally minuscule top. 'I can't possibly wear these,' she breathed.

'Sure you can. Why not?'

'If you think I'm parading around in public wearing something as revealing as this, then you are mistaken.'

'I wonder if you have any idea how potent the appeal of all that indignant innocence is,' he murmured. 'The beach I am planning to take you to is completely private. Not overlooked at all,' he added softly.

'I'm not even going to ask how you knew my size.'

His eyes glinted with unholy humour. 'Probably best not to,' he agreed, handing her another expensive-looking package.

Inside Grace found a light robe which matched the bikini and a gorgeous pair of sandals, which managed to be both delicate yet robust. 'What else are you going to produce, like a rabbit out of a hat?' she questioned, thinking that Christmas morning had never been like *this*.

'How about this?' he said, handing her a tiny box, and Grace's heart missed a beat because it looked like...

Flipping open the lid, she saw a giant yellow stone set in a band of glittering white diamonds, reposing against a backdrop of indigo velvet and her heart skipped another beat. 'Oh, Odysseus, it's...'

'An engagement ring,' he said. 'Go on. Put it on.'

With shaking hands, Grace complied, staring in disbelief as it sparkled like a rectangle of sunlight against her finger. 'It's so beautiful,' she breathed, holding it up to the light.

A forty-carat yellow diamond, cushion-cut, with VS2 clarity,' he informed her, his prosaic words cutting through her delighted response.

She blinked at him, not really understanding him. 'And is that relevant?'

'It will be.' His words were careful. 'When you're thinking about resale value.'

Which was a diplomatic way of putting it, Grace supposed, trying to ward off the crazy crash of disappointment that he was talking about the end of the marriage before it had even started!

But despite this brief swamp of self-doubt, Grace soon cheered up as they made their way towards the sea. A flight of stairs cut into the rock led straight from the villa's gardens to the sheltered cove, and she was startled to discover all manner of things had been put there, ready for their arrival. A small table and chairs. A cool box containing bottles of water, lemonade, and champagne. Chilled cherries, chocolates and grapes. There were even neat piles of soft towels and two comfortable loungers, lying in the shade of the overhanging cliff. She wondered which unseen servants had placed them there and who would give them the signal that it was safe to remove them again.

Most distracting of all was seeing Odysseus in this startlingly new guise, looking more relaxed than she'd ever seen him. She watched hungrily from behind her dark shades—also new—feasting her eyes on the pair of black bathers which clung so definitively to his powerful buttocks and rocky thighs. She couldn't seem to *stop* staring at him and the mocking smile he threw her as he handed her a glass of sweet-sharp lemonade made her realise that he was perfectly aware of being her new obsession. Was that why he walked into sea, letting the transparent water gradually submerge him, before diving beneath the surface and executing a powerful crawl?

Eventually he rose to the surface, shaking droplets of water from his black hair. 'Come on in,' he lured.

'I'm quite happy here,' she said self-consciously, aware that the teeny bikini left more of her body exposed than it covered.

But he was nothing if not persistent and after a while Grace plucked up enough courage to follow him, wading in up to her thighs with a predictable squeal, and he swam over to her.

'The water's good, isn't it?' he murmured.

'It's…incredible.' She dipped down to her shoulders, then bobbed up again. 'And you're a fantastic swimmer.'

'I know,' he agreed, with a complete lack of modesty. 'So why don't I show you how it's done?'

'Odysseus, I am the least sporty person in the universe.'

But he paid her negativity no heed, wrapping his big hands around her hips. 'It's easy. You can stop any time you like. Just lie on your stomach. *Neh*. Like this. The salt in the water will keep you buoyant.' His voice curled with something she didn't recognise. 'Try to relax.'

Relax? How could she possibly relax when he was touching her bare skin, especially when he put his hand underneath her stomach to support her, while encouraging her to kick her legs? But, to Grace's surprise, he was way more patient than she had imagined and her first brief attempt at striking out on her own filled her with a disproportionate amount of giggling pride.

'See?' he murmured. 'I told you it would be easy.'

She didn't answer because now he had slipped his finger inside her bikini bottoms, and the contrast of the water combined with the warm stroke of his finger was almost too sweet to endure. 'Odysseus,' she breathed.

'It's good, isn't it?'

'But what if…what if somebody sees us?'

'Nobody can see us.'

And just like that, all her resistance drained away and Grace was at the willing mercy of what he was doing to her. Suddenly she seemed to be composed of all the elements—of fire and water, of earth and air—and at the centre of all this was him.

Him.

Strong. Powerful. Indomitable. The sunlight was glinting off his broad shoulders as he continued to work his magic, pleasure slowly building, layer upon sweet layer of it, until she was drowning in it. 'Odysseus,' she choked, and his hard kiss silenced her cry.

Slowly, she floated back to earth, and he taught her how to pleasure him beneath the cool waters of the Mirtoan Sea, peeling down his bathers and gripping his silken hardness, hearing his murmur of approval as she experimented. And when he choked out his own low broken moan of fulfilment, Grace was filled with another sense of satisfaction because in that moment she felt like his equal.

They waded back to shore, flopping down on adjoining loungers, screened by the shadow of the overhanging rock and, after a while, he poured them both a glass of champagne. As he touched the crystal flute to hers, Grace realised that she felt supremely comfortable. Thoughtfully, she ate a deliciously cool cherry. For the first time she could really believe that she was going to be his wife and that she was capable of fulfilling that role to both their satisfaction. Yet despite the passionate sex and surprising patience the man she was about to marry remained an enigma. She thought about his choices. His stated refusal to ever contemplate having a family of his own. His marriage to her nothing but an expedient gesture. What had made him so immune to the normal feelings and desires which drove other people? she wondered.

'Odysseus?' Tracing a finger down over his rock-hard belly, she felt him shudder. 'Can I ask you something?'

'Anything,' he said thickly.

It was obvious he was expecting something sensual and she hesitated, loath to shatter the sultry mood which was binding them together with silken ties. But she had to. It wasn't just that she wanted to know him, there was some bone-deep desire inside her which *needed* to know. 'What made you such a loner?'

Odysseus scowled as Grace's unwanted question shattered his burgeoning hunger, because the answer was very simple. And private. He'd lost count of the times women had tried to interrogate him like this over the years and it was always in a similar situation. Glowing in the wake of yet another orgasm, they started erroneously thinking he was in the market for deepening their intimacy in other ways. Inevitably, they went straight for the jugular by asking the intensely personal, which instantly sharpened his defences. His mouth hardened because he had always refused to answer intrusive queries before, and didn't see why that had to change now.

Consequently, the smile he gave was dismissive. 'Is that really relevant?' he drawled carelessly, sliding his hand down to straighten Grace's skewed bikini bottom, making sure he stroked a slick fold of flesh along the way. But although she shivered in response, his attempt to distract her failed because she propped herself up on one elbow and gave him a determined look.

'I think it is, yes. I mean, I've told you plenty about myself, but you haven't exactly reciprocated, have you?'

'I told you plenty,' he answered repressively.

'I don't think so.' She shook her head so that the damp chestnut strands flew around her narrow shoulders. 'Oh, you filled me in on the story about how you made all your money, but that's not what I'm talking about. I'm talking about the other stuff. The young you. How you spent your Christmases. That kind of thing.' She hesitated. 'Because I don't want you to be like a stranger to me.'

Odysseus's scowl deepened. He knew it would be kinder to warn her off. To tell her it wouldn't make the slightest difference if he recounted the cheerless facts about his upbringing. It wouldn't change the way he felt. About women. About life. About everything really, including her. 'I'm not one of those men who enjoy *opening up*,' he informed her silkily. 'That's why I never do it.'

Still she refused to take the hint. 'But we will soon be man and wife, Odysseus.'

'Only on paper,' he snapped.

'What about when we go to Tuloranka and we're staying with the King? Don't you think it will look a bit… well, *weird*, if I don't know anything about you? If something comes up in conversation, for example.' She pursed her lips together. 'Unless you *want* our marriage to look fake, of course.'

He opened his mouth to say he didn't particularly care how it looked, until he reminded himself that the notoriously short-tempered King Kaliman might be irritated by a couple who were enjoying his hospitality under false pretences.

But there was another consideration which he hadn't taken into account before, one which was only just dawning on him. Grace had worked for Vincenzo Contarini and lived in his house for all those years. She knew him better than pretty much anyone else and yet was seemingly unaware of the true depths of his cruelty. Even though their Paris trip had been interrupted by the old man's unreasonable demands, she had been prepared to give him the benefit of the doubt. Hadn't his bodyguard reported back that she'd attempted to say goodbye to the old bully, but he had refused to see her? She was tenderhearted, yes. But wasn't it more accurate to accuse her of suffering from self-delusion? His mouth hardened and a flicker of something cold and unrecognisable wrapped icy fingers around his heart as he stared up at the blue sky. Perhaps it was about time he enlightened her about her ex-boss.

CHAPTER TEN

'So, what *exactly* do you want to know about my life?'
Odysseus drawled, rolling over and staring up into the
vast blue bowl of the Greek sky because that was easier
than meeting the question in Grace's amber eyes. 'How
much I weighed when I was born? How long it took for
me to walk and talk? Because those details aren't on record, I'm afraid. As for Christmases, it may shock you
to know that my father wasn't really into traditional cel-
ebration and was usually passed out drunk by midday.'

But she didn't comment on this and when she did
speak, her voice was very quiet. 'Mostly about your
mum, really,' she said.

Your mum.

Those two words floored him. Drove every other consideration from his brain. He was more used to the Greek
mitera—and the English pet-name of the word hinted at
a simple intimacy which was way outside his comprehension. Suddenly Odysseus was glad he was lying on his
back. It meant Grace couldn't see his face properly. He
could close his eyes and it would appear like perfectly
normal post-sex lethargy. And not like someone trying
to conceal the sudden inexplicable prick of tears.

'Her name was Valentina,' he said at last, dredging up

the grudging scraps of information he had gleaned from his father. 'And she was born out of a brief, unhappy marriage to Vincenzo Contarini, which ended in divorce. No surprise there,' he added bitterly. 'I don't suppose he made a great husband, but he was certainly predictably ruthless when it came to divorce. He paid off his ex-wife very generously, on the condition that she and her family would cut all ties with her only child. Valentina was to be brought up by him, and only him,' he added bitterly. 'And he made sure that she never saw her mother again.'

'Oh, Odysseus,' she whispered. 'That's terrible.'

Did she think he wanted her *sympathy*—meaningless words which bounced off his skin like summer rain? Didn't she realise that this was why he always kept it locked inside him? 'Let's skip the judgement and the interjections, shall we?' he questioned harshly. 'Because if I have to put up with that kind of gushing response to every statement, I'll shut up right now. Do you understand?'

'I think you've made yourself perfectly clear,' she answered stiffly.

Steeling his heart against the obvious hurt in her voice, Odysseus forced himself to continue. 'As you can imagine, growing up with a man like Vincenzo wasn't what you'd call ideal.' His mouth twisted. 'Apparently, my mother begged to go away to boarding school and was sent to the world's most exclusive academy, on the banks of Lake Geneva. But when school ended, so did her life there, and she went back to Venice…'

Grace bit her lip as his words tailed off because she could hear the pain etched on every syllable. She wanted to reach out to him. To offer him all the comfort she possessed. But even if he hadn't already warned her off, his body language was forbidding enough to forestall her. He lay as motionless as marble and as off-limits to her touch as a statue in a museum.

'What happened then?' she ventured.

He took a moment before he answered. 'She was rich and beautiful and, at eighteen, had the world at her feet. There were suitors—' He gave a short laugh. 'Vincenzo told me during my meeting with him that any number of wealthy men were keen to marry her. But then she met my father—'

'And fell in love?' she questioned, eager to provide a positive spin. Was she hoping that acknowledgement of a great passion would provide some solace to a man who was failing to disguise the pain and bitterness in his voice? But she should have kept quiet because when he turned his head to look at her, his shadowed features were dark with contempt.

'*Love?* Let's not give credence to fantasy, shall we?' he negated cuttingly. 'I thought I'd made my feelings clear on that particular subject. Love is just a word which people use as leverage, for money or status, or sex—or all three, as I suspect was my father's motive.'

'So, how did they meet?' she asked in cautious response to this damning statement.

'In a bar. He was a good-looking guy and women flocked to him like wasps on honey. He was "doing" Europe on a shoestring, when he ran across my mother.' He shrugged. 'They had zero in common, but they clicked. It probably would have been no more than a summer fling if my mother hadn't found herself pregnant. And then...'

Grace held her breath.

'Vincenzo kicked her out,' he grated. 'Told her he never wanted to see her again. She had no money and nowhere to go. No choice but to return to Greece with my father—and I don't think he was exactly over the moon about the idea.' He drew in a ragged breath. 'But I don't think she was ever prepared for what she found there. A hot and tiny apartment. A hand-to-mouth existence. She didn't speak the language and the other women viewed her with suspicion. I think the cracks in the relationship had already started to show, when she went into labour. Early,' he expanded. 'And she...'

He swallowed, his words tailing off, the working of his face telling its own bleak story. 'She...'

'She died in childbirth,' Grace supplied into the frozen silence which followed, a shiver of compassion skating over her skin as she heard the raw emotion making his voice crack.

He leaned over her then, his features dark and his blue eyes blazing as his gaze raked over her. 'Who told you that?' he demanded. 'Who *told* you?'

She could feel his heat. His hurt. His anger. She shook her head. 'Nobody told me,' she breathed. 'It was obvious from your face, your voice, your...everything. I'm sorry, Odysseus. So very sorry. That you never knew her. That you—'

'That I'm a poor, scarred man whose mother died in childbirth? Don't bother reaching for the violin, Grace,' he mocked. 'Save your pity for somebody else. I don't need it.'

But Grace didn't rise to the taunt, even though she suspected he wanted her to. Because wouldn't that fuel the undercurrent of lust which was simmering between them again, even now? And wouldn't it be easier if she let him kiss her and drive into her, so that they could both gasp out their pleasure and forget about all the torment of his past and let his revelation slip away? Yes, of course it would. But the easiest solution wasn't always the best one. Instead, she attempted to steer the conversation back on track so he would finish the story—and this was nothing to do with wanting to appear a convincing wife in front of the King, or even for her own curiosity. This was for Odysseus's sake—because mightn't this reluctant revelation provide some kind of catharsis for a man who had clearly buried all his hurt and pain?

'It must have been difficult for your father...bringing up a baby on his own,' she offered. 'Surely Vincenzo must have reached out to help?'

'Don't you know the kind of man he really is, Grace— or have you just blinded yourself to his faults?' he demanded. 'Surely you can guess his reaction? My father phoned to tell him his daughter was dead, but that he had a grandchild and he wasn't sure how he was going to cope without some help.' There was a pause. 'And Vincenzo Contarini told him to go to hell.'

Her hand went to her mouth. 'Oh, Odysseus.'

'No pity,' he warned her sharply. 'Remember?'

Her tongue flicked over bone-dry lips. 'So did your father find another woman to act as a mother figure?' she whispered.

'Let's just say he found a *number* of women who were more interested in sex than looking after a baby who never stopped crying.' He gave a short laugh. 'And a toddler who, apparently, was nothing but trouble.'

So Odysseus had never known unconditional love,

Grace realised. Not for a single second of his life. The maternal bond had been severed by nature's cruelty and that tearing void in his life had been compounded by the absence of a caring father. Was it any wonder the little baby had cried and the toddler who followed had played up? Why the adult he had become was so distant and remote? Her heart went out to him but she didn't show it, just continued to study his face as if he'd been talking about nothing more controversial than the weather.

'It wasn't as bad as it could have been,' he continued. 'I was a curious child, hungry for information—saved by a teacher at the local school, who encouraged my love of reading. And then,' he added, almost reflectively, 'just before I turned sixteen my father married and my stepmother came to live with us. And that's when I realised that three was a crowd.' The crack of his knuckles sounded exceptionally loud against the distant sound of waves beating against the shoreline. 'Only she decided it was my father who was in the way, not me.'

It took a moment or two for the meaning of his words to sink in and when it did, Grace didn't ask him to elaborate, because the contempt in his voice told its own story. You wouldn't need to be a genius to work out that some women might find a handsome, virile teenager preferable to an aging drunk. Had his stepmother actually made a pass at him? she wondered, with a sick feeling at the pit of her stomach.

'So what did you do?' she asked and the tension which made his carved features resemble granite made her wonder if she'd pushed him too far. But after a while he spoke, slowly at first, as if the words were unfamiliar. As if he'd never said them before.

'I left. Slept rough for a couple of nights until I found a job as a security guard, which came with a room—though calling it that was a bit of a stretch.' He gave a hollow laugh. 'The wardrobe I keep my suits in these days is bigger than that room. The rest of the story you've already heard, Grace. The air-brushed, edited version, which illustrates the young colossus going out and conquering the world.' He gave a mocking replica of a smile. 'This version doesn't ever get aired and I'm sure you understand why.'

Yes, she understood why. Grace nodded, trying to get her scrambled thoughts in order. Mostly she was aware that he had confided in her, which meant that on some level he must trust her and that was something she needed to cling on to. But his story threw into sharp relief what had made him the man he was.

No wonder he didn't believe in love. How could he, when he'd never experienced it during the most formative years of his life? A child—certainly up until the age of three—could do without a mother, so long as it received unconditional affection from someone else. But his womanising drunk of a father seemed to have left the young Odysseus to fend for himself.

Suddenly she pictured the man beside her—not as the embodiment of material success, with his handmade suits, his private plane and his billions, but as a lost little boy who nobody had wanted. She felt his pain and wanted to put her arms around him. To cradle him and comfort him. To absorb some of the terrible emptiness which existed inside him, but he would interpret that as pity and she knew exactly how he felt about that.

She met his gaze, aware of those bright blue eyes burning into her—as if daring her to say the wrong thing so that he could push her away. Ever the watchful servant, she wondered how best to react to what he'd told her.

What did Odysseus Diamides want from her?

Sex, obviously. His self-professed obsession with her body was the main reason he was going to slide a golden band on her finger for his upcoming work trip to a country where the cohabiting laws were strict. That, and the quietening of speculation—the normalising of his life through a fake marriage which didn't require him having to put any work in.

But what did he *need* from her? That was the more important question.

He'd never known a mother, his stepmother sounded as perverted as hell and he'd been targeted by the opposite sex for most of his adult life, as if he were a rich, sexy trophy. To say he didn't like or trust women would be an understatement. She wanted him to know that he could trust her, but she wasn't sure how to go about it.

Unless she showed him something he seemed to have been lacking all his life…something as simple as kindness. Couldn't she just be there for him and prove she could be steadfast and true? Couldn't she demonstrate to this powerful but essentially lonely man that she cared about him, without asking for anything in return?

Because she *did* care. That much she knew. A fierce certainty seized her heart. He'd given her the ability to support her beloved nana. He had bared his soul and shown her that he too could be vulnerable and that insight had made her feel closer to him. He'd shown her the real man beneath all the fancy trappings. How could she want to do anything but fight his corner?

But she mustn't be obvious about it. Still smarting from the disclosure of all that pain, he would lash out like a wounded animal if she tried to get too close.

Her pragmatic course of action decided, she rose to her feet and straightened her bikini strap. 'Right, then,' she said, firmly. 'I suppose we'd better think about getting all this stuff cleared away.'

She saw his eyes narrow and felt a momentary flicker of triumph as she observed his surprise. Had he expected her to keep digging into his past when it was obvious he'd reached saturation point?

'*What* are you talking about?'

'This.' The wave of her hand encompassed the debris of their picnic. The half-empty glasses of champagne. The cherry stones and the single chocolate she had consumed, its glittery wrapper completely outsparkled by the spectacular yellow diamond glittering on her finger. 'We can carry some of this stuff up to the house.'

'There's absolutely no need,' he said impatiently. 'I've got staff to do that.'

'But that doesn't mean we can't help, does it?' She looked at him hopefully. 'I'm going to take up these leftovers anyway. Otherwise we'll risk getting a swarm of flies down here.'

'A swarm of flies?' he repeated faintly.

'Or wasps. Nobody likes wasps, do they?'

He started laughing and Grace couldn't help but smile back. And she found herself wanting to hug herself because, for some strange reason, the sound of his laughter felt almost as good as the sex.

CHAPTER ELEVEN

'No, HONESTLY,' GRACE said firmly, even though the stylist was looking at her in some dismay. 'I can't possibly accept all this.'

Her gaze drifted over the abundant offerings, which were occupying every available spot in the bedroom, making it look like an upmarket department store. There were silk dresses. Linen trousers. Fine lawn blouses. Long dresses displaying intricate embroidery, or scatterings of sequins. A shimmering evening coat, and an incredible denim jacket. Handbags for every conceivable occasion. And shoes. She had lost count of the number of shoes. Grace looked at it all askance. A wedding dress and matching lingerie were one thing—but all *this*?

'Can't accept what?' questioned Odysseus imperiously as he walked into the room without knocking, seemingly oblivious to the stylist's instant gushing reaction to his presence. 'What's the matter, Grace?'

'Nothing's the matter. But this is far too much,' she said stubbornly.

With a quick nod he dismissed the stylist, who couldn't quite hide her disappointment at being unable to witness what was obviously going to be a pre-wedding bust-up. And it wasn't until she had left them alone and he had shut the door that Odysseus turned to Grace, his dark eyebrows raised. 'You think your little sundresses and a borrowed hat will suffice for what lies ahead, do you, *poulaki mou*?'

Grace bristled. 'I thought you told me you liked that hat.'

'Which I do. Very much.' He stroked a placatory finger over her cheek. 'It's just not suitable for a stay in a royal palace.'

'Which is why I agreed to have you buy me some clothes—but there's enough here for about a year. Just how long is this job in Tuloranka going to last?'

'I have no idea. It could be one month…it could be two,' he answered smoothly. 'But you will be required to change several times a day and you'll feel inadequate if you aren't able to do that.'

Letting out a small sigh, Grace nodded. 'Okay, then,' she agreed reluctantly. 'If you absolutely insist.'

'How ironic it is…' Odysseus gave a slow smile '… that of all the women I should have chosen as my wife, I seem to have acquired one who remains resolutely unimpressed by what my wealth can buy for her.'

His wife. Grace knew it wasn't for real, but when he said it like that it *felt* real. *Dangerously* real. She wondered if that was inevitable. Was it because women were subtly conditioned from birth to expect high romance, in the form of a wedding? Maybe the choosing of a white dress and flowers was subconsciously reinforcing all those childhood dreams she'd always secretly fought against. Or was it because her feelings for her future husband were growing by the day, despite all her best efforts to quash them?

Because sometimes this felt like a dream from which she never wanted to wake.

Each day, as the sun rose over the glorious Mirtoan Sea, Odysseus made love to her, in rumpled sheets coated in morning colours of coral and pink. After a slow and very erotic shower, they ate breakfast on the terrace—where the air was soft with the scent of orange blossom. To the sound of birdsong and the distant beat of the sea, they feasted on figs and yogurt and honey, before going back upstairs to make love all over again. His sexual appetite was voracious and so too, it seemed, was hers. The more he taught her, the more she wanted to learn—something which made him give a low laugh of pleasure. He called her greedy. He called her insatiable—and she revelled in the mocking words which he breathed so approvingly against her skin.

The physical side of their relationship was perfect—it was the other aspects of it which gave her cause for concern. The unpredictable ice and fire of his nature continued to enchant her in a way which felt addictive... alarmingly so. She'd thought continued exposure to his irascible character would provide her with some kind of immunity against his potent charm but that wasn't happening. And if an impending sense of emotional danger sometimes caused words of alarm to whisper into Grace's ear, she stubbornly chose to ignore them.

She was frustrated with herself for wanting it to be a real marriage. A marriage which lasted—something which had never been on the cards.

Yet Odysseus was the one who was providing such fertile ground on which to grow her fantasy. Work-wise, he'd taken his foot off the brake, which was apparently a

first—or so Evangelia, the housekeeper, had rather indis-
creetly confided. With proprietorial pride he had shown
her around the island, giving her an insider's view of its
natural beauty—the rugged mountains and tall forests,
and the hidden coves, which took her breath away. She
witnessed for herself how highly he was regarded by the
local fishermen and farmers, and how much he was hero-
worshipped by the small boys who ran up with rags to
wash the windscreen of his car.

It was hard not to fall for him. And harder still to
make sure he didn't suspect. Especially as circumstances
seemed to be conspiring against her efforts to dial down
her feelings, as demonstrated by an astonishing fact she'd
learned in bed that very morning.

'Won't Evangelia think we're slightly decadent, the
amount of time we're spending up here?' she remarked
sleepily, her lips drifting little kisses along the soft skin
of his shoulder.

'I don't pay my housekeeper to have opinions on how
I spend my time,' he growled.

'No, of course not. And I suppose…well, I suppose
she must be used to it,' she added, probing a little, trying
not to sound jealous, which of course she was.

There was a heartbeat of a pause, during which he
seemed to be weighing up his next words. 'If you must
know, you're the only woman I've ever brought here,' he
informed her tersely.

For a full minute she was shocked into silence. 'So
where do you usually…?' she asked eventually.

'There are such things as hotels, Grace,' he offered
sardonically. 'You may have heard of them?'

Grace was glad she was lying down because she suspected her knees might have given way if she'd been vertical, but she couldn't help the sudden rush of pleasure which was making her skin feel so warm and glowing.

She was the only woman who had ever slept in his island bed!

'Wow!'

Did he detect the misplaced flattery in her soft exclamation? Was that why he quickly disabused her of any idea that she was in some way special?

'Bringing you here is simply intended to add credence to our sudden marriage, *poulaki mou*. Just like your engagement ring,' he drawled, dropping a light kiss onto the top of her head, presumably to take the sting out of his words. 'It's nothing more complicated than that.'

Grace forced herself to remember that clipped statement later that day, as they made their wedding vows on the roof terrace, in front of the blue blaze of the sea. She wore a white dress, with her hair hanging loose— the way Odysseus liked it, though she had woven fragrant stephanotis into the thick strands as a concession to the occasion. The only witnesses were Odysseus's lawyer, who had flown over from the mainland, along with Christos, one of his assistants. Somehow their businesslike presence emphasised the formal element of the marriage, which was reinforced by the prenup she'd put her signature to the previous day. And *that* had been a strange experience. Odysseus had signed over an eye-watering sum for Nana's welfare, enough for the rest of her life, because… 'If our marriage ends next month, we don't want your grandmother's care being comprised, do we?' he had drawled.

Grace had been unbearably touched and grateful for

his consideration, but after that undeniable sweetener had come his rules.

She was to give no interviews.

She was to make no other financial claims other than the one which stood.

And the real clincher. The one which made her blood run cold...

She was never to contact him again once they were divorced.

It hurt. It hurt more than it should have done and more than he would ever realise, but at least nobody could ever accuse Odysseus Diamides of being anything other than savagely honest with her.

The marriage service was simple and stark and the words weren't supposed to mean anything, but the annoying thing was that, to Grace, they *did*. Despite all her misgivings, she could feel the leap of hope. The warm glow of possibility. She couldn't seem to hold back the embryonic stirrings of love for a man she sensed was badly in need of love. But one look at Odysseus's face was enough to bring her crashing down to earth. His stony features showed nothing but indifference and his cool voice sounded as if he were reciting an inventory. Which she should have *expected*, she told herself fiercely, hoping her face didn't betray her disappointment. In fact, the only thing which surprised her was the sudden appearance of a photographer who fired rapid shots to capture the newly-weds standing in a swirl of white rose petals, enthusiastically thrown by Evangelia and her son, Marinos.

Odysseus's eyes were thoughtful as he brushed one

of the stray petals from her cheek, his thumb lingering fractionally on her skin.

'You look beautiful, by the way.'

'Honestly?'

'Honestly,' he affirmed gravely. He raised his eyebrows. 'You're not regretting it?'

'It?'

'The marriage.'

'Of course not,' she answered, glancing around—relieved nobody was in earshot to hear this less than traditional question from a husband to his new wife. 'I mean, I was a bit freaked out when that photographer suddenly appeared.' She pulled a face. 'I thought you said you wanted the whole thing to be kept low-key.'

'I did. But low-key, not secret.' He raised his eyebrows in mocking query. 'We don't want people thinking you're pregnant, do we?'

To Grace, his words sounded harsh. Or perhaps that was his intention. To remind her that there would not be—nor could there ever be—any children. Why that should cause a sudden twist of sadness was a mystery, but at least it was a wake-up call.

'We most certainly don't,' she said staunchly, peering over the balcony to see that a small wedding feast had been assembled on the dappled terrace below, and Marinos was carrying an ice bucket containing a bottle of champagne towards the two lawyers. The hostile black and white cat she'd discovered was called Gouri, was now being shooed away by the housekeeper. As Evangelia deposited a platter of stuffed vine leaves on the table, Grace wondered what the staff made of their boss's surprise marriage—and whether they could see through it for the farce it really was. Did Odysseus sense the cause of her sudden tension, and was that why he put his hand on her bare arm?

'Let's just go to bed,' he said.

Grace dug her fingers into her bouquet, because the temptation to do exactly that was overwhelming. But she knew how much trouble Evangelia had gone to making a traditional dessert of *masticha chiou* for the newly-weds, which she felt duty-bound to try. And, if she was being brutally honest—didn't she want to cling on to as much of her wedding day as possible, even though deep down she knew it wasn't real? She might never get another one and she was finding it seductively easy to enjoy playing the role of Odysseus's bride. 'The lawyers will think it very odd if we don't even have a toast with them.'

'They're on the payroll, Grace,' he drawled arrogantly. 'Their remit is to please me, not to judge me.'

And that was exactly what could happen if you became impossibly rich and successful, Grace realised furiously. If people were working for you, they were forced to dance to your tune. It meant you didn't have to engage with them on a personal level and hadn't Odysseus spent his whole life taking advantage of that? And not just with servants—her, too!

'I think it would be very bad manners to duck out now,' she admonished.

His sapphire eyes glittered as they acknowledged her forthrightness. 'Oh, do you?' he queried softly.

'Yes, I do. Believe me, I know how frustrating it can be when you've gone to a lot of trouble to prepare something and people just turn their noses up at it.'

'I am talking about a different type of frustration,' he murmured.

'I'm sure you are.' The soft drift of her finger around the edge of his mouth belied the primness in her voice. 'But that can wait until later. Come on, Odysseus. At least show willing.'

Slightly bemused by his petite bride's determination, Odysseus accompanied her to the flower-decorated middle terrace and went through the various wedding rituals. And he couldn't deny that Grace took an element of sunshine with her, wherever she went. As Marinos served drinks and shoed away the ever-persistent cat, he couldn't help but notice that Evangelia was more smiley than usual as she served them.

But as his housekeeper began to explain the significance of the traditional, white-coated sugar almonds known as *koufeta*, Odysseus began to grow impatient and he knew the time for play-acting was over.

'Let's go,' he instructed softly.

Feeling the tremble of her fingers, he led Grace up the marble staircase to the master suite and watched as she put her bouquet down and turned to face him. She really *did* look beautiful, he acknowledged—her young body slim and supple in the simple white dress and her skin glowing with health. But although he was aching to take her to bed, instinct was urging him to delay.

Why was that?

To prolong the anticipation and rack up the sexual tension between them and make the consummation of their marriage especially mind-blowing? Or to demonstrate that, although they were now married, he had lost none of his legendary control?

Yet at times today it had felt exactly like that. As if power was slipping away from him, into the hands of his new wife, and not just because she had overruled him about skipping the reception. When she had stared up at him during the wedding ceremony, so tiny and appealing—those big amber eyes of hers bright with undeniable hope—hadn't he been forced to steel himself against that look and the inexplicable stab to his heart which had accompanied it? Her soft vulnerability had been the reason he had plucked her from his grandfather's house and put her out of the old man's reach, but how could he have underestimated its subliminal effect on him?

How *could* he?

His anger was an aphrodisiac, his mouth hard and hungry as he kissed her, and she answered it with a fierce hunger of her own. The kick to his groin was instant, the throb of blood through his veins unstoppable. Tangling his fingers in the spill of her dark hair, he deepened the kiss—the thrust of his tongue mimicking the more intimate thrust his body so desperately craved. As she writhed restlessly against him, he cupped her breasts through her wedding dress. Her nipples were pushing against his palms like bullets and suddenly the gown represented everything he despised. All those things the white sugar almonds had symbolised. Fertility, and the endurance and sweetness of marriage. When, in reality, both were a trap which didn't mean a damned thing. Because nothing was ever as it seemed, he reminded himself bitterly.

'I want to rip this damned thing off.'

'But it's brand-new,' she whispered.

'You're not planning to wear it again, are you?' he mocked.

'I guess not. G-go ahead, then.'

And God forgive him, but he did. He couldn't seem to stop himself, rending the garment with one sure movement, so that it flapped around her, giving him scope to feast his eyes on her petite frame, clad in snowy lingerie. 'This is new, too,' he observed unevenly, one finger tracing a lingering path over the delicate curve of her lacy bra.

'Y-yes. The...' She shuddered with pleasure as he paid extra attention to her nipple. 'The stylist persuaded me I needed new lingerie, too.'

'The stylist was right,' he concurred smokily.

'But you won't rip that, will you?' she questioned and suddenly her cheeks grew pink. 'Can you...can you leave it on?'

Her shy candour only increased his ardour as he scooped her up and carried her into the bedroom, his disbelieving gaze registering a huge red heart of rose petals lying in the centre of the bed, forcing him to put her down.

'Who the hell put these here?' he demanded, impatiently sweeping aside most of the petals so that they fluttered to the ground in a swirl of scarlet.

'Evangelia must have done. And there's no need to sound so cross,' she reproved softly. 'It's a traditional welcome for honeymooners.'

'But we aren't traditional honeymooners,' he ground out. 'And I'm not a big fan of gestures of cloying sentimentality.'

'Cloying sentimentality?' she repeated. 'What a bad-tempered man you can be at times, Odysseus.'

'Only because I'm as frustrated as hell,' he admitted huskily. And indeed, all his irritation was banished the moment he had Grace lying supine on the mattress, her chestnut hair spread all over the pillow, one knee bent with artless provocation as she looked up at him from between shuttered lashes. He gazed back at her as a rush of desire pulsed through him like a hot tide, and for a moment it threatened to take him under. But this isn't real, he reminded himself dazedly. It's just an arrangement which happens to suit us both.

Kicking off his shoes, he started pulling off his own clothes. His wedding suit, shirt and boxers soon strewn haphazardly all over the floor before he joined her on the bed and began to explore her with a thoroughness which was making his heart thunder. For a while he feasted lavishly on her silken flesh, his teeth nipping the bra she had requested he leave on, his hand sliding between her legs.

'Odysseus,' she whispered, arching her back so that her belly made contact with the weight of his erection.

'You're driving me wild,' he complained hungrily.

'Good.'

Somehow he managed to locate a condom, though his hands were shaking as he tore open the foil. Concentrating fiercely, he slid it over his virile shaft as Grace lay there watching him. She raised her arms above her head, heavy eyes glinting as he positioned himself between her legs.

'Do you realise you look like every man's secret fantasy, lying there in your virginal lingerie, just waiting to be ravished?' he questioned unsteadily, sliding aside the damp panel of her panties.

'Do I?'

'Mmm. Leaving me with no alternative other than to do…this…'

He pushed deep inside her and she gave a little cry of pleasure.

'And *this*.'

'Odysseus,' she gasped.

'It's good?' he asked unnecessarily.

'You wouldn't believe how good,' she breathed.

Oh, but he would, he thought—almost grimly—he most definitely would. It was unbearably erotic to feel the rub of lace against his skin and he could feel the liquid heat at the very heart of her. Shifting her weight to accommodate him, she wrapped her soft thighs around his back as he went deeper, impaling her against the mattress. And suddenly he was lost. It was all about sensation as he felt her body beneath his. Her soft lips covering his with kisses. Her throaty sighs urging him on. He teased her for as long as it took for her to shudder out her orgasm—her petite frame quivering ecstatically. And then all last vestiges of control fell away as he bit out his own incomprehensible words of surrender.

Afterwards he lay there, his mouth still buried in the softness of her hair, his arm slung tightly around her waist, and she turned her head a little, so that he could feel the warmth of her breath against his cheek.

'Can I ask you something, Odysseus?'

'Anything,' he said recklessly.

'Does it feel…different?'

Still basking in the glow of what felt like the most incredible orgasm of his life, he indulged her a little more. 'What, specifically?'

'That's what you said when you found out I was a virgin, because it was the first time,' she added shyly, and he could hear the softness in her voice. 'And since neither of us have been married before, I was just wondering whether the sex felt different. Now that it's legal.'

A flicker of alarm whispered over his skin as he met her complicit smile and suddenly his satisfaction evaporated. Yes, he conceded grimly. It *had* felt different.

It had felt as if she had ripped something from deep inside him. As if she were determined to destroy the control which was the only thing he had ever been able to rely on.

'It was good,' he said, but the cool compliment was deliberately dismissive and he registered the flash of disappointment in her eyes before she closed them. And Odysseus was grateful for the temporary respite. He didn't want that amber gaze surveying him with a tenderness she was so bad at hiding.

He thought about everything he'd done differently since he'd met her, starting with having sex with a total stranger. He'd brought her here and married her. He'd told her about his mother. Was it her gentle probing or her innocent allure which had made him confide in her? Which had allowed her to peel away his armour with such ease and expose the darkness beneath.

Too late to regret it now, for it was a done deal. She was dangerous, he recognised, with a sinking heart. More dangerous than he could ever have anticipated. And something took his mind back six years, when the most hard-hearted man he knew—a man who didn't even *like* cats—had been captivated by a helpless kitten left half dead on the side of an Athens road. Odysseus remembered his sinking sense of responsibility as he'd plucked the weightless scrap of black and white fur from the roar of passing cars, but mostly he remembered the purr it gave when he stroked its ear, just after it had bitten him. He was intending to pay handsomely to have it adopted by a charity had it not mewed so piteously whenever he'd tried to get rid of it. In the end, he had given the cat to Evangelia but the damned thing would still insist on butting her head outside his office door whenever she got the opportunity, trying to get in to wind her tail around his ankle.

And wasn't Grace just like that damned kitten? Trying to burrow herself further and further into his life. Attempting to take from him things he wasn't willing to give up. She needed to understand his boundaries, he reminded himself grimly, and there was only one way to do that.

His mouth curved into a smile he knew was cruel— he had been told so often enough by women. Only this time the smile felt like a life raft, rather than a deliberately distancing measure. He was a master of pushing women away but never had it been more vital than now. Because he would hurt her if she took him into her heart. And he really didn't want to hurt her.

'Odysseus?' she whispered, her soft voice redolent with pleasure and something else—something which was making those alarm bells ring even louder. Any minute now she'd be telling him she loved him, because women had a terrible habit of mistaking orgasm for emotion. Yet

once those words were spoken, you could never go back.
You could never unsay them.

'Hold that thought until I get back,' he murmured.

'You're…going?'

'Mmm.' Yawning, he stretched his arms above his
head. 'I need to look through a few papers,' he added,
dropping a careless kiss on top of her ruffled hair. 'And
then I'm going to take a shower.'

But he had to steel himself against the disappointment which darkened her amber eyes as he threw back
the covers and got out of bed.

CHAPTER TWELVE

'DO YOU HAVE to work *all* day?' Grace tried to remove the pleading note in her voice as Odysseus rose up from the breakfast table, but sometimes it was hard to pretend to be contented when inside you were a bubbling mass of conflicting emotions. When you were trying like mad to temper the stupid feelings which kept growing inside you, no matter how much you knew that it was pointless to care for such a stone-hearted man. She shrugged her shoulders slightly and gave him a hopeful smile. 'Couldn't you at least bunk off for a couple of hours so we could go swimming?'

As the glorious sunshine dappled over his powerful body, he gave her that look she knew so well. Slightly regretful and slightly resigned. As if he could do nothing about the many work-related demands on his precious time, despite being the boss of a massive global business. 'You know I can't. There are a dozen things I must do before we leave for Tuloranka and, unfortunately, these are things I don't really want to delegate. Now come here, *poulaki mou*, and kiss me before I go.'

She wanted to tell him that she wasn't his *little bird*. She was his wife, and she was becoming increasingly frustrated. Not sexually. Oh, no. She certainly had no complaints in that department. How could she when she melted with intoxicating pleasure whenever he so much as laid a finger on her? It was everything else. But she raised her face to his all the same, while he planted a lingering kiss on her lips and told her he would see her later.

As she watched him walk across the beautiful grounds towards his office, she acknowledged a certainty which was growing by the day.

That there were always serpents in paradise.

Always.

Putting the spoon back in the jar of honey, Grace stared out at the unremittingly blue sea. Not that she had anything against the island of Kosmima itself. Her view that this was the prettiest place she'd ever seen remained constant—and if there was a nicer spot to sit eating your breakfast, she couldn't imagine it. And who in their right mind would turn up their nose at the massive infinity pool, stunning grounds and endless beaches of fine sand so close to Odysseus's sprawling villa? Throw into the mix a massive library, a friendly housekeeper who would rustle up anything Grace wanted, no matter how many times she protested that she was perfectly capable of doing it herself, and it felt as if she were staying in a five-star luxury resort.

On her own.

Once again she was the recipient of someone else's wealth and once again she was nothing but a kind of functionary…only this time she wasn't a servant, but a makeshift wife.

It didn't help that she couldn't drive and although her husband had put his chauffeur at her disposal, she hadn't taken him up on the offer. She didn't want to be driven around, sitting like a lemon in the back seat, like some bizarre curiosity as the powerful car moved through the countryside.

She didn't seem to know who she was any more. She was no longer a rich man's housekeeper, but she didn't feel much like a wife either. In fact, she didn't feel like a wife at all.

Because things had changed between her and Odysseus. He had become increasingly distant since the night of their wedding and she wasn't sure how to fix it.

This was *supposed* to be a brief honeymoon before they flew out to Tuloranka, but she'd scarcely seen her husband. Stirring some sugar into her coffee, she willed the stupid lump in her throat to subside. Had she expected marriage to bring them closer? Guilty. But there were plenty of other crimes she could add to her charge sheet of unrealistic expectations. Despite all her best intentions, she knew perfectly well that she'd fallen for him. But was that so very surprising? It wasn't as if she was in a club of one, was it? Not if you read the reports of women who'd been smitten with the Greek billionaire in the past.

He'd explicitly warned her that he didn't *do* love, but Grace had chosen to blot out those warnings. Secretly, she had hoped for more. When he'd told her about his awful childhood, her heart had melted like butter. His bitter disclosure had given her a glimmer of hope that their relationship had the ability to deepen and she'd been longing to show him some of the affection he'd grown up without.

But she hadn't got the chance, because his emotional retreat from her had been immediate and almost tangible. Was he regretting having let his guard down during his bitter revelation about his early years? Was that why he closeted himself away in his office day after day, making it very clear that her presence in his private lair was unwelcome? She'd learnt that any attempts to entice him away from his busy schedule were doomed to failure, so that in the end she'd given up trying. At first she had consoled herself with the knowledge that he would always appear by late afternoon, giving them time for a blissful bout of sex before early-evening drinks. Afterwards, they would dine by candlelight on the sunset terrace and she guessed that, to an observer, everything must have looked just fine.

Sometimes, she even managed to convince herself it *was* fine. His quickness of mind and rare flashes of humour continued to captivate her and his capacity for physical pleasure remained undiminished. He could dissolve her doubts and uncertainties with a single kiss and sometimes, in those moments, she was certain that she loved him. But those kind of thoughts were dangerous. Wouldn't he be horrified if he knew? Of course he would. And the longer this went on, the more she would lose her own identity—hankering after a man who seemed determined to push her away.

More than that, she was lonely. At least in Venice she'd had her friends and the familiarity of a city she'd known most of her life, even if she had been working for the boss from hell. But this loneliness was different. It went bone-deep. She forced herself to read books from the vast library and made serious inroads into learning Greek—sometimes helped by Marinos, who would practise his English on her. Odysseus had employed a female coach to help improve her swimming technique and every morning she used the vast pool, getting more proficient and fitter than she'd been in years. But there was only so much displacement activity you could engage in before your head started wanting to explode.

Finishing her coffee, she went up to their room, where the bed had already been made—the pristine new sheets giving no sign of the previous night's passion. She thought of the way he held her every night. The way he drove into her and buried his face in her hair when it was over, his breathing harsh until he had steadied it enough to whisper her name in a way which made her heart clench. Wasn't it all too easy to feel that she meant something to *him* in those moments? That she was more than just a convenient wife—a tick on the list of requirements for a successful man?

But those longings never lasted—they were banished by the sight of the now-familiar mask Odysseus put on as he got dressed each morning, the stony perfection of his features making him resemble a gorgeous stranger.

This morning, even the vast garden was making her feel claustrophobic and suddenly Grace knew she had to get away from the villa before she drove herself crazy. Cramming on the straw hat which Sofia had gifted her as a wedding present, she prepared for a walk—sensibly covering her shoulders in a cap-sleeved cotton dress before running downstairs to ask Evangelia for some water.

'The master, he knows you are going out?' the housekeeper questioned doubtfully.

The master! An infuriating and outdated description, but not as infuriating as the illicit thrill of pleasure it triggered, as Grace acknowledged its implications of dominance and power. Resisting the impulse to enquire whether she needed the Greek billionaire's permission to actually *leave* the building, Grace shook her head.

'He's busy working,' she said, taking the flask of chilled water Evangelia held out to her, unable to iron the sarcasm from her voice as Gouri the cat arched her back and hissed at her. 'And I'd hate to disturb him.'

But a few minutes of brisk walking soon calmed her ruffled senses and she found her mood automatically lifted by the beauty of the island as she got further away from the villa. The sky was blue and the sea even bluer, glittering like dark sapphires beneath the beat of the sun. She didn't see another soul as she made steady progress along the cliff path and as the sun rose higher, she was cheered by the sight of a small harbour in the distance. Carefully, she began to pick her way towards it, down a winding path edged with an abundance of wild flowers.

The temperature was higher than expected and the village further away than she thought and Grace was boiling by the time she reached the gleaming waterside. Wiping her clammy brow with the back of her hand, she looked around. The place was completely deserted—the fisherman must have returned with their catch hours ago and there was nobody else to be seen. By now her water bottle was almost empty and as she spotted a tiny tav-erna, she decided to get a drink and a refill. Blinking a little as she went inside, she felt as if she were in one of those old Western movies her nana used to watch. Ev-eryone stopped talking and stared at her. Did they know who she was? Did the sparkle of the fabulous yellow dia-mond engagement ring on her finger proclaim her as the new bride of the island's owner?

Using the small amount of Greek she'd learned, she bought a glass of fizzy water and gulped it down while her water bottle was being replenished. Looking around the small bar at the other customers, she was just psyching herself up for the long walk back when she saw someone she recognised. Sitting playing cards at the back of the room was Marinos, Evangelia's son, and Grace's heart lifted as he got up and came towards her.

'Marinos. *Yiasu!*' She smiled. 'I can't tell you how glad I am to see a familiar face.'

'Kyria Diamides.' His smile was rather cautious. 'You are a long way from home.'

She wondered what the shy student would say if she told him that Odysseus's lavish villa didn't feel remotely like home—but she guessed that was the story of her life. 'I've come much further than I thought,' she admitted.

'If you like, I can take you back.'

She opened her mouth to refuse, but making her way back up those cliffs in the soaring heat was the sort of foolhardy escapade which gave the English such a terrible reputation on the continent. 'That'd be great. Have you got a car?'

He shook his head and grinned. 'I have my motorbike.'

Once outside, he handed her a spare helmet which was strapped to the bike, and after cramming it on and folding up her straw hat, Grace climbed gingerly on the back.

'I've never been on a motorbike before,' she warned him.

'It's easy,' he reassured her. 'Once you know how.'

He showed her which way to lean when they went round a bend and, considerately, kept his speed down and Grace found the journey back nothing short of exhilarating. Back at the estate, she thanked him and made her way through the grounds where the glorious air-conditioned cool of the villa greeted her. Slipping off her sandals, she padded barefoot up the delicious cool of the marble staircase and as she pushed open the door of their bedroom, her only thought was to stand beneath the welcome jets of a cold shower and put on a clean dress.

She didn't see him at first.

Why would she, when she hadn't expected him to be there? When he blended so well with the shadows—this man of intense shade, rather than light? He was sitting in an alcove in one corner of the room, a computer open in front of him but he wasn't looking at the screen. Despite her barefooted noiselessness, he must have heard her come in because he turned round, and she could see the flicker of something she didn't recognise glittering in the depths of his blue eyes.

'Good day?' he questioned evenly.

Grace didn't know why she'd been holding her breath, only that it was leaving her mouth in a gentle hiss. But her sense of unease remained and she didn't know why. 'Great, thanks. I went out for a walk only I went further than I intended and nearly ran out of water and I ended up in a taverna and...' She was aware that she was babbling but couldn't seem to stop herself. 'And Marinos was there and he brought me back on his motorbike.'

'So I believe.'

'Oh?' She looked at him in confusion. 'Do you have spies patrolling the island, or something?'

But the unsmiling set of his mouth made clear that her feeble attempt to lighten the atmosphere hadn't worked. 'I heard the sound of his motorbike roaring up the cliff road and I saw you. With your hair streaming behind you,' he added softly.

Grace frowned, because surely the detail about her hair was superfluous. And was that *censure* underpinning his words? She should have let it go, but some stubborn voice of objection was stirring up inside her and refusing to be silenced. 'Why do you say it like that?'

He raised his eyebrows. 'Like what?'

'Oh, come on, Odysseus.' Suddenly all the frustration and fear she'd been suppressing since her wedding night came bubbling to the surface and now it started rushing out in a hot and angry torrent. 'You might do your best never to engage in normal human interaction and most of the time you succeed, but I can tell you're bluffing. You know exactly what I mean. Like you disapprove.'

There was a pause. 'Maybe because I do.'

She drew in an unsteady breath. 'Why?'

'Why do you think, Grace?' He rose to his feet, dominating every atom of space around him, and suddenly some of his habitual composure had slipped. 'You are my wife and it is entirely inappropriate for you to accept rides from the housekeeper's son!'

She shook her head in disbelief. 'I thought—given your experience of life—that the last thing you'd be was a snob!'

'This is nothing to do with snobbery,' he iced out furiously. 'It's about the messages you're sending out.'

'And what messages might they be?' she goaded as his words halted because wasn't there something almost *thrilling* about the anger she could see on his face?

A muscle had begun to work at his temple. 'You don't think that feeling your arms around his waist and knowing the whip of the wind is exposing your creamy thighs might make him regard you differently?'

'Oh, for heaven's sake.' Her mouth fell open. 'He's years younger than me!'

'And?' he demanded dangerously. 'You didn't stop to think that he might get the wrong idea when you leapt onto the back of his motorbike like someone he'd just picked up in a nightclub?'

Maybe it was the unexpectedness of his response which made a slew of thoughts rush through Grace's mind and not all of them were negative. Why, Odysseus sounded *jealous* of the university student and if that were the case, wouldn't it imply he cared about her more than he was letting on? The hopeful stab of her heart lasted only as long as it took to think it through.

Because caring implied thoughtfulness, didn't it? And sensitivity. And neither of those qualities were evident in the forbidding set of her husband's powerful shoulders, or the suddenly rigid composition of his features. This was all about possession, she realised suddenly. As if she were something he owned, just as he owned a plane and a colossal villa and a stack full of stocks and shares. As if she were an object, not a person.

'What are you imagining is happening here?' she whispered. 'That I'm making love to you by night, and plotting to have Marinos in my bed by day, when you're not around? That I've gone from virgin to whore in a few short weeks? Is that what you think, Odysseus? That I'm planning to be unfaithful to you?'

For possibly the first time in his life, Odysseus found himself lost for words, because he didn't know what was happening to him. Only that he had suddenly found himself in the grips of something he didn't recognise. Something he hadn't allowed himself to think about and thus, to identify. But he certainly didn't intend rising to her bait and turning this into the kind of emotional ping-pong he despised.

'No, of course I don't think that,' he conceded coldly.

'How good of you!' she declared sarcastically. 'What is it, then? Should I have run it past you first? Is that what you wanted, which you forgot to lay down in those pre-wedding *rules* of yours? Did you intend to police every single person I speak to? Should I have sought your per-mission like a good, docile wife? No wonder Evangelia looked so shocked when she discovered I was actually leaving the villa without telling you. I know we're married now but this kind of expectation is positively *medieval*!'

'Now you're just being ridiculous.'

'I am not being ridiculous!' she howled.

He frowned, taken aback by the fervour of her attack, and instinct made him step away from it, to coat his words with reason, to behave as if he were in an irksome meeting with a client who was refusing to see sense. But it wasn't easy, not when she looked so magnificent in her righteous rage and all he wanted to do was to kiss her. But not just kiss her, he realised grimly. He wanted to quieten her too. He wanted to quash this kind of dis-cussion and ensure it never happened again. He sucked in a steadying breath. 'It just might have been courteous if you'd let me know.'

'How?' she demanded. 'When you're holed up in your office all day—bringing new meaning to the term work-aholic—and you practically have a sign on the door, tell-ing me to keep out!'

'You know that I have a whole heap of things I need to do before our trip,' he thundered.

'So you keep telling me. So rather than waiting around here all day until the *master* deigned to grace me with his presence, I decided to go for a walk. Is that such a big deal—that I didn't want to get it signed off in triplicate? It was a spur-of-the-moment thing and you're just not a spur-of-the-moment man, Odysseus, are you?'

'Oh, aren't I?' he questioned as her words sank in and every warning cry which was engaging his brain was silenced as he began to walk towards her. In the pin-drop silence which followed he could read the anger blazing from her eyes, but he could see the hunger too, her pupils darkening with desire and making them resemble two big chunks of burning coal. The atmosphere between them was so hot it was almost combustible, but he didn't touch her—dampening down his own desire with characteristic composure. Let her wait, he thought furiously. Just as he had waited—going out of his mind with worry that she might have fallen over the edge of those damned cliffs. As he waited every single day, counting down the cruelly lingering seconds until he could have her in his arms again, because only that way could he reassure himself that he was still *in control*.

'Perhaps, in future, you might let me know your travel plans,' he told her coolly. 'And if you're planning on going out walking, I can easily provide you with a map.'

Grace stared at him with growing incredulity as she silently listed his most irritating faults. His studied politeness. His growing distance from her. His outrageous controlling demands that she keep him informed of her movements at all times. But more than that, his icy control, evident now in the way he was looking at her. As if he were a machine, not a man. A cold and unfeeling machine. 'Why, you...you...' she breathed.

'What is it, *poulaki mou*?' he taunted, his sapphire eyes meeting hers in mocking challenge. 'What names do you want to call me?'

And that was what did it. The flicker which sparked the flame. Which drove all reason from her head and replaced it with a red-hot fury. With a little yelp, she launched herself at him, planning to drum her fists against his chest, or maybe to shove him out of the door to show she didn't need him, or want him. But who was she kidding? Because that wasn't happening. His mouth was on hers—hot and hard and urgent—and she was kissing him back as if her life depended on it. Her hands were all over his body, as if she were discovering it for the first time, and he was doing the same to her. Palming her breasts so that the nipples became hard and painful. Trickling her finger down over his belly, she began scrabbling at his belt, and as she slithered his jeans over his thighs she thought he'd never felt this big before.

'Oh!' she gasped.

'So what are you going to do now, Grace?' he goaded.

'This.'

With the flat of her hand she pushed his accommodating body back until he was lying flat on the floor. He was watching her from between slitted lashes, a muscle working frantically at his cheek as she found a condom on the nightstand and opened it so slowly that some of his control seemed to crack.

'Just hurry, will you?' he husked out.

That urgent plea pleased her more than it should have

done because there was no measured quality in his deep voice now, was there? Grace revelled in his helpless groan as she finished sheathing him with fingers which incited and excited, using skills he had taught her. And then she took off her panties and boldly climbed on top of him, taking him deep inside her, deeper than he'd ever been before—at least, that was how it felt. He was hot and hard. He was beautiful, and he was hers. *Hers*. A wave of emotion swelled up inside her as she cried his name and his hands were on her breasts as she rode him, his bronze fingers splayed decadently over the pale fabric of her sundress. She gripped his shoulders, feeling the pleasure build to a pitch which was sweet and unbearable, until she could resist it no longer. A low, keening sound erupted from the very core of her as suddenly she was torn apart, her body blitzed by sensation as she felt the first pump of his seed.

Dazed, she slumped on top of him, resisting the sleep her body was so desperately craving, remembering the futility of her thoughts in the middle of that frantic lovemaking. Because Odysseus wasn't *hers*, was he? He never had been and never would be.

And that reaction had frightened her.

It was frightening her now. Observing the ebony sweep of his closed lashes and the satiated smile curving his lips, all she could feel was a great swell of misplaced longing, which was totally one-sided. Which was probably going to get worse. Because she was fast discovering that affection, or love, or whatever you wanted to call it, was a funny thing. It grew, even when you didn't want it to. It made you vulnerable and it made you hurt.

She couldn't carry on like this and she needed to tell

him, before their strange marriage whittled away her sense of worth completely. But not here and not now. Not while she was still straddling him and could feel him inside her.

'I'm going to take a shower,' she announced, aware of his lashes fluttering open and his hot blue gaze burning into her as she peeled herself away.

CHAPTER THIRTEEN

THE KNOCK ON the door was unannounced but Odysseus had been expecting it, ever since his wife had left him lying half naked on the floor of their bedroom and slammed her way into the bathroom. A ragged sigh left his lungs. It had been unforgettable sex. Intense. *Theos, neh*. Very intense. But angry, too. So very angry. He had been jealous. He who had never known a moment's jealousy in his life.

But that was part of the trouble, wasn't it? That somehow Grace had the ability to access feelings he didn't even know he possessed. Why else would he have raged about a youth he'd known in his heart that she wouldn't have looked at twice. Because she didn't really want any man but him, did she? That was the disturbing truth of it.

'Come,' he growled reluctantly, the complexity of his thoughts compounded by the sight of Grace walking into his office, because there was something different about her and he couldn't quite put his finger on what it was. He kept his expression impassive enough for her to realise that her presence was unwelcome, because he didn't want this. The last thing he needed was some kind of showdown when he was trying to work Far better to suggest they discuss it reasonably over dinner later, when hopefully she might have had a chance to calm down.

'Can't this wait?' he questioned.

'I'm afraid it can't.' She bit her lip as if unsure how to proceed.

'Well?'

His terse interjection seemed to galvanise her and she sat down on the other side of his desk without asking.

'I want to go to England,' she announced.

He felt an automatic flicker of disquiet. 'I hope your grandmother is not ill?'

'Odysseus, she has dementia. She doesn't know what day of the week it is. Thank you for asking, but that's not...' She drew in a deep breath. 'That's not the reason.'

He raised his eyebrows, aware of the sudden pounding of his heart. 'So what *is* the reason for this unexpected departure?'

'Oh, come on. Is it really so *unexpected*?' she challenged, and then, when he refused to rise to it, she gave a little nod—as if he had just confirmed something she already knew. 'I don't want to continue with this marriage.'

'But you're supposed to be accompanying me to Tuloranka next week,' he informed her with icy logic. 'That was part of the deal.'

She didn't deny his words but her expression remained oddly calm. 'You really are an extraordinary man, Odysseus,' she said slowly. 'Aren't you even going to ask me why?'

Suddenly he realised what was different about her. Her jeans were old and her top much-washed. There was no sign of the fine garments crafted by some of the world's most famous designers which had been heaped on her since her arrival. Instead she was wearing her own clothes. Not only that, but her engagement ring and wedding band were nowhere to be seen. It was as if she had shed the luxurious skin she had acquired when she had become his wife, to reveal the woman she had always been underneath.

And that was when he knew she meant it.

He felt another flicker of disquiet. He should call her bluff. Tell her he didn't care what her reasons were, but that would have been a lie—because he was discovering that his curiosity was almost as intense as his irritation that she was going against his wishes and he was finding it increasingly difficult to keep his feelings in check. 'Why?' he shot out.

Grace licked her lips, trying to stay composed, because any flair of undesired emotion would only work against her, instinct told her that. She wondered why it was so difficult to say this when she knew it was the right thing for her. Was it because her heart was appealing against her logic and she wanted nothing more than to cross to his side of the desk? To run her fingers through his jet-dark hair and bend her face to kiss him and let his lovemaking obliterate all her doubts. She cleared her throat. 'Because there is little point in going from one controlling relationship to another.'

'What the hell are you talking about, Grace?' he asked softly.

Grace bristled. Even the question was patronising! But at least it freed her from the worry of sparing his feelings—he didn't have any! How long would it take for her to learn that and then to accept it? 'I'm talking about men,' she bit out. 'But two men in particular. Both incredibly wealthy and powerful and both of them, in their different ways, pushing me around as if I'm a pawn on a chessboard—'

'If you're suggesting what I think you're suggesting I will not have it. Don't you *dare* compare me to Contarini!' he hissed.

'I *will* dare because it's true!' she retorted and as her composure dissolved, it occurred to her how unusual it was for him to keep losing his rag like this. 'Vincenzo may have provided me with a fancy location and a generous wage but, essentially, I was living in a gilded cage. I had no real freedom. And it's exactly like that, living here with you.'

'How is it like that?' he barked.

'Think about it. You insult me when I go off on my own for the day—'

'I was trying to protect you.'

'Or imprisoning me—isn't that a more accurate description? Telling me I should take a car, or a map, mostly so you can know where I am at all times, tracking me from afar—like someone who's had their phone stolen! And then making snide digs about me being alone with Marinos—as if a man and a woman can't spend time in each other's company without instantly wanting to have sex. Do you want to have sex with every woman you meet, Odysseus?'

'You know damned well I don't,' he conceded, on a growl.

'Well, then. I rest my case!' She swallowed down the annoying lump which kept rising in her throat. 'But anyway, that's history now because I've been thinking...'

As her bravado temporarily deserted her, he looked at her enquiringly, his dark brows elevated in arrogant query, the firm press of his lips not quite managing to hide his rage. He's still angry, she thought—and for some reason that spurred her on. Was it a final remnant of misplaced hope that he might see the error of his ways? Admit defeat and throw himself on her mercy, so that they could all live happily ever after—was she still being a sucker for that elusive sense of romance?

'What have you been thinking, Grace?' he prompted.

'I think you've been fooling yourself about your motives for asking me to marry you.'

'How fascinating,' he murmured sarcastically as her words tailed away. 'Please. Continue.'

'This idea of me accompanying you on a work trip to a strict country so you could have unlimited sex with a woman you couldn't keep your hands off was nothing but a smokescreen. Oh, it might have been one of the reasons, but it certainly wasn't the main one, was it? Not when you've already demonstrated to yourself that you are able to do without sex whenever it suits you, because you have a steely self-will. Be honest, Odysseus,' she finished, her voice becoming a thready little whisper. 'The only reason I am here, married to you, is because you wanted revenge. I think you've never really forgiven your grandfather for kicking your mother out when she was pregnant and vulnerable and you wanted to punish him for all the hurt he had caused.'

At first she wondered if he had heard her because his features remained stony, though maybe the dark glitter in his eyes was an indication that she'd touched a raw nerve. 'That is an absurd accusation,' he said at last, slicing his hand through the air with customary dismissive arrogance. 'I went to see Contarini simply to satisfy my curiosity, not really expecting him to repent or apologise, and my expectation proved to be correct.' He gave a bitter smile. 'Unfortunately, he seemed to have learned nothing from his past behaviour. When he offered me money and shares to stay away from you, I was appalled. And my revulsion that he was prepared to barter you as if you were a sack of rice at the local marketplace was what prompted my proposal.'

'Do you really believe that, Odysseus?'

'Don't you?' he parried coolly.

'Oh, I'm not denying that some shred of altruism may have been involved and I suppose I should be grateful for that.' She gave a bitter laugh. 'But we both know that Vincenzo's offer would be like a drop in the ocean to a man of your wealth and influence. You didn't need or want his money, or his shares, did you? But you knew the very fact that he'd made the offer proved how much he wanted to hang onto his housekeeper—and that was what gave you your brilliant idea. You knew how disruptive it would be if I left and how much it would affect him. And so you took me away from him. As simple as that. Revenge, with plenty of sex thrown in—it's a very potent combination. Win-win.'

As she sat there waiting for a response, Odysseus felt the flicker of a pulse at his temple. Was she waiting for him to deny it? To throw himself on her mercy, perhaps, so that she could *forgive* him?

He sat back in his chair and linked his fingers together on his chest. 'An interesting hypothesis,' he mused. 'And clearly not the foundation for any kind of marriage, no matter how temporary the arrangement is supposed to be.' He raised his eyebrows, before adding thoughtfully,

'Although that doesn't necessarily mean we can't go through with the Tulorankian trip, as originally planned.'

'Are you out of your mind?' She stared at him with disbelieving eyes. 'Do you really think we can go through with such a charade as if nothing has happened?'

He shrugged. 'You'd need to dig into all your acting skills, that's for sure,' he offered drily. 'We certainly wouldn't be able to put on a united front at the royal palace if you make it clear that you think so little of me, Grace.'

She shook her head. 'But that's where you're wrong,' she whispered at last, and her voice was so quiet that he had to lean forward fractionally to hear it. 'I'm not apportioning all the blame to you. Maybe some of what happened was down to me, and the choices I've made.' She shrugged. 'For a long time, I was feeling increasingly trapped working for Vincenzo and your marriage proposal gave me the chance to escape from that cage, without compromising my grandmother's care. But perhaps I should have looked for an alternative solution. I should have known there's no such thing as a free lunch. Maybe I was too keen to opt for what looked like the easier, softer option—only to find that it was anything but.'

He shrugged. 'So now you know.'

'Yeah. Now I know.' She gave a short laugh. 'On that first night I joked that I wanted you to rescue me but, perhaps, deep down—I meant it. And no woman should expect a man to do that.'

His brows rose a little higher. 'Have you quite finished?'

'Not yet.' Her amber eyes were as dark as honey as she fixed him with a trembling look. 'You pushed me away after the wedding—what happened to make you do that, Odysseus? Did I commit the terrible crime of starting to care too much for you? Because I'm afraid I did.' She swallowed. 'I do.'

'But caring was never on the agenda!' he continued remorselessly, steeling himself against the look she was directing at him. Because what she wanted and what he wanted were opposite sides of the coin and it was time she realised that, once and for all. 'You know what we agreed,' he concluded coldly. 'That it was nothing but a marriage of convenience.'

'Yes, of course I know *what we agreed*. But we're human beings—not machines! It doesn't always work like that. At least, for some of us, it doesn't. But anyway, that's all academic now, isn't it?' She rose to her feet. 'Like I said, I want to go back to England. Obviously, I can't just rock up to the airport and buy myself a ticket, because there isn't one. And since the only way off this place is by your helicopter, or one of the fishermen's boats, I'm going to need your help. But if this sudden change of plan makes you unwilling to do that, then I'm prepared to swim if I have to even if I *am* a relative novice!'

Despite her reckless threat, there was a quiet dignity about her which was making his heart clench and suddenly Odysseus realised that his throat had grown so dry that he couldn't speak. And the crazy thing was that he wanted to pull her into his arms. To kiss away the hurt which was making her lips look as tight as the bud of a rose. To transmute that hurt into the desire which always thrummed between them, no matter what they did or said, even now.

And if he did that, then what?

It was obvious.

Nothing would change. Her expectations would increase until, sooner or later, he would be unable to meet them. And then *he* would be the one who had to end it, which she would inevitably find more difficult. He felt the hard punch of his heart. She was a beautiful woman, inside and out, and if he were a different kind of man then maybe he could have believed in some kind of future with her.

But he wasn't. He could never be the kind of man she needed, and even if he could…he didn't want to be. Because what kind of idiot would voluntarily open themselves up to the prospect of pain? It would be like somebody whose flesh had been burned to the bone putting their hand straight back in the fire.

He rose to his feet and felt another twist of his heart as she looked up into his eyes because never had she seemed a more bewitching combination of the strong and the vulnerable.

'I will get you back to England with all speed, Grace,' he said heavily and then managed to give a bitter smile, although his lips felt as if they were made of concrete. 'And believe me, one day you'll thank me for it.'

As he turned away from her, Grace could have wept, but she pursed her lips together hard to ensure that didn't happen. No way was she going to make him aware of the pain which was coursing through her veins like a fierce fever, making her heart pound and her skin shiver. She needed to convince him that all her stupid dreams had been extinguished. She had only to think of his brutal words if she needed any more convincing that he couldn't wait to see the back of her.

'Yes. Do that,' she said tonelessly. 'Get me out of here with all speed.'

CHAPTER FOURTEEN

GRACE HAD LEARNED how to mop the floors *mindfully*—which apparently involved using as many muscles as possible and thinking about nothing more than how shiny the tiles were becoming under her rhymical ministrations. Because it was easier to think about her daily domestic chores than allow herself to be dragged back down into a whirlpool of misery. Outside the rain was bashing against the windows as it seemed to have been doing ever since she'd arrived back in England, and the relentless downpour seemed to echo her mood.

She'd left the island of Kosmima on a high of indignation and hurt, but it had all been downhill from there. She shook her head, impatient with herself. Had she honestly thought she'd be able to wave a magic wand and magically drive Odysseus from her mind? Had she imagined that a man like him would be so easy to forget? Fourteen days into her new life and the aching in her heart seemed to be getting worse instead of better. But time healed, apparently. It was the one thing on which everyone was agreed.

Straightening up from her bucket, she pushed a fist into the small of her back and gave it a little rub, relieved that her long shift would soon be over and she'd be able to put her feet up. Working as a cleaner at the old folks' home was physically much harder than anything she'd ever done at the Contarini house but it was way more rewarding. And, of course, she got to see Nana as often as she wanted.

'Grace?'

She turned round to see the duty manager, who was smiling at her. The kindly, middle-aged woman who had insisted on giving Grace a job when she'd stumbled in one rainy morning, feeling like an alien who had landed from outer space. Who had offered her a job as a domestic cleaner and somehow managed to include a tiny room as part of the package. She'd been so gentle when Grace had been trying hard not to cry and that flicker of kindness had seemed like the single tiny light shining at the end of a long, dark tunnel.

'Yes, Mrs MacCormack?' Grace squeezed out her mop and straightened up. 'I hope everything's to your satisfaction?'

'It certainly is. Sure, and couldn't you see your face in those tiles?' But after her initial burst of enthusiasm, the Irishwoman's smile faded. 'You have a visitor.'

This should have been the moment when Grace blinked in surprise, asking who it was. But she knew who it was, because there was only one person it *could* be. None of her friends from Venice would have just turned up without warning and she hadn't had the chance to make any friends in England yet. Hadn't wanted to, if the truth were known, because she suspected she'd be rotten company at the moment. And though not a day had gone by when she hadn't fantasised about exactly this scenario, now that the moment was here, Grace was filled with an overwhelming sense of trepidation—mostly because of her own reaction, which was one of excitement and, yes, joy. But that was plain stupid. It was probably something to do with the divorce settlement, because what other reason would he have for coming here? Maybe his lawyers had managed to find a loophole in the prenup and he was about to tell her that he wasn't prepared to be as generous as he'd originally stated.

No.

Grace might find it possible to entertain any number of bleak thoughts about her estranged husband, but on some gut level she knew he would never cheat her. 'What did you tell him?' She glanced at her watch. 'I finish in half an hour.'

'Put your bucket away, dear, and you can knock off early. He's waiting in the lobby and he doesn't look like the kind of man who is used to being kept waiting.' Mrs MacCormack hesitated. 'Or would you like me to send him away altogether?'

Yes, thought Grace. Send him as far away as possible, so that I don't have to look at his beautiful face and have my heart broken all over again.

But she wasn't a coward and anyway, something told her that if Odysseus Diamides wanted to see her, then nothing would stand in his way until that mission had been accomplished.

She shivered.

Why the hell should she make it easy for him?

'I'll work until the end of my shift,' she said doggedly and was rewarded with a nod of approval from the older woman. 'Tell him he'll have to wait.'

As it was, she took even longer than she'd planned, washing out her mop with extra care and not even bothering to change out of her polyester uniform. Keeping her severe hairstyle in place, she glanced in the mirror, wondering if she was shooting herself in the foot by presenting him with such a drab appearance.

But what did she think was going to happen? That if she let her hair down and dabbed on a bit of lip gloss, Odysseus would fall to her feet in a swoon and tell her he couldn't live without her? She gave a bitter laugh as she made her way towards the main entrance. No. She was through with having unrealistic expectations.

Yet the crashing of her heart was deafening as she walked into the reception hall and somehow it seemed incongruous to see Odysseus Diamides standing there. Against the cosy backdrop of squashy armchairs and fake houseplants, his masculinity had never seemed more defined. No beautifully cut charcoal suit could possibly disguise the musculature of his powerful body and, despite the lash of rain outside, he was completely dry. Of course he was. His driver would have leapt from the car as soon as it stopped, unfolding a giant umbrella to keep the billionaire protected from the elements. Because that was the sort of life he lived—in his precious bubble of wealth—protected from all the hardship and feelings which normal folk encountered every day of their lives.

She searched his face for disappointment when he registered her mundane appearance but she saw no such thing, only the glint of something in his sapphire eyes as if someone had suddenly shone a light at them. But as she grew closer she could see there were dark shadows beneath the inky lashes and she realised that his raven-dark hair was a tad *too* long, curling ever so slightly over the collar of his silk shirt. And wasn't it insane that she was having to quell her stupid instinct, which was to rush over to him and ask if he was okay?

'Odysseus,' she said, giving him a polite nod. 'Aren't you supposed to be in Tuloranka?'

'I told the King I was no longer available.'

'You told him...*what*?'

'That I was prepared to send one of my associates to do the work, but I could no longer commit to staying indefinitely in his country.'

'Good heavens. How did he take it?'

He shrugged. 'He wasn't best pleased, but I haven't come here to talk about King Kaliman, Grace!'

'No,' she said slowly, trying not to think about the implications of such an uncharacteristic gesture on the part of her workaholic husband and concentrating instead on something else. 'How did you know where to find me?'

'I made a few enquiries.'

'So you *do* have spies!' Politeness now forgotten, she shot him an accusing look. 'Why didn't you tell me you were coming?'

'Because I thought you might absent yourself.'

'Yeah.'

Sapphire eyes bored into her. 'So you would have done?'

Grace shrugged, until she forced herself to be straight with him. She might have been very foolish in the past where Odysseus Diamides was concerned, but she had always been honest and there was no reason to change that now. 'No.'

He nodded, as if storing away this small concession before drawing in a deep breath. 'Could we go somewhere more private to talk?'

It was that moment that Grace spotted one of the residents ambling past on her Zimmer frame, before coming to a halt to stare in awe at Odysseus. But then, that was the effect he had on women. Even ninety-year-olds, it seemed. 'Like where?'

'Don't you have a room here?'

'I'm not sure I'd call it that. Presumably your spies aren't providing a gold-standard service, or they would have told you that I'm living in the equivalent of a shoebox.'

He gave a hollow laugh. 'Ah, but I'm used to those, remember?'

And yes, she did remember but wished she didn't. Inwardly, Grace cursed because she didn't want to think of him as broken and lonely and abandoned. It was much easier if she concentrated on his arrogance and control. She thought about her alternatives. She could take him to the café in the nearby village but it was still tipping down with rain and no way was she going to set a foot inside his limousine. This had to be on *her* territory.

'Very well,' she said woodenly. 'You'd better follow me.'

Odysseus did as she asked, only vaguely aware of a series of brightly lit corridors and plenty of oversized chairs with footrests, because his attention was solely concentrated on the petite woman who marched before him, her head held high. Her hair was drawn back into the most restrictive style he'd ever seen and yet all he noticed was the fiery hint in the chestnut depths. Just like that ugly and rather voluminous uniform, which was managing to brush enticingly against her neat frame and do dangerous things to his blood pressure.

Eventually, they reached a rather gloomy corridor, along which were a row of similar doors, and as she drew a small bunch of keys from her pocket and unlocked one, he couldn't help noticing that her hand was trembling.

'Come in,' she said peremptorily.

The room was indeed minuscule, and as she was shutting the door Odysseus took the opportunity to look around, because it was a long time since he'd been anywhere like this. There was a single bed and a functional locker, on which stood a photo of two women with a small child. A small sink adorned one corner and a suitcase he recognised had been placed on top of the modest wardrobe. It looked like a cell, he thought.

And this was what she had chosen in preference to a life with him.

He turned round to find her studying him, her face giving nothing away. But she wasn't haranguing him, or asking him why he had turned up in the middle of the day, without warning, which surely anyone else in her position would have done.

But Grace wasn't *like* anyone else.

Wasn't that the reason he was here?

'You're probably wondering why I've turned up today like this,' he said, at last.

She shrugged. 'The thought had obviously crossed my mind.'

Odysseus scowled because he didn't want flippant evasion, he *wanted* her to prompt him. To drag the reluctant answers from him, with the determination of someone trying to extract an oyster from its shell. To make *her* do the wanting and him do the giving, so that he would still be in control. But still she said nothing. He gave a ragged sigh as he realised she wasn't going to make this easy for him. And why should she? 'I miss you,' he said thickly.

She nodded. 'That's a bit like what you said just before our wedding, when you made it very plain exactly what it was you'd been missing. But this time we're not going to have sex, Odysseus, no matter how much we want to—because it will only complicate matters.'

She was right. He knew that. He agreed with every word on principle, damn her, yet he had been expecting her to capitulate instantly—as women had been doing all his life. But her face showed no passion, just a soft curiosity shining from her amber eyes. And something about her calm reason made him realise that if he wanted what he had come here for, then she would settle for nothing less than a brutal examination of his feelings.

His feelings.

Something like fear stalled him because all his life he had denied their existence and, to some extent, this had worked in his favour. He'd been able to focus solely on his career. To drag himself out of the sordid poverty of his upbringing and make a new life for himself. But now he recognised that his reticence and closure were no longer working and he had to be prepared to confront all the pain and hurt and confusion if he wanted her.

And he wanted her more than he had ever wanted anything.

Drawing in a deep breath, he prepared to make his pitch—something he had done countless times in his life and yet never had a prospect seemed so daunting and so vital. 'When I met you that night in Venice, you captivated me—nothing less than that. I was utterly entranced by you. Despite the masks and unfamiliar outfits we wore, the chemistry between us was off the scale. I'd never experienced anything like it and I'd certainly never had a one-night hook-up with a woman before.'

He shook his head. 'It was incredible and next morning I kept thinking about how I could contact you again but decided against it because…'

'Because?' she prompted into the silence which followed, but he could hear the surprise in her voice.

'Because I have a track record for breaking women's hearts and I didn't want my sweet virgin lover to be among their number,' he ground out. 'And then I went for my meeting with Vincenzo, and there you were. Dressed in grey with eyes downcast, as if I had summoned you up out of my thoughts.'

'So it was just coincidence that we ended up seeing each other again?' she said quietly. 'A one in a million chance.'

'Or destiny,' he demurred, with a vehemence which was growing by the second. 'Don't you believe in destiny, Grace?'

'I'm not sure—and I'm surprised you do, being such a cynic and all.'

'I'm surprised, too,' he admitted, with a ragged sigh. 'I've been thinking about the accusations you threw at me on Kosmima and whether or not they were true. Yes, I took you away from my grandfather's employment, but it wasn't for revenge.' He shook his head and stared at her with a sudden intensity which flooded through him like fire. 'Do you really think I would have asked you to marry me—with all the implications and possible fallout of such a life-changing course of action—just to derive some sort of meaningless satisfaction from having thwarted a bitter old man I was never going to see again? Apart from anything else, I would never allow him to have that much power or influence over my life. It was something else which made me determined to ask you.'

'What?' she asked quietly, her heavy lids shading the sudden wary look in her eyes.

'The fact that you were supporting your grandmother by working there. Sublimating most of your youth and energy in a position of drudgery because you felt responsible for her. I'd never met a woman who was prepared to put someone else's needs ahead of her own. It made me realise how sweet and good you were. But it suited me to concentrate on our incredible chemistry instead— to try to convince myself that what I felt for you would soon burn itself out. Only it didn't.'

He walked across the room and picked up the photo from the locker. It showed three generations, grandmother, mother and child. The two women had hair of the exact same colour as Grace and the little girl between them was so obviously Grace herself. He could see the future adult in the child. That shy mischief already in her eyes. That sweet tenderness as her chubby little arms clung on to her mother and her nana. They were all laughing, and a fleeting pang of pain ripped at his heart as he acknowledged something he had never known, something he'd never thought he wanted. But now he did. If she would accept him. Because Odysseus recognised that what he really wanted could not be fulfilled with anyone else but Grace.

He put the photo back down. 'When you came out to the island, I realised that a very different kind of life was possible with you. But that scared me.' He gave a short laugh. 'Me, who always imagined I was so fearless. I remembered the chaos of emotions when I was growing up. The mess of my father's affairs. Even worse was the dull ache of loss which had always served as a backdrop, because I was missing a mother I had never known. I didn't want the possibility of feeling that kind of pain and confusion ever again, so I pushed you away— thinking that if we kept our marriage on a purely superficial level it would be satisfactory. But it wasn't. Certainly not for you and ultimately, not for me either. I've missed you so much, Grace. You've weaved your way into my life, like a thread of gold which makes it shine. I can't imagine living without you and that's the truth. I've realised I don't want the empty kind of marriage I offered you,' he added huskily. 'I want the real kind. The only kind which works and which is founded on only one true principle.'

He swallowed as he sucked in a deep and unsteady breath. 'I don't expect you to believe me,' he began slowly and then he could hold onto his composure no longer and his words began to crack. 'But I love you, Grace. I've never said that to another living soul but I'm saying it to you now and I mean it, from the bottom of my heart.'

Grace had grown so still that for a moment she felt as if she were suspended in some unreal state between dreaming and reality. Because this must be a dream, surely? To see Odysseus standing before her, all that icy control replaced by a look of longing and, yes, pleading in his eyes. As if she held the key to his happiness in her humble little hand.

It was a lot to take in. In fact, it was a total realignment of everything she had believed to be true. But she knew one thing above all else. That he would never say something as profound as that unless he meant it. He had stripped his emotions bare before her and that must have taken a lot of courage for a man like him. He had spoken poetically and longingly and lovingly. Her heart turned over, knowing that she must treasure his words but that she must share them, too. That he must never be in any doubt about how much he meant to her.

'I love you too, my darling Odysseus,' she whispered. 'I tried so hard not to fall for you because that was what you wanted—'

'What I *thought* I wanted,' he negated fiercely.

She smiled. 'But despite your best efforts to push me away, I couldn't seem to stop myself, because the chemistry was there for me, too,' she admitted softly. 'Two strangers in masks—but once we removed them, those same powerful feelings were there. Maybe it was fate which brought us together that night, but right now it feels like our destiny.' She swallowed. 'That we will love and care and commit to each other.'

'For the rest of our lives?' he affirmed throatily.

'Oh, yes, my love. A thousand times yes.'

The sound he made might have been tinged with triumph but Grace didn't care. She didn't care about anything right then, other than to hurl herself into his arms as he picked her up by the hips and suspended her in the air—just as he'd done at that masked ball in Venice. And when he set her back down again, he kissed her. Kissed her and kissed her until she had no breath left. And then he was unzipping her uniform dress and tugging her constricted hair out of the tight scrunchy. He was tearing off his own costly clothes and hurling them to the ground until they were both naked on her tiny single bed, his erection hard and proud as it nudged between her thighs, when a scowling look passed over his face.

'What's the matter?'

'I've left the damned condom in my suit trousers,' he growled.

'So what?' she answered demurely. 'I don't care, if you don't care.'

The sound he made was feral as he thrust deep inside her and Grace had never felt anything quite as beautiful as that. Was it because he was unsheathed and the unspoken subtext was that they wanted to have a baby together which made it so incredible? Or that they had finally found the freedom to articulate words of love?

Grace didn't know. All she did know was that afterwards, when they had finally floated back down to earth and Odysseus had finished kissing her, he pulled her closer to him.

'Do you know what I'd like to do in a while?' He yawned.

'Hang your suit up, in case you get mistaken for a tramp?'

He smiled. 'I'd like to go and see your grandmother, to tell her that I love you and that I intend to spend the rest of my life showing you just how much.'

Grace opened her mouth to say that while the idea was incredibly sweet and thoughtful, Nana didn't recognise anyone or anything and there was no way she would understand.

Until she remembered that hearing was the very last of the senses to go and that miracles could happen.

She tightened her arms around him.

Hadn't one just happened right here when they'd declared their love for one another?

'Let's do that,' she said huskily.

EPILOGUE

'Do you think we've done everything?'

Odysseus slanted his wife a slow smile as she stood against the balustrade of the rooftop terrace, bathed in the vivid light of the setting sun. Her coral-tinged hair tumbled to her waist and her petite figure was shown to spectacular advantage by a tiny pair of shorts and a pink camisole. 'Everything looks perfect,' he assured her. 'Including you.'

She smiled. 'Stop it,' she whispered.

'I'm not doing anything.'

'Yes, you are. You're looking at me like…'

'Like what?' he questioned, all faux innocence.

'As if you'd like to eat me up.'

'Ah. That I cannot deny.' He walked towards her, enjoying the darkening of her magnificent eyes and hungry tremble of her lips. 'Eating you up is one of my very favourite pastimes.'

Her cheeks were warm as he pulled her against him. 'Mine, too,' she admitted, reaching up on tiptoes to graze her lips against his jaw. 'Despite the attempts of two little boys to come between us!'

Odysseus's beat of pride was instant, because the love he felt for their twin sons, Apollo and Axis, was powerful and all-consuming. 'Thank heavens for childcare,' he remarked drily, though his words didn't quite tell the whole story. It was true they had plenty of help with their pair of rumbustious toddlers but to everyone's surprise— his own included—he had proved to be a hands-on father. To be around for the boys, but still able to devote as much time as possible to his beautiful wife. Thus, he delegated much more these days and his reputation as a workaholic had taken a severe battering.

'How about we drink some champagne and then go to bed?' he suggested softly. 'We've got a busy day tomorrow.'

'I think I'll pass on the champagne,' she said. 'Just hold me for a little while, will you?'

'That would be my pleasure, *angele mou*,' he purred.

Grace snuggled even closer as Odysseus tightened his arms around her, revelling in the simple joy she found whenever he was near. Sometimes she wondered what she had done to deserve so much happiness, but she never took it for granted. Not once.

She had given birth to their darling boys two years earlier and the twins had been just six weeks old when the family had travelled to England, to say goodbye to her beloved nana. Had the old lady been aware of the new life and continuation of her line? Grace liked to think so—especially as Axis in particular had squalled so loudly, causing Mrs MacCormack to enquire whether he had colic. (He did.)

Afterwards they had returned to Kosmima and although occasionally Odysseus had wondered whether she might find island life too isolating, Grace loved it. Grateful for her linguistic background, she was now fluent in the beautiful Greek language. She was on the board of the tiny cottage hospital and elementary school, where she gave twice-weekly lessons in English to the children. Inevitably, things would change as the boys grew older, but they would cross those particular bridges when they came to them.

Even Gouri, the black and white cat, had finally accepted her—jumping into her lap whenever she got the chance and becoming the fierce guardian of the twins—though it was always Odysseus who made her purr the loudest. It had been Evangelia who had suggested that the rescued feline might actually have been *jealous* of Grace.

And Grace had encouraged her husband to connect with his global scattering of godchildren which meant they now hosted weekends for friends he admitted to having neglected in the past. Their island villa often rang with the sound of laughter and, tomorrow, Kirsty and Sophia were coming to stay.

'Grace?'

Her husband's deep voice had disturbed her reverie and Grace stared up into his beloved face. *'Neh, zoi mou?'*

'Why don't you want any champagne?'

'Am I such a lush that you need to ask?' she joked.

'No.' He traced a thoughtful finger around the edge of her lips. 'But a glass or two on Saturday night is something we usually both enjoy.'

She had been savouring the moment since she'd found out that afternoon, hugging it to herself like the most delicious secret, trying to work out the perfect time to break the news. But he had guessed. She could tell from the light shining from his sapphire eyes. The smile of pure delight on his lips. He knows me so well, she thought contentedly.

'For the avoidance of doubt, yes, I'm pregnant,' she whispered.

He didn't speak for a moment and when he did, his words were tinged with pride and something else. *'Kardia mou,'* he said huskily. 'My heart. My one true love.'

And then effortlessly he picked her up—just as he had done one cold February night in Venice, when her eyes had glittered at him through a jewelled mask and melted the ice around his heart.

* * * * *

Did you fall in love with

Greek's Bartered Bride?
*Then you're sure to enjoy
these other dramatic stories
by Sharon Kendrick!*

Innocent Maid for the Greek
Italian Nights to Claim the Virgin
The Housekeeper's One-Night Baby
The King's Hidden Heir
His Enemy's Italian Surrender

Available now!

KING, ENEMY, HUSBAND

JACKIE ASHENDEN

MILLS & BOON

To Soraya. I miss the GIFs already. :-)

CHAPTER ONE

TIBERIUS MAXIMUS BENEDICTUS of the House of Aquila, in approximately five minutes from now the newly crowned and rightful King of Kasimir, strode down the wide hallway to the throne room, a flock of men consisting of his aides, guards, one general and a priest following on his wake.

The coup that had finally ousted the Accorsi tyrants hadn't been as bloodless as he'd wanted—there had been casualties, though thankfully no civilians had been hurt—but at least his strategies had paid off.

Finally, after twenty years of Accorsi rule that had nearly brought the country to the brink of collapse, the Accorsis had been defeated. And now they were gone. For good.

The one black spot in his otherwise unblemished victory was that unfortunately the Accorsis had managed to evade capture, and the last report he'd received was that they'd fled Kasimir entirely. Much to his fury.

He'd hoped to bring Renzo Accorsi and his advisors before the courts here, to answer for their crimes, but sadly that was not an option. Still, the international authorities had been notified. Renzo would be brought to justice in time, Tiberius had no doubt.

First, though, and most important, was the crown.

He wouldn't be King until it was on his head, and only once it was could he start with the vital work of rebuilding the country that years of mismanagement and civil unrest had torn apart. Nothing was more important than that. Nothing.

The empty hallway echoed with the sound footsteps on the ancient parquet of the floor as Tiberius and his entourage swept into the throne room.

Or at least what remained of the throne room.

It had been home to the rulers of Kasimir in various iterations for centuries. The Accorsi coup that had ousted his parents and caused the death of his mother had occurred when he'd been a baby, so he had never been inside it himself...

Until now.

Growing up in Italy, hidden and forgotten, his father would often bring Tiberius to the mountains that looked over Kasimir. There had been a scenic lookout spot where tourists could pull off the road and take pictures of the picture-perfect European castle and jagged, snow-capped mountains that surrounded it.

'*That* is your legacy, boy,' his father would tell him, pointing at the castle spires. '*That* is yours. *That* is where you belong.'

Well. Now he was here.

In the castle that had been taken from him and his family years before.

His true home.

Tiberius paused in the doorway, then scowled.

The throne room was a bloody mess.

In their rush to leave, the Accorsis had somehow found the time to get their soldiers to desecrate the Kasimiran throne room.

Most of the tapestries had been torn down and were lying in heaps near the walls. Centuries-old paintings were scored and cut with knives. The panelled oak that lined the walls had been kicked in and spray-painted with obscenities, and someone had even tried to light a fire in one corner with the remains of an ornate chair. Smoke drifted across the pitted parquet as one of Tiberius's own guards hurried to douse the fire with water.

Tiberius scanned the mess, trying to rein in his fury at the mess. Because a good strategist never let his feelings get in the way and certainly neither did a king. He turned to one of his aides, issued some sharp orders to get the clean-up started, then strode towards the dais and the huge carved oak throne that sat on top of it.

It was ancient, that throne, the wood smooth and dark with age and wear. The cushions that had likely been on the seat lay slashed open and scattered around the dais, feathers dusting the wood.

Tiberius ignored them as he climbed the stairs of the dais and kicked the remains of the cushions aside. A throne wasn't meant to be padded or comfortable, because once a king was comfortable that was where corruption lay. He wouldn't fall into that trap.

Slowly he turned and sat on the throne.

Finally.

After so long, a Benedictus sat on the throne once more. Now the ghosts of his parents could rest.

A deep, savage satisfaction curled through him, and he let himself feel it for a few seconds, because the road had been hard and long to get here. Years of training in other countries' armies to hone his military skills. Years of planning and political manoeuvring to gather supporters to his cause. Years of anguish watching his people suffer under Accorsi rule...

Now that was done.

Now the real work would begin.

Shoving aside the satisfaction, Tiberius snapped his fingers at the priest and another aide standing in the crowd clustered at the base of the dais.

'Father Domingo,' he said curtly. 'If you please?'

The aide holding the heavy gold circlet carved with oak leaves that was the Kasimir royal crown handed it to the priest, who immediately came up the stairs.

There would be no ceremony, no pomp and definitely no circumstance in this coronation. Tiberius didn't have time for any. His country needed hospitals and schools and new housing, not pointless and expensive ceremonies.

The priest intoned the words of an old prayer, then placed the circlet on Tiberius's brow. And just like that, after twenty years of exile, the crown of Kasimir finally rested on the head of the true King.

Tiberius ignored the weight of it, and this time allowed himself no satisfaction at all. Instead, he waited stoically as the little gathering of people at the foot of the dais cheered and applauded before raising his hand. Silence fell instantly.

He was not a man to be disobeyed.

'In my first act as King,' he began. 'I will—' He broke off abruptly, the back of his neck prickling.

Ten long years of military training had given him sharp senses and a finely honed awareness of threats. He was very aware of when he was being watched, for example, and he was definitely being watched now. And not only by the people gathered in the throne room.

Below him, one of his guards shifted on his feet, boots scuffing on the parquet.

'Quiet!' Tiberius snapped, trying to concentrate on the prickling sensation, scanning the room while his men waited in absolute silence.

Everything was the way it had been before he'd come in here. Nothing had changed. He glanced up at the ceiling to find nothing but painted plaster. Nowhere for anyone to watch him from there, clearly.

Yet, the fact remained that he was being watched.

Like his father, he had a photographic memory, and as part of his training to take back the throne his father had made him memorise the palace floor plans. He knew that one of the Kings in centuries past had constructed a small network of narrow corridors within the thick palace walls, so his spies could secretly observe people.

Perhaps whoever it was, was in there?

Tiberius scanned the wall to his left. One of those corridors lay behind it, if he wasn't much mistaken, and there was a door to it behind one of heavy tapestries.

Well, whoever was lurking in those corridors wouldn't stay hidden for long. Not if he had anything to do with it.

Saying anything would alert whoever was hiding, so he didn't speak, merely glanced at his captain of the guard and jerked his head in the direction of the tapestry. The man knew all his king's wordless commands and instantly strode over to it and jerked aside the heavy fabric. A small, narrow door lay behind it, just as Tiberius suspected. The captain pulled open the door and disappeared into the corridor behind. A soft cry came through the doorway, then a scuffle of footsteps, and an instant later, much to Tiberius's surprise, the captain marched a slip of a girl all in white lace and muslin out into the throne room and over to the dais.

No, not a girl. A woman. A small woman, wearing some kind of flouncy, lacy white dress with a ragged hem and covered in dust. Her hair was a pale mass of curls, half falling out of a pink ribbon and hanging down her back, almost obscuring her face, but from what he could glimpse her features were delicate, precise and sharp.

She was very pale. Was it fear? If so then she *should* be afraid. She might not look like an immediate threat, but she'd been hiding in the walls and watching him, and that he would not tolerate.

His captain, who was holding her by her upper arm, released her, and she made an aggrieved sound, rubbing at her arm as she stood at the foot of dais.

The oddest thought crossed Tiberius's mind then... That she looked like a piece of thistledown coming down to rest on the old parquet of the floor. Either that or a terrified fairy—and, despite that aggrieved noise, she was definitely terrified.

Tiberius stared down at her impassively from his throne.

Who was she and why had she been in those secret corridors? Was she an Accorsi assassin, left behind to launch a surprise attack? Or an Accorsi spy, lying in wait to take back information on the new King?

Whatever she was, she wouldn't be doing it for much longer. She would go before the courts to be tried. The Accorsis and their hangers-on would answer for their crimes. He would make them.

'So,' he said at length. 'I see we have mice in the walls.'

The woman stared up at him, her sharp cheekbones pale as snow. Her curls had fallen back from her face, revealing a pair of the deepest, most luminous blue eyes he'd ever seen.

Something unfamiliar twisted in his gut and he found himself leaning forward, as if to study her more closely. There was fear in them, and yet an odd kind of defiance too.

Intriguing.

She'd been caught spying on him in his newly acquired throne room so she was right to be afraid. Yet this defiance in spite of her fear… It either made her very brave or very stupid.

'A silent mouse,' he murmured. 'You should speak, little mouse. Explain what you're doing, hiding and spying on your king.'

The fine line of her jaw hardened even though fear still lurked in her eyes. 'I am not a mouse,' she said. 'And I was not spying.'

Her voice was precise and clear as glass.

'Then what were you doing?' He studied her intently, looking for signs of a lie, looking for weaknesses. He had a soldier's instinct, alert to anything and everything that might be a threat, and while she might not be an obvious one, looks could be deceiving.

A woman in a flouncy, lacy dress could still cause him problems, no matter how pretty she was—and he had to admit she was very pretty.

Not that he was interested. He had been sexually abstinent for the past six months as he'd entered the final stages of his plan to reclaim the throne, because he'd wanted no distractions. His body hadn't been happy about it, but he was a master of physical control and it would do what he wished.

Perhaps after his project for rebuilding Kasimir had

got underway he'd find himself a willing woman and lose himself for a night or two. But not until then.

Everything had to wait until then.

The woman was holding herself very still, her hands clasped tightly together, and it was clear that she did not like being looked at the way he was looking at her.

Good. She wasn't supposed to like it. If she hadn't wanted to be looked at, she shouldn't have been hiding in the walls.

'Well?' He kept his tone calm, almost gentle. 'You will give me an answer, mouse. And that is an order, not a request.'

Her mouth firmed. 'I was...hiding.'

'Obviously. And who were you hiding from? My soldiers? Or...' Tiberius stopped as a thought came to him. Now he'd taken a good look at her, he saw there was an odd familiarity to her features, as if he'd seen a face like hers before, somewhere...

Yes. He knew where. The photos his father had kept, which he'd showed to Tiberius as he was growing up. Making sure Tiberius memorised the people in them. Making sure he knew who they were and what they'd done.

'These are your enemies,' his father had said. 'Your mother died because of them. Remember them. They took what is ours and it is up to you to get it back.'

Those sharp features, those blue eyes, that pale hair...

She was an Accorsi—of course she was.

A pulse of something hot and fierce lanced through him. So. Not all of them had escaped. One had stayed and here she was, standing before his reclaimed throne.

His prisoner.

His war prize.

'Miss Accorsi,' he said softly, watching her, seeing the flicker of shock in her eyes as he said the name, the delicate rosebud of her mouth opening. 'It is a dangerous thing for someone with your name to be hiding in walls.'

She went even paler, almost the colour of her dusty white dress. 'How do you know—?'

'You're Guinevere Accorsi, are you not?' he interrupted, because she had to be. Renzo had had three children and there was only one girl.

Her gaze flickered, then that sharp little chin of hers lifted, as if she was trying to stare him down, no matter that he was on a throne, on a dais, and she was at his feet.

'Y-Yes,' she said. 'And?'

Tiberius's grip on the arms of his throne tightened as a thought began to take shape in his head. He was a master strategist, all his risks calculated, his gambles fully with the odds in his favour. Being an excellent tactician had given him the crown that was by rights truly his and, while he didn't like surprises, when one presented itself he had no problem adapting it to suit his purposes.

If this woman was indeed Renzo's daughter, then she could be useful to him. There were still those sympathetic to the Accorsis scattered throughout the country—supporters who would no doubt cause trouble now he was King.

He could crush those pockets of resistance, jail the supporters or exile them from the country, but... The Accorsis had done exactly that when they'd taken power, and he was determined not to be like them. He refused. His country didn't need a tyrant intent on suppressing any protest. It needed to heal, and so did his people. The divides needed to be bridged, not deepened.

Which was where the Accorsi daughter came in.

Eventually he would need a queen, and while obtaining one had been the very last thing on his mind certainly when his first priority had been claiming his throne, she was here now and his prisoner. A Benedictus/Accorsi marriage would be the kind of union that Kasimir needed. It would unite the divided families and factions and would categorically underline his intentions for the country going forward.

No more divisions. Only peace and healing for his people.

Guinevere Accorsi was eyeing him warily, as if he was an unknown and potentially dangerous animal—and, to be fair, she was right to view him that way.

He *was* dangerous.

He stared back, turning over the idea slowly in his head. Yes, she was very pretty, but she would definitely need some styling if she was to be Kasimir's queen.

You will also need her consent to the marriage.

Of course. But he would get that. If he gave her a choice between being Queen and a prison cell, he was sure she'd choose the former rather than the latter.

Her eyes were startlingly blue against her white skin, and deep within them he could see her fear looking back at him.

Too bad. She was an Accorsi, of the same wretched lineage responsible for his mother's death and his country's near collapse. The things Renzo had done as King had been appalling, and while this little mouse might not have had a hand in any of it, she was still representative of the corruption that had lived in the heart of Kasimir for far too long.

He had no sympathy for her whatsoever.

Still, there was no reason to be unduly threatening.

Not when it would serve no purpose. And he wasn't a man who did anything without purpose.

'In that case,' he said, after a long period of silence. 'I have a job for you.'

Her eyes widened. 'What kind of job?'

Tiberius held her gaze. 'Being my queen.'

Guinevere had watched Tiberius first enter the throne room from within the walls, safe in her little hiding place.

The enemy was here.

In the days leading up to his entry into Kasimir she'd overheard her father talking about him, calling him trivial, a minor annoyance that he would soon be rid of. Ineffectual and weak, like all the Benedictus family. One look at the Accorsi army and he'd be yelping his way back to Italy with his tail between his legs, Renzo had added.

It hadn't happened that way. Obviously. In fact, her father and her two older brothers had been in such a rush to flee the palace no one had bothered to check on her, and so she'd been able to slip away unnoticed into the secret corridors. She'd waited there, hiding, as her father, her brothers and the remaining guards who were still loyal had all escaped. Leaving her behind.

The relief she'd felt in that moment had been so intense she hadn't been able to quite believe it was real—that she'd finally managed to do what she'd dreamed of doing for so many years: being free of her family.

All she'd needed to do was to slip out through the corridors—no one in her family knew of their existence—and then the palace, and then she'd lose herself in the city streets and just…disappear.

Then he'd walked in and ruined it all.

Tiberius Maximus Benedictus, the rightful King of Kasimir.

She'd watched him sit on the throne, and then watched as the golden crown was lowered onto his short, inky black hair. He wore that crown as if he was wearing cloth of gold and robes of state, not grey army fatigues.

He wasn't exactly handsome—his face was all blunt planes and angles, and deeply carved into hard granite lines—but there was an aura about him that set him apart from other men. An aura of power, of a command so overwhelming that she'd almost felt it seeping through the walls to where she hid.

Utterly terrifying.

She should have made her escape then, while the coronation was happening, but she hadn't. She'd been caught, held fast despite her fear, by some kind of fascination she couldn't adequately describe. Perhaps it had something to do with finally seeing him, this famous enemy of her family, in the flesh and finding him to be not at all what she'd imagined.

This wasn't the beaten dog her father had kept saying he would shoot.

This was a man in total command of himself and his men and he was frightening.

Then his head had turned and he'd stared straight at her, as if he could see through the walls to where she hid, and she'd frozen. His eyes were a light silvery grey, pale and cold as winter snow, standing out starkly beneath his straight black brows and against his olive skin, and they were scalpel-sharp. Being stared at so intently had made her feel as if he was cutting away pieces of her soul, leaving the small, vulnerable parts at the centre of her exposed.

It had scared her so completely that she'd been left trembling. She'd told herself that of course he couldn't see her, and anyway it was time to leave and make her escape. But then, as she'd crept along the hidden corridor towards the exit, the door behind the tapestry had opened and one of his guards had seized her, dragging her before his throne.

She'd almost been sick with fear, while he'd sat there, legs spread arrogantly and that unnerving gaze of his pinning her to the spot. Yet beneath her terror had been a thread of unfamiliar anger too—at him, for finding her before she could disappear, and at herself, for lingering when she shouldn't have.

Hiding was what she did best—she'd been doing it for the past fifteen years—and yet when staying hidden had mattered the most, she'd failed.

Now she was here, standing before the new King, who was now demanding that she be his queen.

She could hardly process it, what with all the fear coursing through her body.

'Wh-What?' she stammered. 'Marry me? Why?'

He didn't move, didn't even blink. 'You are an Accorsi.'

'Yes, but—'

'There are divisions in this country,' he interrupted curtly. 'Deep divides that have hurt Kasimir. And as of today, those divisions will be no more. Your father was responsible for creating them, and since he is not here it will be you who will fix them.'

His voice was deep, resonant and utterly implacable, and something in it made her shiver.

'But I...' She stopped, then tried again. 'I—I can't be your queen.'

'You will.' He said the words as if it was a foregone conclusion. 'The Accorsis nearly destroyed this country, and since Renzo fled rather than face justice, you will answer for his crimes.'

Shock began to move through her in an icy wave. It was true that Renzo was a monster, as were her two older brothers—she'd been the butt of their worst behaviour over the years and they were the reasons she'd never ventured beyond the palace grounds.

It wasn't because she loved living here.

No, she hated it. And all she'd ever wanted to do was leave.

'But I didn't do anything,' she protested, barely able to get out the words she was so afraid. 'I never—'

'You are part of the Accorsi family.' He was relentless, cold as ice. 'Therefore you are complicit. Which means you *will* serve the sentence on behalf of your family.'

A ray of sun shone through the windows on either side of the throne, catching on the golden tips of the crown and glossing his coal-black hair. He looked utterly removed from anything as base as humanity. Untouchable, remote…god-like, almost.

'You have a choice, Guinevere Accorsi,' he went on, a warrior angel handing down divine judgment. 'You can serve your sentence in a jail cell or you can serve it as my queen.'

Guinevere clasped her hands together more tightly to stop them from shaking.

Complicit, he'd said. Cowardly, he'd said.

Her throat closed. Cowardly, yes—she already knew that. But complicit in what? She had no idea. She'd been held a prisoner in the palace since she was a child and knew nothing of the outside world. Her only escape was the books she read.

She'd been hoping that today would be her escape physically, too—except it hadn't. She'd let herself be trapped by her family's enemy, and now she was facing a jail cell for crimes she hadn't committed.

Crimes she knew nothing about.

Because you spent the last fifteen years hiding.

Guinevere shivered. She'd hidden, yes, but there were reasons for that. Very good reasons.

Silence lay heavy over the throne room, the smoke from the recently put-out fire in one corner filling the space with an ashy smell.

Tiberius hadn't looked away from her—not once.

She felt almost crushed by the pressure of his gaze.

'You…can't want to marry me,' she forced out, knowing she had to say something, since it was clear he was waiting for her to do so. 'There must be m-many other—'

'No,' he said, in the same implacable tone with which he appeared to say everything. 'I do not want to marry you. But this isn't about you or me. This is about what is best for Kasimir. I need a queen and you, as an Accorsi, are the most logical choice.'

The tips of her fingers were icy, her chest tight. 'But… but you don't love me.'

The words seemed to echo in the room, the desperate sound of her own voice bouncing off the walls and making her cringe in embarrassment. Why had she said that? What on earth was she thinking? What did love matter anyway?

Of course he didn't love her—not when he'd only just met her.

Love happened in the books she devoured, between

people who respected and accepted one another. It happened in real life too, she knew that, but she'd never seen any evidence of it. Her mother had died while she'd been a baby, and it had been made very clear to her, very early on, that neither her father nor her two older brothers had any kind of feelings for her at all.

Beside her, one of the soldiers shifted on his feet as if uncomfortable.

Up on his throne the King stared down at her with an unwavering gaze. His dark winged brows drew down, making her feel all of two inches high as he studied her from the tip of her head down to the soles of her feet and back up again.

'Love?' He said the word as if it was foreign to him. 'This is not about love, *signorina*, this is about duty. All I require from you is your name on a marriage certificate and your presence at my side for official events. Nothing more and nothing less.'

Well, that was something at least, wasn't it?

She'd grown up the only female in a world of men. Selfish, violent men. She'd never had any gentleness, never any kindness and never any care from any of them. To her father she was a nuisance and to her brothers she was prey, to torment and tease and bully whenever they could.

Men were different in books. Some of them were kind and gentle and caring, protective and loving too, so she knew those types of men existed. But not anywhere she would ever meet one—and certainly this king wasn't one of them.

He was probably just like her father. A man who loved power and bending people to his will. Who believed completely that only the strong survived.

She took a little breath. If he was, indeed, that kind of man, then she knew from experience that it was better not to argue. With those kinds of men your only option was rolling over and playing dead. Either that or hiding.

She couldn't hide now, which meant the only thing left was doing what he said.

Still, it was better than the marriage her father had been in the process of arranging for her, to one of his younger advisors. She'd never met him, but if he was anything like her father's other advisors then she knew he'd be awful. They were all awful.

She hadn't had a choice about that either, and all the hiding in the world wouldn't have got her out of it. Her feelings mattered not at all, as her father had so often said. She was only a tool, to be used by him to solidify his support base—nothing more.

However, that *would* have involved more than a mere legal marriage. She would have had to have been in his wife in every way, and the thought of that had left her cold and very afraid.

Give him what he wants. That's your only option.

Yes, it was. And, looking on the bright side, she wouldn't have to sleep with him at least. Then again, what else did he want to do with her bar public events? Would she be his prisoner? Would she be allowed to go anywhere…do anything?

'Th-then what?' she asked, mustering up a courage she hadn't known she possessed. 'How long would the marriage be for?'

His odd light eyes swept over her. 'It will be for as long as I require it to be.'

'But then you'll let me go?' It was tempting fate to keep questioning him and she was appalled at her own temerity. She should just agree to everything and not draw his attention. Yet she couldn't seem to stop herself. She'd been so close to freedom that she couldn't quite let it go. 'Once you don't need me, I mean.'

His gaze narrowed and he continued to stare at her for what felt like yet another eon. 'Are you trying to bargain with me, mouse?'

An unexpected flickering anger caught at her. Angelo and Alessio, her twin brothers, had called her mouse. Because she was small and insignificant and afraid. She'd hated the nickname but never had the courage to protest at it. She'd told herself that she didn't care what they called her, because mice knew how to hide and that was the main thing.

But to have this man, this terrifying enemy, call her the same thing, tarring her with the same brush her brothers had used, rubbed against a place she hadn't realised was raw.

'Don't call me that,' she snapped, before she could think better of it. 'My name in Guinevere.'

Silence crashed down like a lead curtain.

The guards beside her had frozen and Tiberius, up on his throne, was a figure carved from stone.

She'd spoken out of turn. Yet despite her fear, despite the fact that she was his prisoner, she found she didn't want to take it back. She'd rolled over and played dead before with her brothers, who'd used to hunt her through the palace hallways. She'd been traumatised by that as a child—so much so that most of her childhood had been spent in a haze of fear. And now the freedom that had been so close had been snatched away...

Well. She was angry. After years of hoping and praying for an opportunity to leave the palace she'd finally got one—only for him to stop her at the last moment. And not only that he'd accused her of being complicit in her father's actions—whatever they had been—and now he was demanding that she marry him.

It seemed so unfair.

So she didn't take it back. She said nothing as the silence stretched endlessly, clinging to the flickering anger that had sprung to life inside her like a life raft in a stormy sea.

Then, just when it seemed as if it wasn't possible for the tension to stretch any tighter, Tiberius made a dismissive gesture with his hand. 'Leave us,' he ordered.

Almost as one, the assembled guards and other hangers-on turned and left the throne room, their footsteps scuffing on the parquet as they disappeared through the doorway.

Guinevere turned too, a surge of relief making her knees weak.

'Not you,' Tiberius said.

Guinevere watched as the throne room doors shut behind the vanishing guards with a heavy *thunk*, then took a shaken breath and turned back to the throne.

Tiberius had risen to his full height. And then her mouth dried completely as he began to walk down the steps of the dais towards her, stalking her like a tiger stalked a gazelle.

CHAPTER TWO

TIBERIUS WENT DOWN the stairs of the dais towards her, knowing full well that he didn't have time for idle chatter with an Accorsi. Yet that little show of spirit she'd displayed just before had intrigued him, especially given how white-faced and shaking she'd been only minutes before.

He'd been hoping to give the command for the marriage to go ahead immediately, since the priest was already at hand, but a quick discussion with her privately seemed to be in order. He didn't want to put yet another potential Accorsi tyrant on the Queen's throne, so it would pay to do at least a little due diligence on the kind of woman he intended to marry.

He couldn't believe she'd actually snapped at him.

No one had ever dared take that tone with him—not for many years—and yet this little woman…this apparently terrified little woman…had somehow mustered up the courage to chastise the man who'd just taken back his throne for calling her a mouse.

Interesting.

He preferred women with spirit and backbone—in a queen both were vital—and it appeared that, despite appearances, Guinevere Accorsi seemed to have at least a hint of both. That was promising. After all, it wouldn't do for her to be as pale and trembling in front of the public as she'd been in front of him.

Her big blue eyes widened as he approached, her cheeks ashen. There was dust in her hair and on her dress, and a smear of it across one pale cheekbone. That must have come from the secret corridors she'd been scurrying around in, which wouldn't do. His queen shouldn't look like Miss Havisham waiting in vain for her lover. He would have to instruct her not to go into them again.

Tiberius stopped in front of her. The top of her head only came up to his chest so he had to look down. She really was very small and delicately built, gazing up at him from beneath long, pale lashes. It wasn't a flirtatious look. It was more like a deer staring at a wolf with wide, frightened eyes.

Weren't you supposed not *to be threatening to innocent women?*

He wasn't being threatening. And she wasn't innocent—not the daughter of Renzo Accorsi. She'd grown up here. She must be aware of what kind of person her father was, and how badly he'd mismanaged Kasimir. And who was to say that she wasn't the same? Or at least cut from the same cloth? Her twin brothers certainly were, by all accounts.

'I will not hurt you,' he said, just so she was clear. 'I sent my guards away so we can talk without an audience.'

This did not seem to make any difference to the fear in her eyes. 'T-talk about what?'

'About your suitability as my queen.' He gave her another considering glance. 'And also about showing proper respect for the King, especially in front of my guards.'

That glimpse of spirit he'd seen just before, when she'd snapped at him, glowed like blue embers once again. But all she said was, 'Oh.'

The contrast between her fear and her defiance was fascinating. Was it really bravery? Because, if so, that was an admirable quality in a queen.

'They do not like Accorsis,' he said mildly. 'So it would be as well not to give them any excuse to dislike you even more.'

Her sharp little chin lifted. 'I won't apologise. I don't like being called a mouse.'

Something shifted inside him like the earth settling after an earthquake. A certain...interest. She was his captive, and she was afraid, and surely the most logical thing for her to do now would be to ingratiate herself with him. That was what he was expecting—especially from a cowardly Accorsi.

Yet here she was, doing the opposite.

'A simple *No, Your Majesty, I am not trying to bargain with you* would have sufficed,' he murmured. 'What is it about a mouse you find so distasteful?'

She glanced down at her hands, as if the pressure of his gaze was too much. 'I just don't like it. It implies something small and insignificant and...a-afraid.'

Interesting that she didn't like that...despite the fact that she *was* afraid.

'Yet mice can scare human beings,' he said. 'They can also cause a lot of damage—which is why they are also thought of as pests.'

She kept her gaze on her hands. 'I...am not a pest,' she said finally, the words emphatic.

A silence fell again, and he let it sit there, because silence could be a useful tool. But, unlike most people, she didn't rush to fill it with meaningless chatter. Instead, she gripped her pale hands together even tighter and stared fixedly down at the floor.

'Then what are you?' he asked.

She gave a little shrug. 'No one important.'

He frowned. She'd said the words without any inflection, as if being unimportant wasn't a bad thing, and perhaps it wasn't. The Accorsis had a cruel streak—he knew that for a fact. His mother had died in the coup they'd staged to oust his father Giancarlo. He had been forced to leave his critically injured wife in favour of getting his baby son to safety. She'd been shot by a guard, and the Accorsis had left her to bleed to death in one of the palace hallways. They'd then sent word to his father that that would be his fate if he ever tried to reclaim the throne.

Then there was the treasury Renzo had drained—funnelling money into offshore accounts and into the military, into casinos and palaces and other buildings that no one needed or wanted, while hospitals and schools were forced to operate on less and less every year. Then there were the tax breaks for the rich, and some kind of grand plan to turn Kasimir into a tax haven, which would only be of benefit to his cronies.

A morally bankrupt, corrupt man. And, from the intelligence he'd received, the Accorsi sons had taken on their father's moral compass. Maybe that was true of her too.

Perhaps she'd wanted to be important to them and never had been.

Or perhaps she's lying through her teeth in an attempt to get close to you and assassinate you?

No, that wasn't it. The fear in her eyes had been real, and he'd seen enough of it in his life to know when it was being manufactured and when it wasn't.

She *was* truly afraid. And yet she also had courage enough to snap at him.

Curiosity caught at him along with the urge to test

her courage and her fear, to see how deep they both ran. Because he had to know if he was going to make her queen. She would be merely a figurehead, it was true, but she would need to project an illusion of strength at the very least.

He moved closer. 'You were bargaining with me,' he said. 'Weren't you?'

She shook her head, still staring at the floor.

No, he needed to look into her eyes, see what was going on inside her head. He needed to see that courage again. So he reached out and put a finger under her chin, urging her head up.

Her breath caught audibly as her gaze lifted to his, revealing the deep, endless blue of her eyes.

They were beautiful, those eyes. He'd never seen a colour like it. The sky at twilight, blue darkening into a deeper, almost violet blue, so startling in her pale face. Fear was there—he could see it—but also something else. A flickering anger and a stubborn defiance that seemed to reach inside him and grip a piece of him tight.

Such stark contrasts. He found them fascinating. In fact, he wanted to explore them further, with her skin warm and very soft beneath his fingertip, her blue gaze pinned to his.

'Weren't you?' he repeated softly.

Her blue gaze darkened and he was conscious of the sweet smell of jasmine and something more delicate and feminine that made his body suddenly tight.

It had been months since he'd had a woman—not since he'd put into motion his carefully laid plans for retaking the throne. He hadn't wanted the distraction. He didn't want it now—and certainly not with an Accorsi. But pulling away would be an admission of something he didn't want to admit.

So he stood there, his finger beneath her chin, looking down into her eyes, willing her to reply.

She stayed where she was, though there was still tension in her. 'I'll marry you,' she said at last, her clear voice husky-sounding. 'I will serve my sentence. But at the end of it you will let me go. You will let me leave Kasimir for good.'

Interesting. So she wanted to leave the country? Was it to follow her father and brothers? Because they'd left her behind?

'Making demands in your position is quite the choice,' he said, even as a part of him noted the shape of her mouth and the full pout of her bottom lip. 'You are a prisoner, Guinevere. And after what your father did to this country you should be glad I'm giving you a choice of cell.'

The flicker in her eyes looked like anger, and this time she didn't look away. 'I'm not making demands. I...was going to leave Kasimir. That's all I was intending to do.'

Was that the truth? It seemed to be. Those words, softly spoken with a kind of quiet dignity, weren't something a liar would say, he was sure.

Yet still he couldn't help but ask, 'Why? To go after your family?'

'No. What I want is to escape them.'

Surprise echoed through him. This was the truth. He could see it in those luminous eyes of hers. He wanted to ask her why—wanted to know what had they done to her to send her hiding in the walls where he'd discovered her—but that would be a waste of time. He didn't need to know her. All he needed was her to be his queen.

With an effort of will that was greater than he would

have liked, he took his finger from beneath her chin and stepped back.

'Well,' he said, 'I can see no reason to keep you here any longer than necessary. I can't say how long our marriage will be, but once Kasimir is more settled we will divorce and you may leave. But not until then—understand?'

She didn't look relieved or pleased, her skin still pale. 'And I'll be a prisoner until then?'

Irritation wound through him—partly at himself, for being curious and starting this pointless conversation in the first place, and partly at her, for asking annoying questions.

The decision to marry her had been an opportunistic one and he hadn't had time to think through the implications of it yet—let alone what he would do with her outside official appearances. She wasn't as important as the work of surveying the damage Renzo had done to Kasimir and putting in place plans to fix it. He didn't want to waste time thinking about what to do with an unwanted wife.

'We will discuss that later,' he said dismissively, turning towards the doors. 'I will call the priest in. He can perform the ceremony now.'

Her eyes went wide. 'Now?'

Tiberius paused and lifted a brow. 'Of course, now. There is vital work to be done, and the sooner we are married, the sooner I can start fixing my country.'

'But… But—'

'Need I remind you that your father is responsible for nearly destroying Kasimir? If you want to make up for that, may I suggest no more protests?'

She stared at him for a second, with what looked like bewilderment on her face, then she bent her gaze back down at the floor, whatever spirit that had burned in her before now gone.

'Very well,' she said colourlessly.

For some reason that only increased his irritation, though he couldn't imagine why. Yes, courage and strength were important in a queen, but if she didn't have them, then she didn't have them. He didn't need to fight her. He was tired of fighting anyway. Now was the time for peace and the chance to rebuild.

His country would always be more important than his curiosity about one little Accorsi woman.

Annoyed with himself, he turned and strode to the closed doors of the throne room, throwing them open. His guards and aides were on the other side, waiting patiently for him.

'Father Domingo,' he said curtly. 'You are required.' Then he glanced at his guards. 'I need witnesses. You and you.'

The ceremony commenced at the foot of the throne and was over in approximately five minutes. The rings would come later, as would the licence, but such things were insignificant details. What was important was the marriage certificate and her signature on it.

Guinevere was silent throughout, except when she was required to speak, and then she was as good as her word and didn't protest. But she didn't look at him either, keeping her gaze firmly downcast.

He couldn't have said why that needled at him. Why it made him want to put out a hand, grip her chin once more and have her look at him. See exactly what she was feeling in this moment. Whether it was fear or anger or something else…

But no, he didn't need to see it. This wasn't about her,

anyway, nor even about him either. This was about Kasimir, and doing what he needed to for the good of his country, and that was the only thing that mattered.

Besides, he wasn't going to force her into doing anything she didn't want to do—not beyond having her signature on the marriage certificate. He wouldn't touch her, and they'd only meet for official engagements. She wouldn't find marriage to him…onerous.

As the ceremony finished, Tiberius turned to his new wife. 'Tomorrow we will speak of the details,' he said. 'Tonight I will have my staff ensure you're comfortable.'

There was nothing more to say, and he had a day's important work ahead of him, so before she could speak he turned around and strode out of the throne room, followed by his men.

Guinevere felt almost in a daze as a guard led her through the corridors following the wedding ceremony.

Somehow, she was married.

Somehow, she was a queen.

It was almost inconceivable that the day she'd thought she'd escape the palace and Kasimir for good, instead she'd found herself trapped yet again.

Trapped first by her name and then by his.

Trapped by a crown and by the ring he'd told her he'd get for her later.

She didn't know how the whole thing had happened so fast, or what she'd done to have fate imprison her so completely like this. It was wrong. Even the concession she'd managed to get from him—that he'd let her go once he had no more need of her—didn't feel like one.

But really, the wedding wasn't even the worst part of what had happened in the throne room. The worst part had been when he'd stalked down that dais and come close to her, and then had put a finger beneath her chin and tilted her head back.

He'd seemed so tall to her, and so broad, overshadowing her like an oak tree, and she'd been expecting cold fear to run through her the way it always had whenever she'd caught the notice of her father and brothers.

Except this time it hadn't. The touch of his finger on her skin had felt scorching, creating an odd tension inside her that had fear as one of its components, yet also something else. Something...more. A kind of anticipatory excitement that had made her skin feel tight and her heartbeat sound loud in her ears.

The intensity she'd seen in his silvery eyes as he'd looked at her had called to a part of her she hadn't realised was even there, and abruptly she'd become very, very aware of him. Of not just his height, or the broad width of his shoulders, but the gleam of the crown against his black hair. The curve of his bottom lip. The stretch of his army fatigues over his muscled chest. The warmth of him, so at odds with those icy eyes, and the scent of him—something fresh and outdoorsy, reminding her of the sun and the sea and the wind that blew between them.

She didn't understand why his nearness had felt that way, because by rights she should have been terrified.

Perhaps she was getting braver.

Or perhaps you were just stupid.

Guinevere thrust the thought away and all her strange feelings with it. They didn't matter anyway—not when he'd made it clear that the only times she'd see him was for public appearances. That was a *good* thing. The less she saw of him the better.

The walk back through the winding palace corridors

wasn't easy. They were horribly familiar, these corridors. She'd been walking them all her life and she hated every inch of them. They were a both a maze and a prison, marking the boundaries of the small, insignificant life she'd had within these walls. A prison she'd thought she'd be free of today, and yet—

No, there was no point thinking about that. One day she'd get out of here. Eventually, she would.

She swallowed, shaking her hands to ease the tension that drew tighter and tighter the more they walked. Because she was starting to understand where she was being taken, and every cell of her being rebelled.

'My room is down there,' she said tentatively to the guard as they passed by a branch in the hallway.

'I was not instructed to take you to your room,' the guard answered, without even looking at her.

'But all my things are there and—'

'I was instructed to take you to the royal apartments,' the guard said without inflection, making it clear that he was going to follow those instructions come hell or high water.

Guinevere swallowed again, her throat closing.

The royal apartments. Where her father had lived. Where her brothers had once hunted her down and where she'd hidden, almost wetting herself with fear.

That same fear seemed to grip her now, her breath catching, her fingertips going numb. She hadn't had a panic attack for months, but today she had clearly pushed things too far—because she felt close to one now.

She tried to ignore the feeling as the guard stopped outside the big double doors that led to the royal apartments, yet the fear kept on rising, swamping her.

The guard pulled the doors open and waited, making it clear she was expected to walk inside.

Dread slid through her like a fine sliver of glass, cold and cutting. She wanted to tell the guard that she couldn't possibly stay here, that she needed to go to her own room, but there was no give in the man's expression.

Come on, pull yourself together. It's just a room. Also, there is an escape, don't forget.

Yes, there was. She didn't have to stay if she didn't want to. And also her father was gone, and so were her brothers. There was no one left to frighten her any more.

No one except the King. Your husband.

Guinevere shoved that particular reality aside and forced herself to cross the threshold, walking through the doors into the private receiving room beyond.

This room wasn't as much of a mess as the throne room, but there were signs of a hurried tidy-up. A mound of what looked like shattered pottery in one corner. A priceless Persian silk rug in front of the fireplace stained. There were a few pictures missing, also, and in one place the panelling on the walls had been kicked in.

The doors shut heavily behind her, then the lock clicked, and no matter how much she tried to resist it panic closed cold, sharp talons around her throat.

Oh, God, they were locking her in.

Breathing fast, she whirled around and went to the door, rattling at the handle and of course not getting anywhere because the guard had turned the key.

'You don't need to lock it,' she called through the door, trying not to let her voice shake. 'I—I promise I won't leave. Please. Just…don't lock it.'

'Sorry.' The guard's voice was unapologetic and flat. 'His Majesty's orders.'

A scream rose in her throat, but she fought it down hard. That wouldn't help, she knew, and it would only make her panic worse. And as for the guard—well, no one had ever listened to her screams, so why would he?

But you're the Queen now, remember?

Was she, though? She didn't feel like one. She had a feeling that if she gave an order the guard would only laugh in her face, and she wouldn't blame him.

Closing her eyes, Guinevere rested her forehead against the door, her palms pressed flat to the wood on either side of her. She took a couple of deep breaths, trying to calm herself.

It was only a room. Just a room.

After a moment, her heart still hammering in her ears, she pushed herself away from the door and turned around.

The room was just as it had been, and yet she could also see the past laid over it like a palimpsest.

Over there was the doorway to the bedroom that her mother had used when she was alive. Once Guinevere had been at a curious stage about her, and had wanted to see what was inside, but she'd been found by her father, who'd ripped her away from the door and flung her onto the floor in a rage. He'd screamed at her never to go near that room on pain of a sound thrashing. She'd been six.

Her brothers had known she wasn't allowed to go into the Queen's rooms and so of course they'd tried to chase her there, hunting her down in the palace hallways like dogs after a fox. They were years older than she was, and bigger, and they'd been cruel. Her father had done nothing to stop their bullying of her because she was 'only a girl'.

He'd wanted another son, not a tiny, delicate daughter, and when she'd come to him weeping, after having her hair pulled, or her dresses ruined, or her knees skinned after they'd pushed her over, he'd only told her to stop being a 'fraidy cat' and said that if she didn't want to be bullied she had to stand up to them. But she'd tried to do that once and had been given a black eye for her trouble.

She'd tried very hard after that not put herself at risk of being hunted, but for her brothers it had been their favourite game. They'd liked ruining things that were precious to her—especially any hints of prettiness and femininity. They'd thought pouring oil on her favourite dress was a joke, as was tearing pages out of her favourite books. Once, they'd crept into her bedroom at night when she was ten and fast asleep and cut off all her hair.

She hadn't been able to escape them and no one had done anything to protect her. Sometimes she'd wondered what her life would have been like if her mother had still been alive, and whether her mother would have protected her. But it had been pointless thinking about that. Her mother was dead and being frightened of her brothers all the time had been her constant state of being. Yet some small part of her had refused to be beaten, and so even though her pretty dresses and long, curly hair marked her out for more bullying she'd worn them anyway in a show of defiance.

That hadn't helped her, though.

The only thing that had was finding the secret passageways in the walls. No one knew they were there—certainly her brothers didn't. So when it had got bad she'd simply disappeared into them, finding her way to other hiding places around the palace.

Life had become more bearable then, and although her brothers had tried relentlessly to find out how she managed to disappear, they never had. And after a few years, as they'd grown into men, they'd stopped looking and eventually forgotten about her entirely.

Guinevere took another breath, and then another, willing the fear to go away. Because she wasn't in danger now and there was nothing that could hurt her.

But the panic wouldn't go away, and the knowledge that she was trapped here, the way she'd been trapped in this palace for so many years, began to close in on her.

Staying in these rooms was impossible, the weight of her memories and the terror sitting on her shoulders crushing, and there was only one way to deal with that.

Breathing deeply, Guinevere went into her mother's rooms and into the dressing room where the big carved armoire was. She went over to it and pulled open the doors, then stepped inside.

It was always difficult entering the secret passageways through the armoire, because the only reason she'd found them in the first place had been because she'd taken refuge in the armoire one day when her brothers had been chasing her.

They'd worked out quickly where she was and had locked the door of the armoire, telling her they were going to tell their father where she was and he'd give her a thrashing.

She'd become panicky and had kicked at the back of the armoire, since kicking at the door had failed to open it. The back had turned out to be not solid wood but thin veneer, and her foot had gone straight through it into...nothing.

After she'd kicked more of the veneer away she'd seen that there was a narrow doorway in the wall behind the armoire, and an even narrower pitch-black corridor. The darkness had scared her, but anything was better than being shut in the armoire and waiting for her father to find her, so she hadn't thought twice.

She'd escaped into the corridor beyond.

She did so now, even as the fear continued to lap at her, squeezing her chest and throat, making her feel as if she was suffocating.

Then she was through the armoire and into the safety of the darkness beyond.

It wasn't Narnia, but it was an escape, nevertheless.

Guinevere walked silently down the corridor, turned to the left and continued to walk until she came to the end of it. The darkness didn't bother her now, and she didn't need light to find her way around—not when she knew every inch of these corridors like the back of her hand.

A small lever pulled aside part of the wall and she stepped through the opening and into her favourite place in the whole palace: a tiny, forgotten room that no one knew about except her.

It was a small library, with bookshelves and a fire-place, an ancient, uncomfortable sofa and a deep window seat with a curtain over it that one could pull across and be shielded from anyone who might glance into the room.

Guinevere pulled another lever so that the bookshelf that had slid aside to open the doorway slid back into place. Then she went across to the window seat. Over the years she'd gathered lots of blankets and pillows, and other pretty little things, taking them into the little library, turning the window seat into an extremely comfortable bed where she could sleep or read or do anything else, hidden from everyone.

Safe.

She crawled into it now, making sure the curtain was drawn across so no one would see her, then curled up under a blanket and did what she always did when she couldn't escape her fear.

She fell asleep.

CHAPTER THREE

THE DAY AFTER his somewhat casual coronation Tiberius expected to start the morning with a meeting involving all his advisors, who would then help him with the important work of sorting out the mess Renzo Accorsi had made of Tiberius's kingdom.

What Tiberius did not expect was to be informed that his brand-new wife and queen was missing. That somehow she'd managed to get out of the royal apartments—which had been locked—and had apparently vanished into thin air.

It put him in a foul temper—not helped by the fact that he hadn't slept well the previous night. He never slept all that much as it was, but last night his sleeplessness had been entirely due to his body plaguing him with inappropriate urges. For some reason the little mouse had ignited something within him and he didn't like it one bit.

Clearly neglecting his sexual needs had been a mistake which now had to be fixed. The fact that he was a married man was of no consequence. The union was purely political, and he was sure Guinevere wouldn't have a problem with him satisfying his hunger elsewhere. He had no intention of remaining celibate.

So what he wanted this morning was to start work, then perhaps in the evening find a willing woman to deal with his other needs—not to search the palace for a missing Accorsi.

After their marriage the afternoon before he'd spent the rest of the day and the evening sorting through a game plan for his country, then drafting a public announcement of his marriage with his press secretary, including a date for their first royal appearance. However, there couldn't be a royal appearance if he was missing a royal, so find her he must. If she'd somehow managed to escape the palace entirely, then time was of the essence.

Whether he liked it or not, her presence was needed. She was now a vital emblem of unity, the final piece in the strong foundation he hoped to rebuild Kasimir upon, and he wasn't going to let her escape like the rest of her cowardly family.

Deciding to inspect the royal apartments himself, since apparently his men couldn't keep one small woman from straying, he strode in, his temper vile. But after a close survey of each room he realised he couldn't fault his guards. There did, indeed, appear to be no way for Guinevere Accorsi to have escaped, yet the fact remained that she had.

He stood for a long moment in the Queen's empty bedroom, thinking about how she could have got out. Then it hit him—something he should have thought about before and hadn't because he'd been too busy focusing on other things.

The secret passageways. That was the only way she could have got out of this room unseen, which must mean that there was an entrance to them in the royal apartments somewhere.

Tiberius reviewed the floor plans in his head, piecing together a map of the palace and the corridors in order to determine the most likely place for a secret entrance. Then he started methodically looking around for anything that might give away a secret door.

It didn't take him long. A cursory examination of a huge, ornate wooden armoire revealed a kicked-in panel at the back which led into a gap in the wall behind it. He stepped into the gap and the darkness beyond without hesitation.

He wasn't claustrophobic—which was a good thing, because the corridor was a narrow fit and pitch-black. He didn't find the lack of light a problem either. He'd been in worse situations when he'd been in the military, after all.

A couple of minutes later he came to a branching of the corridor, but after a pause to consult his memorised plans he was pretty sure one branch led to the throne room—and surely she wouldn't have gone there, not when it was full of cleaning staff—so he took the one leading in the opposite direction.

Soon the corridor came to a dead end, but feeling around in the dark, he soon found a lever that must open a door. He pulled it—clearly it had been in recent use, since the mechanism moved smoothly—and the wall in front of him slid aside, dim light spilling into the narrow corridor.

He stepped through the doorway and found himself in a small room—a library from the looks of things. There were bookshelves stuffed full of books, an old couch sitting before a fireplace, magazines and a book of crossword puzzles discarded on the cushions. A jug of wilted flowers was on the mantelpiece, along with a glittering pile of what looked like jewellery, a few crystal bottles of perfume and a silver-backed hairbrush.

He frowned, noting the signs of feminine occupation,

and yet not seeing the little Accorsi anywhere. Then he noticed the curtains drawn across the window—odd, because it was morning—so he went over and pulled them aside.

A deep window seat lay behind them, and curled up on it, in a nest of blankets and pillows, was his new wife.

She was asleep, her hands tucked beneath her cheek, her curly blonde hair lying in tangles all over the cushions. The morning sun spread like liquid gold over her, bathing her in a kind of glow, and despite himself he felt his breath catch.

So. She hadn't left after all. Likely there had been too many guards for her to escape the palace entirely, so she'd found a place to hide. Maybe she'd been waiting for a better opportunity to escape and had fallen asleep before she could.

Her sleep looked to be deep, and there were faint dark circles under her eyes. In fact, if he hadn't known better, he would have said it was the sleep of someone exhausted.

She was wearing the same clothes as she had the day before. The same dusty white lacy dress. And even the streak of dust across one cheekbone was still there. She clearly hadn't bothered to wash.

Why not? Had something driven her from the royal apartments? And why had she come here? Why had she curled up like a cat and gone to sleep?

He stared at her, the curiosity he'd felt the previous day pulling tight once more and deepening.

She was an Accorsi, from the same family that had put Kasimir through hell and destroyed his own family, and yet curled up on the cushions, small and pale, she had an innocence to her, a fragility that belied her family's history. It tugged at something long-forgotten inside him, reminding him of being very young, long before his father had told him who he was and what his destiny was to be. When he too had been innocent, and all that had concerned him was who he was going to play with at school and whether his father would cook something he liked for dinner.

Was it peaceful, this sleep? And if it was, what would it be like to sleep so deeply that not even the presence of another person standing close could wake you? Long years as a soldier had made him all too aware of the threat of deep sleep, and even now, after he'd left his military career, he didn't sleep well. There were too many things to think about, too many things to do.

Sleeping was a waste of time that he only tolerated in order to keep himself physically well. And he needed the strength to keep moving forward, to keep fighting—because the battle was constant. He couldn't put down his burdens, his duty to his country, not even for a moment.

His mother had sacrificed too much, and if he was going to deserve the gift of life that she'd given him, then he had to keep going no matter how tired he was.

She deserved better.

Kasimir deserved better.

He had no idea how his new wife could sleep so deeply, given what her father had done, but she must feel safe, here in this little room, to give herself over to sleep like that. He was a little jealous of that. Sometimes there were days when all he wanted to do was lay down those burdens. To rest. To sleep as Guinevere Accorsi was sleeping, deeply and without fear.

He should wake her, not stand there staring at her, and yet he didn't move. Because he was becoming aware of other things. Things he should not be aware of. Such as how the blanket was half falling off her and how her dress was pulled up, revealing one gently rounded thigh. And the way she was lying made the neckline of her dress gape slightly, giving him a view of the soft darkness between her sweetly curved breasts.

A pretty little thing…

Almost without conscious thought, he let his hand come out to touch the dusty streak across her cheek—perhaps to wipe it away or maybe just to feel the texture of her skin. He wasn't sure. But bare inches from her face he stopped.

His hands were soldier's hands, scarred from missions and battles and roughened from long hours spent training, and he had the oddest thought that if his fingertips brushed her cheek he might harm her. That he might mark her pale skin like the rough point of a nail against sheer silk.

Does that matter? She is an Accorsi. You could touch her…have her. Corrupt her as her family corrupted Kasimir. That would be an apt vengeance.

His body had gone tight, his breath catching hard in his throat.

No, those weren't thoughts worthy of a king. He didn't thirst for vengeance for his mother's death, no matter how many times his father had told him he should. He was a protector, and he protected his subjects. And, Accorsi or not, she was one of those subjects. Corrupting her would end up making him no better than her father and he would not do that.

He would *never* do that.

Besides, regardless that their marriage was only political, she was his wife and his queen, and that made her worthy of his respect.

Tiberius straightened, bringing his recalcitrant body back under ruthless control, and opened his mouth to give her a curt command to wake up.

However, before he could get the words out her silvery lashes fluttered and her eyes opened. She looked up at him, the deep, dark blue of her eyes holding him captive, and her mouth curved in an unexpected welcoming smile, as if he was a friend and she was delighted to see him.

His heart caught hard inside him. No one had ever looked at him the way she was looking at him right now. His army saw a general they were loyal to, his aides a king they must obey. It was always awe and fear and respect—never happiness. Never delight. He hadn't known he'd wanted that until this moment.

Then she blinked a couple of times and her eyes went wide, as if she was only now processing the fact that he was here. Abruptly she sat up, rearing back against the window seat, the smile disappearing, her face going pale with unmistakable terror.

And that caught him too—like the bite of a whip.

She was scared of him.

Are you surprised, when you forced her to marry you? She was scared of you yesterday too.

Disappointment gripped him, though he told himself he didn't feel it. She was right to be scared. She was an Accorsi and she should fear him. Marrying her wasn't quite the vengeance his father wanted, but in a small way it was to punish Renzo. He would certainly not be happy to learn that his daughter had married his enemy.

'Good morning, my queen,' Tiberius said flatly.

'Wh-What are you doing here?' she asked in a shocked voice. 'How did you find me?'

He folded his arms, his mood fraying. 'It wasn't difficult. The door to the royal apartments was locked, and yet you'd disappeared, so I assumed you'd vanished into the secret corridors again.' He glared at her. 'It seems I was correct. And now you have wasted my guards' time and mine by vanishing without a word.'

'I'm sorry.' She remained pale, eyeing him warily. 'I didn't want to stay in the royal apartments. I have my own room in the palace. I did tell the guard that, but he said your orders were to put me in my parents' rooms. I didn't know he was going to lock me in there.' She lifted a hand and pushed the mass of golden curls off her face. 'I would have told someone where I was going, but there was no one around to tell.'

'This isn't a hotel, Signorina Accorsi,' he said severely. 'You cannot pick and choose your rooms. You are the Queen and your place is in the royal apartments.'

She glanced down at her hands, now twisting in her lap the way she'd done the day before in the throne room.

It annoyed him. Did she think that he'd hurt her? That he was the type of man who would raise a fist to someone much more vulnerable than he was?

Preposterous. He was a king, not a bully, and the only people he'd ever hurt physically had been other soldiers during fighting. Never a civilian. Still less a woman.

'I'm not going to hurt you,' he snapped. 'You needn't act like a beaten dog.'

Her shoulders hunched, as if his tone had physically hurt her—which, for reasons he couldn't articulate, only annoyed him further.

'I never would have thought that an Accorsi would protest at being given their due,' he went on. 'You should be grateful I decided to put you here and not in a prison cell.'

She shook her head, but said nothing.

He didn't know why this incensed him. 'Well?' he demanded. 'Give me one good reason why I shouldn't put you in a cell right now.'

Guinevere's heart was beating far too fast and far too hard. The muzzy, sleepy feeling she'd woken up with was long gone, washed away by an icy flood of fear.

She'd been having a lovely dream… She couldn't remember quite what it had been about, but she knew she'd been safe, and it had been years since she'd felt that way. But then she'd woken up to find a very tall man standing beside her window seat, glittering grey eyes looking down her. Her first thought hadn't been one of fear. Only that somehow it was right he should be standing there— that in another life, or in another dream, she knew him, and while he was there nothing bad could get her. She was safe.

Then her brain had kicked into gear and she'd processed exactly who it was standing by her window seat. And the fact that she wasn't safe. She wasn't safe at all.

A burst of adrenaline had hit her then, making her sit bolt-upright and lean back, pressing herself against the window in order to get away from him.

Tiberius. The King. And he was angry.

It was always bad when a man was angry. Always.

He wasn't in fatigues today, nor was he wearing a crown, but he might as well have been, given the aura of power rolling off him.

He was dressed simply and all in black. Black trousers and a perfectly tailored black business shirt, no tie. A lesser man might have looked like a monk, or even a waiter, but no monk or waiter had ever radiated such crackling electricity. It seemed to wind around her and grip her by the throat, making her mouth go dry.

The morning sun was shining full in his face, making his grey eyes glitter like icicles, his black hair glossy as a raven's wing, highlighting his strong nose and the shape of his mouth, the hard lines of his jaw...

She didn't understand why she was noting all this about him, or why she was thinking that 'handsome' was too conventional a word for this man and didn't quite encompass the sheer charisma of his physical presence.

She didn't understand why she felt almost stunned by it, or why she had to look away from him just so her brain would work.

What was happening to her? Why did he have this effect on her? She should be afraid of him—and she was—but that was starting to fade now, especially since she couldn't stop looking at him. It was as if he was a tiger about to take a bite out of her and all she could think about was the beauty of his fur.

You know why. You might be sheltered, but you're not stupid.

Guinevere swallowed. She'd read all about physical attraction. It was there in her favourite books. But she'd never felt it herself. Never met a man who made her feel anything at all apart from afraid. Until now.

It made no sense. He was clearly angry with her—which he had a right to be, she supposed, since she had disappeared without telling him. But still... She hated confrontation, especially when men got into a rage, because when they did, people got hurt. And he was so much larger and stronger than she was...

Yet despite all that her heart was beating fast and her

skin felt tight, and she wanted to keep looking at him because he was also beautiful to her.

Your husband.

There was something flat and so final in the word
'husband', and it made her shiver. She had no examples
of what a husband was—none at all. Her father never
spoke about her mother, so what he felt about her Guinevere had no idea.

'Well?' Tiberius demanded, his deep voice shattering
her thoughts and somehow getting under her skin.

What had he said? Something about this not being a
hotel and wasting his time and being a beaten dog? Oh,
yes, and jail cells. And he was angry.

*He came into your safe place without asking and now
he's demanding yet more things from you. How dare he?*

A small thread of anger began to wind through the cold
grip of fear—because, yes, how dare he come in here,
demanding explanations from her? Calling her names
and threatening her? This was her private space—*hers*.

'I'm sorry,' she forced out, staring at her hands and
ignoring her anger.

Getting angry only made things worse. Apologies,
even if you didn't mean them, were the best thing for
calming angry men. Then again, they'd never worked
on her brothers—not when her very existence had made
them torment her.

'That's all?' The edge in his tone rubbed against the
same raw place it had rubbed against the day before.
'You're sorry?'

She knew it was always a mistake to fight back against
someone more powerful than you, and yet that small
thread of anger grew hotter, brighter, and abruptly she

was sick of him. Sick of his demands and sick of her own weakness at caving in to them.

A beaten dog, he'd called her, with contempt in his tone. And of course he'd be contemptuous. He was tall and strong and physically powerful. He was King.

He'd probably never lived in fear of being hurt or maybe even killed by those who were supposed to love you and protect you. He wouldn't know what it was like to be small and fragile and utterly defenceless. He wouldn't know what it felt like to be hunted like prey.

How dared he judge her when he knew nothing whatsoever about her? How *dared* he?

'Well?' she snapped before she could stop herself, looking up and meeting his silvery, icy gaze. 'What else do you want? I apologised.'

He was standing there, towering over her, muscular arms folded across his broad chest. Obdurate as a mountain.

'You have wasted my time, mouse,' he said flatly. 'I have a country to fix and I do not want to spend the entirety of my morning running around after an Accorsi.'

Beaten dog. Mouse. Small. Insignificant. Powerless.

If he had been either of her brothers she would have cowered, sick with fear. Yet for some reason, just like it had the day before, her anger only flickered higher, hotter, making her lift her chin in unconscious insolence.

'Then don't. No one asked you to run around after me.'

His eyes widened a fraction and she thought she caught a glimpse of surprise there. Clearly he hadn't been expecting her snap back at him. Well, good. She *wasn't* a beaten dog, and she was tired of being treated like one.

He'd said he wouldn't hurt her, and maybe he'd been

telling the truth, but right now she didn't care. She didn't have any energy left for fear.

'I don't like the royal apartments,' she went on, since she might as well while she had the courage. 'There are bad memories there. So if you don't want me to have a panic attack, I suggest that you don't lock me in any more and either let me stay in my old room or here.'

'A panic attack?' he repeated slowly, his black brows drawing down.

'Yes. I presume you know what they are?' She gripped the edge of her blanket, her anger burning higher and hotter at the unfairness of it all. At how he'd had her locked into a place full of past trauma and then been angry with her for trying to leave it. At how he saw her—vulnerable and frightened—and found that contemptible.

'But maybe you don't,' she went on hotly. 'Since you're the King now. And kings don't ever have panic attacks, do they? They never get scared and they're contemptuous of those who do. They never stop to think about the poor dog, or even of why it was beaten in the first place.'

The torrent of words fell into the silence of the room, echoing around her, and immediately she knew she shouldn't have said anything. She shouldn't have confronted him. She should have bowed her head and kept on apologising, kept on appeasing him, done whatever he'd ordered her to do. Because talking back drew attention and attention was never a good thing. It only made everything worse.

Except it was too late. She'd been pushed one too many times, and this man, this enemy of hers with his disturbing presence, who'd made her marry him and talked sternly of prison cells and beaten dogs, had been the last straw.

She might be small and defenceless, but she'd found

some unexpected steel inside her—so too bad if he didn't like what she'd said.

His face was impassive, his gaze sharp, betraying nothing of what he thought about her tirade. But she lifted her chin even higher, just to show him that she didn't care what he thought. Didn't care that she'd snapped at him and wasn't showing him the respect he'd spoken about the day before. Not a bit.

What could he do to her anyway? Put her in a prison cell? She'd been living in one for all twenty-three years of her life, and nothing could be worse than this palace. Nothing.

He was silent for a very long moment. Then he said, 'For a mouse, you have quite sharp teeth.'

'Don't call me that,' she said fiercely. 'I am *not* a mouse. Or a damn dog!'

His gaze glittered, focusing on her with disturbing intensity. 'No,' he murmured. 'Clearly not.'

A curious prickling sensation swept over her skin in response, making it feel tight and hot, as if his icy silver gaze was akin to a physical touch, and a flush of heat crept up her neck and into her cheeks, warming her.

She was blushing and she didn't know why—and it only made her angrier. The way he was looking at her, his irritation with her, and the dismissive way he'd spoken to her kept rubbing against that sore spot, fraying nerves already frayed from what had happened the day before.

She'd been so close to getting away…so very close. But he'd caught her. He'd dragged her from the safety of the shadows and into the light, making her his prisoner, making her marry him, trapping her yet again in this hateful place. And now he was getting angry with her because she'd wasted his time.

All of a sudden she hated him. Hated his silvery gaze and the way it made her feel. Hated the way he called her mouse. And most of all she hated how he assumed she was pathetic and cowardly—and she wasn't.

'And stop looking at me that way,' she said angrily, shoving herself off the window seat, pleased when he took a couple of steps back to give her room. 'You hateful…hateful b-bastard.'

He said nothing, merely tilted his head to look down at her, assessing. And she stared back, all the blood in her veins hot with a fury that had been there all her life, waiting in the shadows like her. But now it was out, bursting its banks like a flood tide, and for the first time since she could remember she felt powerful. She felt strong.

Perhaps if her brothers had been here she wouldn't have cowered.

Maybe she would have punched them in the face.

'No, not a mouse at all,' he said slowly. 'What would you prefer to be, then?'

'Why not try my actual name?'

The look in his eyes shifted, became sharp-edged as an icicle. It moved over her slowly, as if he was taking her in, cataloguing her every feature, and it made her suddenly breathless.

Then he said, his dark, deep voice lingering on each syllable, 'Guinevere.'

A shiver crept over her skin and she nearly trembled. He'd said her name like a poem, or a song, and so slowly—as if he was tasting it, taking his time over it.

She'd never heard anyone say it like that. Mostly because no one had said it at all. She was always and for ever either 'girl' or just 'mouse'.

She stared up at him, her anger slowly ebbing away. It

felt as if he'd given her an unexpected gift and now she didn't know what to say.

The morning sun slid over his night-dark hair, shining full in his face, making his odd light eyes look crystalline, the planes and angles of his features highlighted with exquisite perfection.

She was standing very close to him, she realised then, as close as she had been yesterday, in the throne room, when he'd put his finger beneath her chin. And she felt again what she'd felt back then. The warmth of his body and his scent, an intoxicating mix of sun, salt and warm earth. It made her imagine the wind in her hair, walking in a summer forest, maybe, or on a boat, riding the waves.

Freedom. He smelled like freedom.

Breathing felt difficult, and every thought went out of her head as the air around them became weighted with a tension she didn't understand. Her cheeks burned and her heartbeat sounded far too loud. And in place of her anger was something else. Something hotter and more demanding.

He had gone very still, that intensity back in his eyes.

If she lifted her hand, she could touch him. She wouldn't have to reach far, since there was barely any distance between them. What would he feel like if she did? If she laid her hand on his chest? Would he be as hard as she imagined? Would he feel as hot? What would he do if she did?

She felt dizzy at the thought, and breathless too, as if she'd run a long way and very fast.

What are you doing?

She had no idea. She had no idea why she even felt this way. And yet she felt consumed by it. By him.

An eon seemed to pass. All the air in the little library

was vanishing, bit by bit, and she knew it had something to do with him—with his height and the broad width of his shoulders and that glitter in his eyes, which weren't quite as icy as they had been. No, if she wasn't much mistaken, it looked as if there were silver flames burning there instead.

Then, quite abruptly, he turned away. 'I have no time this morning to discuss our marriage,' he said in curt tones. 'It will have to be this evening. I will send for you.'

Then, before she could say another word, he stalked out.

CHAPTER FOUR

TIBERIUS PACED BEFORE the fireplace in his office, restless, impatient and vaguely out of sorts. He'd spent all day in meetings with his aides and advisors, sorting through the difficult task of imposing a new government upon a nation that had been under martial rule for the last twenty years.

A parliament needed to be reinstated and elections held—because he had no intention of holding on to power. He was no dictator. Then budgets needed to be looked at and press releases drafted. And naturally there was the issue of a public appearance.

He needed to do that as quickly as possible, so that his people would be reassured that Kasimir was once more being governed by someone responsible. There had been reports of unrest, which he'd expected, but that only made him even more impatient to get to the task of delivering reassurance to his subjects.

There weren't enough hours in the day…that was the problem.

He came to the end of the long silken rug that lay on the parquet before the fireplace, turned around, and paced back to the other end of it.

There were other things that needed to be done too. Such as the clearing up of the palace. The King's office hadn't been vandalised, as the other rooms had, and it hadn't taken more than half an hour for a couple of the palace cleaning staff to get it in order. Just as well. He needed a place to work with no distractions.

The room held an antique carved oak desk, a fireplace, oak bookshelves standing against the walls, and had a huge window behind the desk that looked out over the crags of the mountains that surrounded Kasimir.

A utilitarian room, with very little in the way of frills, but it suited his soldier's temperament.

He came to the other end of the rug, turned, and paced back once more.

Then there was the other question. The one he'd been trying not to think about all day and yet had pushed to the front of his thoughts far more often than he'd wanted it to.

The little Accorsi. The mouse who was clearly not a mouse—as she'd demonstrated so admirably this morning.

He couldn't stop thinking about the unexpected fury in her eyes when he'd confronted her about escaping. Or about how she'd shoved herself off the window seat to stand before him, curls spilling everywhere, dust on her cheek and anger blazing in her deep blue eyes.

Panic attacks, she'd said. Bad memories, she'd said. That was why she'd escaped from the royal apartments and into the hidden corridors.

Tiberius turned once more and paced another circuit in front of the fire.

Then the look in her eyes had changed…blue becoming violet as something hot and electric had arced between them.

She hadn't been a beaten dog or a mouse then.

She'd been a woman.

He gritted his teeth, his muscles tightening once more in response to the memory.

Yes, he couldn't deny it. The way she'd stood up to him, the way she'd blazed defiance at him and then the way her eyes had darkened had been…exciting. It had been obvious to him that she'd felt the same electricity, and with her standing so close, all spirit and fire, he'd had the almost overwhelming urge to take that sharp little chin in one hand and cover her mouth with his, taste all that fire for himself.

You could. She's your wife. You could make her yours in every way. You could make her want you…crave you. Put her on her knees before you. That would be a fitting revenge for what the Accorsis did to your country…

A growl escaped him as all the blood in his body rushed below his belt. Yes, Renzo Accorsi's forgotten daughter on her knees, naked before him… She'd have all those pretty curls loose, giving him something to hold on to as he defiled all that innocence, all that sweetness—

No. *No.* Why was he thinking of this again? He'd dismissed those base thoughts this morning, back in that little library, so why they should be returning again he had no idea.

He wasn't that type of man. He was a king. And a king didn't indulge in anything as petty as revenge—still less with some innocent.

Perhaps she's not innocent?

Perhaps so. But still their marriage was for Kasimir only, and that did not involve anything physical. Besides, he preferred women less fragile, women who liked their sex hard and rough, and the little Accorsi was definitely not a hard and rough type of woman. She'd mentioned panic attacks, for God's sake, and she'd certainly been terrified of him, which rendered her immediately off-limits.

So no, even if she hadn't been an Accorsi he wouldn't have touched her.

And as for this…chemistry. Well, he'd ignore it. Physical attraction was easy to control—and besides, if it proved too distracting he'd find himself one of those women who liked it rough. It didn't need to be his new wife.

Speaking of…

He stopped pacing for a moment and glanced at his watch. He'd sent her a message earlier that afternoon, instructing her to present herself in his office at six p.m. sharp. Dinner would be served and they would discuss their little…arrangement.

It was now five minutes past six and she was not here.

His restlessness intensified, eating at him, and he broke from his pacing, headed over to the door, intending to go and find her. He pulled it open only to see her standing on the other side of the doorway, her hand raised to knock.

Her eyes widened, her mouth opened, and much to his annoyance he found himself staring at it. Because it was a pretty mouth. He could think of many things he could do with that mouth…

Another growl almost escaped him at his own wayward thoughts, but he managed to wrestle them into submission.

Guinevere was not in the same dusty lacy dress she'd worn this morning, but a light blue one, with lots of frothy tiered skirts that made her look as if she had a fountain falling down on either side of her. She had her hair tied back, curls cascading down her back in a more orderly fashion than it had been this morning, and the dust on her cheekbone had gone.

She still looked delicate, like a fairy, if a much more tidy one than she had the previous day, and despite the control he had himself under he found his gaze coming to rest on the neckline of her dress, which was low and scooped, providing a perfect showcase for the swell of her breasts.

She will be soft. How long has it been since you've had any softness?

Too long. His life had been nothing but hard, relentless action, always moving forward, always onwards to the next plan, the next strategy. There had been no time for rest, for anything gentle or light or soft.

There was still no time for it.

And he should *not* be thinking about this as constantly as he was.

Forcing his gaze away from the neckline of her dress, Tiberius stepped back from the doorway. 'You're late,' he said tersely.

She blinked. 'By five minutes.'

'Five minutes is time enough for someone to lose their life.'

'Really? I had no idea this meeting was a matter of life and death.'

Acid laced her words as she stepped into the room. So. It seemed the little mouse was definitely a thing of the past.

He shouldn't respond. She knew nothing about what he'd gone through to get here and it wasn't worth arguing about. That didn't stop the words from coming out of his mouth, however.

'You have no idea about many things, Guinevere Accorsi, and that is why you are here—so I can discuss them with you.'

Hot blue flames leapt in her eyes, turning her once more into the fiery, spirited woman who'd stood up to him in the library that morning. The polar opposite to the quiet, terrified girl who'd kept staring at her hands, too afraid to look at him.

Maybe she isn't as fragile as you thought.

He did not need that thought in his head. No, he most certainly did not. Because now he was intrigued by the contrast, and by how, for all her delicacy and fragility, there appeared to be a fire burning in her. A fire he found fascinating.

She put her chin in the air and moved past him, going over to the chair in front of his desk and sitting herself down in it like the little Queen she was. 'Well, then, Your Majesty,' she said. 'Here I am.'

Tiberius shut the door and walked over to the fireplace, where he'd been pacing not moments before. He stopped, folding his arms as he looked at her.

She had her hands once again clasped in her lap, but for a change she wasn't looking at them. She was looking at him, anger still leaping and flickering in her deep blue eyes.

This evening she was a lioness, perhaps. A lioness in a pretty blue dress…

'First,' he began, starting with his most pressing concern, 'I cannot have you disappearing again. The entirety of the palace was in an uproar this morning, because you'd decided to vanish without warning.'

'I told you why I did,' she said hotly. 'I told you that I—'

'Yes, yes,' he interrupted, impatient. 'However, you

must understand that I've only recently taken power, and there is still unrest in this country. I married you to end division and create stability, and you vanishing without a word significantly undermines that.'

She glowered at him, her pretty mouth tight.

'You do understand that, don't you?' he demanded insistently. 'Or does the wellbeing of our country not matter to you?'

All at once her hands came out of her lap and she gripped the arms of her chair, shoving herself out of it in a furious movement. 'Of course it matters to me!' Her voice was so fierce it shook slightly. 'But I didn't know what was happening. I wasn't ever allowed to leave the palace, and all my father said about the state of Kasimir was that everyone loved him as King.'

Her vehemence took him by surprise, and for a moment he only stared at her. What did she mean, she hadn't been allowed to leave the palace? And did she really not know what Renzo had done to Kasimir? How could she not?

Guinevere stood in front of her chair, fingers clenched into fists at her sides, her cheeks pink, fury blazing in her eyes.

He'd hit a nerve, that was clear, and in that moment a cold awareness swept over him. That fury wasn't fake or manufactured. It was the truth.

Her father really *had* never let her out of the palace. And perhaps she really *hadn't* known what was happening in Kasimir either. But how could that be?

The awareness deepened into shock. He forced it back. Renzo was a monster, but she was a grown woman. She must have had some inkling about what kind of ruler her father was.

You say that like you expected her to have stopped him, somehow, or done something about it.

Perhaps. He needed to know more—and not just for himself, but for Kasimir. He needed to know if the woman he'd married so abruptly was indeed the right Queen for his country. Possibly it was something he should have questioned her more thoroughly on the day before, but it was too late to regret that now.

'I'm not accusing you of anything,' he said coolly. 'That's not what I was saying.'

She was still trembling with emotion. 'Then what were you saying?'

His first instinct was not to be comforting. He had no experience of it. He was a leader, a commander, a soldier. A man of quick, decisive action. He left the job of reassurance and comfort to others more skilled in giving it than he was.

Yet it was clear that Guinevere needed more than decisive action, and since there was no one else around to reassure or give comfort, his would have to suffice.

Pushing his impatience aside, he took a step towards her, then stopped and gestured to the chair. 'Sit,' he said, in what he hoped was a gentle tone, though it came out sounding more like an order than he'd wished. 'Please,' he added.

Her chin was jutting at a stubborn angle, but after a moment she let out a breath, unclenched her hands and sat back down again.

'This is about Kasimir,' he said. 'The short answer is that your father mismanaged the treasury, spent too much money on palaces and monuments and not enough on infrastructure or on basic social services. The country is in a terrible state, and it is my job to rebuild what he almost destroyed.'

She glanced away, her shoulders hunching, as if what he'd said was another attack.

'Marrying you is part of that,' he went on. 'As I told you yesterday, there are still deep divisions within Kasimir and people still sympathetic to your father. I want to unify this country, heal those wounds, and our marriage is a potent symbol of that healing.'

Again, she said nothing, her head bent, her gaze on her hands, and before he knew what he was doing, he'd come over to her chair and reached out, taking one of her hands in his. He had no idea what prompted the urge to touch her. It hadn't ever occurred to him before to touch another person in comfort.

She didn't pull away, and because her fingers were cold he began to rub them gently with his thumb. 'I should not have implied that the wellbeing of our country was of no importance to you,' he allowed. 'Especially when I don't know anything about your life.'

Now her gaze was fixed on her hand in his, and he became conscious that her skin had warmed. It felt smooth and silky beneath the brush of his thumb. A familiar electric awareness swept through him, tightening his muscles, and he wondered if she was as smooth and silky all over...whether that faint, sweetly feminine scent that surrounded him was her hair or her body or a combination of the two.

Not that he should be thinking about her body. He should not be thinking such thoughts at all. And he definitely should *not* be touching her.

With an effort of will that cost him far more than it should, Tiberius let go of her hand and stepped back, ignoring how the warmth of her skin lingered on his fingertips.

'I think you need to tell me, Guinevere,' he said. 'About what your life was like here.'

Guinevere could still feel the warmth of his hand around hers. His skin had been so hot, and there had been a slight roughness to the pad of his thumb as he'd stroked it over the back of her hand.

It had been unexpected, and she'd had to steel herself not to flinch, since the last touch she'd had from anyone male—her brother Alessio—had involved a chunk of her hair being torn out.

But there had been nothing violent about the way Tiberius had taken her hand within his. Nothing rough about the gentle chafe of his thumb. The feel of it had sent the most delicious shivers down her spine.

She couldn't think when he was near her…her thoughts getting as slow and heavy as thick treacle.

That afternoon, because of a couple of things Tiberius had said, she'd found one of his aides and pestered him into telling her what her father had done to Kasimir. He'd always boasted about the good things he'd done for the country, and how his subjects loved him, and while she'd doubted that—because she'd certainly never loved him—she hadn't seen anything to the contrary and hadn't been able to get any information from anyone.

Finding out the truth had been like a sliver of glass in her heart. It had made her feel dreadful, and complicit in some way, even though she'd had no choice about her imprisonment. And then Tiberius accusing her of knowing what had gone on and not doing anything about it had shoved that sliver even deeper.

It had hurt, his accusation. But it had been his admission of regret for the way he'd spoken to her that had taken the wind completely out of her sails. No one had ever apologised to her for anything. Not her brothers for their treatment of her, and certainly not her father.

For Tiberius to reach out and touch her had further shocked her. Not so much the fact that he'd done it as her own reaction to it. Being touched with gentleness was a new experience for her, and there had been something infinitely warm and reassuring about his hand around hers. A big hand, and scarred, yet it had held hers carefully, as if it were precious.

She hadn't known men could be capable of gentleness. Her father hadn't been, for example, and neither had either of her brothers. They'd taken pleasure in having power over others, as if cruelty were a kind of strength, and they'd encouraged it in the guards they had surrounded themselves with too.

Guinevere had spent all day anticipating this meeting and not in a good way—especially after hearing what had happened to Kasimir. She'd known Tiberius would be angry, and that he might be accusatory, and so she'd dreaded facing him.

But part of her knew that she had to face up to what her father had done, even though it wasn't her fault, so she'd showered and changed into one of her favourite dresses to give herself courage. And then she'd forced herself to meet him here in the King's study.

He had been angry and accusatory, as she'd known he would be, but what had surprised her was the anger that he'd woken in her that morning had once again ignited, roaring up inside her like a bonfire.

She should have kept it locked down and away, because arguing and making a scene drew attention to herself, and that had never ended well for her, but she hadn't been able to control it. She'd expected him to retaliate in kind—because men like him always did. Except...

He hadn't.

Instead, he'd apologised and taken her hand in his, asked her to tell him about her life.

She had no idea how to respond.

He'd let go of her now, and was standing back, putting distance between them, his back to the fireplace, silver eyes betraying nothing. But she could still feel the brush of his thumb scorching her skin. Why had he done that? Was it because he felt sorry for her?

She was tempted to ask him, but then decided she didn't want to know. She didn't want any sympathy—and definitely no pity. She'd ignore it, pretend it hadn't happened. That seemed the safest route.

'There isn't much to tell,' she said. 'I was born here and grew up here. I was educated here too, along with my brothers. But... I wasn't allowed to leave the palace. My father told me it was because he was concerned for my safety.'

Tiberius's dark brows drew down. 'Even when you were older?'

'My brothers were allowed out, but not me. I was a...a girl. And I was to be protected.'

Except there had been no protection from the monsters within the palace walls. She'd had to protect herself, because there had been no one else. But she didn't want to tell him that. He'd only pity her even more and she couldn't bear it.

She didn't know what he thought about her imprisonment. He gave no sign. His features were impassive.

'And you truly didn't know anything about what was happening in Kasimir while your father was in power?'

There was no accusation in his voice this time, only a note of puzzlement—as if he couldn't quite conceive that she hadn't known.

Well, he could believe what he liked. She knew the truth of her childhood.

'No,' she said flatly. 'I didn't. The only thing I was told was that Kasimir was returned to its former glory and that everyone loved the King. I wasn't allowed electronic communications until I was eighteen, and even then my access to the web was tightly controlled.'

He was still frowning. 'You must have heard rumours...'

Guinevere let out a breath, thinking about the whispers she'd overheard while hiding in the passageways. Whispers from the staff, from the guards, from guests. Whispers about the state of the economy and joblessness, about the statue that had gone up in one of the city's central piazzas that had cost millions—money the country could ill afford to spend.

It had struck fear into her heart, listening to them, because it had sounded so awful. And because there had been nothing she could do to help. She was only one small mouse in the walls, whom everyone had forgotten.

'I heard things,' she admitted. 'Once I tried to talk to my father about it, but he told me that it wasn't my business and to stay out of it. So... There was nothing I could do.' Tearing her gaze from the flat expression in Tiberius's eyes, she glanced down at her hands yet again, acid collecting in her stomach. 'So, I suppose you're right, in a way. I was complicit in my father's crimes.'

A silence fell over the room.

She could feel him looking at her—judging her, no doubt. And he had a right to. Her father *had* almost ruined Kasimir, while all she'd been worried about was her own safety. She wasn't any better than he was. Because she too had fled and hid.

'How did you know about the passageways?' His tone was impossible to read. 'My father used to tell me stories about them, but he said no one else knew about them.'

She didn't want to tell him the truth—that she'd merely been a toy her brothers had used to hone their bullying skills on, and that instead of standing up to them she'd hidden in the walls. She could only imagine what he would think of that. He was tall and strong and powerful. He wouldn't understand fear. He would think her a coward, just like her father, and he'd be right.

'I discovered them when I was playing hide and seek with my brothers.' It wasn't exactly a lie...merely a variation of the truth. 'The armoire in my mother's rooms was locked, and I couldn't get out, so I kicked open the back of it and found the opening behind.'

'The lock is on the outside of the armoire doors,' he said, his tone expressionless. 'It would require someone to actually turn the key to lock you in.'

Guinevere swallowed and looked down at her hands, twisted in her lap. She didn't want to tell him. Didn't want that icy silver gaze to judge her the way he judged her father.

'I don't know how that happened,' she said carefully.

There was a silence.

'I think you do.' His voice was soft, but there was something hard and unyielding in his tone.

In spite of herself, Guinevere glanced up. The expression on his face now was frightening in its intensity, his silver eyes sharp as knives, and even though she knew that he likely wouldn't hurt her, she couldn't help her instinctive flinch.

'What did they do to you?' he asked, in the same unyielding tone. 'And they definitely did something. I can see it in your eyes.'

There was no judgment in his face, but there was certainly anger, and she wondered why. What did he care what had happened to her? No one else had.

You should tell him the truth.

She didn't want to, but it was clear he suspected what the truth was, and she had a feeling he wasn't going to let her leave until he had it. And, really, what did his judgement matter anyway? Yes, he was her husband, but it wasn't as if they loved each other—not when they'd only just met.

'My father didn't touch me,' she said, choosing her words carefully. 'But my brothers liked to…tease me.'

The hard glitter in Tiberius's gaze didn't falter, but a muscle leapt in the side of his strong jaw. 'How? By locking you in the armoire?'

'Yes,' she admitted.

'Were there other things they did?'

Her mouth was dry, but she forced herself to speak. 'They liked to…chase me through the palace. And pull my hair. Sometimes, when I was much younger, they'd break my toys.' The look on his face had changed, and now it frightened her. 'It wasn't anything too bad,' she added quickly.

'Did they hurt you?'

'Please…' she said without thinking. 'Please, don't be angry.'

His eyes widened for a moment, as if what she'd said

had surprised him, before narrowing into glittering silver slits as he studied her. 'I'm not angry with you, Guinevere,' he said quietly. 'I am angry with those who hurt you.'

Something inside her eased at that, and she realised she'd been sitting there tensely, as if waiting for him to explode in a furious rage, preparing to run from the room in fright.

He's not going to do that, and you know it.

Perhaps she did know it. He seemed to be in a constant state of annoyance, and yet he did not throw anything or scream obscenities the way her father did, or say cruel things and laugh the way her brothers did.

He was contained, she thought. Self-possessed and impervious. And for some reason that made her feel safe.

'They...did hurt me,' she said in a rush—because he'd asked for the truth and she wanted to give it to him, especially since he'd already guessed. 'That's why I hid in the passageways. So they wouldn't find me.'

Tiberius's expression remained hard as stone. 'They will pay for it,' he said, pronouncing the words like a vow. 'They will pay for what they did to this country and for what they did to you.'

Surprise rippled through her. 'Why should you care about what they did to me?'

'You are my queen, and as King it is my duty to protect you as I do all my subjects.'

She heard it then. The steel beneath his tone. He stood before the empty fireplace, muscular arms folded, a severe expression on his face and his light grey eyes glittering with intention. A strange kind of thrill went through her. She'd never had anyone state that they would protect her—not one single person. But, looking at his fierce expression, she believed him.

He absolutely *would* protect her.

That made her feel warm, and immensely reassured, and for the first time in what felt like years her muscles relaxed. She let out a breath. 'Thank you,' she said, and she meant it, though she didn't know what else to say—she didn't want to keep talking about her brothers. 'But you didn't ask me here to talk to me about my life. You wanted to discuss our marriage.'

At that moment there was a knock on the door. Tiberius gave her one long, sharp glance, then turned to answer it.

A minute later the room was full of serving staff who unloaded food onto the huge wooden desk that was the only available flat surface in the room. They arranged it along with a bottle of wine from the palace cellars, and then left as discreetly as they'd come.

'I've had dinner brought to us,' Tiberius said. 'The main dining room has yet to be cleaned and, given your feelings about the royal apartments, I thought you would prefer to eat here.'

Another little shock went through her. She hadn't expected him to think about that. She hadn't expected him to think about her feelings at all.

'Thank you,' she repeated, which appeared to be her standard response.

'Eat.' He gestured at the food. 'You must be hungry.'

It was true—she was. She hadn't bothered with lunch. She'd stayed in the safety of the little library, too out of sorts and uncomfortable with Tiberius's intense electric presence to leave it.

She still felt that he might be a danger to her in some way, but it wasn't the same as the sick dread that used to fill her whenever she heard her brothers' voices. No, his danger felt almost exciting…which was very strange. Anyway, the food was there, and her stomach was empty, so it seemed silly to refuse.

Rising from the chair, she went over and helped herself. It was a simple meal—salad and fresh bread and roasted chicken.

Tiberius poured her a glass of wine as she pulled a chair up to the desk and began to eat.

'There will be some making do until the palace has been fully restored,' he said, pouring a glass for himself too. 'As you can see.'

'I'm sorry,' she felt compelled to say. 'For the condition my father left the palace in.'

'Did you spray paint the walls and burn the tapestries?' he asked mildly.

'No, but—'

'Then you have nothing to apologise for.' His silver gaze was very direct. 'We must present a united front as rulers, Guinevere. I have been thinking on this and I have decided that our marriage must at least look cordial, if not joyful. We will need to be seen together, as well as making official public appearances together. I want our union to look strong and steadfast—do you understand?'

A tight, hot feeling prickled over her skin. 'Strong and steadfast? How?'

'The King's bedroom is part of the royal apartments, which means we will have to share them.'

The prickling feeling deepened. 'Sh-share?'

Tiberius finally picked up his glass of wine, slowly swirling the deep red liquid inside it. 'Not the bedrooms. We'll keep those separate. But we should be seen to retire to the royal apartments together, at least initially, as any newly married couple would.'

Her stomach tightened for reasons she didn't care to examine too closely.

'You don't have to sleep there if you don't wish to,' he continued. 'No one knows about the corridors, which means no one will know if you choose to sleep in that little room.'

The warmth that had been sitting inside her ever since he'd touched her hand and then said he'd protect her deepened. She might be his prisoner, but he was granting her a space that was hers and hers alone, free of the memories that soaked through every other part of the palace. It was almost as if he was taking her feelings into account.

She could feel colour rise into her face, but she didn't look away from him this time. 'You really won't mind?'

'I don't see why not. You shouldn't have to deal with memories that upset you.'

'I…appreciate that.'

He gave her a regal nod in acknowledgement. 'And another thing… You'll need some preparation, I think, before our first public appearance.'

'Preparation? What kind of preparation?'

'You say you haven't ever left the palace. Not once. But public appearances will involve not only leaving the palace, but visiting various Kasimiran cities. There will also be international engagements we will need to attend.'

An unfamiliar excitement filled her, even as the thought of venturing outside made her nervous. There was embarrassment there, as well, at how sheltered she must seem to him—backward, even. Though why she should feel embarrassed about something she hadn't had a choice in, she didn't know.

'Good,' she said, forcing away the odd mix of feelings.

'That won't be a problem. It's not as if I wanted to spent the last twenty-three years stuck in here.'

His gaze was considering. 'I don't want to throw you into the deep end straight away—especially not with the public looking on. Perhaps we can acclimatise you to the outside world a little before then.'

You'll be going outside. Actually outside!

A quiver ran through her. 'Acclimatise how?'

'We can start somewhere within the palace grounds. The forest...or the orchards, perhaps.'

The orchards she'd seen out the windows of her little room, full of many different fruit trees. Sometimes she'd imagine herself being able to walk amongst the trees, reaching up to pick herself an orange or a peach.

'I was only allowed in the courtyard gardens and on some of the terraces,' she offered hesitantly. 'I haven't been to the orchards or the forest.'

'In that case,' Tiberius said, 'we shall start there.' Then, unexpectedly, a faint smile turned one side of his mouth. 'Now. I was told my new queen didn't touch her lunch today, so eat—please.'

That smile. It turned him from charismatic to utterly beautiful in seconds flat. And it felt to her as if she'd been given a gift...a glimpse of the man behind the hard, stern King. A warmer, easier kind of man.

But then the smile vanished.

As if it had never been.

CHAPTER FIVE

TIBERIUS DIDN'T REALLY have the time to spare to acclimatise his new queen to the outside world. There were too many other, more important things to do. Yet the thought of one of his aides or guards accompanying her on her first venture beyond the palace walls was unacceptable.

He hadn't been able to stop thinking of her sitting in his study the night before, white-faced and delicate, hesitantly telling him that her brothers had hurt her.

He'd known, maybe subconsciously, that something like that must have occurred—especially given her terror of him. But her confession, veiled as it was, had filled him with the most intense rage on her behalf. That anyone had dared lay a hand on her, so fragile as she was, was incomprehensible to him. Though he knew men did such things and worse every day.

That it had been her brothers, her family, who should have protected her and cared for her, made it even more egregious, and he burned to know what they'd done to her and why her father hadn't stopped them. But he'd bitten down on the questions. He hadn't wanted to upset her further with intrusive questions, especially since his knowing wouldn't change anything for her.

But when he'd told her he would protect her he'd meant

it. Her brother and her father would pay. And if anyone else laid a hand on her they would answer to him.

Bullying behaviour was unconscionable in royal princes and most definitely in a king, and he would never be like that. Never.

Her first time outside the palace walls would be with him, so he could watch over her—as he should his queen. Also, she would be at his side for their public appearances, and he needed to see how she reacted, so that if she was overwhelmed he'd know what to do and have some solutions. The eyes of the world's press would be on them and, as he'd told her, he wanted their marriage to at least look as if it was solid.

Taking her outside himself would also kill two birds with one stone—he could get her used to being out of the palace and also to being with him. It would not do for her to flinch away if he put an arm around her, for example.

Eventually, a few days after their dinner together in his office, he found a couple of hours free in the late afternoon.

He hadn't seen her since then because he'd been working from dawn till midnight every day, wrestling with the thorny issues of getting his country back on track. The damage the Accorsis had done to the Kasimiran treasury was considerable, though not as bad as he'd expected, so that was something at least.

He sent word to Guinevere to meet him by the doors to the back gardens, and when the hour came he strode down the echoing hallways, expecting to see his queen waiting promptly outside the specified doors. Only she wasn't.

It took him a moment to realise that the tension in his muscles and the accelerated beat of his heart was anticipation.

For the past two days he'd been good, and he hadn't thought about her once. There hadn't been room in his head for her anyway. But late at night, when he finally left his study for bed, he'd come into the royal apartments to find a tantalising sweet scent hanging in the air, one that made his body go tight with want.

He'd ignored it, thinking that hard work and late nights would mean he was too tired to think about his new wife. Sadly, he'd been wrong. That delicate scent would greet him and instantly he'd start to think about her, naked and at his feet—which was a terrible fantasy for him to have about a woman who'd been hurt as she had.

It had frayed his temper, put him on edge, and had helped him with his sleep not at all.

Which meant that by the time Guinevere finally arrived, five minutes after the time he'd specified, his mood was dark and irascible.

That she was in another of her pretty flouncy dresses, this one soft pink, with full skirts and a heart-shaped neckline, only added to his annoyance. Her hair was completely loose, in a cotton-soft cloud around her head and down her back, and he was conscious of an unbearable need to wrap those curls around his fingers and tug lightly. Then maybe not so lightly...

No, that was a mistake. He should not be thinking any of this.

Unlike the previous times they'd talked, when she had been either white-faced with fear or angry, today Guinevere smiled at him as she approached, her deep blue eyes lighting up and something deep inside him stilled.

People smiled at him—of course they did. But not like this. Not as if they were pleased to see him. As if his presence gave them joy.

He was a leader, and his advisors, his guards and his army respected him. Feared him. Admired him. But they never looked at him the way she was looking at him…as if he was simply a man she liked and liked being with.

'I know, I know,' she said as she came towards him. 'I'm late. Sorry. I was trying to find a ribbon for my hair and couldn't, and then…' She trailed off, noticing the scowl on his face.

'I have limited time,' he snapped. 'I do not have it to waste, waiting for you.'

She reddened, her smile fading. 'I said I was sorry.'

The loss of that smile angered him even more. Because he knew he was being unreasonable, that she probably had had enough of men being angry. But knowing he had no one to blame for that except himself only made it worse.

Other people's feelings had never concerned him, and his own he kept under strict control. Emotions were irrelevant, his father had always said. The only thing of any importance was Kasimir and his duty to it, and everything else should come second.

Except right now his sharpness had hurt her, and he didn't like it that he was the cause. She'd no doubt been hurt enough, and she didn't need him adding to her trauma.

'There is much to be done,' he felt compelled to explain. 'Time is of the essence. The people of Kasimir have suffered enough under your father's rule, and the longer I take to fix the problems, the longer the people will suffer.'

She frowned. 'Surely it's not *all* dependent on you?'

'Of course it is.' He tried to rein in the sharp note in his voice. 'I am the King now. The ultimate responsibility for our people is mine.'

She studied him. 'That seems…an awful lot for one person to bear.'

The observation hit him uncomfortably, though he wasn't sure why. Yes, it *was* a lot for one person to bear. Which was why his father had started early in preparing him for it.

From the age of ten he'd been told what his purpose in life was: to reclaim his father's stolen crown and rescue his country.

His journey to the throne room had been a long and hard one, but he'd survived it. His father had died before he could see Tiberius reclaim what had been lost, but now he was here and had begun the process of rescuing his country. His father's ghost could be at peace now.

And now you can make the Accorsis pay—especially for what was done to her.

No, regardless of how furious he was about that, vengeance was a petty action and he was above it.

'Not for me,' he said shortly. 'I was born to do this.'

Her brow furrowed, as if she found this worrying. 'I… I could help,' she said a little hesitantly. 'If you like.'

His instinctive reaction was to snap that he didn't want help, especially not from an Accorsi, and how could she help him anyway? But he simply couldn't countenance letting his temper get the better of him any more than he had already.

It wasn't her fault that he was letting her get under his skin. The blame lay with him entirely.

'You can help by being at my side as my queen,' he said carefully, impatient with her questions and the unwanted emotions they brought. 'So, are you ready to walk to the orchards?'

'Yes.' Her hands were once again clasped tightly in

front of her, which he was beginning to see was a sign of her anxiety. 'I'm not agoraphobic or anything. Just so you know.'

She might not be, but it was clear to him that she was nervous.

'We will take it slowly.' He turned to the big double doors, opening them so they could step out onto the terrace. 'The orchards aren't far.'

He took the lead, stepping through the doors, then turning around to face her.

Guinevere stood still in the doorway, blue eyes slightly wary, the set of her shoulders betraying her nervous tension.

Without thinking, he held out his hand to her. 'Come.'

She reached for it without hesitation, and for some reason that satisfied him. As if her taking his hand meant something. It didn't, of course, he was only trying to reassure her. And yet he didn't let go of it as she stepped through the doors to join him on the terrace, and the satisfaction deepened when, instead of pulling away, she held on tighter.

He met her gaze. 'Are you ready?'

She took a little breath, then nodded, and they began to walk slowly to the end of the terrace and then down the stairs to the path into the gardens. Guinevere's blue eyes were wide and she kept looking around—at the sky, the grass, the gardens, then back at the palace, its towers soaring into the heavens, mirroring the mountain peaks around them.

She was brave, this little mouse of an Accorsi. Despite what had happened to her—which he suspected was a lot worse than she'd said—she had a thread of courage running through her that gave her unexpected steel.

He watched her keenly, alert for signs of fear, yet there were none. Her cheeks had gone pink, the sun was striking golden sparks from her hair, and when she looked at him her smile was full of delight.

'I'm outside,' she said breathlessly, as if she couldn't believe it herself. 'I'm really outside!'

Tiberius hadn't found much to smile about in life—the stakes had always felt too high for levity—but the simple joy on Guinevere's face touched something long-forgotten inside him.

Back when he was boy, before his father had laid the heavy burden of kingship on his shoulders, he'd often gone out into the scrubby garden of his father's rundown house after he should have been in bed. And he'd lie on his back, looking up at the stars. Pinpricks of light against the black background of space. Whole worlds, whole galaxies spinning above his head. He'd felt that simple joy then, at the beauty above him, and a sense of wonder that he too was a tiny part of those galaxies.

He'd forgotten what it felt like to experience joy…to find wonder in such a simple thing as being outside in the sun.

And you *did this for her.* You *gave her this.*

The things he did for his country helped his subjects as a whole, but this was personal. Now he'd given this one woman joy, and it made his heart tighten in a way he wasn't used to.

And it shouldn't—that was the problem. The way she was getting under his skin felt like…more, somehow. Beyond physical. And that was *not* allowed.

His father had told him time and time again that a ruler's feelings didn't matter. That what was good for the country mattered more.

'Patience, Tiberius,' Giancarlo would say sternly, when Tiberius, burning with anger at his mother's death and desperate to put things right, had tried to argue his father into action, instead of waiting, as his father had counselled. 'Kasimir will not be served best by impatience and a desire for vengeance. You must put your feelings aside and do what is right for the country, not what is right for you.'

Emotion had no place in a king's rule and he knew it, and he'd decided long ago that it was easier not to have any at all. Or rather to learn to channel his grief at being deprived of a mother he didn't remember and his anger at a father who had put an impossible burden on his shoulders at far too young an age and then waited too long to take back what was his. All that rage and grief he'd channelled into reclaiming the throne, and now he'd channel those same feelings into rebuilding his country.

There wasn't room for him to be concerned with the emotions of one small woman, no matter how brave she was.

He let her hand go, since she apparently didn't need any reassurance, though it was difficult to keep any distance between them with the warmth of her skin against his fingertips.

'How are you feeling?' he asked.

She frowned, her fingers clenching into a fist, as if she wanted to keep the touch of his skin against hers with her. Then her expression relaxed and she lifted her face to the sky, clearly enjoying the sun on her skin.

'I feel...' she murmured. 'I feel as if I can breathe again.'

He couldn't stop looking at that little fist. Holding on to his warmth.

You affect her.

Tiberius turned away abruptly. He didn't need that thought in his head...he really didn't.

They continued on through the lavish palace gardens where fountains filled the air with a soft music, then went down more stairs and through a small gate. The orchards lay beyond, situated on a sunny slope.

Guinevere made a delighted sound and ran past him, heading straight to the orange trees. They were in season, and the branches were heavy with fruit.

He followed more slowly, watching her. How childish of her...to run like a little girl to the tree. He almost expected her to hike up her dress and start climbing it.

Was that what it was like to have no burdens whatsoever? To be free to enjoy the sun and the grass and the trees without having the weight of other people's expectations on you? Guinevere had her own burdens, it was true, and they were terrible ones, but now it was as if she'd simply shrugged them off and sprung free, weightless in the sun.

Suddenly he burned to know how she did it—how she made it look so easy to just...step away. To lay down the weight of those burdens and spend a few moments without it crushing you down.

He watched her with a kind of wonder as she stood at the base of a tree, reaching up to try and pick one of oranges hanging just out of her reach. Even on her tiptoes, with her hand outstretched, she couldn't reach it.

She turned then, her face alight. 'This might sound crazy, but I could see these trees from the window of my room. And I used to have this fantasy of being able to go outside and pick an orange if I wanted to.' She glanced back up at the fruit above her. 'So now I'm here, I'd really like to pick that orange. Could you give me a boost?'

The request was so out of left field it took him a few moments to understand. 'You…you want me to lift you up?'

She'd gone up on her tiptoes again, reaching up to touch the orange hanging from the branch above her, laughing at little as she tried and failed to touch it. 'Yes, please.'

He didn't think it through. He moved over to where she stood, coming to stand in front of her. Then he put his hands on her hips and lifted her so she could pick the orange.

And it was only once she was in his arms, the warmth of her body pressed to his, the sweet, feminine scent of her curling around him, that he realised his mistake. Because it *was* a mistake. She felt soft…so very soft… and he'd almost forgotten what soft felt like. His life had been hard and from a young age he'd been driven, his father forging him like a blade on the anvil of hardship, of struggle.

He hadn't missed gentleness, hadn't missed softness, because he'd never known either. But he could feel both in her, and the dark craving inside him deepened, intensified.

'You can put me down now,' Guinevere said breathlessly, holding her fruit and looking down at him with a triumphant expression.

He stared up into her depthless blue eyes, alight with a joy he hadn't thought was still possible. Her cheeks were pink and she was warm against him and he didn't want to put her down. He wanted to keep hold of her, feel that warmth and softness against him for a little longer, even though he knew he shouldn't.

Reluctantly he lowered her, doing so slowly, because he couldn't help himself, easing her down the length of his body so her pretty curves pressed against his...the giving swell of her breasts and hips in his hands, the softness of her thighs sliding down over his.

Her eyes widened, the blue deepening into the most fascinating violet, a blush rose beneath her skin and her lips parted. At the base of her throat he could see the beat of her pulse, hard and fast. She was still clutching her orange, but she wasn't looking at it. She was looking at him as if mesmerised.

Had she liked the feel of him as much as he'd liked the feel of her?

For a second neither of them spoke, then her gaze dipped to his mouth and an arrow of pure desire punched him hard in the stomach, stealing his breath. He should step back, let her go, put some distance between them. But the way she was looking at him was intoxicating.

She wants you. You know she does.

He released her hips and took the orange from her hands. 'Here,' he murmured. 'Let me.'

And he began to peel it slowly.

She didn't make any effort to step back, remaining where she was, standing close, with barely an inch between them, watching him peel the orange.

It was dangerous to have her so close, to do what he was intending, yet he couldn't stop. And once he'd finished with the peel and discarded it onto the grass he pulled apart the fruit, holding a segment between his fingers.

'Open your mouth,' he ordered softly, letting her see what was in his eyes, making no secret of the desire that tightened every muscle in his body.

This was a challenge—that was all. A test of his own control. He had no doubt he would pass it. He only wanted to see what would happen if he made it clear that he could feel this electricity between them. He wanted to know what she'd do. In his head he'd already pictured her blushing deeply and stumbling back—because, after all, her interactions with men hadn't been pleasant ones.

But she didn't.

Instead she opened her mouth, her gaze fixed on his.

Desire flared bright inside him, and before he knew what he was doing he'd lifted the segment of orange to her mouth and her small white teeth were taking a bite out of it. She chewed and swallowed and then took the rest of segment from his fingers, the softness of her mouth brushing against his skin, followed by the touch of her tongue as she licked the juice from his thumb.

An electric shock arced straight through him, stealing his breath, stealing all thought. And then, obeying an urge he couldn't have resisted if he'd tried, he took her chin in a firm grip and bent his head to taste the sweetness of her mouth.

Guinevere knew he was going to kiss her. She could feel it…could see the intention laid bare in his silver eyes. Perhaps it had been a mistake to get him to lift her up so she could pick the orange, but she hadn't been thinking straight. She'd just wanted to pick the fruit. Then, as he'd eased her down the length of his body until she was on her feet again, she hadn't been thinking at all.

There had been only him and the granite press of his chest against her sensitive breasts. The hard feel of his thighs. The heat of his skin and the smell of him, salt and sea and dry earth, now overlaid with a musky, masculine scent that made her mouth go dry with a new and painful desire.

When he'd taken the orange from her and begun to peel it she hadn't been able to drag her gaze away from the movement of his hands. Long, blunt fingers…scars on his skin. Large, rough hands and yet gentle enough remove the peel without tearing the delicate skin of the orange itself.

The contrasts in him fascinated her.

Her heart had begun to beat loudly in her head, prickles of heat sweeping over her. She'd known that it was a mistake to stay so close to him, but she hadn't been able to bring herself to move away. And then, when he'd offered her the orange segment, she'd seen desire in his intense grey gaze, a flame burning, and along with it a challenge.

She wasn't sure what had possessed her to obey his order and open her mouth, but she hadn't been able to stop herself. Maybe it was the sudden surge of bravery that had swept over her as she'd stepped out of the palace and into the gardens, her hand in his. Or the delight of having the sun on her face and the wind in her hair, the rich scent of the forest and the slight tinge of snow on the mountains.

It had all been thrilling, amazing, and for the first time in her life she hadn't felt afraid—not of anything.

She wasn't afraid of him either. Nor of the blatant heat in his eyes.

That was thrilling too, and a deep part of her was flooded with a sudden sense of power. That this warrior, this enemy, this king, should look at her like that. Her, the forgotten mouse hiding in the walls of the palace. The girl no one had ever cared about enough to protect, or even just not to hurt.

He wanted her.

And, while she'd never known what it was to want anyone physically before, she *was* certain that right now she wanted him. Honestly, why wouldn't she? He was dangerous, but so beautiful, and even though that should have made her feel threatened, it didn't.

He would never hurt her. She knew it the way she knew her own name.

He was in dark suit trousers today, with a deep blue shirt that made his eyes glow blue-silver, standing out starkly against his olive skin. He'd been terse when she'd arrived late, explaining to her with some severity exactly what his issue with time was. She hadn't expected that. She hadn't expected, either, the rush of sympathy she'd felt when he'd told her that he was responsible for his country. It had seemed like such a heavy burden, and she'd told him so. But he'd shrugged it away.

Then he'd held out his hand to her to help her step outside, despite the glower on his compelling features, and she hadn't even thought why that might not be a good idea, she'd just taken it.

He was a severe man, vibrating with a taut, impatient energy she found absolutely mesmerising. His hand was warm, and so was his body. And when she'd bitten through that segment, and the juice had run down his thumb, she hadn't been able to stop herself from licking it, tasting the sweetness of the orange and the salt on his skin.

She could taste those same things now, with his mouth on hers...oranges and salt and something darker, richer. Delicious. He smelled like freedom and tasted of courage, and she wanted those two things more than she wanted her next breath.

Thought was difficult, and his kiss was hot, and she could barely take in anything else. Then the kiss turned even hotter, became demanding, and she couldn't resist opening her mouth beneath his.

He took advantage, his tongue exploring hers, making her tremble all over.

Somehow her hands were pressed to his chest and she could finally feel the hard muscle beneath the cotton of his shirt. She'd had no idea he would feel so wonderful. No idea that the rough demand of his kiss would be so incredible.

His fingertips holding her chin tightened and she felt his other hand slide to the small of her back, the orange falling unnoticed on the ground. His hand slid further down, over her rear, cupping her, easing her hips against his, and the hard length of his erection pressed to the unbearably sensitive place between her thighs.

A helpless whimper escaped her as a shock of pleasure sent sparks along every nerve-ending. She'd had no idea it would feel like this. She'd imagined it—yes, she had. Kisses. Touches. Desire. This was what she'd read about. *This.* This magical feeling of being wanted and of wanting herself. But it was better than she'd ever imagined…so much better.

The kiss turned feverish and he released her chin, sliding one hand into her hair and closing his fingers into a fist, tugging back her head, exploring her mouth deeper and with even more demand. She was shaking now, and the hard press of him between her thighs was almost unbearable. She wanted his hand there—wanted something more… More friction. Yes. She needed it.

He moved, walking her insistently backwards until she felt the rough trunk of the orange tree pressed against her spine, his hands on her hips holding her against it. Then he tore his mouth from hers and she found herself looking up into his face, half dizzy with desire and breathing fast. He was breathing fast too, the look in his eyes blazing with want, and with something else that looked like fury.

'Is this what you want?' he demanded suddenly. 'To debase yourself with me?'

Guinevere blinked up at him, not understanding. 'Wh-what do you mean…debase myself?'

'You want me to have you up against this tree? Your skirt hiked up and me inside you? Because I will, little Accorsi. Say the word and that's exactly what will happen.'

She stared at him, noting the hard lines of his face and the anger—yes, it *was* anger—flaming in his eyes. 'I… I…' she stammered, hating how she couldn't get the words out. 'Wh-what did I do?'

'Nothing. But I like it rough, mouse.' He growled the words, pressing his hips suddenly against hers, letting her feel the hard length of him through her dress. 'And you don't even know what you're doing when you look at me that way.'

Guinevere's pulse pounded in her ears, her cheeks burning. She still didn't understand his anger. 'What way?'

'Like all you want me to do is put you on your back in the grass, spread your thighs and eat you alive.'

The words sent a hot shock through her. She knew what he was talking about—she might be sheltered, but she'd read enough about physical passion to understand. The thought of him doing that to her excited her, thrilled her, even as it made her want to go up in flames with embarrassment.

She took a shuddering breath. 'But… I don't understand. Would that be wrong? Why are you so angry?'

Abruptly, Tiberius shoved himself away, then pushed a distracted hand through his black hair, glancing away, a muscle leaping in the side of his strong jaw. Then he looked back, his gaze a silver spear piercing her right through. 'I have never had a problem with controlling myself, Guinevere Accorsi. Never. Doing my duty to Kasimir is the most important task I can conceive of and I should be thinking about it—not of ripping your clothes off.'

Her mouth opened, but no sound came out.

'I don't know why, or what it is about you that is driving me to distraction, but let me be very clear. Nothing can happen between us. I am not the man for a virgin who has lived her entire life within the walls of a palace—and especially not if that virgin is vulnerable, fragile and has been badly treated by the people who were supposed to protect her.'

The way he said it all, so dismissively, caught at something inside her, igniting her own anger. He was acting as if *she* was the problem, and yet she'd done nothing. Nothing at all. It wasn't her fault that her brothers had been monsters, that they'd hurt her. It wasn't her fault her father had failed to protect her, either.

And as for the 'virgin' stuff—well, again, that wasn't her fault. Even if by some miracle she'd met a man she liked, she wouldn't have had the opportunity to rid herself of her virginity anyway.

'Why not?' she shot back, stepping forward. 'You make me sound like a sad little victim, and I'm not.'

The scorching silver of his gaze swept over her. 'No, perhaps not. But the problem isn't you—it's me. I'm afraid of what I want to do to you. I want to punish you, corrupt you, take my revenge out on you for what your father did to my family.' The flames in his eyes were cold now. 'But I am a king, and a king is above such pettiness. He does not put his own desires before those of his country. To do so would make me no better than Renzo, and I will not be that man.'

A shiver passed over her, and she didn't know whether it was because of the ice in his voice or the flames in his eyes.

Punish you...corrupt you...

She swallowed, her mouth dry. 'If you're worried about hurting me, you won't. You would never make me do anything I didn't want.'

She knew that was true. He could have done what he'd just said to her at any point over the past few days and he hadn't. Even when he'd been angry.

His eyes glittered, sharp as swords. 'But I can make you want it, little mouse. I can make you do anything I command. And that's why nothing can ever happen between us.'

'What if I wasn't a virgin? If I was experienced?'

That muscle jumped in the side of his jaw. 'A moot point, since you are neither of those things.'

There was no use in denying it. Her inexperience must be obvious. 'I know that, but...' She tried to think. 'I mean, I'm your wife. So are you planning on being celibate for the entirety of our marriage?'

An emotion she didn't understand flickered over his face and he gave a low, mirthless laugh. 'No. No, I am not.'

A strange feeling lanced through her then—a kind of pain.

You're jealous now?

She wanted to deny it, tell herself that she felt nothing for him so of course it couldn't be jealousy. And yet... The thought of him with someone else made her hurt deep inside. 'You'll...take a lover, then? Is that what you're saying?'

There was a darkness in his eyes now. 'I will not be staying celibate just for you, little lioness.'

Lioness.

Brave as a lion. That was what he meant, wasn't it? He thought she was brave.

She took another step, wanting to prove it both to herself and to him. 'You have made demands of me since we met, and I've given you everything you wanted. I married you. I gave you my name and promised to be at your side for public appearances, for the sake of our people. So you've already punished me for my father's crimes.' The words kept on spilling out, even though she'd had no idea she was going to say them. 'But it's my turn now. I want to demand one thing of you.' She took another step, then another, the last one carrying her straight to him. 'Don't find a lover, Your Majesty. If you want one, your wife is right here.'

His gaze flickered, then blazed with a bright, hot, fierce emotion that again she didn't understand. He was breathing fast, as she was, his hands in fists at his sides.

Was that her effect on him? Had she driven him to this point?

They stared at each other for what felt like one long, aching eon.

Then abruptly he turned around without a word and strode away.

Disappointment gripped her as she watched his tall figure vanish up the path and into the gardens, along with another tight, hot feeling that was almost unbearable.

He might think her brave, but he still thought of her as fragile and vulnerable too, thought that she needed to be protected. She liked it that he wanted to protect her, but she didn't want him to put her in the 'delicate and fragile' box. It aggravated her.

She was tired of being thought of as a victim, of being powerless and weak. Throughout her childhood she'd accepted those labels because it had been safer. But they chafed now. He'd called her a lioness, he thought she was brave, and she wanted to prove that to him—show him that she wasn't as fragile as he thought.

She wanted him, his touch, his kiss. She wanted the passion she'd read about in books and the pleasure too. And she didn't see why she couldn't have it.

Yes, she was inexperienced, and he'd been very clear about what he liked sexually, but it hadn't frightened her. It had made her curious, made her want to find out exactly what he meant by 'rough'. Because she wasn't some shy, wilting flower—or a bloody mouse.

She took a slow breath, determination hardening inside her.

He wanted her. She excited him—she could see that. But he was also denying himself, because he was a good man, with strong principles, and no matter what he said, he wasn't like her father—not even a little bit.

He would make her want it, he'd said. Well, that was a two-way street. She could make him want it too. Why shouldn't she?

Why shouldn't she, for the first time in her life, actually take what she wanted for herself instead of hiding away in the dark? Also, it wasn't just about her. It was clear he needed what she could offer. In a way, convincing him to sleep with her would be helping her country. A distracted king wasn't ideal, after all, and from the looks of him he needed some relief. He'd been working so hard. She'd seen the shadows beneath his eyes.

Guinevere walked over to where the rest of the orange lay and picked it up. She tore off a segment and put in her mouth, and as she walked back to the palace she began to plan.

CHAPTER SIX

THE REST OF the day was a nightmare. Tiberius threw himself back into the endless list of tasks he had to do, along with all the interminable meetings he had to attend. But it didn't seem to matter how hard he tried to distract himself—and he tried *very* hard—all he could think about was her.

Her mouth. The sweet taste of her. The warmth and softness of her body against his. The unexpected fire in her eyes as she'd told him that she wanted him. That, should he want a lover, she was right there.

His wife. His lovely, lovely wife.

The devil on his shoulder whispered to him all day, giving him good reasons for why he should take her, indulge himself with her. She wanted him. Everyone likely thought they were sleeping together already. And besides, he'd need an heir at some point, and she would be a good candidate to give him one. Also, his concentration was shot, so if he really wanted to put his country first he shouldn't be hesitating.

They were already married, for God's sake, and he wanted her...

He had to resist, though. Because if he could not control his own appetites, how could he put some distance between his rule and that of Renzo Accorsi? How could he do justice to what his father had taught him?

And then there was the way Guinevere had been traumatised by her brothers and by her father. The last thing she needed was a man like him forcing his desires on her.

Even now, he still couldn't believe his behaviour in the orchard, when he hadn't been able to control himself, letting go the leash and gripping her so tightly, holding him to her as if he wanted to cover himself with her softness and sweetness and warmth…

No, he shouldn't be thinking about this. At all.

The meetings went on all day and he was surly to everyone, no matter how hard he tried to keep his temper under control.

He should have found himself a lover, of course, but that was impossible now. He'd told her the truth—that he'd never intended to be celibate—and she'd made her wishes very plain. Now, if he took a lover, not only would it be an admission of weakness he couldn't allow, it would also hurt his new wife, and he didn't want to do that.

How he was going to last until the time came for a divorce, he had no idea…

It was very, very late by the time his last meeting of the day ended and he finally let all his exhausted advisors retire to their beds. Tiberius considered visiting the palace gym, to work off a little of his agitation, but he was tired too, and he'd be useless tomorrow if he didn't get at least one full night of sleep.

He strode through the dark palace hallways to the royal apartments. His guards were the only people still awake. He wouldn't encounter Guinevere, he was certain. She'd have long since gone back down the secret corridors to her little nest in the room where she slept every night.

Sure enough, when he entered the apartments and shut the doors behind him they were dark and silent. He could smell the lingering scent of her, though, all sweet femininity and delicate musk that made his body tighten with want.

Ridiculous to be pushed to the edge by one woman. He couldn't understand it.

In his private bathroom, he pulled off his clothes and showered. Then he towelled himself dry before heading into the darkness of his bedroom.

Only to stop in the doorway, every one of his threat senses going into high alert.

Someone else was in the room, he knew it. And there was that scent again, sweet, feminine...

He stilled for a second, then reached out and hit the light switch.

Kneeling in the centre of his bed, wearing nothing at all, was his queen.

Guinevere.

Blonde curls cascaded over her pale shoulders, the ends caressing the most beautiful pair of rounded breasts he'd ever seen. Soft pink nipples, creamy skin, the delicious curve of her hip and the pale expanse of her thighs. And between them the sweetest little thatch of curls...

His body went instantly hard, every muscle drawn tight.

Her deep blue gaze met his and there was absolutely no fear in it, only sparks of the passionate fire he'd seen earlier that day when he'd kissed her.

'Guinevere,' he said roughly. 'What are you doing? I told you nothing could happen between us.'

She lifted her sharp little chin. 'I've been in the dark for a long time, Tiberius. Hiding in the walls. But I've decided I don't want to do that any more. What I want is my husband. What I want is a wedding night.'

It had been a very long day, and he was tired, and all of a sudden it felt as if he'd been doing nothing but fighting. Fighting for his throne, his crown, his country. Fighting for years without a break. And fighting himself most of all.

He was weary of it.

She was his wife. No one would know if they slept together—in fact everyone would be surprised that they hadn't already. And he'd given her a taste of his own passion back there in the orchard and she hadn't pulled away. He'd told her that he wasn't the man for a sheltered virgin and she hadn't cared.

What was he trying to prove anyway? And who was he trying to prove it to?

Yes, he was supposed to be setting an example, to be better than Renzo Accorsi, but what went on in his bedroom had nothing to do with his country, and both his father and his mother were gone.

It was only sex. Sleeping with his wife wouldn't destroy his throne.

Anyway, she'd made the decision to put herself in his way, naked and on her knees. She wanted him and had made no secret of it. So now she'd have to accept the consequences.

He kicked the door shut behind him and walked over to the bed. It was gratifying to see how her gaze roved over his naked form, as if she liked what she saw as much as he did when he looked at her.

'You want me to be your husband, then?' he asked, pinning her with his gaze. 'In every way?'

She nodded, the pulse at the base of her pale throat beating frantically. 'Yes.'

He let himself look at her finally. Taking his time as

he scanned every inch of her lovely body. She was so very, very pretty.

She is yours. Claim her.

Perhaps he would. Perhaps he'd claim her completely, permanently. He needed a wife anyway, to provide heirs, and any children they had would be the ultimate union of Benedictus and Accorsi. So why not this woman he already knew he wanted?

Of course they might not suit sexually, but he didn't think that would be the case. Even now he knew that one night wouldn't be enough for him, and a king couldn't be seen to be taking new lovers every couple of weeks. No, it was better to have one woman, and to have that woman be his wife.

'If you want this,' he said—because these would be his terms and she had to agree to them—'then understand that if we sleep together I will not give you a divorce later. You will remain my queen and carry my heirs.'

Her eyes widened. 'Oh, I—'

'I will not have a parade of lovers going in and out of my bedroom. That won't set the example I want for my rule or for my people. Also…' He paused so she would see his intention clearly in his face, so there would be no mistake. 'Now I have the throne, I will not give it up. The same goes for my queen. I keep what is mine, Guinevere Accorsi. So if you want me to be a husband to you, that is what you'll have to accept.'

She stared at him for a long moment and he watched in fascination as goosebumps rose on her skin. He wanted to touch her, stroke her, lick her all over like an ice cream. It felt almost impossible to hold himself back. But he wasn't going to touch her unless she accepted this. Because he had the feeling that if he did he wouldn't be able to give her up.

Slowly Guinevere nodded, and he could see fire in her blue gaze now, building higher and hotter. Little lioness. She was brave—he'd already seen evidence of that—but now he knew it to be true. Brave and passionate.

'I accept it,' she said in a husky voice. 'But I want something in return. For the duration of our marriage there will be no other women for you but me.'

As if he would want another woman. Looking at her, he couldn't even remember what other women looked like, and it satisfied him that she was asking for fidelity. He didn't want a doormat for a wife. He wanted a woman who demanded the same things of him that he did of her. A match for him. A meeting of equals. A queen had to be as strong as a king.

'I accept,' he said. 'There will no other women but you.'

She nodded, then slowly held out her arms to him. 'Then come to me, my king.'

My king...

The blood pumped hard in his veins at the husk in her voice, and at the way she held her arms out to him, welcoming him.

He came to the edge of the bed, looking down at her, kneeling before him, naked except for the veil of her hair.

His wife.

Lifting a hand, he threaded his fingers through her curls. Soft, like silk against his skin. 'You are mine,' he murmured. 'You are my war prize, little Accorsi, and so you must do whatever I tell you.'

She was trembling now, but it wasn't with fear—he could see that. No, there was nothing but hungry anticipation in her wide blue eyes.

'I will,' she whispered. 'What do want you me to do?'

He tightened his grip in her hair and then bent, answering her by taking her mouth in a hot, deep kiss. She tasted of oranges and sunshine and something else sweet, a flavour that he found the more he tasted, the more he wanted.

He kissed her deeper, hotter, and she made a small sound of hunger in the back of her throat that went straight to his groin. Before he knew what he was doing, he'd pushed her onto her back across the mattress and he was over her, tracking hot kisses down her neck and the delicate architecture of her throat, his hands tracing her curves as he went.

He lingered over her breasts, stroking, squeezing, weighing them in his hands, before tracing the shape of them with his tongue, flicking over one hard little nipple before drawing it into his mouth. She cried out, her body arching against his, making him grit his teeth against the need to sink inside her straight away. He didn't want to do that yet. She was a virgin, and she was sheltered, and she'd been ill-treated. And despite all of that she'd chosen him to give herself to. And even though he'd told her he liked it rough, she deserved better from him than that. Certainly this first time. And besides, it was the perfect opportunity to drive her as mad as she'd driven him all day.

He licked and kissed and nipped her sensitive nipples, then worked his way down further, gripping her shuddering hips in his hands as he kissed his way over her stomach and finally down between her thighs.

Guinevere gave another hoarse cry as he tasted her, sweet yet tart at the same time, holding her writhing body as he explored. She panted and moaned, her hands in his hair, holding on to him as if she was drowning and he was the only thing keeping her afloat. He kept her there, exploring her deeper, drawing more and more desperate sounds from her as she moved restlessly beneath him, the grip she had in his hair almost painful.

She was as soft as he'd thought she'd be, and as hot, and she tasted like the sweetest treat. It felt as if he'd been years without a woman, years since he'd had anyone this responsive, this passionate. She'd abandoned herself to him without self-consciousness, not hiding her pleasure or holding back. It made him feel like a god that he could do this to her.

His little lioness.

She called his name in the end, as he brought her to the peak and held her there, making her plead, making her beg, and then he took her over it, her screams of release echoing in his ears.

Guinevere lay on her back in Tiberius's bed, staring blankly at the ceiling, trying to remember what her actual name was. It came back to her slowly as the aftershocks of that incredible climax faded, leaving her heavy and sated and yet strangely still hungry.

Guinevere. That was right. That was what her name was. And she was here in Tiberius's bed because she'd had the brilliant idea of giving herself to him in a way that would make it very difficult for him to refuse.

In fact, she'd gone through many scenarios after those moments in the orchard, trying to think of the best approach when it came to seducing her husband. But, considering how little experience she'd had with men, she'd decided that being as direct as possible was the key.

Of course he'd been working late, since that was what he'd been doing every night since he'd married her, so she'd had lots of time to prepare. Not that she'd needed it, since her plan had been basically to turn up naked in his bed.

She'd already been there a quite a while before he'd entered the bedroom, sitting on the bed, vacillating between wild excitement and a sick dread that he'd laugh at her, or simply send her away.

Anxiety had gripped her when she'd heard him enter the royal apartments, and then the shower in the bathroom next door had been turned on. Her heart beating fast, she'd come up onto her knees on the mattress, trying to calm her ragged nerves as she'd heard the door open.

Then he'd turned on the light and she'd seen him in the doorway.

Naked.

Her mouth had dried, her nerves forgotten, and she hadn't been able to look away. Because he was beautiful. So achingly beautiful. Broad shoulders. Muscled chest and stomach. Narrow hips and powerful thighs. All encased in smooth, satiny olive skin. And the most male part of him, hard and thick, making no secret of how much he wanted her.

She'd thrilled to it, even as a sudden attack of nerves had nearly undone her.

She'd thought he might turn around and walk away, leaving her kneeling in his bed all alone. She'd had no idea what she would do if that happened.

But it hadn't.

Instead, he'd told her that there would be no divorce. That if she wanted this then she had to accept that she would be his wife in every way, including bearing his heirs. She understood why. Knew that he wanted to set an example for his people. It wasn't about her specifically. It was about what she represented as his wife and queen.

She'd known a moment's hesitation when he'd laid it all out for her, because she hadn't been expecting that.

Hadn't been expecting more than a night and hadn't thought about anything beyond that.

Yet he had.

She'd also known that this was the moment of truth. That if she didn't give this to him she'd get nothing at all. And looking at him, standing there, she hadn't been sure she could stand having nothing.

If she agreed, she would be his, and there was reassurance in being someone's…in being claimed. No one had ever wanted her to be theirs, even when she was a child, long before she'd decided that hiding was better than being noticed. Her value as a daughter, as her father had often said, was only in her ability to make a good marriage, nothing more.

Certainly no one had loved her, and while she knew that it wasn't love with Tiberius, she would settle for being desired. He'd promised to protect her too, and after all it would hardly be a hardship to share his bed every night.

Of course she'd said yes.

And then everything had happened very fast.

His lips on hers, his hands on her body, and then she'd been pushed onto her back and his marauding mouth had been everywhere. On her throat, her nipples, her thighs and then between.

Pleasure had gripped her like music as he'd turned her body into an instrument that he played with the most incredible precision. She hadn't known that so many different sounds could be drawn from her.

He hadn't been rough like he'd warned her earlier that day. Instead he'd been decisive, firm and unhesitating, which had thrilled her…excited her. She'd loved him taking charge, because she wouldn't have even known where to start.

Now she lay there, gasping, and he was moving again, sliding between her thighs, one hand braced beside her head as the other slipped through her slick folds, spreading her open for him. She stared up into his silver eyes as he shifted once again, pushing against her and then into her, sliding in deeply, slowly, watching her as he did so, gauging her reaction.

'Does this hurt?' he asked, his voice almost guttural.

She was panting, the feeling of him inside her almost too much and yet also not enough. 'No… It's just…strange.'

His hand slipped beneath her rear, lifting her, letting him slide even deeper, and then he paused. The feel of his hot, bare skin against hers and the weight of him on her was intensely erotic. She wanted to hold him there, never let him go.

Unexpectedly, he put out a hand and pushed a curl behind her ear, the movement tender, making her frantically beating heart catch fire. And then he leaned down and kissed her, tasting her, and at the same time he began to move, making her blaze.

She'd had no idea she could be so hungry for him again, and so soon, but she was. Desperate and feverish. Wanting more.

Looking up into his face, at the harshly carved lines of it drawn taut with desire, she felt the flames inside her burn higher and hotter. It was strange to be so surrounded by a person. To have him over her and inside her, the heat of his body against hers, the scent of his skin everywhere.

It was thrilling. Intoxicating.

She didn't know what to do with her hands, so she put them on his powerful shoulders, loving the feeling of hard muscle moving under his skin. The hand beneath her rear shifted again, tilting her hips, and somehow the hunger deepened, becoming fierce. Then it slid away as he reached down to grip her behind her knee, drawing her leg up and around his hip, opening her more to him.

'Better?' he asked roughly.

'Yes…' It came out on a gasp, the acuteness of the pleasure making her moan. 'Yes… More.'

Tiberius bent and kissed her, then his mouth moved down to her throat, the sharp edges of his teeth grazing the delicate cords of her neck. 'You enjoy this?' he growled, and the deep velvet sound of it was like a stroke against her skin. 'Giving yourself to a Benedictus? To your father's enemy?'

Maybe it was wrong to find that so erotic, but she did. 'Yes,' she moaned again. 'I like it. I want more.'

He moved faster, harder, and she began to understand what he meant by roughness, because he wasn't gentle. His grip was almost painful. But she loved it. It made her feel strong that he didn't hold himself back. It made her feel powerful.

'More,' she repeated, turning it into a demand. 'Don't hold back from me, my king. I'm not as delicate as you think.'

He growled then, and before she could take another breath he pulled out of her, flipping her over onto her front. Then he gripped her hips hard and slid back inside her from behind, moving faster, harder, deeper.

Guinevere pressed her hot face into the pillow as pleasure drew into a tight knot inside her, the pressure almost unbearable. Then he slipped a finger beneath her, finding the most sensitive part of her, stroking firmly. And that hard, tight knot burst suddenly apart.

She screamed against the pillow as the orgasm crashed over her, and as she shook and shook she dimly felt him move faster, then fall out of rhythm, heard his own harsh roar of release in her ears.

She lay there for several stunned seconds, listened to both of them breathing hard. Then with firm hands he withdrew from her, before pulling her into the warmth of his body, turning her over onto her back and taking her chin between his fingers. His burning gaze swept over her, as if checking she was unharmed, before settling on her face.

'Did I hurt you?' he asked. 'Give me the truth, now, lioness.'

'No,' she said huskily, tremors still shaking her. 'Not at all.'

He said nothing for a long moment, and she was distracted by the dark shadows beneath his eyes, the lines around his mouth. He had been working hard. Perhaps too hard.

Without thinking, she reached up and touched his cheek. 'You look tired.'

'I am.' He made no move to avoid her touch, only stared down at her as if he couldn't look away. 'But I couldn't go to sleep because someone was already in my bed.'

The faint trace of humour in his voice was unexpected, and she smiled. 'Sorry. I thought the direct approach was better.'

'I'm not complaining.' He turned his head against her hand, brushing her fingertips with his mouth. 'You're very brave, though. To beard me in my den, so to speak. Especially after what I told you today.'

'I think your bark is worse than your bite.'

His eyes glinted wickedly. 'How can you know when I haven't bitten you yet?'

A delicious shiver ran through her. 'When you said that you like it rough…is biting a part of that?'

'Sometimes.' He leaned down and kissed her again. 'I meant what I said,' he murmured against her mouth. 'You will be in my bed every night, and you will be my wife in every way from now on. Do you understand?'

She sighed, the feel of his mouth on hers like a cold drink of water in a parched desert. 'Yes.'

He trailed kisses down her throat. 'And I will not divorce you. You will stay my queen from now on.'

Another sigh escaped her as, unbelievably, her body began to wake once more. 'Yes,' she repeated.

He lifted his mouth from hers, then took her hand, guiding it to the hard, flat plane of his stomach and down. His skin was hot, and it felt like satin, and she was once more hungry.

'Shall I show you the proper respect that a war prize should give to her king?'

Her mouth went dry as he wrapped her fingers around the rapidly hardening length of his shaft. 'P-please…'

So he showed her how to touch him, how to caress him—and, no, she didn't have to be gentle. She could be rough as she wanted. Then he guided her mouth to him, so she could worship him there, as he'd worshipped her, and she loved it.

He tasted good, and the feel of him in her mouth was good too, and when that got too much he pulled her up and lifted her, settling her down on him and showing her how to ride him.

In fact, he showed her many other things too, keeping her up well into the night. And she didn't even think about going to her little room, not once. Instead she fell asleep in his arms, exhausted.

CHAPTER SEVEN

THE LIMO DROVE slowly through the streets of Kasimir's capital city, with Tiberius gazing out through the windows at the crowds thronging the footpaths. They were cheering and waving Kasimiran flags, children were being lifted up by their parents to catch a glimpse of the King's car.

It was gratifying to find the people so excited to see him. Certainly his aides had mentioned that the mood of the country was high—far better than it had been when the Accorsis were in power, which pleased him.

Of course there was still much work to be done, but this public appearance—a tour of the city's main hospital—would be the start of many, and would hopefully provide the people with much-needed reassurance.

Guinevere sat beside him. She was in a yellow dress today, gauzy and pretty, wrapping around her curves lovingly, while her hair was piled on top of her head, with a couple of loose curls trailing around her ears.

She looked delicate and beautiful, like a splash of sunshine sitting beside him, and already anticipation was gathering tight inside him at the thought of showing this lovely, lovely woman to his subjects and introducing her as his new queen.

There would no doubt be some trepidation about the

fact that she was an Accorsi, and he'd already anticipated that, but they would soon come to see that she was nothing like her father.

He knew that now for the truth, having spent the past week with her.

It had been a revelation.

He'd still been working every hour, closeted with his advisors and talking over things like taxes and elections, but every night he'd found himself hurrying back to the royal apartments and to Guinevere.

She slept in his bed every night, in his arms, languorous and sated as a cat after hours of extremely satisfying sex. She was passionate and curious, responsive and generous, and he'd never had a lover like her. It seemed the more he had of her, the more he wanted, and he certainly had no regrets about his decision to keep her as his wife.

Not that they'd spoken about the future of their marriage. He simply hadn't had the time. And in the hours he did spend with her he preferred to pursue their physical hunger for each other over anything else.

She hadn't argued, seemingly as hungry for him as he was for her.

A couple of days earlier she'd asked him if he'd have some time to talk about her role as queen, but he hadn't yet followed that up. There always seemed to be more important, more vital things to do.

He glanced at her now, assessing her. She was looking out of the window too, her cheeks a little pale, her hands clasped tightly in her lap, lines of tension around her eyes.

Reaching out, he took one of her hands in his. Her fingertips were cold. 'Nervous?' he asked softly.

She glanced away from the window and back at him. 'Yes, a little.'

'What about?'

'Oh…the crowds. I haven't ever been among so many people at one time. And also…' She let out a breath. 'I'm an Accorsi.'

The protective urge he felt whenever he was around her stirred again, and he squeezed her hand gently in re-assurance. 'I will allow no one to hurt you, remember?' He put the force of all his considerable authority behind the words. 'And I will allow no one to show you any dis-respect. You are my queen and I expect everyone to treat you accordingly.'

She looked down at where her hand was enclosed by his. 'I don't feel like your queen,' she said. 'I feel like your dirty little secret.'

The comment came out of the blue, and for a moment he could only stare at her in surprise. 'What? What makes you say that?'

She didn't reply immediately, still staring at her hands. Then she sighed. 'Sorry, I didn't mean it to come out sounding that way. It's just… You're not around during the day, and I only see you at night, only in bed. And we don't talk. We just have sex.'

He frowned. 'Is that a problem?'

'Yes. I would like to talk to you, Tiberius. I want to know what kind of marriage we're going to have—es-pecially since you were so demanding about it before we slept together. And I want to know what kind of role I'll have in the palace, because at the moment I don't have one.'

He was conscious then of a slight shock—because these were things he hadn't considered. He'd been so consumed with getting his country in order that he hadn't had the time to consider anything personal.

'I sent an aide to you yesterday,' he pointed out—because he had. 'To prepare you for today's appearance.'

'Yes, you did,' she allowed. 'But...'

Annoyance was starting to creep through him—mostly at himself for not sparing a moment to think about her. 'But what?' he asked, trying not to let his irritation show. 'I have had a great deal to manage, Guinevere. Naturally I apologise if I've neglected you, but the wellbeing of my country takes precedence.'

She looked at him for a long moment, then abruptly pulled her hand from his. 'I'm not asking you to ignore the wellbeing of Kasimir. In fact, I want to be a part of helping you rebuild it. But I don't know how to be a queen and I don't know what's required. I don't know what your plans for the future are, or what my place is in that future.' Her chin came up. 'It feels as if you're ashamed of me.'

Tiberius was conscious of not a little astonishment. 'Ashamed of you?' he repeated. 'Why would I be ashamed of you?'

'Because I'm an Accorsi,' Guinevere said. 'Because I'm sheltered and I don't know anything. Because I'm not—'

Tiberius laid a gentle finger over her soft mouth, silencing her. 'I'm not ashamed of you,' he said. 'I married you *because* you were an Accorsi. Because I wanted Kasimir to be whole, not divided.'

That hot blue flame of her temper had begun to burn in her eyes and she reached up, gripped his wrist and pulled his finger away. 'I don't want to be a symbol, Tiberius. I want to do something. I've spent years being trapped in that damn palace, and if I'm to be your queen I need to know how. I already know what it's like to be forgotten and I'm tired of it.'

Then, as if to emphasise her point, she nipped the end of his finger, sending a bolt of white heat through him and making his breath catch.

'If you do not wish to give our people a ringside seat for what I do to you at night,' he growled, 'I would advise against doing things like that.'

She dropped his hand, but gave him an unrepentant look. 'If you want your war prize ready, willing and eager every night, then I would advise giving me something to do.'

Stubborn little Accorsi!

She's not wrong.

Looked at from her point of view, that was of course how she would see it. And, no, she wasn't wrong. He hadn't given her any time this past week, nor spared her a thought beyond what they did in bed together. Of course there were things they needed to discuss, he just…

You just don't want to think about her. You don't want to think about another person's needs.

And how could he when the needs of his subjects mattered more? Then again, if she was to be his queen, then not teaching her what she needed to know was shortsighted. Especially if she could help him in his endeavours. He wasn't used to sharing the burden, it was true, but that wasn't because he didn't want to share it with someone.

He met her gaze and held it. 'I see your point. For the record, I am genuinely *not* ashamed of you, little lioness. I have just been very busy with trying to fix everything that is broken in Kasimir—and there is so much that is broken.'

The sparks of her temper faded, her blue gaze turning softer. 'I know,' she said quietly. 'I do know that. But the state Kasimir is in is not your fault, Tiberius. You understand that, don't you?'

Another little shock went through him, as if she'd somehow found a vulnerable place inside him. 'I know that,' he said tersely, sounding far more defensive than he wished. 'Of course it isn't my fault. Why would you think I believe that?'

She ignored his tone. 'Because of the way you're trying to fix it. As if you alone are responsible for it.'

'But isn't it my responsibility? I am the King. It is my job to protect and care for my subjects.' And before he could stop himself, he added, 'If it hadn't taken me so long to reclaim the crown, there wouldn't have been—'

'No,' Guinevere interrupted, gently but very firmly. 'You can't think that. My father stole the crown and he is to blame for what happened—not you. Also, you can't take the burden of repairing an entire country upon yourself. That's ridiculous. Besides, how can you take care of anyone else if you don't take care of yourself?'

'I don't need taking care of,' he said, again far too tersely.

'Of course you do,' she disagreed. 'You're working yourself to the bone and everyone else around you too. The burden can be shared, you know.'

It was as if she'd reached inside his head and plucked out that very thought.

Of course it could be shared. Except no one had ever offered to do so because they were worried about *him*… as if *his* wellbeing mattered to them. His father had made sure he was fed and clothed, and had taught him all he needed to know about being a king. But his father hadn't been concerned for Tiberius himself. All that had been important was being strong enough to take the crown and then to take responsibility for the country. His own wellbeing had always come last.

'I do not matter,' he said. 'Only Kasimir does.'

Guinevere's deep blue eyes were soft. 'You do matter,' she said quietly. 'You matter to me.'

That softness, the way she was looking at him, rubbed against a raw place inside him—a place he hadn't thought was vulnerable. 'Why should you care?' he demanded, unable to keep the edge out of his voice. 'You barely know me.'

'Why should I care?' she repeated, her eyes widening in surprise. 'Because I'm your wife and your queen and because someone has to, Tiberius. You can't do this all on your own.'

He wasn't sure why he wanted to argue with her—tell her that he'd been doing this all on his own since his father had died and he'd succeeded very well, thank you very much. He wasn't sure, either, why there was a curious leaden feeling in his gut…as if he'd wanted her to say something else, though what, he didn't know.

Right then, though, the limo came to a stop outside the hospital and it was time for them to get out.

'I am not doing this on my own,' he said curtly. 'Now it's your turn to help.'

Guinevere's mouth had gone dry and her stomach was unsettled with nerves. The conversation with Tiberius had distracted her from the upcoming appearance, but unfortunately it hadn't made her feel any more settled.

She'd spent the past week roaming around the palace, familiarising herself with going outside, as well as looking up on a computer all the articles about the state of Kasimir she could find, and then looking in vain for aides who could give her information about what she was supposed to be doing.

She'd hoped Tiberius would give her some time so she could discuss with him her thoughts, but he'd been incommunicado for most of the week. Busy, his aides would tell her. His Majesty had no time to spare.

Except for the nights, of course, when he had plenty of time to spare, and when all discussions fell by the way-side in favour of the physical pleasure they could give one another. She had only herself to blame for that, she supposed, but he made her feel so good, and it was easier in the end to let her body do the talking.

As the week had gone on she'd started to feel more and more annoyed with both herself and him, but it wasn't until now, when she had him for a length of time out of the bedroom, that she'd thought she might as well take advantage of that.

She hadn't meant to sound so cross, but that had been her nerves talking. But then, when he'd told her about his responsibilities, all her annoyance at him had just leaked away.

Because all it had taken was one look into his fierce silver gaze to see that he believed utterly that, being the King, it was his responsibility to repair the country and his alone. That he cared about it and cared very deeply. That he worried for his subjects. That the length of time it had taken for him to get rid of the tyrants ate at him. And whether he knew it or not, some part of him must blame himself for that. Otherwise why would he be so impatient to fix everything?

It made her feel petty for being angry with him at not

giving her any time—but, petty or not, the fact remained that there were things they needed to discuss.

Also, she wanted to help. Kasimir was her country too, and if she was going to be its queen she wanted to be a practical one, not a mere figurehead. Her father had nearly run the country into the ground, therefore it was her responsibility to fix it as well as Tiberius's.

Being with him, telling him what she wanted, had given her courage, and she didn't want to go back to hiding safely in the walls of the palace any more—even though she might be nervous about what the people would think of her.

Those nerves were certainly making themselves felt now, as the limo door opened, letting in the noise and the cheering of the crowd.

Tiberius got out first, the cheers rising in volume as he appeared, and no wonder.

He wore a dark suit today, with a plain white shirt and a silvery grey silk tie that set his eyes off to perfection. He was astonishingly charismatic, and she couldn't help but watch him, mesmerised, as he acknowledged the crowds, a smile turning his beautiful mouth.

She shivered, unable to help herself, still tasting the salt from his skin where she'd nipped him. She shouldn't have done it, but she hadn't been able to resist, because he was irresistible. Even when she was arguing with him she wanted to touch him, kiss him. Wanted to be close to him.

He turned back to the limo and his dark head bent as he leaned down to offer her his hand. And then she was being drawn out of the car to stand beside him, the roar of the crowd in her ears.

It was almost overwhelming, the number of people and the noise, and she didn't know quite where to look—

especially when she heard a couple of boos in amongst all the cheering. A few people were even carrying signs that had derogatory statements about her family on them.

She couldn't blame those people, but it made her feel anxious. Not so much that they would hurt her, but that her presence at Tiberius's side would damage his political standing as King. Yes, marrying her would show his willingness to move on as a whole country rather than as one divided, and that was a good thing, but there would always be those who would view that as a betrayal.

Abruptly, the thought of her presence undermining his rule made her feel afraid. Although he hadn't told her anything about his life in exile, she had got the impression that it had been a hard and long journey back to his crown, and certainly the time and effort he'd put into his first week as King could not be understated.

She hoped her presence wouldn't put all that work at risk.

Why would you care?

Good question. But it was one she knew the answer to, and one she'd given to him already. He mattered to her. And whether that was because of the sex or something else, she didn't know. But matter to her he did.

His hand was warm around hers, and he didn't let it go as she came to stand beside him. So when he moved over to where some of the crowds were standing behind the barriers she had no choice but to follow him.

Had he heard the people booing her? Had he seen those signs?

'Don't be afraid,' he murmured in her ear, showing her that, yes, indeed, he had seen the signs. 'They are only a small proportion of this crowd and they do not know you.'

'I don't want to undermine you,' she whispered back. 'And I'm afraid my presence here will.'

He paused for a moment, in full view of the crowd, though she was pretty sure no one could actually hear them.

'Your presence undermines nothing.' His gaze was fierce. 'You are strong and beautiful and brave—everything our people require in a queen. So show them, my little lioness. Show them what kind of queen they are getting.'

He had taken to calling her that whenever she lay in his arms, and she liked it a lot. She liked the conviction in his eyes too. He wasn't a man for idle words, and he meant what he said when he said it.

The way he looked at her made her feel as if she was every one of those things, and the nerves in her stomach settled. And so, obeying an impulse she hadn't seen coming, she went on her toes and kissed him in front of the crowd.

The cheers were almost deafening as she came back down on her feet, and when she looked up into his face and saw the look of shock there she smiled at him. Then, gripping hard to her courage, she approached the crowd, smiling at them too, speaking a few words to some of the people.

A little girl pushed some flowers into her hands and said breathlessly, 'You're so pretty!' And another young woman wanted a selfie.

Tiberius joined her, and together they moved towards the hospital entrance, pausing to speak to as many people as they could.

By the time they got through the hospital doors Guinevere was breathless. Her face hurt from smiling, and she felt energised in a way she'd never felt before.

It might only have been a small proportion of the population here today, but there had been more who'd welcomed her than who hadn't, and it had been wonderful.

For so long she'd felt powerless and alone, but here, at Tiberius's side, she didn't feel like his dirty little secret now. She felt like his queen.

This is how you can make a difference. This is how you can right the wrongs done to you and your country. This is how you can defeat the ghosts of your father and your brothers.

Determination settled inside her as they were introduced to the hospital management. She was an Accorsi, and while what had happened to her country hadn't been her fault, or Tiberius's, it was something she wanted to fix, nevertheless. It was right that an Accorsi should help to put right all the wrongs. It was how it should be. And she wasn't going to be put off by Tiberius any longer.

Tonight she wasn't going to let him sequester himself away with his aides. She was going to demand they discuss all things to do with their marriage, and then she was going to join him in his meetings.

And she was not going to take no for an answer.

The hospital visit was appalling in some ways, because it made clear the depth of underfunding for critical health services. But it was good for both her and Tiberius to know, because once they did they could do all they could to fix it.

The visit took up most of the day, and by the time they got back to the palace it was close to evening. As they got out of the limo, Tiberius said, 'I have a meeting to attend. I don't know what time—'

'No,' she interrupted, looking at him stubbornly. 'That can wait. The meeting you have to attend is one with me.'

He frowned. 'It is to discuss taxation. That will end up funding the hospital we just saw, which desperately needs the money.'

Guinevere let out a breath. 'There will always be something more important, Tiberius. The taxation discussion can wait for at least one hour, can't it?'

He regarded her silently for a moment. 'Very well,' he said at last. 'I can spare you an hour.'

They retired to his office, with Tiberius pausing outside the door to ask for some food to be brought to them, since they hadn't eaten since the lunch the hospital had put on.

Then he gestured for Guinevere to come in, before shutting the door firmly behind them.

'Very well,' he said, coming to stand in front of the fireplace, his muscular arms folded. 'You want a discussion…so let us discuss.'

He looked forbidding standing there, and very stern. The smile she'd seen him give to so many people today was absent now. He didn't want to be here, she could tell, and she could almost sense the tightly leashed impatient energy crackling around his tall figure.

He still looked tired, and unexpectedly her heart ached. He was so driven. It couldn't be easy to think that you were ultimately responsible for an entire country, and to be so conscious of it with every passing second. He could afford some time here and there just for himself, couldn't he?

Then another thought struck her. If he didn't look after himself, who was there to do it for him? Who did he have to turn to when things were hard? Who did he talk to honestly and openly? Did he have anyone he trusted? Anyone at all?

You know he doesn't.

Oh, she knew that. She knew all too well. Just as she knew what it was like to be lonely. To have no one. She'd had no one for so very long and it had been so very difficult.

Perhaps if he truly had no one she could be that person for him?

All of a sudden she wanted to be. She very much wanted to be.

'When was the last time you had a break?' she asked.

His black brows drew down. 'A break? What do you mean by "a break"?'

'A holiday, Tiberius. Time off to relax.'

'A holiday?' he echoed, repeating the words as if they were in a foreign language. 'You think that I have time for...holidays?'

'I think you tell yourself you don't have time for them. But be honest. How long have you been working for Kasimir without a break?'

CHAPTER EIGHT

TIBERIUS STOOD IN FRONT of the fireplace, his arms folded across his chest, staring at his wife, who was staring back as she stood in a patch of late-afternoon sunlight looking as if she glowed from within.

She'd been remarkable today. Yes, she'd been nervous, but when she'd stepped out of the limo and had joined him on a walkabout with the crowd she'd been…amazing. Warm and open and approachable, radiating her beautiful smile.

He'd seen the signs of a few dissenters within the crowd, had heard them booing her. As he'd told her, they were only a small percentage, and even though he'd burned to do something incredibly inappropriate, such as punching them in the face, he'd controlled himself and ignored them instead.

He'd appreciated her sharing her worries with him, about how her presence might undermine what he was trying to do, but she needn't be concerned.

While she might be an Accorsi, she was one who wasn't known to the world's press, and thus there was no gossip about her. No rumours. No hidden videos or toxicity that might rear its ugly head online at the worst possible time.

There was only her, beautiful in her yellow dress, her

smile like the promise of summer on a cold winter day. She was honest and open, not a shred of darkness in her.

As his queen, she was perfect.

Really, he shouldn't begrudge her this time she wanted for a discussion, since if she wanted to take an active part in ruling they would need to talk about it. But this mention of holidays...

What on earth was she talking about? Who could think of breaks or holidays when they had a country to run? A country where people had suffered and were suffering still?

A holiday implied personal whim, and Giancarlo had been very clear that kings did not indulge in personal whims. There was no rest for a king. Responsibility was a heavy weight that had to be endured.

'I have been working for Kasimir since the day I was born,' he said severely. 'My mother died in the coup— you know this, yes?'

She nodded slowly. 'I do know. I'm sorry that—'

'It's not your fault. She died before you were born. Renzo's guards shot her as she was escaping with my father, and to save me he had to leave her behind.'

Her eyes darkened. 'That's awful.'

'Your father didn't offer her any medical help so she bled to death.' He hadn't meant for the words to sound so stark, especially when an expression that looked like pain crossed her features. But he didn't take them back. That was what had happened—no more and certainly no less.

'That must have been dreadful,' she said softly.

He shrugged, ignoring the pain that sat inside him. 'I don't remember her, but certainly doing the best for Kasimir that I can is how I will make her and my father's sacrifice worth it.'

She nodded slowly. 'And then you went into exile with your father?'

'Yes, we escaped into Italy. But I did not have a normal childhood. My responsibilities were made clear to me before I'd even started school.'

Her brow creased. 'Did no one help you? Did no one…?'

'What? Interfere politically with a tiny European nation? No, no one helped. And, no, my father didn't take me on holiday anywhere. He was of the opinion that a king has no personal life. He is a servant of his people and they come before him every time.'

Her gaze flickered briefly at that, but all she said was, 'So…what? You've been training to be a king all this time?'

'Of course. Did you think I just strolled into the palace the day we met? No, my father and I had to find supporters, work to raise funds, and then get sympathisers from within Kasimir itself, because we didn't want a civil war.'

'So…you never had a chance just to be a boy?'

There was something soft in her eyes that felt dangerous, though he wasn't sure why.

'No. People were dying here. People were suffering. There was no time "just to be a boy".'

She took a small step towards him. 'When will it end, Tiberius? This concern? This frantic need to fix everything?'

What strange questions she was asking him. Questions she should know the answers to if she thought long enough about them.

'It won't ever end,' he said. 'People will always suffer and something will always be broken. The responsibility of a king is a burden without end.'

That soft expression on her face deepened, and it looked like concern. 'But,' she murmured, 'is there any time in all of that for yourself? For joy? For happiness?'

Joy. Happiness.

He couldn't remember ever feeling either of those emotions. Maybe once, when he was a child, lying on his back looking at the stars, he'd felt something akin to them. But it had been so long ago now he couldn't remember what they felt like. And anyway, he'd managed well enough without them so far. Why would he need them now? Why should he have them when some of his subjects could not?

He'd always been cognisant of the fact that his life was not his own and never had been. He was the son of a dispossessed king. His mother had given up her own life for him. And then his father had died of cancer, five years ago, and now he had to make those deaths meaningful. He had been saved for a reason, his father had told him from his hospital bed, just before he'd died. And that reason was to restore the crown, help the people of Kasimir.

'No,' he said impatiently. 'Why should I have either of those when many of my subjects do not? I have power, Guinevere, and I do not take that lightly. Nor can I rest on it. The work is always there and must always be done— so, no, there can be no rest from it.'

She swallowed, a flicker of what looked like anguish crossing her features. 'Is that what our marriage will be, then?' she asked quietly. 'You working until midnight every night and then rising at dawn the next day? Where is there time for children in that? Where is there time for a marriage? A life?'

Something caught at his heart then, giving a small, painful tug. 'There will be time for children,' he said, ignoring it. 'I will have a schedule and they'll be looked after. We will engage the services of a nanny, naturally.'

'But what about time as a family?' She was searching his face as if looking for something. 'Surely there will be time for that?'

'Not at the expense of the work I must do for Kasimir.' He was getting impatient now, because these conversations weren't important right now—couldn't she see that? They could be had later. 'Our family will not look like those of other people because we are a royal family,' he added. 'As I said, our purpose is to serve our country, not vice versa.'

'So, what you're saying is that there is no time for any kind of personal happiness?' she said, an edge in her voice now. 'No time for joy?'

'You may have joy and happiness.' He was holding on to his patience by a thread. 'I am not saying you can't have that. But you need to understand that the lives of rulers are hard ones, contrary to what most people think. It is our cross to bear and our privilege.'

A strange expression crossed her face, one that he couldn't interpret. 'That seems very bleak.'

'Struggle is the anvil we temper ourselves upon,' he said, quoting his father's favourite line. 'And my father gave me plenty of struggle to help prepare me for my role.'

'He didn't…?' She stopped, pain in her voice.

Tiberius knew what she was asking, though. 'No,' he said, this time softening his tone. 'He was never cruel. But he expected a lot from me, and I admit there were times when it was…difficult.' He paused a moment, wanting to give her something that wasn't as bleak, because he was sure it actually hadn't been as terrible as all that. 'Sometimes, as a child, I had difficulty sleeping, so I'd get up and go outside, lie down in the grass to watch the stars. It was…peaceful.'

'That's the only good thing you remember?'

He stared back at her. 'Why does it matter that there were good things? My father did what he had to—which was to put his country first by training me, so my mother's death wouldn't be for nothing.'

She held his gaze a moment, then looked away. 'It just sounds hard,' she said after a moment.

'It was hard,' he agreed. 'But life is not meant to be easy. You yourself know this already, Guinevere. It isn't as if you had an ideal childhood either.'

He wasn't sure why she seemed to find his past quite so painful, especially in comparison to the prison of hers.

'No, I didn't.' She glanced down at the floor. 'My brothers were not…kind.'

Tiberius frowned at the catch in her voice. He hadn't wanted to press her about exactly what her brothers had done to her, but now he couldn't stop himself from asking, 'What did they do, lioness?'

She looked wordlessly at him then, blue eyes dark.

'You don't have to tell me,' he went on. 'Not if you don't want to.'

And he meant it. He found he didn't want to cause her any unnecessary pain.

She stayed silent for a long time, and he thought that maybe she wouldn't, but then she said, 'It…doesn't sound bad…not compared to what some people have to suffer, but… They terrified me and I think they…liked that. They used to h-hunt me in the hallways—that's what they called it, Hunt the Mouse—just to scare me. And they pulled my hair, broke my toys, pushed me into walls, and once Alessio gave me a black eye.'

Tiberius was almost stupefied by a hot rush of fury so intense he could hardly keep still. He'd not heard any rumours about Renzo's sons, but this wasn't a rumour. This was the truth, he could hear the ring of it in her voice.

They'd *hunted* her. *Terrified* her. And all for fun, by the sounds of it.

He'd never wanted to hurt anyone as badly as he wanted to hurt her brothers.

'And your father?' he forced out, his voice hoarse with fury. 'What did he do about it?'

She shook her head. 'Nothing. He indulged them… told me that's what brothers did.'

'Guinevere,' he said roughly, taking a step towards her to take her hand, offer her something—he didn't know what.

But then she lifted her head and looked at him, her blue eyes clear. 'I hid from them in the end, because that was safer, and then they forgot about me. It wasn't all bad, though—and I mean that. I had moments of happiness. Reading good books in my little room. Listening to music. Watching movies. Learning about the outside world. I just loved that.'

He could see her as little girl. Long golden curls and wide blue eyes alight with the same joy he'd seen when he'd showed her the orchard. Her ready laugh and her smile, despite what she'd been through.

She was made for joy, he thought suddenly. Standing there in her yellow dress, she was made for sunshine and summer and moments of happiness.

You cannot give her that. You will never give her that.

The thought came out of nowhere, startling him, pulling at something painful inside him. It was true. He couldn't give her that. He barely even recognised happiness, let alone would be able to give it to her.

Yet you have tied her to you for ever.

That painful thing tugged harder, and he almost growled at it. Yes, he *had* made the decision to keep her—and he didn't regret it. She was a strong woman. She would find her own happiness, her own joy. It didn't have to come from him. That was one of the downsides of marrying a king: the work always had to come first. He'd given her a choice, anyway. She hadn't had to choose to stay married to him.

A part of him told him snidely that that was specious reasoning, but he didn't want to dig into it any further. It was what it was.

'Well,' he said, when she didn't say anything more, 'is there something else you wish to discuss?'

She stared at him a moment longer, then said, 'I want to take part in your meetings. If I am to be your queen, then I want to be more than just a symbol to the people. I want to actually do something.'

She had mentioned something similar in the limo that morning, and he'd found her desire to be involved admirable.

You will need to spend time with her, teaching her.

He didn't have the time to show her personally, but he could spare an aide to show her the ropes.

'Of course,' he said. 'I will have someone come to you tomorrow morning, if you like. They can spend some time with you and—'

'No,' Guinevere interrupted, for the second time that day. 'I don't want one of your aides. I want you to do it.'

By the set of Tiberius's mouth and the flash of temper in his silver eyes Guinevere knew that he didn't like that idea at all. But that was too bad. If that was the only way she could get her husband out of his meetings and spending time with her, then that was what she'd do.

The idea had come to her as they'd discussed his utter disdain for holidays. Not that she'd expected anything else—especially given what he'd said about his father driving him and his mother's death. She felt sorry for that little boy whose only peace had been looking at the stars. Such a heavy burden to put on his shoulders.

It made her understand him a little bit better, though. Gave her some insight into why he was so driven, why everything was of such vital importance, and why he had to be the one to fix it.

He was inured to fighting now, to struggle—she could see it in his eyes just as clearly as she saw his weariness.

He didn't know what joy was, what happiness was, either. And for some reason that hurt. He was a prickly, driven man, who desperately needed some kind of surcease. More than what she gave him in bed, certainly.

Perhaps she shouldn't have told him about what her brothers had done to her, because that hadn't helped—she hadn't missed the hot leap of rage in his gaze in response. But he'd called her lioness, and that had made her brave, and while he might not have been aware of it, telling him the truth had been a gift of trust. And he'd reined in his protector's rage, not burdening her with it.

He didn't know what he'd given her—didn't know why being able to tell him and not suffer any judgment was important. She wasn't sure he'd want to hear it anyway. But she wanted to give him something in return. If not happiness, then peace. Rest. A moment of lightness amidst the hard grind of his work.

But she was going to have to teach him. She knew it deep inside. Because if she didn't, this was what the shape of her marriage would be. Seeing him at night only, with his country constantly taking and taking from him. It wasn't the kind of marriage that people had in the books she'd read, and it certainly wasn't the kind of marriage she wanted to bring her children up in.

Why do you want that with him, though?

Because she'd married him. No, he hadn't given her much of a choice in the beginning, but he'd given it to her the night they'd first slept together. She'd told herself then, in a haze of desire, that she was fine with that—and she was still fine with it. But she was starting to want more. More of him. A chance to dig beneath the surface of the King and find the passionate man who lost himself in her arms every night.

And there was more there—she could sense it. He was like a fire burning in a cosy room and she was only looking at it through the window. She wanted to get closer to that fire…see how hot it really burned.

And even if those concerns were for herself, there were also potential children to consider. She wanted to give them a better childhood than the one she'd had, and certainly better than what Tiberius's father had given him. Was that really too much to ask?

So, yes, she would have to teach him what joy and happiness looked like, and she'd likely have to do it by stealth. She'd have to make him give her some time every day, and if she couched it in terms of it being for Kasimir's aid then surely he couldn't say no.

'No,' said Tiberius shortly. 'I do not have the time.'

'I'm not asking for much. A couple of hours every day. Perhaps in the morning, when we wake up, or at night before bed?'

'Like I said—'

'It has to be you, Tiberius,' she said insistently. 'You're so passionate about Kasimir and none of your aides could teach me about being a queen better than you could. We have to rule together, remember? So wouldn't it be best for you to show me how you do it, so I can match you?'

His gaze narrowed, clearly looking for reasons to disagree, but she knew he couldn't argue with her last statement. After all, there *was* no one more passionate about Kasimir than he was, and if there was one thing she knew about him, it was that he was a control freak.

Perhaps he just doesn't want to spend time with you.

The thought made a sharp sliver of glass slide under her skin, cutting her in a way she hadn't been expecting, but she ignored it. If he didn't, he didn't—but she was going to make him give her this despite that. This wasn't about her and her needs. It was about him.

'A couple of hours...' he murmured, still eyeing her narrowly. 'That's not nearly enough time to learn how to be a queen. It took me many years before I fully grasped what being King meant.'

'Yes, it might take time,' she allowed. 'But I'll learn more directly from you than anyone else. Also, I could get further instruction from your aides when you're busy.' She gave him a sunny smile. 'I'm a quick study. I've been reading all I can about Kasimir—all the things that my father didn't tell me—so I'm familiar with its difficulties.'

He said nothing, still looking at her as if he was debating.

Guinevere moved over to him and placed her hands on his broad chest, loving the feel of him beneath her palms. He really was the most eminently touchable man... 'If you like,' she murmured, 'we could do it bed in the mornings. Or, if you'd prefer, before we retire at night.' She looked up at him from beneath her lashes. 'There must be more I need to learn about how to show proper respect for my king.'

As she'd hoped, the silver flames she'd become addicted to ignited, burned suddenly and intensely in his eyes. She really was getting the hang of flirting with him.

'Perhaps,' he said, his voice hot and rough. 'Perhaps there are…certain things I can teach you.'

Guinevere rose up on her toes and pressed her mouth gently to his. A soft, butterfly kiss. 'I'm sure you can, Your Majesty,' she whispered. 'I can hardly wait.'

His hands settled on her hips, holding her close. 'How about I give you a few tips now? Here?'

A shiver ran through her. He was never physically demanding outside of the bedroom. He would be absent all day and only at night would her take her, often in a wild rush, as if his desire was a river he kept behind a dam and only at night would he open the floodgates.

It felt intoxicating to ignite his passion this way…to make him forget his never-ending workload with only a kiss.

'I thought you had more important things to do?' she said, teasing just a little. 'Taxation, I think you mentioned.'

He frowned, his gaze dipping to her mouth and back up again. She could feel him hardening against her, and the hot press of his body made her feel dizzy, as if she'd had too much champagne far too quickly.

'That can wait for a few minutes.'

A few minutes…

At night, when finally the day was done and they came together in bed, it was a flash fire. But they never indulged in any lazy aftermath, any idle conversation.

Never simply enjoyed being together. He would take what he wanted, give her what she wanted, and then, inevitably, he would fall asleep. Because he was exhausted.

It would be like that now, she knew. They would take their pleasure, and it would be quick, hurried and intense, and then he would leave for yet another meeting, likely not coming back to bed until much later that night.

You are giving him everything he wants and he is giving you nothing in return.

That wasn't quite true. He gave her as much pleasure as she could handle, and then some. He wasn't a selfish lover by any stretch of the imagination. But she was starting to realise she wanted more than mere physical release. She wanted his time too.

Her own body was starting to wake, her hunger for him building, but she forced it away. He'd always been demanding about his own needs, but now it was time to give him a taste of his own medicine.

Guinevere reached down to where his hands gripped her hips and gently but firmly removed them. Then she forced herself to step back, her heart beating uncomfortably fast. 'No,' she said. 'I want more than just a few minutes.'

She had never denied him before, and it was gratifying to see his temper flare, a bright burst of silver. It made her aware of her own power to affect him, and that was satisfying too.

'What do you mean, more than a few minutes?' His voice was calm, but a muscle jumped in the side of his strong jaw.

'I mean exactly that.' She stepped back again. 'I don't want a few hurried minutes of pleasure.'

The muscle at the side of his jaw leapt again, the lines

of his face growing tight with annoyance. 'We will have tonight also.'

'You mean with you falling asleep because you're exhausted?' She shook her head. 'I want more than that, Tiberius, and I think you owe it to me. I've given you everything you asked for. I haven't denied you a thing. So don't you think it's time for me to ask something of you?'

'I've just agreed to give you a couple of hours—'

'To teach me about being a queen, yes. I'm talking about us being together as husband and wife. Not me being the mistress you come to every night and leave before she wakes up every morning.'

He did not like that, it was clear. His whole body was tense. His hands had dropped to his sides and were clenched into fists. A week ago the signs of his anger would have terrified her, but since then she'd discovered the steel inside her—and besides, she knew he'd never hurt her.

'Guinevere,' he said roughly. 'You…make me unable to think. I cannot concentrate on anything else when you kiss me. How can I be expected to give the taxation system the proper amount of attention when all I can think about is taking you to bed?'

It was heady, having this power over him. In fact, it was surprising how much she liked it.

She smiled at him. 'I'm sure you'll think of something.'

His expression darkened. 'I do not appreciate you using sex to manipulate me.'

Sometimes she could tease him and sometimes she couldn't. Now was clearly one of the times she couldn't.

'I'm not trying to manipulate you,' she said, letting her smile fade to show him how serious she was. 'Marriage is a two-way street. This whole time it's been about you, and now I want something for me. I want to feel like a wife, not a mistress.'

'You already are a wife.'

'Yes, but you don't treat me like one,' she said firmly. 'I'm not your partner—I'm your comfort object. Your toy. You play with me when you feel like it, then put me away when you're done. I'm tired of it, Tiberius. You were the one who wanted to marry me, so I married you. Now I'm saying I want our marriage to be more than sex at night and public appearances.'

His gaze was fierce, his temper flaming, but she only stared back at him.

She wasn't afraid of him and she wasn't afraid of his temper. He would never do anything to hurt her, never do anything she didn't want. She knew that. In fact, the thing she was perhaps a little anxious about was that he might do something she *did* want—in which case her determination not to give in on this point might be undermined.

But he didn't move. Then like a door being shut on a fire, the heat in his gaze vanished, the light, crystalline grey becoming frosty.

'Very well,' he said, his tone as cool as his gaze. 'Perhaps we can discuss this during your instruction.'

Then, before she could say another word, he turned on his heel and went out.

CHAPTER NINE

TIBERIUS WENT TO his taxation meeting angry, and as he'd feared he found it difficult to concentrate. His body refused to go back to sleep, his hunger for his wife invading his every thought. He couldn't let his mind wander—not even for a second. Because if he did, it would return to the feel of her against him, the warmth of her hips beneath his palms. The soft brush of her mouth against his.

The determination in her blue eyes as she refused him.

He was beginning to both love and hate that determination of hers.

Love it because she was stubborn, and there was a strength in her that he found both fascinating and devastatingly attractive.

Hate it because he couldn't argue with her about the way he was treating her.

He *was* using her like a mistress or a toy. Coming to her at night, hungry and desperate for the sweet oblivion only she could give him, and then falling asleep in her arms. He'd never slept so well as in the past couple of weeks with her. But he always woke before she did, and then he'd leave the bed, driven by his need to keep progressing with his country's rebuild.

She wanted more than that from him. And, given the terrible childhood she'd suffered at the hands of her father and brothers, she deserved more. But he wasn't sure he could give her more. There was only so much of him to go around, and Kasimir needed him more than she did.

Still, her denial shouldn't have put him in such a vile temper. It was only sex, and he'd always been able to control his urges with ease. Except he was still furious about it. And he wasn't sure why.

Maybe it was about her demanding his time to teach her about being a queen—time he could ill afford. Then again, he hadn't liked the idea of someone else handling it. What she'd said about it being in his interest to do the teaching himself made sense—really, who better to teach her about being a queen than her king?

You like the idea. Admit it.

That was true. The idea of teaching her, spending a couple of hours a day in her presence that weren't about sex was…attractive. And he was curious about what kind of queen she would make. He had his own ideas about that, but he wanted to see if he was right.

He thought about it all evening, and as usual went to bed late that night, his body already waking, coming to aching, hungry life in anticipation of the pleasure to come.

But when he pushed open the door to his bedroom there was no sweet scent lingering in the air, and no warm, silky little body in his bed.

It was clear that she had gone elsewhere to sleep, and though he told himself it was her right, and that he wouldn't go searching for her, it was hours before he finally slept. Even giving himself relief didn't help. It was as if some part of him was still hungry for her. A part that had nothing to do with his need for sex. A part that wanted more.

The next morning he rose at dawn and spent yet another day in meetings, still trying and failing to get his new wife out of his head.

At midday an aide approached him with a message from the Queen, reminding him that he'd promised to give her a couple of hours of his time and that she'd be waiting for him in the orchard that afternoon.

He had no idea why she'd chosen the orchard, and knew he'd made her no such promises, yet when the hour approached he found himself watching the clock, felt his body gathering itself in anticipation, his heartbeat accelerating.

Ludicrous to feel this way about a meeting with his wife. And yet no matter how ludicrous he told himself it was, that didn't stop his excitement from building. Or stop him from excusing himself when the time came with far more alacrity that he should have.

He made his way quickly to the orchard—it was a gorgeous, sun-drenched day—and found her sitting under the orange tree he'd pushed her against the week before, on a rug spread out over the grass. She was in one of her pretty dresses, this one loose and floaty, the colour of fresh lavender. The front of her blonde curls had been tied back, the rest flowing down her back, and she looked so lovely and delicate and fairy-like that his heart almost stopped beating.

She was in the process of laying out food from a basket, and when she sensed his presence she looked up and gave him the sunniest, most devastatingly pretty smile. His heart, in fact, did stop.

'I hope you're hungry,' she said. 'I had the kitchen put together some afternoon tea for a picnic.'

His muscles tensed and he felt obscurely angry for

some reason—as if her sitting there, pretty as a picture, with a delicious picnic all around her, was an affront. Maybe it was. Because, deep inside him, the part of him that had missed her the night before wanted nothing more than to sit on the rug and enjoy her picnic.

But he couldn't. It felt wrong. His mother hadn't died for him so that he could sit in the sun without a care in the world, and neither had his father. There was too much work to be done.

'Come and sit down,' she invited when he didn't move. 'Would you like some coffee? Or maybe a glass of champagne?'

'A picnic is not—'

'A picnic,' she interrupted calmly, 'is exactly what you need. I promise this will take no more than two hours, and if you're going to be teaching me all about being a queen then it won't matter if we sit in the sun with a picnic. You'd have to spend that two hours with me somewhere, hmm?'

He couldn't argue with that, so he found himself moving over to the rug and sitting down on it, watching her put some sandwiches on a plate and then leaning over to put it on the rug beside him.

'Why here?' he asked shortly as she piled food onto a second plate. 'My study would be more appropriate.'

'More appropriate, yes, but I'm tired of being inside.' She twinkled at him. 'It's much nicer being outside in the sun and the fresh air, don't you think? Especially when you've been cooped up inside all day.'

He wanted to deny it, but that was difficult when the sun shining down was warm on the back of his neck and the air was full of the smell of warm grass and oranges and the cool tang of the mountains around them.

Letting out a breath, he picked up a sandwich from the plate and began to eat, because he was actually quite hungry. 'Where were you last night?' he asked, even though he'd told himself he wasn't going to and that he didn't care.

'I felt like some time to myself,' she said. 'I didn't think it would matter to you if I wasn't there.'

'It didn't,' he replied, knowing it was a lie even as he said it. 'I only wanted to know where you were.'

She regarded him for a moment, her blue gaze assessing. 'I slept in the little room. You could have come to find me.'

Tiberius finished the sandwich, then picked up another. 'It was late. I didn't want to wake you.'

'Okay.' She ate her sandwich in tiny bites, and his gaze was drawn to the softness of her mouth and her small white teeth as she bit into the bread.

'You will be there tonight.' He'd meant it to sound like a question and instead it came out as a command.

'Will I?' She popped the rest of the sandwich into her mouth and chewed thoughtfully. 'That will depend on whether you're going to treat me as a wife or a toy.'

This again. Annoyance twisted inside him. 'I am treating you as a wife.'

'No, you're not. A husband and wife generally spend time together, and we do not.'

'Because we're the rulers of a nation. Our marriage will not be like other people's.'

She gave him a level look. 'And if I want it to be?'

Everything in him drew tight. 'What are you saying?'

'I'm saying that I want our marriage to be more, Tiberius. Like I told you yesterday, I want it to be more than just sleeping together at night.'

Tension crawled through him, though he wasn't sure why. 'It is more. You wear my ring, you are at my side, you are my queen.'

'That is not a relationship, and a relationship is what I want. And not one based entirely on sex. I don't think that's too much to ask for, especially if and when we decide to have children.' One fair brow arched. 'Or do you really want your children to have the kind of upbringing you did?'

That washed over him like a cold shock. He hadn't spared a thought for children beyond knowing that he'd need heirs, and he certainly hadn't thought about what kind of childhood he wanted for them.

One like yours? Crushed under the weight of other people's expectations?

His chest grew tight with instinctive denial. 'No,' he said tersely. 'I do not want that.'

'Good. Then we agree on one thing, at least.' She leaned forward and reached for the bottle of champagne sitting in the basket. 'Let's have a toast.'

'We should be discussing what you need to do as queen,' he growled. 'Not drinking in the sun and talking about children.'

She only shrugged and uncorked the bottle with a deft movement. 'Okay, then. Let's talk about me being a queen.'

She handed him a glass, which he had no choice but to take, then she poured some sparkling liquid into it before doing the same for herself. Putting the bottle down, she picked up her glass and knocked it gently against his.

'To the future.'

Then she lifted it to drink, and somehow managed to spill nearly all of it down the front of her pretty dress.

Tiberius sat there, unable to move, his gaze pinned to the wet fabric and the way it stuck to her skin, clinging to the curves of her breasts, making it very clear that she wasn't wearing a bra.

'Oh, no...' She put down her glass and looked at him wide-eyed. 'I'm all wet.'

He was suddenly painfully hard, with visions of himself peeling the damp silk from her and licking the champagne from her skin before checking to see just how wet she really was reeling through his brain.

Her deep blue gaze met his, and he knew that she could read the desire in his eyes because her own leapt to meet it.

'This is a seduction, isn't it?' he asked roughly.

'Is it?'

She made no move to dry herself, sitting there with the silk clinging to her, making it clear that her nipples were hard.

'I'm already seduced. You don't need to do this now. Couldn't it wait until tonight?'

'We're talking about you teaching me how to be a queen, Tiberius. Nothing else.'

Except she wasn't looking at him that way, and before he quite knew what he was doing he'd reached out, hauling her into his lap so she was facing him, her legs on either side of his hips.

'Time for your first lesson, then,' he said and lifting his hands, plunged them into her hair and took her mouth like he owned it.

It was reckless to do this out in the open, but Guinevere had decided that Tiberius wasn't the only master strategist. She was one too. She'd organised the picnic with the kitchen, then given instructions to both the staff and the palace guards that the orchard was to be out of bounds for the next couple of hours.

She'd wondered if he'd even come, but when his tall figure had come striding through the trees her heart had leapt. He'd looked devastatingly attractive, in dark trousers and a black shirt, and it had been all she could do not to lay hands on him the moment he'd sat down.

He'd missed her the night before—she could see it in his face, hear it in his voice. If it truly hadn't mattered to him then he wouldn't have asked, but he had. And the truth was she'd missed him too. It had taken all her of considerable will to stay in the library the night before, to deny him the pleasure of her body. But this was part of the lesson she wanted to teach him—that he couldn't have everything his own way—and that was a difficult lesson for a man like him.

Nevertheless, he had to learn. He had to understand that he could have moments for himself. That life wasn't all about work or the burden of kingship. That there could be moments of joy and happiness.

She wasn't sure when his wellbeing had come to matter to her so much, but it had, and so here, in the sunlight of the orchard, on a beautiful day, she'd spread before him a picnic and determined that for a couple of hours he could relax.

Then she'd thought that maybe that relaxation should be physical. They weren't in bed, for a change, and maybe in the sun, after some pleasure, he'd lose some of the tension she could sense in the air around him.

She probably needn't have indulged in the performance of spilling perfectly good champagne over herself, but she'd wanted him to be hungry for her. She'd wanted him to forget everything but her.

And certainly the wet fabric of her dress was doing that work for her.

The flare of desire in his eyes had been the only warning she'd had before he'd leaned forward and dragged her into his lap.

Now she didn't pull away from his hungry kiss, pressing her body to his instead, and kissing him back just as hungrily.

The feral growl he made in the back of his throat delighted her, and she wasn't displeased when he ripped apart the thin silk of her dress. He put one hand between her shoulder blades to support her as he bent her back, pulling the fabric aside, kissing his way down her throat, over her collarbones to her breasts, still damp with champagne. She gasped as pleasure lanced through her. His mouth had found one of her nipples and was drawing hard on it.

His free hand tugged at more of the dress fabric, ripping it all the way down so that there was nothing between them but his clothing and the little lacy pair of knickers she wore beneath the dress.

His arms came around her, supporting her as he bent her back further, his mouth resting in the hollow of her throat as he shifted one hand down between her thighs, stroking her, making pleasure ripple everywhere.

She sighed, giving herself up to him, to the movement of his hands and the way he kissed and tasted her body, hot and hungry. But he often took the lead in the bedroom, and while she enjoyed that very much, since her experience was limited, she was starting to get more confident.

This was about him, and she wanted to give to him as much as he gave to her.

So she took his hands and held them still. 'Let me,' she murmured. 'Let me give you pleasure, Your Majesty.'

He stilled, his gaze full of flames. He was such an intense man and he felt things so deeply, she could see it. It was his love for his country that drove him, but maybe there was also something else. Something deeper. She wanted to know what it was, what motor kept driving him on. And perhaps if she gave him some release he'd tell her.

She lifted her hands to his face and cupped it gently between her palms, then she leaned in and began to kiss him…butterfly-light kisses on his forehead, the strong bridge of his nose, his eyelids, his cheekbones. Raining down soft, tender kisses that ended with the brush of her lips against his.

'No,' he murmured in protest. 'I need you now, lioness.'

'And you can have me. Just be patient.'

She kept on kissing his face, then his throat, her hands moving to the buttons of his shirt and undoing them. Then she was stroking his chest, tracing the hard muscle beneath his satiny skin, worshipping him.

'Guinevere,' he growled in warning as her hands strayed to his stomach, and then further, flicking open the button of his trousers and then the zip, sliding her hand beneath the cotton of his underwear and finding him long and thick and hard.

'*Guinevere,*' he said again, his voice guttural.

'Shh…' she murmured, stroking him gently, tracing the length of him with her fingers. She kissed his mouth as she did so, tasting him lightly. A tender kiss, slowly—very slowly—deepening into something sweeter and hotter.

He made a sound deep in his throat, but he didn't move. He'd gone very still, and she could feel the tension in his muscles. But it wasn't denial. It was almost as if he'd never felt like this before and wasn't sure what to do.

And perhaps he hadn't. Had anyone ever been tender with him? Had anyone ever been soft? Had anyone ever touched him as if he was beautiful, a work of art you had to be careful with?

His breathing was fast, and normally that was a sign that he'd take charge, put her on her back and thrust inside her. Yet he remained still. As if he was waiting.

She reached down between them, slipping aside her underwear, then gripped him and positioned him before raising herself slightly, easing down, feeling the delicious glide of him as he slid inside her.

'Guinevere,' he whispered again, his voice roughened and yet soft. But it wasn't a warning this time. It was something else. Something that held a note that made her heart tighten in response.

She looked into his beautiful face, met the glorious silver blaze in his eyes. And then she moved, watching the flames in his eyes burn higher and higher. Kissing him tenderly and gently, she let her hands stroke his shoulders and his chest, loving the feel of him. Surrounding herself with him.

The pleasure grew, building high and hot, and there was an urgency to it but also a gentleness, and a sweetness that made her want to stay like this for ever. Then, just as it began to get too much for her, he slipped his hand between her thighs, down to where they were joined, and stroked her. At the same time his other hand settled heavily into the small of her back, holding her to him.

The pleasure broke, exploding slowly and beautifully

like a firework, a peaceful, inexorable tide that made them both shake before touching down lightly back to earth.

She put her head against his shoulder, leaning bonelessly against him as his hand cupped the back of her head, his thumb moving gently over the curve of her skull.

He didn't speak, and neither did she, both of them content to sit in the small bubble of peace they'd created for themselves. And beneath her hands she felt the hard muscles of his shoulders and chest finally relax.

'I can't help feeling,' he said, his voice deep and rough with the after-effects of their passion, 'that I have been expertly seduced by my own wife.'

She smiled against his shoulder. 'Yes, you have. And I'll have you know I'm quite pleased with myself.'

'So you should be.' His hand slid down to the back of her neck, stroking her idly. 'I'm sorry about your pretty dress. I will get you another.'

'I don't care.' She peeked up at him. 'It sacrificed itself for a good cause.'

He glanced down and smiled, his gaze sparking with something that wasn't physical desire, yet had elements of it. And also elements of something warm and tender and utterly glorious.

Her heart tightened painfully, and a kind of wonder moved through her that he'd chosen to give such a smile to her.

'I'll buy you many sacrificial victims, in that case,' he said. 'You can offer one up to me every evening.'

'Please do.'

She sighed, then moved, shifting herself off him and wrapping the remains of her dress around her. He made a growl of protest, reaching for her to pull her down with him as he lay on his back on the rug. She propped her head up with her hand and she leaned an elbow on his chest.

'Did you really spend all your childhood learning how to be a king?' she asked idly—though the question wasn't idle in the slightest. She was taking advantage of his relaxation.

'Yes,' he said. 'My father knew it would take time to get the throne back, so he had to start early. He'd initially planned to take it back himself, but then he got sick.'

'So you had to be the one, then?' She picked up an olive from the bowl nearby and fed it to him. 'That must have been difficult.'

'It was. It took longer than we'd hoped, since getting support for our cause took some time.'

She thought for a moment, then picked up a grape and fed that to him. 'My father used to make fun of you. As a way to reduce the threat you presented, I think. He called you weak and ineffectual.'

There was a satisfied expression on Tiberius's face that she secretly thought looked far too good on him. 'I'm glad he did. It meant your father's supporters underestimated me.'

Guinevere picked up another olive and ate it, trying to decide what to ask him next. Something that wouldn't make him tense up or scare him away. But she burned to know so much.

'I'm sorry about your mother,' she said carefully. 'It must have been hard to grow up without her.'

'I was too young to remember her—and my father didn't talk much about her—but I certainly felt the lack when I was younger.'

She watched him, noting the shadows cast over his face by the sun and the branches of the tree above them. Gilding the long, sooty length of his lashes, highlighting the strong lines of his forehead and nose.

'My mother died young, too,' she said after a moment. 'And I don't remember her either.'

His gaze rested on hers and there was concern in his eyes. 'Did you have anyone, lioness? Anyone to care for you?'

A lump rose unexpectedly in her throat and she had to swallow hard because, again, this was supposed to be about him, not her. 'No. I was safer being alone.'

He reached out and brushed her cheek with his fingertips. 'I'm sorry you had to deal with that. But know that you're not alone now. And that you're not a prisoner here. You may leave the palace whenever you wish.'

She badly wanted him to tell her that she had him, but he didn't, and that made her heart clench unexpectedly.

'You know that you're not alone either, don't you?' she couldn't help saying, leaning into his touch. 'That I am here?'

His mouth curved and the warmth in it made the tightness in her heart clench into a strange kind of pain. 'And I'm glad of it. Speaking of which…shouldn't we be discussing your role as Queen?'

She smiled back. 'Yes. But have another olive first.'

He didn't protest when she fed it to him, nipping at her fingertips instead, and soon they were too distracted to discuss anything at all.

CHAPTER TEN

TIBERIUS GLANCED AT his watch yet again, to check the time. It wasn't quite five, but it would be soon—though not soon enough for the anticipation gathering inside him.

At five a messenger would come and hand him a note, telling him where to meet his wife. He never knew where she was going to hold their daily two hours of queenship teaching—she always picked the place—but it came as a pleasant surprise every time.

They'd been doing this for a couple of weeks now, and while initially he'd been impatient for the two hours to end, after that first time—on the rug in the orchard, with her warm body against his, her touching him slowly and with care, then feeding him olives and grapes—now he was almost disappointed when it was over.

Those first few times they'd ended up getting distracted by sex—which he hadn't minded—and then, in the lazy aftermath, indulging in some idle conversation. He'd always hated small talk and meaningless discussion—it felt like a waste of time. Why talk pleasantries when there were important conversations to be had? But for some reason, after meeting with Guinevere, he found himself in no hurry to get back to the palace.

Their discussions ranged over books, art, science and politics. He started to enjoy their conversations. She was very knowledgeable about a host of different subjects, due to reading her way through the palace library. She was also curious, and interested in what he had to say, though his own knowledge of certain subjects was limited, given the narrowness of his upbringing.

She also met him in a variety of different places. First the orchard, then a clearing in the forest. One day it rained, so he met her in her little library, and then there was the time when the sky was bright blue and she met him by the pool. There were cocktails and delicious finger foods that time, then they'd swum—which had soon evolved into extremely hot sex, both of them slippery with water, on one of the sun loungers.

He'd begun to look forward to their meetings, begun to find the length of time he spent in other meetings an imposition. He had to be very stern with himself not to be distracted when he was working, but it was difficult.

He'd also started to look forward to their public appearances together, which he found a delight when she was by his side. She was beginning to win over those few stalwarts who didn't like her because she was an Accorsi, with her smile and the natural way she talked to people. Little girls in particular loved their new and pretty queen, and there was always a little posse of them waiting for Guinevere whenever they appeared together.

It wasn't all idle conversation, naturally. They discussed Kasimir, and her role as queen—though he'd soon discovered that she didn't need much in the way of instruction. Her natural empathy, her curiosity and quick wit had helped her pick up the subtleties of queenly duties with relative ease. She had initiative too. It had only been a few days before one of his aides had told him that the Queen was involving herself in various charities, as well as taking a special interest in health services.

She was a remarkable woman, and every day he found there were new aspects of her to respect and admire. Really, marrying her was turning out to be one of his better decisions.

At last, five came, and the door of the meeting room opened to admit the Queen's aide. The man came quickly over to Tiberius and handed him a note. Tiberius unfolded it.

Meet me on our bedroom balcony tonight. Seven p.m.

He was conscious of a slight disappointment that he'd have to wait another few hours—he'd never been good at waiting—but her choice of meeting place was intriguing. The balcony... Why on earth there?

He retired to his office, to finish looking through the endless pile of documents that required his signature, but couldn't concentrate.

In the end he found himself striding to the royal apartments to meet his queen a good ten minutes before she'd said.

There were still palace staff on the balcony when he arrived, laying out food on the stone table there, as tealight candles in glass holders cast a soft, flickering glow.

Guinevere, who'd been directing the staff, gave him a surprised look as he appeared. 'Oh!' she exclaimed. 'You're early.'

She wore a light linen wrap dress of deep blue, her hair loose over her shoulder, and looked so unutterably lovely that he felt ravenous for her.

'I was impatient,' he said, dismissing the staff with a wave of his hand.

Once they'd gone, he crossed over to where Guinevere stood and took her hands in his.

'Why the balcony?'

She smiled. 'I thought you'd enjoy watching the sun set while you give me more instruction.'

The mention of 'instruction' made him hard, and that was strange. Because it wasn't as if they only had sex during these meetings. They also did it at night, in bed together. He most certainly wasn't abstinent.

She hadn't absented herself from his bed again, the way she had done that one night, so he couldn't fathom why the more time he spent with her, the more he wanted.

Somewhere in the depths of him a warning bell tolled, but he ignored it. This was purely a physical infatuation, nothing more, and as long as he continued to make progress with rebuilding his country, why shouldn't he enjoy more time with his wife?

'Also,' she added, threading her fingers through his and leading him over to the table, 'you need dinner.'

She was always feeding him. Not that he objected. It was just strange to have someone invested in his well-being. It wasn't that his aides weren't, but with them it wasn't about him, but his role as King. Guinevere, though, saw past his crown to the man he was behind it, and some part of him took deep satisfaction in that.

'This looks delicious,' he said as he sat down on the cushioned chair at the head of the table.

It was a long table, meant for more than two people, but instead of sitting opposite him, Guinevere sat beside him.

'I hope so.' She got a plate and began to serve him, as she always did at these meetings. 'I had the kitchen make all your favourites.'

Tiberius watched her. 'You know my favourites?'

'Of course.' She gave him a grin. 'I asked the staff what you liked and they told me.'

She has made an effort to know you, but what do you know of her?

What did he know?

He knew she was curious and passionate. That she was empathic and intelligent. That her childhood had been awful and yet it hadn't turned her into a terrible person. She'd been quiet and terrified when he'd first met her, but she'd blossomed since, revealing the warm, generous and caring woman she was beneath the fear. Clearly she was thriving in her new role.

There were many things he knew about her...more than he'd realised.

'I should be doing this for you,' he said as she handed him the plate. 'You are spoiling me, lioness.'

She lifted a shoulder as she began getting food for herself. 'I enjoy spoiling you,' she said, flashing him a smile. 'You deserve to be spoiled.'

Do you?

The thought came out of nowhere, and he felt as if a chill breeze had moved over his skin. He ignored it. It didn't matter what he did or didn't deserve. She'd chosen to do these little things for him, and he wouldn't hurt her by rejecting them.

What about what she deserves?

She deserved much—which he'd give her when he had time for it. Besides, it wasn't as if he didn't do anything for her. Every night he made her scream with the pleasure he gave her, and that wasn't nothing.

'Tell me about your day,' she said, as she did every time they met.

So while they ate he told her about what he and his

aides had discussed that day, and about the current is-sues they were facing, as well as the ones they'd have to deal with in the near future.

'I'm going to get my events team to organise a national tour,' he said after they'd eaten. 'But before that we have an international meeting to attend in Geneva.'

Guinevere put an elbow on the table and leaned her chin in her hand. '"We"?'

'Of course, "we". You will naturally be by my side.'

Her cheeks went pink, and she gave him another of her heartbreaking smiles. 'Oh, that sounds amazing. Have you been there before?'

He had, and told her so, and they discussed travelling for a bit before he asked her how her day had gone. He always asked, and he always found it interesting. In fact, he was starting to find everything about her interesting.

After they'd watched the sunset on the balcony, Guine-vere took his hand and led him inside, telling him she had a surprise for him.

It was full dark by the time they stepped outside the palace, following the path to the orchard once more. There, Guinevere put a rug down on the grass and pulled him down to sit beside her.

'What is this all about?' he asked, as she lay on her back on the rug.

She was smiling as she patted the rug beside her. 'Lie down and I'll tell you.'

So he did, lying on his back, watching the stars wheel-ing above their heads.

'I want you to tell me about the stars, Tiberius,' she said.

He realised what she'd done then. She'd taken him back to his boyhood, to those stolen moments of quiet and peace when he hadn't been the saviour of a country, but only a boy. A boy who was part of something greater... the entire living universe.

Something inside him relaxed in that moment...something that had been tense for a long time. Strangely, it felt as if he hadn't been able to breathe properly, but now, right here, he could draw a full breath for the first time.

The stars glittered in the black velvet of the sky and he lifted a hand, pointing out the different constellations, feeling memories of his childhood interest in astronomy flooding back.

She nestled against him, her voice full of wonder as she asked him questions and then listened to him talk, and he realised that for the first time since he could remember he was utterly relaxed. Content to be in this moment. The relentless engine inside him finally still.

Guinevere lay with her head pillowed on Tiberius's shoulder, listening to him talk about the stars. He knew a great deal about them, and for a change he talked without the edge of impatience that usually coloured his voice.

There was no tension in him, she could feel it in his body. And that made her feel good in turn, that she'd managed to give him this. Two hours of every day when he didn't have to be a king, where he could be free of his burdens if only for a little time.

He needed it. And perhaps the worst part about it was that he didn't even know he needed it, that she'd had to give him these hours by stealth.

After the first couple of days she'd wondered if he'd realise what she was doing, and perhaps stop coming, but he didn't. And if he did indeed understand what she was doing, he certainly didn't question it.

One thing was sure, though. She loved organising their meetings. Loved choosing places to have them—places he'd enjoy—and choosing food too, since he often forgot to eat, or so the palace staff told her. She loved spending time with him, talking with him. He was an interesting and highly intelligent man. He told her all about his plans for Kasimir—how he hoped to develop certain aspects of it for carefully managed tourism and also create export opportunities for Kasimiran products.

It was clear that he loved his people, loved his country, and that his whole life was directed to one purpose. Making things better. And that desire to make things better, to protect his people, came from a deep empathy, she could tell.

An empathy that came from the man rather than the King.

She wanted to know more about that man, that person, rather than about the role he played, so often their conversations would stray onto other topics as she tried to draw out of him glimpses of who he was deep down.

She discovered that he liked good food, and enjoyed wine, but that he had no hobbies. His interests were entirely bent to one purpose. Being a king. She needed to find out more, she decided, which was why today she'd organised to meet him later at night, so that after dinner they could lie in the grass and watch the stars, the way he'd done as a boy.

And she decided that there was nothing nicer than lying here next to him, listening to his deep voice telling her about the rings of Saturn, and how far away the moon was, and other such things.

'Next time I'll bring a telescope,' she said. 'So you can show me some of the planets.'

'I'll get one of my staff to find one.'

They lay in companionable silence for a moment, then he said, 'Why did you bring me out here?'

She let out a breath, debating whether or not to tell him the truth. 'I wanted to remind you that there was more to life than being a king,' she said at last—because why not tell him the truth? He should hear it. 'You said that those moments when you were a boy, looking up at the stars, were the most peaceful you ever had, and I just…wanted to give you that and to remind you what it felt like.'

He said nothing for a long moment. 'Thank you,' he murmured eventually. 'It's been a…long time since I've done anything like this.'

She turned her head, looking up at his face, all silver light and shadows under the moon. 'Why, Tiberius? Why do you drive yourself so hard?'

'Because there is a lot at stake.' His voice wasn't impatient for a change, but almost meditative. 'Because it's taking far too long for me to change things.' There was another pause, then he added, 'Because my mother died to protect me. Instead of saving her, my father had to leave her behind in order to save me. She insisted, apparently.'

Guinevere's heart clenched in her chest. 'And your father?'

'Before he died of cancer, five years ago, he made me promise that I would dedicate my life to claiming back the crown and rebuilding what your father broke.'

'What about you?' She asked the question almost hesitantly. 'Is that something you want to do?'

'It isn't a question of what I want,' he said simply. 'It is what I have to do. It's the right thing to do.'

Was that regret in his tone? She couldn't tell.

'Did you never want to do something else?'

He was looking up at the sky, the expression on his face unreadable. 'No,' he said. 'When I was a child I wanted to be an astronaut—like every other little boy, no doubt. But that wasn't my destiny.'

The pain in her heart seemed to deepen. There was no wistfulness in his voice, only a flat note that excluded any possibility of him wanting to be anything other than what he was.

'So you were told very early on what you had to be?' she said.

'Yes. From the age of ten I knew that that one day I would be King.'

'Did you ever…wish for it to be different?'

He turned his head, looking down at her. 'Different? What do you mean?'

'Did you ever wish that you weren't heir to the throne, I mean?'

He looked thoughtful. 'I don't remember,' he said at last. 'I don't remember ever having the choice—not that I would have chosen any differently if I had.' Something flickered in his eyes then that she couldn't read. 'My mother died to save me. She sacrificed herself and I have to make that sacrifice mean something. The same for my father too. On his death bed he made me swear that I would reclaim the crown and be a good king for Kasimir.'

She'd told him what a terrible burden she thought that was before, and she still believed it. That the purpose of his entire life was to make his parents' deaths mean something seemed a terrible burden to have to carry.

'You can make their deaths mean something and not drive yourself into an early grave,' she said. 'And you can allow yourself other interests that have nothing to do with being a king.'

His gaze flicked back to hers. 'Speak plainly, lioness. What is it you're trying to say?'

She paused for a moment, debating the wisdom of discussing this with him again. But she had to try and make him understand—for both their sakes.

'You're working too hard, Tiberius,' she said at last. 'You're not allowing yourself any time off or even time out. If you burn yourself out you'll no longer be able to do much of anything.'

'Why don't you let me be the judge of that, hmm?'

Guinevere held his darkened silver gaze. 'You're not going to disappoint them, Tiberius. You do know that, don't you?'

He frowned. 'Disappoint who?'

'Your parents. They put a lot of expectations on you, didn't they?'

'No more than any other parent. And no more than was necessary.' He eased her head off his shoulder gently and sat up. 'Being King is a high-pressure role—so, yes, of course the expectations will end up being heavy.'

That edge was back in his voice again, and she could have kicked herself for making things awkward. That wasn't what tonight was supposed to be about.

She shouldn't have asked difficult questions, shouldn't she?

'I understand,' she said quickly. 'And I'm not attacking them or criticising them. I just want you to know that you don't have to be strong all the time...that you don't have to push yourself constantly.'

'You're very invested in my wellbeing.'

'Of course I am. I'm your wife and you matter to me.'

The words came out sounding a lot more emphatic than they should have. A lot more.

He stared at her, studying her face as if it was map he was trying to read. 'Guinevere,' he said at last. 'Our marriage is not like other people's, remember?'

She frowned, not understanding. 'What? What do you mean?'

'I mean,' he went on gently, 'that we did not marry for love.'

'I know that,' she said, unsure why the declaration should hurt. 'What has that got to do with you mattering to me?'

'I don't want you to expect things from me that you will never get. For example, you also matter to me—but not more than Kasimir. The country always comes first.'

It was the answer she'd expected, and yet the moment he said it the hurt inside her grew a little more, cut a little deeper.

'I know that,' she said reflexively. 'I'm not asking you to put me ahead of the country.'

'No, I can see you're not. I just need you to know that should you want more from me, you will never get it— understand?'

She wanted to ask him what he meant by 'more', but she had a horrible feeling she knew already. Love. That was what he meant, wasn't it? Love would never be a part of their marriage, because he was already in love with Kasimir.

You can't ask him to put you ahead of the country.

No, she couldn't. She could never be that selfish. Yet a part of her desperately wished she could.

Why? Why does he matter so much?

But she thought she knew the answer to that already. It

was an answer that had been steadily forming itself deep in her heart for the past three weeks. That grew every time she spent time with him…every time he held her in his arms. That wanted more and more of him until she knew that nothing would ever be enough. That had her dreaming of him, and staring at him, and had her heart beating fast whenever they met.

You're falling in love with him.

Of course she was, and she hadn't known because it had never happened to her before. Nevertheless, she knew what this powerful current was, a tide that responded to him as if he was the moon and she the sea, rushing in when he was here, only to retreat when he wasn't.

It was love.

She was in love with her husband.

CHAPTER ELEVEN

THE BALLROOM WAS full of people. Royalty and nobility from other European nations, as well as heads of state. Music played, and the interior of the old castle on Lake Geneva, where the international meeting was being held, lit up.

Tiberius had had a satisfactory few days, meeting with other leaders, making valuable political alliances. He and Guinevere were due to fly back to Kasimir the next day, and he was almost sorry about it.

Not far from where he stood, chatting with some other leaders, was Guinevere, resplendent in a ballgown of pale silvery-blue silk. It was strapless, revealing her slender shoulders and pale throat, the fabric cupping her breasts lovingly. Her curls were piled on her head with a few loose, artfully tumbling around her ears, held in place with a couple of diamond combs that glittered and sparkled in the light.

He'd given her the necklace she wore of pale sapphires and diamonds, circling the slender column of her throat, and that glittered too. She seemed even more fairy-like tonight, sparkling like a delicate snow crystal in the lights of the ballroom.

He watched her, unable to take his gaze from her.

She needed a tiara, he decided. Many of other ladies

present were wearing one, and after all she was a queen, even if she hadn't been formally crowned.

For the past two weeks he'd been thinking and thinking about what he could do for her—something as special as what she'd given him in those two hours he reserved for her every day. Those two hours that he'd begun to crave more and more with every day that passed. They were special, those hours. They were sacrosanct. And he'd even begun to wonder if he could afford to stretch them to three.

He wanted to reciprocate—show her that he appreciated what she did for him, that he admired and respected her, that she was everything he'd ever wanted in a queen and more. But he hadn't thought of the perfect thing... until now.

A coronation—that's what she should have. He didn't care that his own had been perfunctory, but for her... She should be feted. She should have all the attention she deserved. His fairy princess should be made into a queen with all the pomp and ceremony at his disposal.

It would be a good thing too, for the people. A happy event to boost their spirits after the long years of Accorsi rule. He would decree a public holiday and Guinevere would be crowned in the cathedral in the central city.

He watched as she laughed at something someone had said to her, her smile lighting up her face, making her even more lovely than she was already.

Yes, she should wear a silver gown, or pale gold, and she would look impossibly beautiful in the Kasimiran Queen's crown, all diamonds and sapphires. He would invite the world's media, livestream the whole thing to the rest of the globe. It would be a major event and she would finally get all the attention she deserved.

Impatient to tell her of his plans, he moved over to where she stood, slipping an arm around her waist and drawing her close. 'Spare me five minutes, my queen,' he murmured in her ear.

She glanced up at him, smiling, and his chest tightened. Her smiles were truly the loveliest he'd ever seen.

'As long as it's only five,' she said, teasing, before excusing herself from the little group she'd been chatting with.

'What is it?' she asked, as he drew her over to one of the windows that overlooked the magnificent lake.

'I have an idea,' he said. 'You've been such a delight over the past couple of weeks, and I've been very remiss as a husband. I have not given you anything in return.'

'You've given me your time, Tiberius,' she said. 'That's the most important thing. That's all I need.'

'But you deserve more, little lioness. So much more.' He took her hands in his and held them. 'I'd like to hold a formal coronation for you. In the cathedral. With the world's media looking on, and naturally all our people. A symbol of what our union and you being queen means to Kasimir.'

Her smile flickered momentarily, though he wasn't sure what that meant. 'A coronation? I don't need a coronation, Tiberius.'

'Perhaps not, but I'd like you to have one all the same. Don't you think our people and the world should see the lovely woman who is Queen of Kasimir?'

She squeezed his fingers, then let them go. 'They already know who I am. Besides, it's a lot of money to spend. Money that could better be spent on the hospital, for example.'

Irritation caught at him. This was not the response

he'd expected, he had to admit. He'd thought she'd be pleased, at the very least.

'The people could do with a happy event.' He tried to keep the annoyance from his voice. 'And I will decree a public holiday, which should boost morale even further. It will be for them, not just you.'

Her smile seemed strained now. 'Oh. That does sound like it could be something…worthwhile, then.'

They were in a crowded ballroom, and he didn't particularly want to cause a scene, but her muted reaction had got under his skin.

'You don't like the idea?' he asked, trying to keep his voice level. 'I wanted to do something nice for you.'

Her lashes fell, veiling her gaze. 'If you want to do something nice for me, you could give me another hour of your time. It doesn't need to be anything else.'

Instantly he felt defensive. 'This will be for our people, Guinevere.'

Her lashes rose again, her blue gaze meeting his. 'So it's not really for me at all, is it?'

A curious anger was growing in him—part defensiveness, part disappointment and part an odd pain that his suggestion had been rejected. Yet it seemed ridiculous to be so angry about that. Why should he care?

'Of course it is,' he said curtly. 'But it will help our people also.'

'So you'd rather organise a hugely expensive coronation for me than give me another hour of your time. Is that what you're saying?'

Frustration joined the mix of emotions inside him. He had no more time to give, and she should understand that. 'Why is that a problem?'

Her blue gaze darkened, her smile just a memory. 'You

don't understand, do you? That I might enjoy spending time with you and want more of it.'

'We've talked about this,' he said, trying to mask his impatience. 'Kasimir is the most—'

'Important thing. Yes, I know,' she interrupted, the blue sparks of her temper beginning to show. 'But it's possible to do both, Tiberius. You can rule your country and be a husband at the same time.' She gestured at the crowded ballroom. 'There are plenty of people here who are great examples of that.'

His anger built and he was conscious of it being out of proportion to what she'd actually said, and yet he seemed to be powerless to ignore it.

'Those people do not have the same history we do,' he said through gritted teeth. 'And neither do their countries.'

Guinevere's gaze came back to his. 'You mean me being the daughter of your enemy?'

'No,' he snapped, forgetting himself. 'Our marriage being one of convenience.'

'Yes, until you made it real.' She turned to face him fully now, standing small and indomitable before him. 'You were the one who didn't want a divorce, Tiberius.'

'And you agreed,' he shot back.

She looked away abruptly, her hands clasped in front of her now, a sure sign of her distress.

You are ruining this for her.

Pain threaded through him at the sight of her small hands, holding on to each other so tightly. It was a pain he didn't understand. Because it hurt him that she was distressed. It hurt him to think that he was ruining this evening for her, too, especially when he'd been trying to make things better.

'Little lioness,' he said softly, taking her hands once more and drawing her behind one of the columns. 'I don't want to fight with you. If you don't want a coronation, then we won't have one. I only thought you'd like it.'

She stared up at him, her gaze luminous, and much to his shock he saw tears in her eyes.

'Guinevere?' He drew her closer. 'What's wrong?'

'It's not the coronation,' she said after a moment, her voice thick and shaky. 'I don't...don't need any of that. What I need is you, Tiberius. More of your time, more of your company, just...more of you.'

'Lioness,' he murmured, tightening his grip. 'You know I can't—'

'I need it because I'm in love with you.'

The stunned look on his face told her everything she needed to know about how he felt. There was no joy, no happiness. Only shock.

She'd known it would be a difficult thing to tell him, but she hadn't been able to mask her feelings about his coronation offer well enough. His offer to do something for her, that she'd hoped would be about spending more time with her, only for it to be about a coronation had been too sharp a disappointment.

It wasn't that she didn't appreciate it, it was that the thing he'd chosen wasn't really about her at all. It was about what she represented as his wife, his queen, and their marriage as a symbolic union for all of Kasimir.

It wasn't about her.

It wasn't about Guinevere, who was in love with her husband and who only wanted to spend time with him.

But of course time was his most precious commodity, and he didn't have enough of it to spare for her and her alone.

She shouldn't have told him the real reason for her disappointment, but not telling him the truth would only cause more trouble between them, especially when she wasn't good at hiding her feelings.

But she'd said it now, the the truth that had been sitting there all this time since that moment under the stars in the orchard.

She loved him, and over the past two weeks spending more time with him, and now coming to Switzerland, had only made it more clear to her. She loved being with him, talking to him, arguing with him, having him at her side whenever they were in public and then being held in his arms at night in their bed.

She loved him and she didn't know what to do. Because while she'd realised she was in love with him that night, he'd made it very clear that love would not be a part of this marriage. That Kasimir would always come first and there was no room in his heart for anything else.

There was no room in his heart for her.

He was a king, and his first responsibility was to his country. Not her.

She could give him an ultimatum—tell him she was leaving him if he didn't put her first, but that was something she'd never do. It would force him into an impossible position and that felt terribly unfair.

'I'm sorry,' she murmured, pulling her hands from his. 'I know that's not what you want to hear. I'm sorry. I shouldn't have said it.'

Slowly the shock ebbed from his expression, leaving his eyes hard, cold chips of diamond. 'Guinevere. That is not what our marriage is about—you know that.'

Her throat felt tight. 'Yes, I know,' she forced out. 'Don't worry, I'm not going to ask you for anything. I only wanted you to know that that's how I feel.'

'It's not something I'll ever be able to reciprocate.' Now his voice sounded hard too. 'You know why.'

'Yes.' She couldn't quite mask her bitterness. 'You have to sacrifice yourself on Kasimir's altar and that of your parents' deaths.'

Anger leaped in his eyes, as she had known it would since it had been a terrible thing for her to say.

'Their deaths have nothing to do with this.'

She shouldn't argue. They were in a public ballroom, for God's sake. And yet she couldn't stop the words that spilled from her. 'Don't they, though? Isn't that why you can't afford to take your eye off the crown? Not even for a moment? You're so desperate to prove you're worth your mother's sacrifice—and your father's too.'

His expression became forbidding. 'How is that wrong?' he demanded. 'She died protecting me and my father sacrificed his wife for me. Shouldn't I prove to them that they didn't die for nothing?'

At that, her eyes filled with tears. 'You've already proved that, Tiberius. You've reclaimed the crown and you're getting Kasimir back on track. You have some wonderful plans for the future. And they're gone now. What more do you need to prove?'

Tension had begun to roll off him like a wave. 'Every-thing,' he said harshly. 'My father was clear that a king couldn't have anything else in his life but his country… that anything else was a distraction. And that doesn't end simply because I have a wife and a family.'

She blinked, her throat getting tight. 'There should be room in your life for happiness as well, Tiberius. There should be room in your life for love. Don't you think that's what your mother would have wanted?'

'You know nothing about what my mother would have wanted.'

'No,' she said softly. 'But neither do you. I'm sure she would want what's best for you, and running yourself into the ground for a country that doesn't care about you isn't it.'

'So what are you saying? That I give up everything? Give up the crown I worked for so long to claim just for you?'

That hurt, as he must know it would.

'No, that's not what I'm saying.' She pulled her hands from his, swallowing past the unbearable tightness in her throat. 'You're a king, but don't forget you're also a man, and one doesn't cancel out the other. How can a king make his people happy if he doesn't even know what happiness feels like?'

His expression shuttered. 'I don't need to know. Happiness is irrelevant.'

'It's not,' she said, unable to stop a tear from sliding down her cheek. 'It's important, and it's only been in the past couple of weeks with you that I've realised how important.'

But he ignored her, glancing down at his watch. 'I'm sorry, Guinevere. But this is a pointless discussion. I suggest we have it at a later date, and not in such a public place.'

He was right. Of course he was right.

Another tear joined the second, falling to stain the silk of her gown. 'I don't care if you don't love me back.' She had to say it so he knew. 'I don't care about me. I only want what's best for you.'

Just for a second the cold diamond of his eyes flared as his gaze tracked her tears. 'But you should care,' he said suddenly, low and fierce. 'And you should have someone who can give you what's best for you too.'

She brushed away a tear, not caring where it fell, not understanding. 'What do you mean?'

Tiberius muttered a low curse, that muscle in his jaw leaping. 'I mean that I should never have married you, Guinevere Accorsi. You'd have been better off if I'd just let you go.'

Guinevere stared up at him in shock, her heart feeling as if it was full of broken glass. 'But I wouldn't,' she whispered. 'I would have been still hiding in the walls, too afraid to come out.'

He said nothing to that, only stared at her for one long, aching moment.

Then he turned on his heel and left her standing alone by the column.

CHAPTER TWELVE

TIBERIUS PUSHED HIS WAY through the crowd, abruptly unable to bear being in the ballroom any longer. A hot, painful feeling was pressing against his chest, making it feel as if he was suffocating, and he was desperate to get outside and breathe the cold mountain air.

He found some doors that led to an outside terrace and managed to get them open, stepping out into the clear night, his chest heaving.

But even taking deep breaths of the cold Swiss night didn't relieve the burning sensation, or the tightness. It was as if something enormous was sitting on his sternum.

It was all to do with Guinevere, and he knew it.

Her dark blue eyes looking up at him as she told him that she was in love with him. The wild rush of joy that had filled his veins in that moment, and then the aching bitterness that had followed it, because love wasn't for kings. Or at least not the kind of love that she deserved.

He'd hurt her, bastard that he was. He'd made her cry. He'd told her that she would be better off without him, and she would. She needed someone who could give her their whole heart, not just a small piece of it. She'd had nothing all her life—nothing but her brothers' fists and her father's indifference. It was incredible how her bright, warm, effervescent spirit hadn't buckled under the fear and violence she'd experienced, or at least crumbled away.

But it hadn't.

Despite how her father and brothers had treated her, she was undaunted. And he'd watched her turn from a mouse into a lioness, all beautiful, strong, brave and caring.

A woman like that deserved the entire world—not to be tied to a man who'd never be able to put her first. A man who'd never tasted happiness and had no idea what joy looked like. What could he offer her? Pleasure in bed, that was all.

He walked over to the stone parapet and gripped it, looking out over the lake at the mountains looming dark and forbidding in the night, the caps of snow gleaming.

He didn't know where that left him.

Divorcing her felt impossible, and yet that was the only option he could see. The only option that would give her the freedom she needed and deserved. Freedom from him and from Kasimir.

Free to make her own choices—choices that hadn't been forced on her the way he'd forced them on her at the very beginning, by demanding that she marry him, that she pay for her family's crimes.

The pain in his chest deepened, excoriating him.

He couldn't bear the thought of letting her go, and yet he had to.

To be a ruler required sacrifice, his father had told him. Both of his parents had made that sacrifice. And so would he.

He had to follow their example, otherwise what was he?

An empty, hollow man. A man without purpose, whose whole life had been for nothing.

Tiberius stepped back from the parapet. He'd go and find her now and tell her that she had to leave him, that she should be free, and he had to do it quickly. Make it swift and hard, like ripping off a sticking plaster, so she could heal faster.

He turned around, moved back to the doors.

And found Guinevere standing there, shining in the moonlight, sparkling and glittering like the fairy she was, her eyes, dark in the night, burning with her lioness courage.

He froze, the pain in his chest an agony. 'I told you we'd have this conversation later,' he said, his voice rough and raw.

'It is later,' she said levelly, and stepped outside into the night. 'But we don't need to have this conversation at all. You've said your piece, I've said mine, and we'll agree to disagree.'

That was not what he'd expected.

'Guinevere,' he said, forcing the word out. 'I have made a decision. I can't give you what you need, and as such I can't ask you to stay with me. So I'm going to start divorce proceedings—'

'No,' she interrupted flatly, and crossed the space between them, coming straight up to him and putting her arms around him, her head on his chest. 'You can start proceedings, if you want, but I'm not leaving you. I'm never leaving you.'

He couldn't bear to push her away, yet he also couldn't bear to touch her because if he did, he knew he'd never let her go.

'You have to.' His voice was wooden. 'You deserve a man who can love you the way—'

'And I have found him,' she interrupted yet again, lifting her head and looking up at him. 'What I deserve is to be with the man I love, and that's you. So, no. I'm not leaving, Tiberius.'

His heart felt like it was chained in barbed wire, little hooks digging into it, tearing it. 'Lioness, I can't...'

'I'm not going to ask you to put me first,' she said. 'I would never ask that of you. All I want is a little corner of your heart that is mine. That's all.'

A little corner of his heart...

'Guinevere...'

'You love an entire country,' she said. 'Are you telling me you really can't spare a small piece of that great heart of yours?'

He looked down into her eyes and he could feel the fear wrapping around him, squeezing tight. The fear that she hadn't just claimed a small piece, that she'd claimed all of it. All of him. And he was afraid, because where did that leave him?

'If I love you,' he began roughly, 'then what is there left for Kasimir?'

Her eyes were midnight-blue and her arms around him were warm as she said, 'Why do you think love is limited? That if you give it to your country there's nothing left for anything else? Think bigger, my king. Love is boundless. I can love you and love my country. It's just a different kind of love.'

His will was fading, his strength to put her from him failing. 'I can't make you happy, Guinevere. I don't even know what that looks like.'

Strangely, she smiled at him. 'Yes, you do. It's me and you in the orchard, lying on our backs and looking at the stars.'

She's right.

It burst through him then, in a brilliant flash of light. Yes, he *had* been happy with her that day in the orchard. He'd been happy with her in every one of their daily two-hour meetings, and he'd been happy because of her. Because she'd showed him what it felt like. And it was lying on his back with her in his arms, looking at the stars. It was her in his lap, kissing him and touching him as if he was precious.

It was her smile—the one she gave him every day—and it was her in her yellow dress, looking like a splash of sunshine.

And it was her, her eyes dark, telling him she loved him.

She was happiness.

Which must mean that the agonising pressure in his heart was love.

Because he did love her, even though he'd been telling himself he didn't. Even though he'd been telling himself it was impossible to love her and his country at the same time.

In fact it was perfectly possible, and he'd been doing it for at least a couple of weeks now.

He lifted his hands and cupped her face between them. 'Guinevere…little lioness…it cannot be just about me. You need happiness in your life too. You *deserve* it.'

Guinevere looked up into his beautiful face, her arms tight around his narrow waist. There was anguish there, and something fierce and hot and bright.

Her king. Her enemy. Her husband.

The man she loved without limit and without reservation.

She'd known that the minute he'd walked away from

her, leaving her standing alone in the ballroom. After telling her that he couldn't give her what she deserved and that she'd be better off if she'd never met him.

But she'd told him the truth—that she'd still have been hiding in the walls if he hadn't come along and shown her the courage that had always been there inside her.

And as he'd walked away from her she'd known she couldn't let him. That he needed to learn a lesson too, and one that only she could teach him.

A lesson about the love she knew lay in his heart. The love for his parents that had translated into a driving need to make their deaths matter. The love for his country and for his people that had kept him on the path to the crown.

This king was made of love. And it wasn't a distraction. And loving his country didn't mean he couldn't love her.

Not that she needed him to love her, she'd decided as his tall form disappeared in the crowded ballroom. It didn't matter in the end. Because what she wanted was his happiness, and that was all that mattered to her. He had no one. His parents were gone, he had no siblings, no friends. He was an island, in splendid isolation, and she was his only bridge.

He might decide to divorce her and he probably would—'for her own good'. But she didn't care if he did. She wasn't going to leave him. She couldn't leave him. And she'd rather be trapped inside the walls of the palace with him than be free to go wherever she wanted, because his happiness was her happiness and there was no freedom without him.

So she'd gone after him, to tell him that she wouldn't be leaving him, and had found him on the balcony alone, a look of despair on his face.

He'd muttered something about divorce, but she'd ignored that, showing him, then telling him, that she wasn't going to leave.

Her heart felt barbed and sharp, but the pain wasn't as bad as when she'd stood in the ballroom, because she'd made a decision. It hurt now, though, with his warm palms against her cheek, his expression fierce, silver eyes blazing as he told her she deserved happiness.

'Yes,' she said. 'I do. And luckily I already have it here with you.'

'Guinevere...'

'You make me happy, my king. And you don't need to do anything more and you don't need to be anything else. Just you, as you are.'

'Two hours a day,' he said roughly. 'You wanted more than two hours.'

She tightened her arms around him, holding him fast. 'If you can only give me two hours, then I will be happy with that.' Her eyes prickled with the force of her emotions. 'I will never be happy without you, Tiberius. Don't you understand that?'

The look on his face intensified, and the silver flames in his eyes burned impossibly bright, and for a long time he just looked down at her. Then he said, his voice hot and deep, 'You told me that love isn't something that's finite and I think you're right. I've been afraid that I can't love you and my country at the same time, but I think I've been doing so for the past two weeks.'

A hot wash of shock went through her, her painful heart igniting into flame. 'You...love me?'

Tiberius smiled, natural and brilliant, like the sun coming out. 'Yes, little lioness. I love you.' Then he bent his head and kissed her, his mouth hot and demanding, and when he came up for air, he growled, 'Two hours, my queen. I demand two hours of your time every day. Two hours for the rest of my life.'

'Two hours? My king, I will give you eternity.'

And she did.

EPILOGUE

'THERE,' TIBERIUS SAID, adjusting the telescope. 'Can you see Venus? It's very bright.'

Standing beside him under the orange trees, on the grass of the orchard, his lioness peered through the high-powered telescope Tiberius had brought with him.

'Oh, yes!' she exclaimed in wonder. 'You're right. It's amazingly bright.'

It was their little ritual—to come out here at night once a month, to look at the stars and remind themselves of the whole beautiful universe that they were only tiny parts of.

Plus, Tiberius simply liked astronomy, and had been pursuing it whenever he had a moment. Which was more often than he'd expected.

Being a king was hard work, as his father had said, but it was work that he shared with his lovely wife—and a burden shared was a burden halved.

He glanced down at the baby who slept peacefully in the crook of his arm. His gorgeous daughter and his heir, barely three weeks old and already proving to be a lioness, just like her mother.

He'd thought it wasn't possible to love his wife and his country at the same time, but it was eminently possible. Just as it was possible for that love to grow to include his new daughter, and any more children they would have together.

And there would be more. He'd already decided.

Love expands, he thought, slipping his free arm around his wife, and holding her close.

Love was as infinite as the stars.

* * * * *

Were you blown away by
King, Enemy, Husband?
Then why not explore these other steamy reads
from Jackie Ashenden?

Spanish Marriage Solution
Italian Baby Shock
The Twins That Bind
Boss's Heir Demand
Newlywed Enemies

Available now!

MILLS & BOON®

Coming next month

TWINS FOR HIS MAJESTY
Clare Connelly

'The baby is fine?'

'Oh, the baby is fine. In fact, both babies are fine,' she snapped, almost maniacally now. 'It's twins,' she added, and then she sobbed, lifting a hand to her mouth to stop the torrent of emotion from pouring out in a large wail.

Silence cracked around them but she barely noticed. She was shaking now, processing the truth of the scan, the reality that lay before her.

'Well, then.' His voice was low and silky, as though she hadn't just told him they were going to have *two babies* in a matter of months. 'That makes our decision even easier.'

'What decision?' she asked, whirling around to face him.

'There is no way on earth you are leaving the country whilst pregnant with my children, so forget about returning to New Zealand.'

She flinched. She hadn't expected that.

'Nor will my children be born under a cloud of illegitimacy.'

Her heart almost stopped beating; his words made no sense. 'I—don't—what are you saying?'

'That you must marry me—and quickly.'

Continue reading

TWINS FOR HIS MAJESTY
Clare Connelly

Available next month
millsandboon.co.uk

COMING SOON!

We really hope you enjoyed reading this book.
If you're looking for more romance
be sure to head to the shops when
new books are available on

Thursday 17th July

To see which titles are coming soon, please visit

millsandboon.co.uk/nextmonth

MILLS & BOON

afterglow BOOKS

Afterglow Books is a trend-led, trope-filled list of books with diverse, authentic and relatable characters, a wide array of voices and representations, plus real world trials and tribulations. Featuring all the tropes you could possibly want (think small-town settings, fake relationships, grumpy vs sunshine, enemies to lovers) and all with a generous dose of spice in every story.

♪ @millsandboonuk
◎ @millsandboonuk
afterglowbooks.co.uk

#AfterglowBooks

For all the latest book news, exclusive content and giveaways scan the QR code below to sign up to the Afterglow newsletter:

SCAN ME

afterglow BOOKS

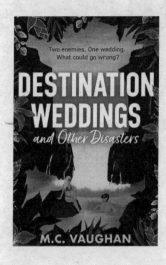

✈ International

♥ Enemies to lovers

((♥)) Forced proximity

👪 Friends to lovers

✈ International

△ Love triangle

OUT NOW

Two stories published every month. Discover more at:
Afterglowbooks.co.uk

LET'S TALK
Romance

For exclusive extracts, competitions and special offers, find us online:

- **f** MillsandBoon
- **X** @MillsandBoon
- **◎** @MillsandBoonUK
- **♪** @MillsandBoonUK

Get in touch on 01413 063 232

OUT NOW!

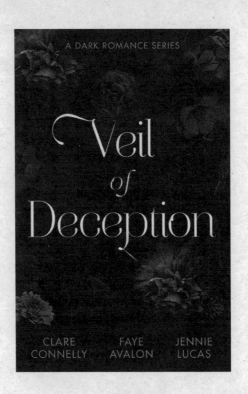